This Novel Journal Belongs to:

_____

And you're sharing it with L. Frank Baum

Write between the lines of some of the best literature the world has to offer with your Novel Journal. Whether you're an aspiring writer crafting the next great novel or a journaler recording life's memorable events, you'll be able to write over, under, and within the words of the world's greatest writers. Each Novel Journal contains the complete text of the classic work; in some cases, that text repeats to allow for standard journal lengths. Important quotes and lines from each novel are highlighted in a different color throughout so that the inspiring words of your favorite authors are never far away.

CHAPTER I The Cyclone Dorothy lived in the midst of the great Kansas prairies, with Uncle Henry, who was a farmer, and Aunt Em, who was the farmer's wife. Their house was small, for the lumber to build it had to be carried by wagon many miles. There were four walls, a floor and a roof, which made one room; and this room contained a rusty-looking cookstove, a cupboard for the dishes, a table, three or four chairs, and the beds. Uncle Henry and Aunt Em had a big bed in one corner, and Dorothy a little bed in another corner. There was no garret at all, and no cellar—except a small hole dug in the ground, called a cyclone cellar, where the family could go in case one of those great whirlwinds arose, mighty enough to crush any building in its path. It was reached by a trapdoor in the middle of the floor, from which a ladder led down into the small, dark hole. When Dorothy stood in the doorway and looked around, she could see nothing but the great gray prairie on every side. Not a tree nor a house broke the broad sweep of flat country that reached to the edge of the sky in all directions. The sun had baked the plowed land into a gray mass, with little cracks running through it. Even the grass was not green, for the sun had burned the tops of the long blades until they were the same gray color to be seen everywhere. Once the house had been painted, but the sun blistered the paint and the rains washed it away, and now the house was as dull and gray as everything else. When Aunt Em came there to live she was a young, pretty wife. The sun and wind had changed her, too. They had taken the sparkle from her eyes and left them a sober gray; they had taken the red from her cheeks and lips, and they were gray also. She was thin and gaunt, and never smiled now. When Dorothy, who was an orphan, first came to her, Aunt Em had been so startled by the child's laughter that she would scream and press her hand upon her heart whenever Dorothy's merry voice reached her ears; and she still looked at the little girl with wonder that she could find anything to laugh at. Uncle Henry never laughed. He worked hard from morning till night and did not know what joy was. He was gray also, from his long beard to his rough boots, and he looked stern and solemn, and rarely spoke. It was Toto that made Dorothy laugh, and saved her from growing as gray as her other surroundings. Toto was not gray; he was a little black dog, with long silky hair and small black eyes that twinkled merrily on either side of his funny, wee nose. Toto played all day long, and Dorothy played with him, and loved him dearly. Today, however, they were not playing. Uncle Henry sat upon the doorstep and looked anxiously at the sky, which was even grayer than usual. Dorothy stood in the door with Toto in her arms, and looked at the sky too. Aunt Em was washing the dishes. From the far north they heard a low wail of the wind, and Uncle Henry and Dorothy could see where the long grass bowed in waves before the coming storm. There now came a sharp whistling in the air from the south, and as they turned their eyes that way they saw ripples in the grass coming from that direction also. Suddenly Uncle Henry stood up. "There's a cyclone coming, Em," he called to his wife. "I'll go look after the stock." Then he ran toward the sheds where the cows and horses were kept. Aunt Em dropped her work and came to the door. One glance told her of the danger close at hand. "Quick, Dorothy!" she screamed. "Run for the cellar!" Toto jumped out of Dorothy's arms and hid under the bed, and the girl started to get him. Aunt Em, badly frightened, threw open the trapdoor in the floor and climbed down the ladder into the small, dark hole. Dorothy caught Toto at last and started to follow her aunt. When she was halfway across the room there came a great shriek from the wind, and the house shook so hard that she lost her footing and sat down suddenly upon the floor. Then a strange thing happened. The house whirled around two or three times and rose slowly through the air. Dorothy felt as if she were going up in a balloon. The north and south winds met where the house stood, and made it the exact center of the cyclone. In the middle of a cyclone the air is generally still, but the great pressure of the wind on every side of the house raised it up higher and higher, until it was at the very top of the cyclone; and there it remained and was carried miles and miles away as easily as you could carry a feather. It was very dark, and the wind howled horribly around her, but Dorothy found she was riding quite easily. After the first few whirls around, and one other time when the house tipped badly, she felt as if she were being rocked gently, like a baby in a cradle. Toto did not like it. He ran about the room, now here, now there, barking loudly; but Dorothy sat quite still on the floor and waited to see what would happen. Once Toto got too near the open trapdoor, and fell in; and at first the little girl thought she had lost him. But soon she saw one of his ears sticking up through the hole, for the strong pressure of the air was keeping him up so that he could not fall. She crept to the hole, caught Toto by the ear, and dragged him into the room again, afterward closing the trapdoor so that no more accidents could happen. Hour after hour passed away, and slowly Dorothy got over her fright; but she felt quite lonely, and the wind shrieked so loudly all about her that she nearly became deaf. At first she had wondered if she would be dashed to pieces when the house fell again; but as the hours passed and nothing terrible happened, she stopped worrying and resolved to wait calmly and see what the future would bring. At last she crawled over the swaying floor to her bed, and lay down upon it; and Toto followed and lay down beside her. In spite of the swaying of the house and the wailing of the wind, Dorothy soon closed her eyes and fell fast asleep. CHAPTER II The Council with the Munchkins She was awakened by a shock, so sudden and severe that if Dorothy had not been lying on the soft bed she might have been hurt. As it was, the jar made her catch her breath and wonder what had happened; and Toto put his cold little nose into her face and whined dismally. Dorothy sat up and noticed that the house was not moving; nor was it dark, for the bright sunshine came in at the window, flooding the little room. **She sprang from her bed and with Toto at her heels ran and opened the door.** The little girl gave a cry of amazement and looked about her, her eyes growing bigger and bigger at the wonderful sights she saw. The cyclone had set the house down very gently—for a cyclone—in the midst of a country of marvelous beauty. There were lovely patches of greensward all about, with stately trees bearing rich and luscious fruits. Banks of gorgeous flowers were on every hand, and birds with rare and brilliant plumage sang and fluttered in the trees and bushes. A little way off was a small brook, rushing and sparkling along between green banks, and murmuring in a voice very grateful to a little girl who had lived so long on the dry, gray prairies. While she stood looking eagerly at the strange and beautiful sights, she noticed coming toward her a group of the queerest people she had ever seen. They were not as big as the grown folk she had always been used to; but neither were they very small. In fact, they seemed about as tall as Dorothy, who was a well-grown child for her age, although they were, so far as looks go, many years older. Three were men and one was a woman, and all were oddly dressed. They wore round hats that rose to a small point a foot above their heads, with little bells around the brims that tinkled sweetly as they moved. The hats of the men were blue; the little woman's hat was white, and she wore a white gown that hung in pleats from her shoulders. Over it were sprinkled little stars that glistened in the sun like diamonds. The men were dressed in blue, of the same shade as their hats, and wore

well-polished boots with a deep roll of blue at the tops. The men, Dorothy thought, were about as old as Uncle Henry, for two of them had beards. But the little woman was

doubtless much older. Her face was covered with wrinkles, her hair was nearly white, and she walked rather stiffly. When these people drew near the house where Dorothy

was standing in the doorway, they paused and whispered among themselves, as if afraid to come farther. But the little old woman walked up to Dorothy, made a low bow

and said, in a sweet voice: "You are welcome, most noble Sorceress, to the land of the Munchkins. We are so grateful to you for having killed the Wicked Witch of the East,

and for setting our people free from bondage." Dorothy listened to this speech with wonder. What could the little woman possibly mean by calling her a sorceress, and saying

she had killed the Wicked Witch of the East? Dorothy was an innocent, harmless little girl, who had been carried by a cyclone many miles from home; and she had never

killed anything in all her life. But the little woman evidently expected her to answer; so Dorothy said, with hesitation, "You are very kind, but there must be some mistake. I

have not killed anything." "Your house did, anyway," replied the little old woman, with a laugh, "and that is the same thing. See!" she continued, pointing to the corner of

the house. "There are her two feet, still sticking out from under a block of wood." Dorothy looked, and gave a little cry of fright. There, indeed, just under the corner of

the great beam the house rested on, two feet were sticking out, shod in Silver Shoes with pointed toes. "Oh, dear! Oh, dear!" cried Dorothy, clasping her hands together in

dismay. "The house must have fallen on her. Whatever shall we do?" "There is nothing to be done," said the little woman calmly. "But who was she?" asked Dorothy. "She

was the Wicked Witch of the East, as I said," answered the little woman. "She has held all the Munchkins in bondage for many years, making them slave for her night and

day. Now they are all set free, and are grateful to you for the favor." "Who are the Munchkins?" inquired Dorothy. "They are the people who live in this land of the East

where the Wicked Witch ruled." "Are you a Munchkin?" asked Dorothy. "No, but I am their friend, although I live in the land of the North. When they saw the Witch of

the East was dead the Munchkins sent a swift messenger to me, and I came at once. I am the Witch of the North." "Oh, gracious!" cried Dorothy. "Are you a real witch?"

"Yes, indeed," answered the little woman. "But I am a good witch, and the people love me. I am not as powerful as the Wicked Witch was who ruled here, or I should have

set the people free myself." "But I thought all witches were wicked," said the girl, who was half frightened at facing a real witch. "Oh, no, that is a great mistake. There were

only four witches in all the Land of Oz, and two of them, those who live in the North and the South, are good witches. I know this is true, for I am one of them myself, and

cannot be mistaken. Those who dwelt in the East and the West were, indeed, wicked witches; but now that you have killed one of them, there is but one Wicked Witch in all

the Land of Oz—the one who lives in the West." "But," said Dorothy, after a moment's thought, "Aunt Em has told me that the witches were all dead—years and years

ago." "Who is Aunt Em?" inquired the little old woman. "She is my aunt who lives in Kansas, where I came from." The Witch of the North seemed to think for a time, with

her head bowed and her eyes upon the ground. Then she looked up and said, "I do not know where Kansas is, for I have never heard that country mentioned before. But tell me, is it a civilized country?" "Oh, yes," replied Dorothy. "Then that accounts for it. In the civilized countries I believe there are no witches left, nor wizards, nor sorceresses,

nor magicians. But, you see, the Land of Oz has never been civilized, for we are cut off from all the rest of the world. Therefore we still have witches and wizards amongst

us." "Who are the wizards?" asked Dorothy. "Oz himself is the Great Wizard," answered the Witch, sinking her voice to a whisper. "He is more powerful than all the rest

of us together. He lives in the City of Emeralds." Dorothy was going to ask another question, but just then the Munchkins, who had been standing silently by, gave a loud

shout and pointed to the corner of the house where the Wicked Witch had been lying. "What is it?" asked the little old woman, and looked, and began to laugh. The feet of

the dead Witch had disappeared entirely, and nothing was left but the Silver Shoes. "She was so old," explained the Witch of the North, "that she dried up quickly in the sun.

That is the end of her. But the Silver Shoes are yours, and you shall have them to wear." She reached down and picked up the shoes, and after shaking the dust out of them

handed them to Dorothy. "The Witch of the East was proud of those Silver Shoes," said one of the Munchkins, "and there is some charm connected with them; but what it

is we never knew." Dorothy carried the shoes into the house and placed them on the table. Then she came out again to the Munchkins and said: "I am anxious to get back to

my aunt and uncle, for I am sure they will worry about me. Can you help me find my way?" The Munchkins and the Witch first looked at one another, and then at Dorothy,

and then shook their heads. "At the East, not far from here," said one, "there is a great desert, and none could live to cross it." "It is the same at the South," said another, "for

I have been there and seen it. The South is the country of the Quadlings." "I am told," said the third man, "that it is the same at the West. And that country, where the Winkies

live, is ruled by the Wicked Witch of the West, who would make you her slave if you passed her way." "The North is my home," said the old lady, "and at its edge is the

same great desert that surrounds this Land of Oz. I'm afraid, my dear, you will have to live with us." Dorothy began to sob at this, for she felt lonely among all these strange

people. Her tears seemed to grieve the kindhearted Munchkins, for they immediately took out their handkerchiefs and began to weep also. As for the little old woman, she

took off her cap and balanced the point on the end of her nose, while she counted "One, two, three" in a solemn voice. At once the cap changed to a slate, on which was

written in big, white chalk marks: "LET DOROTHY GO TO THE CITY OF EMERALDS." The little old woman took the slate from her nose, and having read the words

on it, asked, "Is your name Dorothy, my dear?" "Yes," answered the child, looking up and drying her tears. "Then you must go to the City of Emeralds. Perhaps Oz will

help you." "Where is this city?" asked Dorothy. "It is exactly in the center of the country, and is ruled by Oz, the Great Wizard I told you of." "Is he a good man?" inquired

the girl anxiously. "He is a good Wizard. Whether he is a man or not I cannot tell, for I have never seen him." "How can I get there?" asked Dorothy. "You must walk. It is

a long journey, through a country that is sometimes pleasant and sometimes dark and terrible. However, I will use all the magic arts I know of to keep you from harm."

"Won't you go with me?" pleaded the girl, who had begun to look upon the little old woman as her only friend. "No, I cannot do that," she replied, "but I will give you my

kiss, and no one will dare injure a person who has been kissed by the Witch of the North." She came close to Dorothy and kissed her gently on the forehead. Where her lips touched the girl they left a round, shining mark, as Dorothy found out soon after. "The road to the City of Emeralds is paved with yellow brick," said the Witch, "so you cannot miss it. When you get to Oz do not be afraid of him, but tell your story and ask him to help you. Good-bye, my dear." The three Munchkins bowed low to her and wished her a pleasant journey, after which they walked away through the trees. The Witch gave Dorothy a friendly little nod, whirled around on her left heel three times, and straightway disappeared, much to the surprise of little Toto, who barked after her loudly enough when she had gone, because he had been afraid even to growl while she stood by. But Dorothy, knowing her to be a witch, had expected her to disappear in just that way, and was not surprised in the least. CHAPTER III How Dorothy Saved the Scarecrow When Dorothy was left alone she began to feel hungry. So she went to the cupboard and cut herself some bread, which she spread with butter. She gave some to Toto, and taking a pail from the shelf she carried it down to the little brook and filled it with clear, sparkling water. Toto ran over to the trees and began to bark at the birds sitting there. Dorothy went to get him, and saw such delicious fruit hanging from the branches that she gathered some of it, finding it just what she wanted to help out her breakfast. Then she went back to the house, and having helped herself and Toto to a good drink of the cool, clear water, she set about making ready for the journey to the City of Emeralds. Dorothy had only one other dress, but that happened to be clean and was hanging on a peg beside her bed. It was gingham, with checks of white and blue; and although the blue was somewhat faded with many washings, it was still a pretty frock. The girl washed herself carefully, dressed herself in the clean gingham, and tied her pink sunbonnet on her head. She took a little basket and filled it with bread from the cupboard, laying a white cloth over the top. Then she looked down at her feet and noticed how old and worn her shoes were. "They surely will never do for a long journey, Toto," she said. And Toto looked up into her face with his little black eyes and wagged his tail to show he knew what she meant. At that moment Dorothy saw lying on the table the Silver Shoes that had belonged to the Witch of the East. "I wonder if they will fit me," she said to Toto. "They would be just the thing to take a long walk in, for they could not wear out." She took off her old leather shoes and tried on the silver ones, which fitted her as well as if they had been made for her. Finally she picked up her basket. "Come along, Toto," she said. "We will go to the Emerald City and ask the Great Oz how to get back to Kansas again." She closed the door, locked it, and put the key carefully in the pocket of her dress. And so, with Toto trotting along soberly behind her, she started on her journey. There were several roads near by, but it did not take her long to find the one paved with yellow bricks. Within a short time she was walking briskly toward the Emerald City, her Silver Shoes tinkling merrily on the hard, yellow road-bed. The sun shone bright and the birds sang sweetly, and Dorothy did not feel nearly so bad as you might think a little girl would who had been suddenly whisked away from her own country and set down in the midst of a strange land. She was surprised, as she walked along, to see how pretty the country was about her. There were neat fences at the sides of the road, painted a dainty blue color, and beyond them were fields of grain and vegetables in abundance. Evidently the Munchkins were good farmers and able to raise large crops. Once in a while she would pass a house, and the people came out to look at her and bow low as she went by; for everyone knew she had been the means of destroying the Wicked Witch and setting them free from bondage.

The houses of the Munchkins were odd-looking dwellings, for each was round, with a big dome for a roof. All were painted blue, for in this country of the East blue was the favorite color. Toward evening, when Dorothy was tired with her long walk and began to wonder where she should pass the night, she came to a house rather larger than the rest. On the green lawn before it many men and women were dancing. Five little fiddlers played as loudly as possible, and the people were laughing and singing, while a big table near by was loaded with delicious fruits and nuts, pies and cakes, and many other good things to eat. The people greeted Dorothy kindly, and invited her to supper and to pass the night with them; for this was the home of one of the richest Munchkins in the land, and his friends were gathered with him to celebrate their freedom from the bondage of the Wicked Witch. Dorothy ate a hearty supper and was waited upon by the rich Munchkin himself, whose name was Boq. Then she sat upon a settee and watched the people dance. When Boq saw her Silver Shoes he said, "You must be a great sorceress." "Why?" asked the girl. "Because you wear Silver Shoes and have killed the Wicked Witch. Besides, you have white in your frock, and only witches and sorceresses wear white." "My dress is blue and white checked," said Dorothy, smoothing out the wrinkles in it. "It is kind of you to wear that," said Boq. "Blue is the color of the Munchkins, and white is the witch color. So we know you are a friendly witch." Dorothy did not know what to say to this, for all the people seemed to think her a witch, and she knew very well she was only an ordinary little girl who had come by the chance of a cyclone into a strange land. When she had tired watching the dancing, Boq led her into the house, where he gave her a room with a pretty bed in it. The sheets were made of blue cloth, and Dorothy slept soundly in them till morning, with Toto curled up on the blue rug beside her. She ate a hearty breakfast, and watched a wee Munchkin baby, who played with Toto and pulled his tail and crowed and laughed in a way that greatly amused Dorothy. Toto was a fine curiosity to all the people, for they had never seen a dog before. "How far is it to the Emerald City?" the girl asked. "I do not know," answered Boq gravely, "for I have never been there. It is better for people to keep away from Oz, unless they have business with him. But it is a long way to the Emerald City, and it will take you many days. The country here is rich and pleasant, but you must pass through rough and dangerous places before you reach the end of your journey." This worried Dorothy a little, but she knew that only the Great Oz could help her get to Kansas again, so she bravely resolved not to turn back. She bade her friends good-bye, and again started along the road of yellow brick. When she had gone several miles she thought she would stop to rest, and so climbed to the top of the fence beside the road and sat down. There was a great cornfield beyond the fence, and not far away she saw a Scarecrow, placed high on a pole to keep the birds from the ripe corn. Dorothy leaned her chin upon her hand and gazed thoughtfully at the Scarecrow. Its head was a small sack stuffed with straw, with eyes, nose, and mouth painted on it to represent a face. An old, pointed blue hat, that had belonged to some Munchkin, was perched on his head, and the rest of the figure was a blue suit of clothes, worn and faded, which had also been stuffed with straw. On the feet were some old boots with blue tops, such as every man wore in this country, and the figure was raised above the stalks of corn by means of the pole stuck up its back. While Dorothy was looking earnestly into the queer, painted face of the Scarecrow, she was surprised to see one of the eyes slowly wink at her. She thought she must have been mistaken at first, for none of the scarecrows in

Kansas ever wink; but presently the figure nodded its head to her in a friendly way. Then she climbed down from the fence and walked up to it, while Toto ran around the pole and barked. "Good day," said the Scarecrow, in a rather husky voice. "Did you speak?" asked the girl, in wonder. "Certainly," answered the Scarecrow. "How do you do?" "I'm pretty well, thank you," replied Dorothy politely. "How do you do?" "I'm not feeling well," said the Scarecrow, with a smile, "for it is very tedious being perched up here night and day to scare away crows." "Can't you get down?" asked Dorothy. "No, for this pole is stuck up my back. If you will please take away the pole I shall be greatly obliged to you." Dorothy reached up both arms and lifted the figure off the pole, for, being stuffed with straw, it was quite light. "Thank you very much," said the Scarecrow, when he had been set down on the ground. "I feel like a new man." Dorothy was puzzled at this, for it sounded queer to hear a stuffed man speak, and to see him bow and walk along beside her. "Who are you?" asked the Scarecrow when he had stretched himself and yawned. "And where are you going?" "My name is Dorothy," said the girl, "and I am going to the Emerald City, to ask the Great Oz to send me back to Kansas." "Where is the Emerald City?" he inquired. "And who is Oz?" "Why, don't you know?" she returned, in surprise. "No, indeed. I don't know anything. You see, I am stuffed, so I have no brains at all," he answered sadly. "Oh," said Dorothy, "I'm awfully sorry for you." "Do you think," he asked, "if I go to the Emerald City with you, that Oz would give me some brains?" "I cannot tell," she returned, "but you may come with me, if you like. If Oz will not give you any brains you will be no worse off than you are now." "That is true," said the Scarecrow. "You see," he continued confidentially, "I don't mind my legs and arms and body being stuffed, because I cannot get hurt. If anyone treads on my toes or sticks a pin into me, it doesn't matter, for I can't feel it. But I do not want people to call me a fool, and if my head stays stuffed with straw instead of with brains, as yours is, how am I ever to know anything?" "I understand how you feel," said the little girl, who was truly sorry for him. "If you will come with me I'll ask Oz to do all he can for you." "Thank you," he answered gratefully. They walked back to the road. Dorothy helped him over the fence, and they started along the path of yellow brick for the Emerald City. Toto did not like this addition to the party at first. He smelled around the stuffed man as if he suspected there might be a nest of rats in the straw, and he often growled in an unfriendly way at the Scarecrow. "Don't mind Toto," said Dorothy to her new friend. "He never bites." "Oh, I'm not afraid," replied the Scarecrow. "He can't hurt the straw. Do let me carry that basket for you. I shall not mind it, for I can't get tired. I'll tell you a secret," he continued, as he walked along. "There is only one thing in the world I am afraid of." "What is that?" asked Dorothy; "the Munchkin farmer who made you?" "No," answered the Scarecrow; "it's a lighted match." CHAPTER IV The Road Through the Forest After a few hours the road began to be rough, and the walking grew so difficult that the Scarecrow often stumbled over the yellow bricks, which were here very uneven. Sometimes, indeed, they were broken or missing altogether, leaving holes that Toto jumped across and Dorothy walked around. As for the Scarecrow, having no brains, he walked straight ahead, and so stepped into the holes and fell at full length on the hard bricks. It never hurt him, however, and Dorothy would pick him up and set him upon his feet again, while he joined her in laughing merrily at his own mishap. The farms were not nearly so well cared for here as they were farther back. There were fewer houses and fewer fruit trees, and the farther they went the more dismal and lonesome the country became. At noon they sat down by the roadside, near a little brook, and Dorothy opened her basket and got out some bread. She offered a piece to the Scarecrow, but he refused. "I am never hungry," he said, "and it is a lucky thing I am not, for my mouth is only painted, and if I should cut a hole in it so I could eat, the straw I am stuffed with would come out, and that would spoil the shape of my head." Dorothy saw at once that this was true, so she only nodded and went on eating her bread. "Tell me something about yourself and the country you came from," said the Scarecrow, when she had finished her dinner. So she told him all about Kansas, and how gray everything was there, and how the cyclone had carried her to this queer Land of Oz. The Scarecrow listened carefully, and said, "I cannot understand why you should wish to leave this beautiful country and go back to the dry, gray place you call Kansas." "That is because you have no brains" answered the girl. "No matter how dreary and gray our homes are, we people of flesh and blood would rather live there than in any other country, be it ever so beautiful. There is no place like home." The Scarecrow sighed. "Of course I cannot understand it," he said. "If your heads were stuffed with straw, like mine, you would probably all live in the beautiful places, and then Kansas would have no people at all. It is fortunate for Kansas that you have brains." "Won't you tell me a story, while we are resting?" asked the child. The Scarecrow looked at her reproachfully, and answered: "My life has been so short that I really know nothing whatever. I was only made day before yesterday. What happened in the world before that time is all unknown to me. Luckily, when the farmer made my head, one of the first things he did was to paint my ears, so that I heard what was going on. There was another Munchkin with him, and the first thing I heard was the farmer saying, 'How do you like those ears?' "'They aren't straight,' answered the other. "'Never mind,' said the farmer. 'They are ears just the same,' which was true enough. "'Now I'll make the eyes,' said the farmer. So he painted my right eye, and as soon as it was finished I found myself looking at him and at everything around me with a great deal of curiosity, for this was my first glimpse of the world. "'That's a rather pretty eye,' remarked the Munchkin who was watching the farmer. 'Blue paint is just the color for eyes.' "'I think I'll make the other a little bigger,' said the farmer. And when the second eye was done I could see much better than before. Then he made my nose and my mouth. But I did not speak, because at that time I didn't know what a mouth was for. I had the fun of watching them make my body and my arms and legs; and when they fastened on my head, at last, I felt very proud, for I thought I was just as good a man as anyone. "'This fellow will scare the crows fast enough,' said the farmer. 'He looks just like a man.' "'Why, he is a man,' said the other, and I quite agreed with him. The farmer carried me under his arm to the cornfield, and set me up on a tall stick, where you found me. He and his friend soon after walked away and left me alone. "I did not like to be deserted this way. So I tried to walk after them. But my feet would not touch the ground, and I was forced to stay on that pole. It was a lonely life to lead, for I had nothing to think of, having been made such a little while before. Many crows and other birds flew into the cornfield, but as soon as they saw me they flew away again, thinking I was a Munchkin; and this pleased me and made me feel that I was quite an important person. By and by an old crow flew near me, and after looking at me carefully he perched upon my shoulder and said: "'I wonder if that farmer thought to fool me in this clumsy manner. Any crow of sense could see that you are only stuffed with straw.' Then he hopped down at my feet and ate all the corn he wanted. The other birds, seeing he was not harmed by me, came to eat the corn

too, so in a short time there was a great flock of them about me. "I felt sad at this, for it showed I was not such a good Scarecrow after all; but the old crow comforted me,

saying, 'If you only had brains in your head you would be as good a man as any of them, and a better man than some of them. Brains are the only things worth having in this

world, no matter whether one is a crow or a man.' "After the crows had gone I thought this over, and decided I would try hard to get some brains. By good luck you came

along and pulled me off the stake, and from what you say I am sure the Great Oz will give me brains as soon as we get to the Emerald City." "I hope so," said Dorothy

earnestly, "since you seem anxious to have them." "Oh, yes; I am anxious," returned the Scarecrow. "It is such an uncomfortable feeling to know one is a fool." "Well," said

the girl, "let us go." And she handed the basket to the Scarecrow. There were no fences at all by the roadside now, and the land was rough and untilled. Toward evening they

came to a great forest, where the trees grew so big and close together that their branches met over the road of yellow brick. It was almost dark under the trees, for the branches

shut out the daylight; but the travelers did not stop, and went on into the forest. "If this road goes in, it must come out," said the Scarecrow, "and as the Emerald City is at

the other end of the road, we must go wherever it leads us." "Anyone would know that," said Dorothy. "Certainly; that is why I know it," returned the Scarecrow. "If it

required brains to figure it out, I never should have said it." After an hour or so the light faded away, and they found themselves stumbling along in the darkness. Dorothy

could not see at all, but Toto could, for some dogs see very well in the dark; and the Scarecrow declared he could see as well as by day. So she took hold of his arm and

managed to get along fairly well. "If you see any house, or any place where we can pass the night," she said, "you must tell me; for it is very uncomfortable walking in the

dark." Soon after the Scarecrow stopped. "I see a little cottage at the right of us," he said, "built of logs and branches. Shall we go there?" "Yes, indeed," answered the child.

"I am all tired out." So the Scarecrow led her through the trees until they reached the cottage, and Dorothy entered and found a bed of dried leaves in one corner. She lay

down at once, and with Toto beside her soon fell into a sound sleep. The Scarecrow, who was never tired, stood up in another corner and waited patiently until morning

came. CHAPTER V The Rescue of the Tin Woodman When Dorothy awoke the sun was shining through the trees and Toto had long been out chasing birds around him

and squirrels. She sat up and looked around her. There was the Scarecrow, still standing patiently in his corner, waiting for her. "We must go and search for water," she said

to him. "Why do you want water?" he asked. "To wash my face clean after the dust of the road, and to drink, so the dry bread will not stick in my throat." "It must be

inconvenient to be made of flesh," said the Scarecrow thoughtfully, "for you must sleep, and eat and drink. However, you have brains, and it is worth a lot of bother to be

able to think properly." They left the cottage and walked through the trees until they found a little spring of clear water, where Dorothy drank and bathed and ate her

breakfast. She saw there was not much bread left in the basket, and the girl was thankful the Scarecrow did not have to eat anything, for there was scarcely enough for herself

and Toto for the day. When she had finished her meal, and was about to go back to the road of yellow brick, she was startled to hear a deep groan near by. "What was that?"

she asked timidly. "I cannot imagine," replied the Scarecrow; "but we can go and see." Just then another groan reached their ears, and the sound seemed to come from behind them. They turned and walked through the forest a few steps, when Dorothy discovered something shining in a ray of sunshine that fell between the trees. She ran to the place and then stopped short, with a little cry of surprise. One of the big trees had been partly chopped through, and standing beside it, with an uplifted axe in his hands, was a man made entirely of tin. His head and arms and legs were jointed upon his body, but he stood perfectly motionless, as if he could not stir at all. Dorothy looked at him in amazement, and so did the Scarecrow, while Toto barked sharply and made a snap at the tin legs, which hurt his teeth. "Did you groan?" asked Dorothy. "Yes," answered the tin man, "I did. I've been groaning for more than a year, and no one has ever heard me before or come to help me." "What can I do for you?" she inquired softly, for she was moved by the sad voice in which the man spoke. "Get an oilcan and oil my joints," he answered. "They are rusted so badly that I cannot move them at all; if I am well oiled I shall soon be all right again. You will find an oilcan on a shelf in my cottage." Dorothy at once ran back to the cottage and found the oilcan, and then she returned and asked anxiously, "Where are your joints?" "Oil my neck, first," replied the Tin Woodman. So she oiled it, and as it was quite badly rusted the Scarecrow took hold of the tin head and moved it gently from side to side until it worked freely, and then the man could turn it himself. "Now oil the joints in my arms," he said. And Dorothy oiled them and the Scarecrow bent them carefully until they were quite free from rust and as good as new. The Tin Woodman gave a sigh of satisfaction and lowered his axe, which he leaned against the tree. "This is a great comfort," he said. "I have been holding that axe in the air ever since I rusted, and I'm glad to be able to put it down at last. Now, if you will oil the joints of my legs, I shall be all right once more." So they oiled his legs until he could move them freely; and he thanked them again and again for his release, for he seemed a very polite creature, and very grateful. "I might have stood there always if you had not come along," he said; "so you have certainly saved my life. How did you happen to be here?" "We are on our way to the Emerald City to see the Great Oz," she answered, "and we stopped at your cottage to pass the night." "Why do you wish to see Oz?" he asked. "I want him to send me back to Kansas, and the Scarecrow wants him to put a few brains into his head," she replied. The Tin Woodman appeared to think deeply for a moment. Then he said: "Do you suppose Oz could give me a heart?" "Why, I guess so," Dorothy answered. "It would be as easy as to give the Scarecrow brains." "True," the Tin Woodman returned. "So, if you will allow me to join your party, I will also go to the Emerald City and ask Oz to help me." "Come along," said the Scarecrow heartily, and Dorothy added that she would be pleased to have his company. So the Tin Woodman shouldered his axe and they all passed through the forest until they came to the road that was paved with yellow brick. The Tin Woodman had asked Dorothy to put the oilcan in her basket. "For," he said, "if I should get caught in the rain, and rust again, I would need the oilcan badly." It was a bit of good luck to have their new comrade join the party, for soon after they had begun their journey again they came to a place where the trees and branches grew so thick over the road that the travelers could not pass. But the Tin Woodman set to work with his axe and chopped so well that soon he cleared a passage for the entire party. Dorothy was thinking so earnestly as they walked along that she did not notice when the Scarecrow stumbled into a hole and rolled over to the side of the road. Indeed he was obliged to call to her to help him up again. "Why didn't you walk around the hole?" asked the Tin Woodman. "I

don't know enough," replied the Scarecrow cheerfully. "My head is stuffed with straw, you know, and that is why I am going to Oz to ask him for some brains." "Oh, I see,"

said the Tin Woodman. "But, after all, brains are not the best things in the world." "Have you any?" inquired the Scarecrow. "No, my head is quite empty," answered the

Woodman. "But once I had brains, and a heart also; so, having tried them both, I should much rather have a heart." "And why is that?" asked the Scarecrow. "I will tell you

my story, and then you will know." So, while they were walking through the forest, the Tin Woodman told the following story: "I was born the son of a woodman who

chopped down trees in the forest and sold the wood for a living. When I grew up, I too became a woodchopper, and after my father died I took care of my old mother as long

as she lived. Then I made up my mind that instead of living alone I would marry, so that I might not become lonely. "There was one of the Munchkin girls who was so

beautiful that I soon grew to love her with all my heart. She, on her part, promised to marry me as soon as I could earn enough money to build a better house for her; so I set

to work harder than ever. But the girl lived with an old woman who did not want her to marry anyone, for she was so lazy she wished the girl to remain with her and do the

cooking and the housework. So the old woman went to the Wicked Witch of the East, and promised her two sheep and a cow if she would prevent the marriage. Thereupon

the Wicked Witch enchanted my axe, and when I was chopping away at my best one day, for I was anxious to get the new house and my wife as soon as possible, the axe

slipped all at once and cut off my left leg. "This at first seemed a great misfortune, for I knew a one-legged man could not do very well as a woodchopper. So I went to a

tinsmith and had him make me a new leg out of tin. The leg worked very well, once I was used to it. But my action angered the Wicked Witch of the East, for she had

promised the old woman I should not marry the pretty Munchkin girl. When I began chopping again, my axe slipped and cut off my right leg. Again I went to the tinsmith,

and again he made me a leg out of tin. After this the enchanted axe cut off my arms, one after the other; but, nothing daunted, I had them replaced with tin ones. The Wicked

Witch then made the axe slip and cut off my head, and at first I thought that was the end of me. But the tinsmith happened to come along, and he made me a new head out

of tin. "I thought I had beaten the Wicked Witch then, and I worked harder than ever; but I little knew how cruel my enemy could be. She thought of a new way to kill my

love for the beautiful Munchkin maiden, and made my axe slip again, so that it cut right through my body, splitting me into two halves. Once more the tinsmith came to my

help and made me a body of tin, fastening my tin arms and legs and head to it, by means of joints, so that I could move around as well as ever. But, alas! I had now no heart,

so that I lost all my love for the Munchkin girl, and did not care whether I married her or not. I suppose she is still living with the old woman, waiting for me to come after

her. "My body shone so brightly in the sun that I felt very proud of it and it did not matter now if my axe slipped, for it could not cut me. There was only one danger—that

my joints would rust; but I kept an oilcan in my cottage and took care to oil myself whenever I needed it. However, there came a day when I forgot to do this, and, being

caught in a rainstorm, before I thought of the danger my joints had rusted, and I was left to stand in the woods until you came to help me. It was a terrible thing to undergo, but during the year I stood there I had time to think that the greatest loss I had known was the loss of my heart. While I was in love I was the happiest man on earth; but no

one can love who has not a heart, and so I am resolved to ask Oz to give me one. If he does, I will go back to the Munchkin maiden and marry her." Both Dorothy and the

Scarecrow had been greatly interested in the story of the Tin Woodman, and now they knew why he was so anxious to get a new heart. "All the same," said the Scarecrow,

"I shall ask for brains instead of a heart; for a fool would not know what to do with a heart if he had one." "I shall take the heart," returned the Tin Woodman; "for brains

do not make one happy, and happiness is the best thing in the world." Dorothy did not say anything, for she was puzzled to know which of her two friends was right, and she

decided if she could only get back to Kansas and Aunt Em, it did not matter so much whether the Woodman had no brains and the Scarecrow no heart, or each got what he

wanted. What worried her most was that the bread was nearly gone, and another meal for herself and Toto would empty the basket. To be sure neither the Woodman nor

the Scarecrow ever ate anything, but she was not made of tin nor straw, and could not live unless she was fed. CHAPTER VI The Cowardly Lion All this time Dorothy and

her companions had been walking through the thick woods. The road was still paved with yellow brick, but these were much covered by dried branches and dead leaves from

the trees, and the walking was not at all good. There were few birds in this part of the forest, for birds love the open country where there is plenty of sunshine. But now and

then there came a deep growl from some wild animal hidden among the trees. These sounds made the little girl's heart beat fast, for she did not know what made them; but

Toto knew, and he walked close to Dorothy's side, and did not even bark in return. "How long will it be," the child asked of the Tin Woodman, "before we are out of the

forest?" "I cannot tell," was the answer, "for I have never been to the Emerald City. But my father went there once, when I was a boy, and he said it was a long journey

through a dangerous country, although nearer to the city where Oz dwells the country is beautiful. But I am not afraid so long as I have my oilcan, and nothing can hurt the

Scarecrow, while you bear upon your forehead the mark of the Good Witch's kiss, and that will protect you from harm." "But Toto!" said the girl anxiously. "What will

protect him?" "We must protect him ourselves if he is in danger," replied the Tin Woodman. Just as he spoke there came from the forest a terrible roar, and the next moment

a great Lion bounded into the road. With one blow of his paw he sent the Scarecrow spinning over and over to the edge of the road, and then he struck at the Tin Woodman

with his sharp claws. But, to the Lion's surprise, he could make no impression on the tin, although the Woodman fell over in the road and lay still. Little Toto, now that he

had an enemy to face, ran barking toward the Lion, and the great beast had opened his mouth to bite the dog, when Dorothy, fearing Toto would be killed, and heedless of

danger, rushed forward and slapped the Lion upon his nose as hard as she could, while she cried out: "Don't you dare to bite Toto! You ought to be ashamed of yourself, a

big beast like you, to bite a poor little dog!" "I didn't bite him," said the Lion, as he rubbed his nose with his paw where Dorothy had hit it. "No, but you tried to," she retorted.

"You are nothing but a big coward." "I know it," said the Lion, hanging his head in shame. "I've always known it. But how can I help it?" "I don't know, I'm sure. To think

of your striking a stuffed man, like the poor Scarecrow!" "Is he stuffed?" asked the Lion in surprise, as he watched her pick up the Scarecrow and set him upon his feet, while she patted him into shape again. "Of course he's stuffed," replied Dorothy, who was still angry. "That's why he went over so easily," remarked the Lion. "It astonished me

to see him whirl around so. Is the other one stuffed also?" "No," said Dorothy, "he's made of tin." And she helped the Woodman up again. "That's why he nearly blunted

my claws," said the Lion. "When they scratched against the tin it made a cold shiver run down my back. What is that little animal you are so tender of?" "He is my dog,

Toto," answered Dorothy. "Is he made of tin, or stuffed?" asked the Lion. "Neither. He's a—a—a meat dog," said the girl. "Oh! He's a curious animal and seems

remarkably small, now that I look at him. No one would think of biting such a little thing, except a coward like me," continued the Lion sadly. "What makes you a coward?"

asked Dorothy, looking at the great beast in wonder, for he was as big as a small horse. "It's a mystery," replied the Lion. "I suppose I was born that way. All the other animals

in the forest naturally expect me to be brave, for the Lion is everywhere thought to be the King of Beasts. I learned that if I roared very loudly every living thing was

frightened and got out of my way. Whenever I've met a man I've been awfully scared; but I just roared at him, and he has always run away as fast as he could go. If the

elephants and the tigers and the bears had ever tried to fight me, I should have run myself—I'm such a coward; but just as soon as they hear me roar they all try to get away

from me, and of course I let them go." "But that isn't right. The King of Beasts shouldn't be a coward," said the Scarecrow. "I know it," returned the Lion, wiping a tear

from his eye with the tip of his tail. "It is my great sorrow, and makes my life very unhappy. But whenever there is danger, my heart begins to beat fast." "Perhaps you have

heart disease," said the Tin Woodman. "It may be," said the Lion. "If you have," continued the Tin Woodman, "you ought to be glad, for it proves you have a heart. For

my part, I have no heart; so I cannot have heart disease." "Perhaps," said the Lion thoughtfully, "if I had no heart I should not be a coward." "Have you brains?" asked the

Scarecrow. "I suppose so. I've never looked to see," replied the Lion. "I am going to the Great Oz to ask him to give me some," remarked the Scarecrow, "for my head is

stuffed with straw." "And I am going to ask him to give me a heart," said the Woodman. "And I am going to ask him to send Toto and me back to Kansas," added Dorothy.

"Do you think Oz could give me courage?" asked the Cowardly Lion. "Just as easily as he could give me brains," said the Scarecrow. "Or give me a heart," said the Tin

Woodman. "Or send me back to Kansas," said Dorothy. "Then, if you don't mind, I'll go with you," said the Lion, "for my life is simply unbearable without a bit of

courage." "You will be very welcome," answered Dorothy, "for you will help to keep away the other wild beasts. It seems to me they must be more cowardly than you are

if they allow you to scare them so easily." "They really are," said the Lion, "but that doesn't make me any braver, and as long as I know myself to be a coward I shall be

unhappy." So once more the little company set off upon the journey, the Lion walking with stately strides at Dorothy's side. Toto did not approve this new comrade at first,

for he could not forget how nearly he had been crushed between the Lion's great jaws. But after a time he became more at ease, and presently Toto and the Cowardly Lion

had grown to be good friends. During the rest of that day there was no other adventure to mar the peace of their journey. Once, indeed, the Tin Woodman stepped upon a

beetle that was crawling along the road, and killed the poor little thing. This made the Tin Woodman very unhappy, for he was always careful not to hurt any living creature;

and as he walked along he wept several tears of sorrow and regret. These tears ran slowly down his face and over the hinges of his jaw, and there they rusted. When Dorothy presently asked him a question the Tin Woodman could not open his mouth, for his jaws were tightly rusted together. He became greatly frightened at this and made many motions to Dorothy to relieve him, but she could not understand. The Lion was also puzzled to know what was wrong. But the Scarecrow seized the oilcan from Dorothy's basket and oiled the Woodman's jaws, so that after a few moments he could talk as well as before. "This will serve me a lesson," said he, "to look where I step. For if I should kill another bug or beetle I should surely cry again, and crying rusts my jaws so that I cannot speak." Thereafter he walked very carefully, with his eyes on the road, and when he saw a tiny ant toiling by he would step over it, so as not to harm it. The Tin Woodman knew very well he had no heart, and therefore he took great care never to be cruel or unkind to anything. "You people with hearts," he said, "have something to guide you, and need never do wrong; but I have no heart, and so I must be very careful. When Oz gives me a heart of course I needn't mind so much." CHAPTER VII The Journey to the Great Oz They were obliged to camp out that night under a large tree in the forest, for there were no houses near. The tree made a good, thick covering to protect them from the dew, and the Tin Woodman chopped a great pile of wood with his axe and Dorothy built a splendid fire that warmed her and made her feel less lonely. She and Toto ate the last of their bread, and now she did not know what they would do for breakfast. "If you wish," said the Lion, "I will go into the forest and kill a deer for you. You can roast it by the fire, since your tastes are so peculiar that you prefer cooked food, and then you will have a very good breakfast." "Don't! Please don't," begged the Tin Woodman. "I should certainly weep if you killed a poor deer, and then my jaws would rust again." But the Lion went away into the forest and found his own supper, and no one ever knew what it was, for he didn't mention it. And the Scarecrow found a tree full of nuts and filled Dorothy's basket with them, so that she would not be hungry for a long time. She thought this was very kind and thoughtful of the Scarecrow, but she laughed heartily at the awkward way in which the poor creature picked up the nuts. His padded hands were so clumsy and the nuts were so small that he dropped almost as many as he put in the basket. But the Scarecrow did not mind how long it took him to fill the basket, for it enabled him to keep away from the fire, as he feared a spark might get into his straw and burn him up. So he kept a good distance away from the flames, and only came near to cover Dorothy with dry leaves when she lay down to sleep. These kept her very snug and warm, and she slept soundly until morning. When it was daylight, the girl bathed her face in a little rippling brook, and soon after they all started toward the Emerald City. This was to be an eventful day for the travelers. They had hardly been walking an hour when they saw before them a great ditch that crossed the road and divided the forest as far as they could see on either side. It was a very wide ditch, and when they crept up to the edge and looked into it they could see it was also very deep, and there were many big, jagged rocks at the bottom. The sides were so steep that none of them could climb down, and for a moment it seemed that their journey must end. "What shall we do?" asked Dorothy despairingly. "I haven't the faintest idea," said the Tin Woodman, and the Lion shook his shaggy mane and looked thoughtful. But the Scarecrow said, "We cannot fly, that is certain. Neither can we climb down into this great ditch. Therefore, if we cannot jump over it, we must stop where we are." "I think I could jump over it," said the Cowardly Lion, after measuring the distance carefully in his mind. "Then we are all right," answered the

Scarecrow, "for you can carry us all over on your back, one at a time." "Well, I'll try it," said the Lion. "Who will go first?" "I will," declared the Scarecrow, "for, if you

found that you could not jump over the gulf, Dorothy would be killed, or the Tin Woodman badly dented on the rocks below. But if I am on your back it will not matter so

much, for the fall would not hurt me at all." "I am terribly afraid of falling, myself," said the Cowardly Lion, "but I suppose there is nothing to do but try it. So get on my

back and we will make the attempt." The Scarecrow sat upon the Lion's back, and the big beast walked to the edge of the gulf and crouched down. "Why don't you run and

jump?" asked the Scarecrow. "Because that isn't the way we Lions do these things," he replied. Then giving a great spring, he shot through the air and landed safely on the

other side. They were all greatly pleased to see how easily he did it, and after the Scarecrow had got down from his back the Lion sprang across the ditch again. Dorothy

thought she would go next; so she took Toto in her arms and climbed on the Lion's back, holding tightly to his mane with one hand. The next moment it seemed as if she

were flying through the air; and then, before she had time to think about it, she was safe on the other side. The Lion went back a third time and got the Tin Woodman, and

then they all sat down for a few moments to give the beast a chance to rest, for his great leaps had made his breath short, and he panted like a big dog that has been running

too long. They found the forest very thick on this side, and it looked dark and gloomy. After the Lion had rested they started along the road of yellow brick, silently

wondering, each in his own mind, if ever they would come to the end of the woods and reach the bright sunshine again. To add to their discomfort, they soon heard strange

noises in the depths of the forest, and the Lion whispered to them that it was in this part of the country that the Kalidahs lived. "What are the Kalidahs?" asked the girl. "They

are monstrous beasts with bodies like bears and heads like tigers," replied the Lion, "and with claws so long and sharp that they could tear me in two as easily as I could kill

Toto. I'm terribly afraid of the Kalidahs." "I'm not surprised that you are," returned Dorothy. "They must be dreadful beasts." The Lion was about to reply when suddenly

they came to another gulf across the road. But this one was so broad and deep that the Lion knew at once he could not leap across it. So they sat down to consider what they

should do, and after serious thought the Scarecrow said: "Here is a great tree, standing close to the ditch. If the Tin Woodman can chop it down, so that it will fall to the other

side, we can walk across it easily." "That is a first-rate idea," said the Lion. "One would almost suspect you had brains in your head, instead of straw." The Woodman set to

work at once, and so sharp was his axe that the tree was soon chopped nearly through. Then the Lion put his strong front legs against the tree and pushed with all his might,

and slowly the big tree tipped and fell with a crash across the ditch, with its top branches on the other side. They had just started to cross this queer bridge when a sharp growl

made them all look up, and to their horror they saw running toward them two great beasts with bodies like bears and heads like tigers. "They are the Kalidahs!" said the

Cowardly Lion, beginning to tremble. "Quick!" cried the Scarecrow. "Let us cross over." So Dorothy went first, holding Toto in her arms, the Tin Woodman followed, and

the Scarecrow came next. The Lion, although he was certainly afraid, turned to face the Kalidahs, and then he gave so loud and terrible a roar that Dorothy screamed and the Scarecrow fell over backward, while even the fierce beasts stopped short and looked at him in surprise. But, seeing they were bigger than the Lion, and remembering that there were two of them and only one of him, the Kalidahs again rushed forward, and the Lion crossed over the tree and turned to see what they would do next. Without stopping an instant the fierce beasts also began to cross the tree. And the Lion said to Dorothy: "We are lost, for they will surely tear us to pieces with their sharp claws. But stand close behind me, and I will fight them as long as I am alive." "Wait a minute!" called the Scarecrow. He had been thinking what was best to be done, and now he asked the Woodman to chop away the end of the tree that rested on their side of the ditch. The Tin Woodman began to use his axe at once, and, just as the two Kalidahs were nearly across, the tree fell with a crash into the gulf, carrying the ugly, snarling brutes with it, and both were dashed to pieces on the sharp rocks at the bottom. "Well," said the Cowardly Lion, drawing a long breath of relief, "I see we are going to live a little while longer, and I am glad of it, for it must be a very uncomfortable thing not to be alive. Those creatures frightened me so badly that my heart is beating yet." "Ah," said the Tin Woodman sadly, "I wish I had a heart to beat." This adventure made the travelers more anxious than ever to get out of the forest, and they walked so fast that Dorothy became tired, and had to ride on the Lion's back. To their great joy the trees became thinner the farther they advanced, and in the afternoon they suddenly came upon a broad river, flowing swiftly just before them. On the other side of the water they could see the road of yellow brick running through a beautiful country, with green meadows dotted with bright flowers and all the road bordered with trees hanging full of delicious fruits. They were greatly pleased to see this delightful country before them. "How shall we cross the river?" asked Dorothy. "That is easily done," replied the Scarecrow. "The Tin Woodman must build us a raft, so we can float to the other side." So the Woodman took his axe and began to chop down small trees to make a raft, and while he was busy at this the Scarecrow found on the riverbank a tree full of fine fruit. This pleased Dorothy, who had eaten nothing but nuts all day, and she made a hearty meal of the ripe fruit. But it takes time to make a raft, even when one is as industrious and untiring as the Tin Woodman, and when night came the work was not done. So they found a cozy place under the trees where they slept well until the morning; and Dorothy dreamed of the Emerald City, and of the good Wizard Oz, who would soon send her back to her own home again. CHAPTER VIII The Deadly Poppy Field Our little party of travelers awakened the next morning refreshed and full of hope, and Dorothy breakfasted like a princess off peaches and plums from the trees beside the river. Behind them was the dark forest they had passed safely through, although they had suffered many discouragements; but before them was a lovely, sunny country that seemed to beckon them on to the Emerald City. To be sure, the broad river now cut them off from this beautiful land. But the raft was nearly done, and after the Tin Woodman had cut a few more logs and fastened them together with wooden pins, they were ready to start. Dorothy sat down in the middle of the raft and held Toto in her arms. When the Cowardly Lion stepped upon the raft it tipped badly, for he was big and heavy; but the Scarecrow and the Tin Woodman stood upon the other end to steady it, and they had long poles in their hands to push the raft through the water. They got along quite well at first, but when they reached the middle of the river the swift current swept the raft downstream, farther and farther away from the road of yellow brick. And the water grew so deep that the long poles would not touch the bottom. "This is bad," said the Tin Woodman, "for if we cannot get to the land we shall be carried into the country of the Wicked Witch of the West, and she will enchant us and make us her slaves." "And then I should get no brains," said the Scarecrow. "And I should get no courage," said the Cowardly Lion. "And I should get no heart," said the Tin Woodman. "And I should never get back to Kansas," said Dorothy. "We must certainly get to the Emerald City if we can," the Scarecrow continued, and he pushed so hard on his long pole that it stuck fast in the mud at the bottom of the river. Then, before he could pull it out again—or let go—the raft was swept away, and the poor Scarecrow left clinging to the pole in the middle of the river. "Good-bye!" he called after them, and they were very sorry to leave him. Indeed, the Tin Woodman began to cry, but fortunately remembered that he might rust, and so dried his tears on Dorothy's apron. Of course this was a bad thing for the Scarecrow. "I am now worse off than when I first met Dorothy," he thought. "Then, I was stuck on a pole in a cornfield, where I could make-believe scare the crows, at any rate. But surely there is no use for a Scarecrow stuck on a pole in the middle of a river. I am afraid I shall never have any brains, after all!" Down the stream the raft floated, and the poor Scarecrow was left far behind. Then the Lion said: "Something must be done to save us. I think I can swim to the shore and pull the raft after me, if you will only hold fast to the tip of my tail." So he sprang into the water, and the Tin Woodman caught fast hold of his tail. Then the Lion began to swim with all his might toward the shore. It was hard work, although he was so big; but by and by they were drawn out of the current, and then Dorothy took the Tin Woodman's long pole and helped push the raft to the land. They were all tired out when they reached the shore at last and stepped off upon the pretty green grass, and they also knew that the stream had carried them a long way past the road of yellow brick that led to the Emerald City. "What shall we do now?" asked the Tin Woodman, as the Lion lay down on the grass to let the sun dry him. "We must get back to the road, in some way," said Dorothy. "The best plan will be to walk along the riverbank until we come to the road again," remarked the Lion. So, when they were rested, Dorothy picked up her basket and they started along the grassy bank, to the road from which the river had carried them. It was a lovely country, with plenty of flowers and fruit trees and sunshine to cheer them, and had they not felt so sorry for the poor Scarecrow, they could have been very happy. They walked along as fast as they could, Dorothy only stopping once to pick a beautiful flower; and after a time the Tin Woodman cried out: "Look!" Then they all looked at the river and saw the Scarecrow perched upon his pole in the middle of the water, looking very lonely and sad. "What can we do to save him?" asked Dorothy. The Lion and the Woodman both shook their heads, for they did not know. So they sat down upon the bank and gazed wistfully at the Scarecrow until a Stork flew by, who, upon seeing them, stopped to rest at the water's edge. "Who are you and where are you going?" asked the Stork. "I am Dorothy," answered the girl, "and these are my friends, the Tin Woodman and the Cowardly Lion; and we are going to the Emerald City." "This isn't the road," said the Stork, as she twisted her long neck and looked sharply at the queer party. "I know it," returned Dorothy, "but we have lost the Scarecrow, and are wondering how we shall get him again." "Where is he?" asked the Stork. "Over there in the river," answered the little girl. "If he wasn't so big and heavy I would get him for you," remarked the Stork. "He isn't heavy a bit," said

Dorothy eagerly, "for he is stuffed with straw; and if you will bring him back to us, we shall thank you ever and ever so much." "Well, I'll try," said the Stork, "but if I find he is too heavy to carry I shall have to drop him in the river again." So the big bird flew into the air and over the water till she came to where the Scarecrow was perched upon his pole. Then the Stork with her great claws grabbed the Scarecrow by the arm and carried him up into the air and back to the bank, where Dorothy and the Lion and the Tin Woodman and Toto were sitting. When the Scarecrow found himself among his friends again, he was so happy that he hugged them all, even the Lion and Toto; and as they walked along he sang "Tol-de-ri-de-oh!" at every step, he felt so gay. "I was afraid I should have to stay in the river forever," he said, "but the kind Stork saved me, and if I ever get any brains I shall find the Stork again and do her some kindness in return." "That's all right," said the Stork, who was flying along beside them. "I always like to help anyone in trouble. But I must go now, for my babies are waiting in the nest for me. I hope you will find the Emerald City and that Oz will help you." "Thank you," replied Dorothy, and then the kind Stork flew into the air and was soon out of sight. **They walked along listening to the singing of the brightly colored birds and looking at the lovely flowers which now became so thick that the ground was carpeted with them.** There were big yellow and white and blue and purple blossoms, besides great clusters of scarlet poppies, which were so brilliant in color they almost dazzled Dorothy's eyes. "Aren't they beautiful?" the girl asked, as she breathed in the spicy scent of the bright flowers. "I suppose so," answered the Scarecrow. "When I have brains, I shall probably like them better." "If I only had a heart, I should love them," added the Tin Woodman. "I always did like flowers," said the Lion. "They seem so helpless and frail. But there are none in the forest so bright as these." They now came upon more and more of the big scarlet poppies, and fewer and fewer of the other flowers; and soon they found themselves in the midst of a great meadow of poppies. Now it is well known that when there are many of these flowers together their odor is so powerful that anyone who breathes it falls asleep, and if the sleeper is not carried away from the scent of the flowers, he sleeps on and on forever. But Dorothy did not know this, nor could she get away from the bright red flowers that were everywhere about; so presently her eyes grew heavy and she felt she must sit down to rest and to sleep. But the Tin Woodman would not let her do this. "We must hurry and get back to the road of yellow brick before dark," he said; and the Scarecrow agreed with him. So they kept walking until Dorothy could stand no longer. Her eyes closed in spite of herself and she forgot where she was and fell among the poppies, fast asleep. "What shall we do?" asked the Tin Woodman. "If we leave her here she will die," said the Lion. "The smell of the flowers is killing us all. I myself can scarcely keep my eyes open, and the dog is asleep already." It was true; Toto had fallen down beside his little mistress. But the Scarecrow and the Tin Woodman, not being made of flesh, were not troubled by the scent of the flowers. "Run fast," said the Scarecrow to the Lion, "and get out of this deadly flower bed as soon as you can. We will bring the little girl with us, but if you should fall asleep you are too big to be carried." So the Lion aroused himself and bounded forward as fast as he could go. In a moment he was out of sight. "Let us make a chair with our hands and carry her," said the Scarecrow. So they picked up Toto and put the dog in Dorothy's lap, and then they made a chair with their hands for the seat and their arms for the arms and carried the sleeping girl between them through the flowers. On and on they walked, and it seemed that the great carpet of deadly flowers that surrounded them would never end. They followed the bend of the river, and at last came upon their friend

the Lion, lying fast asleep among the poppies. The flowers had been too strong for the huge beast and he had given up at last, and fallen only a short distance from the end

of the poppy bed, where the sweet grass spread in beautiful green fields before them. "We can do nothing for him," said the Tin Woodman, sadly; "for he is much too heavy

to lift. We must leave him here to sleep on forever, and perhaps he will dream that he has found courage at last." "I'm sorry," said the Scarecrow. "The Lion was a very good

comrade for one so cowardly. But let us go on." They carried the sleeping girl to a pretty spot beside the river, far enough from the poppy field to prevent her breathing any

more of the poison of the flowers, and here they laid her gently on the soft grass and waited for the fresh breeze to waken her. CHAPTER IX The Queen of the Field Mice

We cannot be far from the road of yellow brick, now," remarked the Scarecrow, as he stood beside the girl, "for we have come nearly as far as the river carried us away." The

Tin Woodman was about to reply when he heard a low growl, and turning his head (which worked beautifully on hinges) he saw a strange beast come bounding over the

grass toward them. It was, indeed, a great yellow Wildcat, and the Woodman thought it must be chasing something, for its ears were lying close to its head and its mouth was

wide open, showing two rows of ugly teeth, while its red eyes glowed like balls of fire. As it came nearer the Tin Woodman saw that running before the beast was a little gray

field mouse, and although he had no heart he knew it was wrong for the Wildcat to try to kill such a pretty, harmless creature. So the Woodman raised his axe, and as the

Wildcat ran by he gave it a quick blow that cut the beast's head clean off from its body, and it rolled over at his feet in two pieces. The field mouse, now that it was freed from

its enemy, stopped short; and coming slowly up to the Woodman it said, in a squeaky little voice: "Oh, thank you! Thank you ever so much for saving my life." "Don't speak

of it, I beg of you," replied the Woodman. "I have no heart, you know, so I am careful to help all those who may need a friend, even if it happens to be only a mouse." "Only

a mouse!" cried the little animal, indignantly. "Why, I am a Queen—the Queen of all the Field Mice!" "Oh, indeed," said the Woodman, making a bow. "Therefore you

have done a great deed, as well as a brave one, in saving my life," added the Queen. At that moment several mice were seen running up as fast as their little legs could carry

them, and when they saw their Queen they exclaimed: "Oh, your Majesty, we thought you would be killed! How did you manage to escape the great Wildcat?" They all

bowed so low to the little Queen that they almost stood upon their heads. "This funny tin man," she answered, "killed the Wildcat and saved my life. So hereafter you must

all serve him, and obey his slightest wish." "We will!" cried all the mice, in a shrill chorus. And then they scampered in all directions, for Toto had awakened from his sleep,

and seeing all these mice around him he gave one bark of delight and jumped right into the middle of the group. Toto had always loved to chase mice when he lived in Kansas,

and he saw no harm in it. But the Tin Woodman caught the dog in his arms and held him tight, while he called to the mice, "Come back! Come back! Toto shall not hurt

you." At this the Queen of the Mice stuck her head out from underneath a clump of grass and asked, in a timid voice, "Are you sure he will not bite us?" "I will not let him,"

said the Woodman; "so do not be afraid." One by one the mice came creeping back, and Toto did not bark again, although he tried to get out of the Woodman's arms, and would have bitten him had he not known very well he was made of tin. Finally one of the biggest mice spoke. "Is there anything we can do," it asked, "to repay you for saving

the life of our Queen?" "Nothing that I know of," answered the Woodman; but the Scarecrow, who had been trying to think, but could not because his head was stuffed with

straw, said, quickly, "Oh, yes; you can save our friend, the Cowardly Lion, who is asleep in the poppy bed." "A Lion!" cried the little Queen. "Why, he would eat us all up."

"Oh, no," declared the Scarecrow; "this Lion is a coward." "Really?" asked the Mouse. "He says so himself," answered the Scarecrow, "and he would never hurt anyone

who is our friend. If you will help us to save him I promise that he shall treat you all with kindness." "Very well," said the Queen, "we trust you. But what shall we do?" "Are

there many of these mice which call you Queen and are willing to obey you?" "Oh, yes; there are thousands," she replied. "Then send for them all to come here as soon as

possible, and let each one bring a long piece of string." The Queen turned to the mice that attended her and told them to go at once and get all her people. As soon as they

heard her orders they ran away in every direction as fast as possible. "Now," said the Scarecrow to the Tin Woodman, "you must go to those trees by the riverside and make

a truck that will carry the Lion." So the Woodman went at once to the trees and began to work; and he soon made a truck out of the limbs of trees, from which he chopped

away all the leaves and branches. He fastened it together with wooden pegs and made the four wheels out of short pieces of a big tree trunk. So fast and so well did he work

that by the time the mice began to arrive the truck was all ready for them. They came from all directions, and there were thousands of them: big mice and little mice and

middle-sized mice; and each one brought a piece of string in his mouth. It was about this time that Dorothy woke from her long sleep and opened her eyes. She was greatly

astonished to find herself lying upon the grass, with thousands of mice standing around and looking at her timidly. But the Scarecrow told her about everything, and turning

to the dignified little Mouse, he said: "Permit me to introduce to you her Majesty, the Queen." Dorothy nodded gravely and the Queen made a curtsy, after which she became

quite friendly with the little girl. The Scarecrow and the Woodman now began to fasten the mice to the truck, using the strings they had brought. One end of a string was

tied around the neck of each mouse and the other end to the truck. Of course the truck was a thousand times bigger than any of the mice who were to draw it; but when all

the mice had been harnessed, they were able to pull it quite easily. Even the Scarecrow and the Tin Woodman could sit on it, and were drawn swiftly by their queer little

horses to the place where the Lion lay asleep. After a great deal of hard work, for the Lion was heavy, they managed to get him up on the truck. Then the Queen hurriedly

gave her people the order to start, for she feared if the mice stayed among the poppies too long they also would fall asleep. At first the little creatures, many though they were,

could hardly stir the heavily loaded truck; but the Woodman and the Scarecrow both pushed from behind, and they got along better. Soon they rolled the Lion out of the

poppy bed to the green fields, where he could breathe the sweet, fresh air again, instead of the poisonous scent of the flowers. Dorothy came to meet them and thanked the

little mice warmly for saving her companion from death. She had grown so fond of the big Lion she was glad he had been rescued. Then the mice were unharnessed from

the truck and scampered away through the grass to their homes. The Queen of the Mice was the last to leave. "If ever you need us again," she said, "come out into the field and call, and we shall hear you and come to your assistance. Good-bye!" "Good-bye!" they all answered, and away the Queen ran, while Dorothy held Toto tightly lest he

should run after her and frighten her. After this they sat down beside the Lion until he should awaken; and the Scarecrow brought Dorothy some fruit from a tree near by,

which she ate for her dinner. CHAPTER X The Guardian of the Gates It was some time before the Cowardly Lion awakened, for he had lain among the poppies a long

while, breathing in their deadly fragrance; but when he did open his eyes and roll off the truck he was very glad to find himself still alive. "I ran as fast as I could," he said,

sitting down and yawning, "but the flowers were too strong for me. How did you get me out?" Then they told him of the field mice, and how they had generously saved him

from death; and the Cowardly Lion laughed, and said: "I have always thought myself very big and terrible; yet such little things as flowers came near to killing me, and such

small animals as mice have saved my life. How strange it all is! But, comrades, what shall we do now?" "We must journey on until we find the road of yellow brick again,"

said Dorothy, "and then we can keep on to the Emerald City." So, the Lion being fully refreshed, and feeling quite himself again, they all started upon the journey, greatly

enjoying the walk through the soft, fresh grass; and it was not long before they reached the road of yellow brick and turned again toward the Emerald City where the Great

Oz dwelt. The road was smooth and well paved, now, and the country about was beautiful, so that the travelers rejoiced in leaving the forest far behind, and with it the many

dangers they had met in its gloomy shades. Once more they could see fences built beside the road; but these were painted green, and when they came to a small house, in

which a farmer evidently lived, that also was painted green. They passed by several of these houses during the afternoon, and sometimes people came to the doors and looked

at them as if they would like to ask questions; but no one came near them nor spoke to them because of the great Lion, of which they were very much afraid. The people

were all dressed in clothing of a lovely emerald-green color and wore peaked hats like those of the Munchkins. "This must be the Land of Oz," said Dorothy, "and we are

surely getting near the Emerald City." "Yes," answered the Scarecrow. "Everything is green here, while in the country of the Munchkins blue was the favorite color. But the

people do not seem to be as friendly as the Munchkins, and I'm afraid we shall be unable to find a place to pass the night." "I should like something to eat besides fruit," said

the girl, "and I'm sure Toto is nearly starved. Let us stop at the next house and talk to the people." So, when they came to a good-sized farmhouse, Dorothy walked boldly

up to the door and knocked. A woman opened it just far enough to look out, and said, "What do you want, child, and why is that great Lion with you?" "We wish to pass

the night with you, if you will allow us," answered Dorothy; "and the Lion is my friend and comrade, and would not hurt you for the world." "Is he tame?" asked the woman,

opening the door a little wider. "Oh, yes," said the girl, "and he is a great coward, too. He will be more afraid of you than you are of him." "Well," said the woman, after

thinking it over and taking another peep at the Lion, "if that is the case you may come in, and I will give you some supper and a place to sleep." So they all entered the house,

where there were, besides the woman, two children and a man. The man had hurt his leg, and was lying on the couch in a corner. They seemed greatly surprised to see so

strange a company, and while the woman was busy laying the table the man asked: "Where are you all going?" "To the Emerald City," said Dorothy, "to see the Great Oz."

"Oh, indeed!" exclaimed the man. "Are you sure that Oz will see you?" "Why not?" she replied. "Why, it is said that he never lets anyone come into his presence. I have

been to the Emerald City many times, and it is a beautiful and wonderful place; but I have never been permitted to see the Great Oz, nor do I know of any living person who

has seen him." "Does he never go out?" asked the Scarecrow. "Never. He sits day after day in the great Throne Room of his Palace, and even those who wait upon him do

not see him face-to-face." "What is he like?" asked the girl. "That is hard to tell," said the man thoughtfully. "You see, Oz is a Great Wizard, and can take on any form he

wishes. So that some say he looks like a bird; and some say he looks like an elephant; and some say he looks like a cat. To others he appears as a beautiful fairy, or a brownie,

or in any other form that pleases him. But who the real Oz is, when he is in his own form, no living person can tell." "That is very strange," said Dorothy, "but we must try,

in some way, to see him, or we shall have made our journey for nothing." "Why do you wish to see the terrible Oz?" asked the man. "I want him to give me some brains,"

said the Scarecrow eagerly. "Oh, Oz could do that easily enough," declared the man. "He has more brains than he needs." "And I want him to give me a heart," said the Tin

Woodman. "That will not trouble him," continued the man, "for Oz has a large collection of hearts, of all sizes and shapes." "And I want him to give me courage," said the

Cowardly Lion. "Oz keeps a great pot of courage in his Throne Room," said the man, "which he has covered with a golden plate, to keep it from running over. He will be

glad to give you some." "And I want him to send me back to Kansas," said Dorothy. "Where is Kansas?" asked the man, with surprise. "I don't know," replied Dorothy

sorrowfully, "but it is my home, and I'm sure it's somewhere." "Very likely. Well, Oz can do anything; so I suppose he will find Kansas for you. But first you must get to see

him, and that will be a hard task; for the Great Wizard does not like to see anyone, and he usually has his own way. But what do *you* want?" he continued, speaking to Toto.

Toto only wagged his tail; for, strange to say, he could not speak. The woman now called to them that supper was ready, so they gathered around the table and Dorothy ate

some delicious porridge and a dish of scrambled eggs and a plate of nice white bread, and enjoyed her meal. The Lion ate some of the porridge, but did not care for it, saying

it was made from oats and oats were food for horses, not for lions. The Scarecrow and the Tin Woodman ate nothing at all. Toto ate a little of everything, and was glad to

get a good supper again. The woman now gave Dorothy a bed to sleep in, and Toto lay down beside her, while the Lion guarded the door of her room so she might not be

disturbed. The Scarecrow and the Tin Woodman stood up in a corner and kept quiet all night, although of course they could not sleep. The next morning, as soon as the sun

was up, they started on their way, and soon saw a beautiful green glow in the sky just before them. "That must be the Emerald City," said Dorothy. As they walked on, the

green glow became brighter and brighter, and it seemed that at last they were nearing the end of their travels. Yet it was afternoon before they came to the great wall that

surrounded the City. It was high and thick and of a bright green color. In front of them, and at the end of the road of yellow brick, was a big gate, all studded with emeralds

that glittered so in the sun that even the painted eyes of the Scarecrow were dazzled by their brilliancy. There was a bell beside the gate, and Dorothy pushed the button and

heard a silvery tinkle sound within. Then the big gate swung slowly open, and they all passed through and found themselves in a high arched room, the walls of which glistened with countless emeralds. Before them stood a little man about the same size as the Munchkins. He was clothed all in green, from his head to his feet, and even his skin was of a greenish tint. At his side was a large green box. When he saw Dorothy and her companions the man asked, "What do you wish in the Emerald City?" "We came here to see the Great Oz," said Dorothy. The man was so surprised at this answer that he sat down to think it over. "It has been many years since anyone asked me to see Oz," he said, shaking his head in perplexity. "He is powerful and terrible, and if you come on an idle or foolish errand to bother the wise reflections of the Great Wizard, he might be angry and destroy you all in an instant." "But it is not a foolish errand, nor an idle one," replied the Scarecrow; "it is important. And we have been told that Oz is a good Wizard." "So he is," said the green man, "and he rules the Emerald City wisely and well. But to those who are not honest, or who approach him from curiosity, he is most terrible, and few have ever dared ask to see his face. I am the Guardian of the Gates, and since you demand to see the Great Oz I must take you to his Palace. But first you must put on the spectacles." "Why?" asked Dorothy. "Because if you did not wear spectacles the brightness and glory of the Emerald City would blind you. Even those who live in the City must wear spectacles night and day. They are all locked on, for Oz so ordered it when the City was first built, and I have the only key that will unlock them." He opened the big box, and Dorothy saw that it was filled with spectacles of every size and shape. All of them had green glasses in them. The Guardian of the Gates found a pair that would just fit Dorothy and put them over her eyes. There were two golden bands fastened to them that passed around the back of her head, where they were locked together by a little key that was at the end of a chain the Guardian of the Gates wore around his neck. When they were on, Dorothy could not take them off had she wished, but of course she did not wish to be blinded by the glare of the Emerald City, so she said nothing. Then the green man fitted spectacles for the Scarecrow and the Tin Woodman and the Lion, and even on little Toto; and all were locked fast with the key. Then the Guardian of the Gates put on his own glasses and told them he was ready to show them to the Palace. Taking a big golden key from a peg on the wall, he opened another gate, and they all followed him through the portal into the streets of the Emerald City. CHAPTER XI The Wonderful Emerald City of Oz Even with eyes protected by the green spectacles, Dorothy and her friends were at first dazzled by the brilliancy of the wonderful City. The streets were lined with beautiful houses all built of green marble and studded everywhere with sparkling emeralds. They walked over a pavement of the same green marble, and where the blocks were joined together were rows of emeralds, set closely, and glittering in the brightness of the sun. The windowpanes were of green glass; even the sky above the City had a green tint, and the rays of the sun were green. There were many people—men, women, and children—walking about, and these were all dressed in green clothes and had greenish skins. They looked at Dorothy and her strangely assorted company with wondering eyes, and the children all ran away and hid behind their mothers when they saw the Lion; but no one spoke to them. Many shops stood in the street, and Dorothy saw that everything in them was green. Green candy and green popcorn were offered for sale, as well as green shoes, green hats, and green clothes of all sorts. At one place a man was selling green lemonade, and when the children bought it Dorothy could see that they paid for it with green pennies. There seemed to be no horses nor animals of any kind; the men carried things around in little green carts, which they pushed before them. Everyone seemed happy and contented and prosperous. The Guardian of the Gates led them through the streets until they came to a big building, exactly in the middle of the City, which was the Palace of Oz, the Great Wizard. There was a soldier before the door, dressed in a green uniform and wearing a long green beard. "Here are strangers," said the Guardian of the Gates to him, "and they demand to see the Great Oz." "Step inside," answered the soldier, "and I will carry your message to him." So they passed through the Palace Gates and were led into a big room with a green carpet and lovely green furniture set with emeralds. The soldier made them all wipe their feet upon a green mat before entering this room, and when they were seated he said politely: "Please make yourselves comfortable while I go to the door of the Throne Room and tell Oz you are here." They had to wait a long time before the soldier returned. When, at last, he came back, Dorothy asked: "Have you seen Oz?" "Oh, no," returned the soldier; "I have never seen him. But I spoke to him as he sat behind his screen and gave him your message. He said he will grant you an audience, if you so desire; but each one of you must enter his presence alone, and he will admit but one each day. Therefore, as you must remain in the Palace for several days, I will have you shown to rooms where you may rest in comfort after your journey." "Thank you," replied the girl; "that is very kind of Oz." The soldier now blew upon a green whistle, and at once a young girl, dressed in a pretty green silk gown, entered the room. She had lovely green hair and green eyes, and she bowed low before Dorothy as she said, "Follow me and I will show you your room." So Dorothy said good-bye to all her friends except Toto, and taking the dog in her arms followed the green girl through seven passages and up three flights of stairs until they came to a room at the front of the Palace. It was the sweetest little room in the world, with a soft comfortable bed that had sheets of green silk and a green velvet counterpane. There was a tiny fountain in the middle of the room, that shot a spray of green perfume into the air, to fall back into a beautifully carved green marble basin. Beautiful green flowers stood in the windows, and there was a shelf with a row of little green books. When Dorothy had time to open these books she found them full of queer green pictures that made her laugh, they were so funny. In a wardrobe were many green dresses, made of silk and satin and velvet; and all of them fitted Dorothy exactly. "Make yourself perfectly at home," said the green girl, "and if you wish for anything ring the bell. Oz will send for you tomorrow morning." She left Dorothy alone and went back to the others. These she also led to rooms, and each one of them found himself lodged in a very pleasant part of the Palace. Of course this politeness was wasted on the Scarecrow; for when he found himself alone in his room he stood stupidly in one spot, just within the doorway, to wait till morning. It would not rest him to lie down, and he could not close his eyes; so he remained all night staring at a little spider which was weaving its web in a corner of the room, just as if it were not one of the most wonderful rooms in the world. The Tin Woodman lay down on his bed from force of habit, for he remembered when he was made of flesh; but not being able to sleep, he passed the night moving his joints up and down to make sure they kept in good working order. The Lion would have preferred a bed of dried leaves in the forest, and did not like being shut up in a room; but he had too much sense to let this worry him, so he sprang upon the bed and rolled himself up like a cat and purred himself asleep in a minute. The next morning, after breakfast, the green maiden came to fetch Dorothy, and she dressed her in one of the prettiest gowns, made of green brocaded satin. Dorothy put on a green silk apron and tied a green ribbon around Toto's neck, and they started for the Throne Room of the Great Oz. First they came to a great hall in which were many ladies and gentlemen of the court, all dressed in rich costumes. These people had nothing to do but talk to each other, but they always came to wait outside the Throne Room every morning, although they were never permitted to see Oz. As Dorothy entered they looked at her curiously, and one of them whispered: "Are you really going to look upon the face of Oz the Terrible?" "Of course," answered the girl, "if he will see me." "Oh, he will see you," said the soldier who had taken her message to the Wizard, "although he does not like to have people ask to see him. Indeed, at first he was angry and said I should send you back where you came from. Then he asked me what you looked like, and when I mentioned your Silver Shoes he was very much interested. At last I told him about the mark upon your forehead, and he decided he would admit you to his presence." Just then a bell rang, and the green girl said to Dorothy, "That is the signal. You must go into the Throne Room alone." She opened a little door and Dorothy walked boldly through and found herself in a wonderful place. It was a big, round room with a high arched roof, and the walls and ceiling and floor were covered with large emeralds set closely together. In the center of the roof was a great light, as bright as the sun, which made the emeralds sparkle in a wonderful manner. But what interested Dorothy most was the big throne of green marble that stood in the middle of the room. It was shaped like a chair and sparkled with gems, as did everything else. In the center of the chair was an enormous Head, without a body to support it or any arms or legs whatever. There was no hair upon this head, but it had eyes and a nose and mouth, and was much bigger than the head of the biggest giant. As Dorothy gazed upon this in wonder and fear, the eyes turned slowly and looked at her sharply and steadily. Then the mouth moved, and Dorothy heard a voice say: "I am Oz, the Great and Terrible. Who are you, and why do you seek me?" It was not such an awful voice as she had expected to come from the big Head; so she took courage and answered: "I am Dorothy, the Small and Meek. I have come to you for help." The eyes looked at her thoughtfully for a full minute. Then said the voice: "Where did you get the Silver Shoes?" "I got them from the Wicked Witch of the East, when my house fell on her and killed her," she replied. "Where did you get the mark upon your forehead?" continued the voice. "That is where the Good Witch of the North kissed me when she bade me good-bye and sent me to you," said the girl. Again the eyes looked at her sharply, and they saw she was telling the truth. Then Oz asked, "What do you wish me to do?" "Send me back to Kansas, where my Aunt Em and Uncle Henry are," she answered earnestly. "I don't like your country, although it is so beautiful. And I am sure Aunt Em will be dreadfully worried over my being away so long." The eyes winked three times, and then they turned up to the ceiling and down to the floor and rolled around so queerly that they seemed to see every part of the room. And at last they looked at Dorothy again. "Why should I do this for you?" asked Oz. "Because you are strong and I am weak; because you are a Great Wizard and I am only a little girl." "But you were strong enough to kill the Wicked Witch of the East," said Oz. "That just happened," returned Dorothy simply; "I could not help it." "Well," said the Head, "I will give you my answer. You have no right to expect me to send you back to Kansas unless you do something for me in return. In this country everyone must pay for everything he gets. If you wish me to use my magic power to send you home again you must do something for me first. Help me and I will help you." "What must I do?" asked the girl.

"Kill the Wicked Witch of the West," answered Oz. "But I cannot!" exclaimed Dorothy, greatly surprised. "You killed the Witch of the East and you wear the Silver Shoes,

which bear a powerful charm. There is now but one Wicked Witch left in all this land, and when you can tell me she is dead I will send you back to Kansas—but not before."

The little girl began to weep, she was so much disappointed; and the eyes winked again and looked upon her anxiously, as if the Great Oz felt that she could help him if she

would. "I never killed anything, willingly," she sobbed. "Even if I wanted to, how could I kill the Wicked Witch? If you, who are Great and Terrible, cannot kill her yourself,

how do you expect me to do it?" "I do not know," said the Head; "but that is my answer, and until the Wicked Witch dies you will not see your uncle and aunt again.

Remember that the Witch is Wicked—tremendously Wicked—and ought to be killed. Now go, and do not ask to see me again until you have done your task." Sorrowfully

Dorothy left the Throne Room and went back where the Lion and the Scarecrow and the Tin Woodman were waiting to hear what Oz had said to her. "There is no hope

for me," she said sadly, "for Oz will not send me home until I have killed the Wicked Witch of the West; and that I can never do." Her friends were sorry, but could do nothing

to help her; so Dorothy went to her own room and lay down on the bed and cried herself to sleep. The next morning the soldier with the green whiskers came to the

Scarecrow and said: "Come with me, for Oz has sent for you." So the Scarecrow followed him and was admitted into the great Throne Room, where he saw, sitting in the

emerald throne, a most lovely Lady. She was dressed in green silk gauze and wore upon her flowing green locks a crown of jewels. Growing from her shoulders were wings,

gorgeous in color and so light that they fluttered if the slightest breath of air reached them. When the Scarecrow had bowed, as prettily as his straw stuffing would let him,

before this beautiful creature, she looked upon him sweetly, and said: "I am Oz, the Great and Terrible. Who are you, and why do you seek me?" Now the Scarecrow, who

had expected to see the great Head Dorothy had told him of, was much astonished; but he answered her bravely. "I am only a Scarecrow, stuffed with straw. Therefore I have

no brains, and I come to you praying that you will put brains in my head instead of straw, so that I may become as much a man as any other in your dominions." "Why should

I do this for you?" asked the Lady. "Because you are wise and powerful, and no one else can help me," answered the Scarecrow. "I never grant favors without some return,"

said Oz; "but this much I will promise. If you will kill for me the Wicked Witch of the West, I will bestow upon you a great many brains, and such good brains that you will

be the wisest man in all the Land of Oz." "I thought you asked Dorothy to kill the Witch," said the Scarecrow, in surprise. "So I did. I don't care who kills her. But until she

is dead I will not grant your wish. Now go, and do not seek me again until you have earned the brains you so greatly desire." The Scarecrow went sorrowfully back to his

friends and told them what Oz had said; and Dorothy was surprised to find that the Great Wizard was not a Head, as she had seen him, but a lovely Lady. "All the same,"

said the Scarecrow, "she needs a heart as much as the Tin Woodman." On the next morning the soldier with the green whiskers came to the Tin Woodman and said: "Oz has

sent for you. Follow me." So the Tin Woodman followed him and came to the great Throne Room. He did not know whether he would find Oz a lovely Lady or a Head, but he hoped it would be the lovely Lady. "For," he said to himself, "if it is the head, I am sure I shall not be given a heart, since a head has no heart of its own and therefore cannot feel for me. But if it is the lovely Lady I shall beg hard for a heart, for all ladies are themselves said to be kindly hearted." But when the Woodman entered the great Throne Room he saw neither the Head nor the Lady, for Oz had taken the shape of a most terrible Beast. It was nearly as big as an elephant, and the green throne seemed hardly strong enough to hold its weight. The Beast had a head like that of a rhinoceros, only there were five eyes in its face. There were five long arms growing out of its body, and it also had five long, slim legs. Thick, woolly hair covered every part of it, and a more dreadful-looking monster could not be imagined. It was fortunate the Tin Woodman had no heart at that moment, for it would have beat loud and fast from terror. But being only tin, the Woodman was not at all afraid, although he was much disappointed. "I am Oz, the Great and Terrible," spoke the Beast, in a voice that was one great roar. "Who are you, and why do you seek me?" "I am a Woodman, and made of tin. Therefore I have no heart, and cannot love. I pray you to give me a heart that I may be as other men are." "Why should I do this?" demanded the Beast. "Because I ask it, and you alone can grant my request," answered the Woodman. Oz gave a low growl at this, but said, gruffly: "If you indeed desire a heart, you must earn it." "How?" asked the Woodman. "Help Dorothy to kill the Wicked Witch of the West," replied the Beast. "When the Witch is dead, come to me, and I will then give you the biggest and kindest and most loving heart in all the Land of Oz." So the Tin Woodman was forced to return sorrowfully to his friends and tell them of the terrible Beast he had seen. They all wondered greatly at the many forms the Great Wizard could take upon himself, and the Lion said: "If he is a Beast when I go to see him, I shall roar my loudest, and so frighten him that he will grant all I ask. And if he is the lovely Lady, I shall pretend to spring upon her, and so compel her to do my bidding. And if he is the great Head, he will be at my mercy; for I will roll this head all about the room until he promises to give us what we desire. So be of good cheer, my friends, for all will yet be well."

The next morning the soldier with the green whiskers led the Lion to the great Throne Room and bade him enter the presence of Oz. The Lion at once passed through the door, and glancing around saw, to his surprise, that before the throne was a Ball of Fire, so fierce and glowing he could scarcely bear to gaze upon it. His first thought was that Oz had by accident caught on fire and was burning up; but when he tried to go nearer, the heat was so intense that it singed his whiskers, and he crept back tremblingly to a spot nearer the door. Then a low, quiet voice came from the Ball of Fire, and these were the words it spoke: "I am Oz, the Great and Terrible. Who are you, and why do you seek me?" And the Lion answered, "I am a Cowardly Lion, afraid of everything. I came to you to beg that you give me courage, so that in reality I may become the King of Beasts, as men call me." "Why should I give you courage?" demanded Oz. "Because of all Wizards you are the greatest, and alone have power to grant my request," answered the Lion. The Ball of Fire burned fiercely for a time, and the voice said, "Bring me proof that the Wicked Witch is dead, and that moment I will give you courage. But as long as the Witch lives, you must remain a coward." The Lion was angry at this speech, but could say nothing in reply, and while he stood silently gazing at the Ball of Fire it became so furiously hot that he turned tail and rushed from the room. He was glad to find his friends waiting for him, and told them of his terrible interview with the Wizard. "What shall we do now?" asked Dorothy sadly. "There is only one thing we can do," returned the Lion, "and that is to go to the land of the Winkies, seek out the Wicked Witch, and destroy her." "But suppose we cannot?" said the girl. "Then I shall never have courage," declared the Lion. "And I shall never have brains," added the Scarecrow. "And I shall never have a heart," spoke the Tin Woodman. "And I shall never see Aunt Em and Uncle Henry," said Dorothy, beginning to cry. "Be careful!" cried the green girl. "The tears will fall on your green silk gown and spot it." So Dorothy dried her eyes and said, "I suppose we must try it; but I am sure I do not want to kill anybody, even to see Aunt Em again." "I will go with you; but I'm too much of a coward to kill the Witch," said the Lion. "I will go too," declared the Scarecrow; "but I shall not be of much help to you, I am such a fool." "I haven't the heart to harm even a Witch," remarked the Tin Woodman; "but if you go I certainly shall go with you." Therefore it was decided to start upon their journey the next morning, and the Woodman sharpened his axe on a green grindstone and had all his joints properly oiled. The Scarecrow stuffed himself with fresh straw and Dorothy put new paint on his eyes that he might see better. The green girl, who was very kind to them, filled Dorothy's basket with good things to eat, and fastened a little bell around Toto's neck with a green ribbon. They went to bed quite early and slept soundly until daylight, when they were awakened by the crowing of a green cock that lived in the backyard of the Palace, and the cackling of a hen that had laid a green egg. CHAPTER XII The Search for the Wicked Witch The soldier with the green whiskers led them through the streets of the Emerald City until they reached the room where the Guardian of the Gates lived. This officer unlocked their spectacles to put them back in his great box, and then he politely opened the gate for our friends. "Which road leads to the Wicked Witch of the West?" asked Dorothy. "There is no road," answered the Guardian of the Gates. "No one ever wishes to go that way." "How, then, are we to find her?" inquired the girl. "That will be easy," replied the man, "for when she knows you are in the country of the Winkies she will find you, and make you all her slaves." "Perhaps not," said the Scarecrow, "for we mean to destroy her." "Oh, that is different," said the Guardian of the Gates. "No one has ever destroyed her before, so I naturally thought she would make slaves of you, as she has of the rest. But take care; for she is wicked and fierce, and may not allow you to destroy her. Keep to the West, where the sun sets, and you cannot fail to find her." They thanked him and bade him good-bye, and turned toward the West, walking over fields of soft grass dotted here and there with daisies and buttercups. Dorothy still wore the pretty silk dress she had put on in the palace, but now, to her surprise, she found it was no longer green, but pure white. The ribbon around Toto's neck had also lost its green color and was as white as Dorothy's dress. The Emerald City was soon left far behind. As they advanced the ground became rougher and hillier, for there were no farms nor houses in this country of the West, and the ground was untilled. In the afternoon the sun shone hot in their faces, for there were no trees to offer them shade; so that before night Dorothy and Toto and the Lion were tired, and lay down upon the grass and fell asleep, with the Woodman and the Scarecrow keeping watch. Now the Wicked Witch of the West had but one eye, yet that was as powerful as a telescope, and could see everywhere. So, as she sat in the door of her castle, she happened to look around and saw Dorothy lying asleep, with her friends all about her. They were a long distance off, but the Wicked Witch was angry to find them in her country; so she blew upon a silver whistle that hung around her neck. At once there came running to her from all directions a pack of great wolves. They had long legs

and fierce eyes and sharp teeth. "Go to those people," said the Witch, "and tear them to pieces." "Are you not going to make them your slaves?" asked the leader of the

wolves. "No," she answered, "one is of tin, and one of straw; one is a girl and another a Lion. None of them is fit to work, so you may tear them into small pieces." "Very

well," said the wolf, and he dashed away at full speed, followed by the others. It was lucky the Scarecrow and the Woodman were wide awake and heard the wolves coming.

"This is my fight," said the Woodman, "so get behind me and I will meet them as they come." He seized his axe, which he had made very sharp, and as the leader of the

wolves came on the Tin Woodman swung his arm and chopped the wolf's head from its body, so that it immediately died. As soon as he could raise his axe another wolf

came up, and he also fell under the sharp edge of the Tin Woodman's weapon. There were forty wolves, and forty times a wolf was killed, so that at last they all lay dead in

a heap before the Woodman. Then he put down his axe and sat beside the Scarecrow, who said, "It was a good fight, friend." They waited until Dorothy awoke the next

morning. The little girl was quite frightened when she saw the great pile of shaggy wolves, but the Tin Woodman told her all. She thanked him for saving them and sat down

to breakfast, after which they started again upon their journey. Now this same morning the Wicked Witch came to the door of her castle and looked out with her one eye

that could see far off. She saw all her wolves lying dead, and the strangers still traveling through her country. This made her angrier than before, and she blew her silver

whistle twice. Straightway a great flock of wild crows came flying toward her, enough to darken the sky. And the Wicked Witch said to the King Crow, "Fly at once to the

strangers; peck out their eyes and tear them to pieces." The wild crows flew in one great flock toward Dorothy and her companions. When the little girl saw them coming

she was afraid. But the Scarecrow said, "This is my battle, so lie down beside me and you will not be harmed." So they all lay upon the ground except the Scarecrow, and he

stood up and stretched out his arms. And when the crows saw him they were frightened, as these birds always are by scarecrows, and did not dare to come any nearer. But

the King Crow said: "It is only a stuffed man. I will peck his eyes out." The King Crow flew at the Scarecrow, who caught it by the head and twisted its neck until it died.

And then another crow flew at him, and the Scarecrow twisted its neck also. There were forty crows, and forty times the Scarecrow twisted a neck, until at last all were lying

dead beside him. Then he called to his companions to rise, and again they went upon their journey. When the Wicked Witch looked out again and saw all her crows lying in

a heap, she got into a terrible rage, and blew three times upon her silver whistle. Forthwith there was heard a great buzzing in the air, and a swarm of black bees came flying

toward her. "Go to the strangers and sting them to death!" commanded the Witch, and the bees turned and flew rapidly until they came to where Dorothy and her friends

were walking. But the Woodman had seen them coming, and the Scarecrow had decided what to do. "Take out my straw and scatter it over the little girl and the dog and the

Lion," he said to the Woodman, "and the bees cannot sting them." This the Woodman did, and as Dorothy lay close beside the Lion and held Toto in her arms, the straw

covered them entirely. The bees came and found no one but the Woodman to sting, so they flew at him and broke off all their stings against the tin, without hurting the

Woodman at all. And as bees cannot live when their stings are broken that was the end of the black bees, and they lay scattered thick about the Woodman, like little heaps of fine coal. Then Dorothy and the Lion got up, and the girl helped the Tin Woodman put the straw back into the Scarecrow again, until he was as good as ever. So they started upon their journey once more. The Wicked Witch was so angry when she saw her black bees in little heaps like fine coal that she stamped her foot and tore her hair and gnashed her teeth. And then she called a dozen of her slaves, who were the Winkies, and gave them sharp spears, telling them to go to the strangers and destroy them. The Winkies were not a brave people, but they had to do as they were told. So they marched away until they came near to Dorothy. Then the Lion gave a great roar and sprang towards them, and the poor Winkies were so frightened that they ran back as fast as they could. When they returned to the castle the Wicked Witch beat them well with a strap, and sent them back to their work, after which she sat down to think what she should do next. She could not understand how all her plans to destroy these strangers had failed; but she was a powerful Witch, as well as a wicked one, and she soon made up her mind how to act. There was, in her cupboard, a Golden Cap, with a circle of diamonds and rubies running round it. This Golden Cap had a charm. Whoever owned it could call three times upon the Winged Monkeys, who would obey any order they were given. But no person could command these strange creatures more than three times. Twice already the Wicked Witch had used the charm of the Cap. Once was when she had made the Winkies her slaves, and set herself to rule over their country. The Winged Monkeys had helped her do this. The second time was when she had fought against the Great Oz himself, and driven him out of the land of the West. The Winged Monkeys had also helped her in doing this. Only once more could she use this Golden Cap, for which reason she did not like to do so until all her other powers were exhausted. But now that her fierce wolves and her wild crows and her stinging bees were gone, and her slaves had been scared away by the Cowardly Lion, she saw there was only one way left to destroy Dorothy and her friends. So the Wicked Witch took the Golden Cap from her cupboard and placed it upon her head. Then she stood upon her left foot and said slowly: "Ep-pe, pep-pe, kak-ke!" Next she stood upon her right foot and said: "Hil-lo, hol-lo, hel-lo!" After this she stood upon both feet and cried in a loud voice: "Ziz-zy, zuz-zy, zik!" Now the charm began to work. The sky was darkened, and a low rumbling sound was heard in the air. There was a rushing of many wings, a great chattering and laughing, and the sun came out of the dark sky to show the Wicked Witch surrounded by a crowd of monkeys, each with a pair of immense and powerful wings on his shoulders. One, much bigger than the others, seemed to be their leader. He flew close to the Witch and said, "You have called us for the third and last time. What do you command?" "Go to the strangers who are within my land and destroy them all except the Lion," said the Wicked Witch. "Bring that beast to me, for I have a mind to harness him like a horse, and make him work." "Your commands shall be obeyed," said the leader. Then, with a great deal of chattering and noise, the Winged Monkeys flew away to the place where Dorothy and her friends were walking. Some of the Monkeys seized the Tin Woodman and carried him through the air until they were over a country thickly covered with sharp rocks. Here they dropped the poor Woodman, who fell a great distance to the rocks, where he lay so battered and dented that he could neither move nor groan. Others of the Monkeys caught the Scarecrow, and with their long fingers pulled all of the straw out of his clothes and head. They made his hat and boots and clothes into a small bundle and threw it into the top branches of a tall tree. The remaining Monkeys

threw pieces of stout rope around the Lion and wound many coils about his body and head and legs, until he was unable to bite or scratch or struggle in any way. Then they

lifted him up and flew away with him to the Witch's castle, where he was placed in a small yard with a high iron fence around it, so that he could not escape. But Dorothy

they did not harm at all. She stood, with Toto in her arms, watching the sad fate of her comrades and thinking it would soon be her turn. The leader of the Winged Monkeys

flew up to her, his long, hairy arms stretched out and his ugly face grinning terribly; but he saw the mark of the Good Witch's kiss upon her forehead and stopped short,

motioning the others not to touch her. "We dare not harm this little girl," he said to them, "for she is protected by the Power of Good, and that is greater than the Power of

Evil. All we can do is to carry her to the castle of the Wicked Witch and leave her there." So, carefully and gently, they lifted Dorothy in their arms and carried her swiftly

through the air until they came to the castle, where they set her down upon the front doorstep. Then the leader said to the Witch: "We have obeyed you as far as we were

able. The Tin Woodman and the Scarecrow are destroyed, and the Lion is tied up in your yard. The little girl we dare not harm, nor the dog she carries in her arms. Your

power over our band is now ended, and you will never see us again." Then all the Winged Monkeys, with much laughing and chattering and noise, flew into the air and were

soon out of sight. The Wicked Witch was both surprised and worried when she saw the mark on Dorothy's forehead, for she knew well that neither the Winged Monkeys

nor she, herself, dare hurt the girl in any way. She looked down at Dorothy's feet, and seeing the Silver Shoes, began to tremble with fear, for she knew what a powerful

charm belonged to them. At first the Witch was tempted to run away from Dorothy; but she happened to look into the child's eyes and saw how simple the soul behind them

was, and that the little girl did not know of the wonderful power the Silver Shoes gave her. So the Wicked Witch laughed to herself, and thought, "I can still make her my

slave, for she does not know how to use her power." Then she said to Dorothy, harshly and severely: "Come with me; and see that you mind everything I tell you, for if you

do not I will make an end of you, as I did of the Tin Woodman and the Scarecrow." Dorothy followed her through many of the beautiful rooms in her castle until they came

to the kitchen, where the Witch bade her clean the pots and kettles and sweep the floor and keep the fire fed with wood. Dorothy went to work meekly, with her mind made

up to work as hard as she could; for she was glad the Wicked Witch had decided not to kill her. With Dorothy hard at work, the Witch thought she would go into the

courtyard and harness the Cowardly Lion like a horse; it would amuse her, she was sure, to make him draw her chariot whenever she wished to go to drive. But as she opened

the gate the Lion gave a loud roar and bounded at her so fiercely that the Witch was afraid, and ran out and shut the gate again. "If I cannot harness you," said the Witch to

the Lion, speaking through the bars of the gate, "I can starve you. You shall have nothing to eat until you do as I wish." So after that she took no food to the imprisoned Lion;

but every day she came to the gate at noon and asked, "Are you ready to be harnessed like a horse?" And the Lion would answer, "No. If you come in this yard, I will bite

you." The reason the Lion did not have to do as the Witch wished was that every night, while the woman was asleep, Dorothy carried him food from the cupboard. After he had eaten he would lie down on his bed of straw, and Dorothy would lie beside him and put her head on his soft, shaggy mane, while they talked of their troubles and tried

to plan some way to escape. But they could find no way to get out of the castle, for it was constantly guarded by the yellow Winkies, who were the slaves of the Wicked Witch

and too afraid of her not to do as she told them. The girl had to work hard during the day, and often the Witch threatened to beat her with the same old umbrella she always

carried in her hand. But, in truth, she did not dare to strike Dorothy, because of the mark upon her forehead. The child did not know this, and was full of fear for herself and

Toto. Once the Witch struck Toto a blow with her umbrella and the brave little dog flew at her and bit her leg in return. The Witch did not bleed where she was bitten, for

she was so wicked that the blood in her had dried up many years before. Dorothy's life became very sad as she grew to understand that it would be harder than ever to get

back to Kansas and Aunt Em again. Sometimes she would cry bitterly for hours, with Toto sitting at her feet and looking into her face, whining dismally to show how sorry

he was for his little mistress. Toto did not really care whether he was in Kansas or the Land of Oz so long as Dorothy was with him; but he knew the little girl was unhappy,

and that made him unhappy too. Now the Wicked Witch had a great longing to have for her own the Silver Shoes which the girl always wore. Her bees and her crows and

her wolves were lying in heaps and drying up, and she had used up all the power of the Golden Cap; but if she could only get hold of the Silver Shoes, they would give her

more power than all the other things she had lost. She watched Dorothy carefully, to see if she ever took off her shoes, thinking she might steal them. But the child was so

proud of her pretty shoes that she never took them off except at night and when she took her bath. The Witch was too much afraid of the dark to dare go in Dorothy's room

at night to take the shoes, and her dread of water was greater than her fear of the dark, so she never came near when Dorothy was bathing. Indeed, the old Witch never

touched water, nor ever let water touch her in any way. But the wicked creature was very cunning, and she finally thought of a trick that would give her what she wanted.

She placed a bar of iron in the middle of the kitchen floor, and then by her magic arts made the iron invisible to human eyes. So that when Dorothy walked across the floor

she stumbled over the bar, not being able to see it, and fell at full length. She was not much hurt, but in her fall one of the Silver Shoes came off; and before she could reach

it, the Witch had snatched it away and put it on her own skinny foot. The wicked woman was greatly pleased with the success of her trick, for as long as she had one of the

shoes she owned half the power of their charm, and Dorothy could not use it against her, even had she known how to do so. The little girl, seeing she had lost one of her

pretty shoes, grew angry, and said to the Witch, "Give me back my shoe!" "I will not," retorted the Witch, "for it is now my shoe, and not yours." "You are a wicked

creature!" cried Dorothy. "You have no right to take my shoe from me." "I shall keep it, just the same," said the Witch, laughing at her, "and someday I shall get the other

one from you, too." This made Dorothy so very angry that she picked up the bucket of water that stood near and dashed it over the Witch, wetting her from head to foot.

Instantly the wicked woman gave a loud cry of fear, and then, as Dorothy looked at her in wonder, the Witch began to shrink and fall away. "See what you have done!" she

screamed. "In a minute I shall melt away." "I'm very sorry, indeed," said Dorothy, who was truly frightened to see the Witch actually melting away like brown sugar before her very eyes. "Didn't you know water would be the end of me?" asked the Witch, in a wailing, despairing voice. "Of course not," answered Dorothy. "How should I?"

"Well, in a few minutes I shall be all melted, and you will have the castle to yourself. I have been wicked in my day, but I never thought a little girl like you would ever be able

to melt me and end my wicked deeds. Look out—here I go!" With these words the Witch fell down in a brown, melted, shapeless mass and began to spread over the clean

boards of the kitchen floor. Seeing that she had really melted away to nothing, Dorothy drew another bucket of water and threw it over the mess. She then swept it all out

the door. After picking out the silver shoe, which was all that was left of the old woman, she cleaned and dried it with a cloth, and put it on her foot again. Then, being at last

free to do as she chose, she ran out to the courtyard to tell the Lion that the Wicked Witch of the West had come to an end, and that they were no longer prisoners in a strange

land. CHAPTER XIII The Rescue The Cowardly Lion was much pleased to hear that the Wicked Witch had been melted by a bucket of water, and Dorothy at once

unlocked the gate of his prison and set him free. They went in together to the castle, where Dorothy's first act was to call all the Winkies together and tell them that they were

no longer slaves. There was great rejoicing among the yellow Winkies, for they had been made to work hard during many years for the Wicked Witch, who had always

treated them with great cruelty. They kept this day as a holiday, then and ever after, and spent the time in feasting and dancing. "If our friends, the Scarecrow and the Tin

Woodman, were only with us," said the Lion, "I should be quite happy." "Don't you suppose we could rescue them?" asked the girl anxiously. "We can try," answered the

Lion. So they called the yellow Winkies and asked them if they would help to rescue their friends, and the Winkies said that they would be delighted to do all in their power

for Dorothy, who had set them free from bondage. So she chose a number of the Winkies who looked as if they knew the most, and they all started away. They traveled that

day and part of the next until they came to the rocky plain where the Tin Woodman lay, all battered and bent. His axe was near him, but the blade was rusted and the handle

broken off short. The Winkies lifted him tenderly in their arms, and carried him back to the Yellow Castle again, Dorothy shedding a few tears by the way at the sad plight

of her old friend, and the Lion looking sober and sorry. When they reached the castle Dorothy said to the Winkies: "Are any of your people tinsmiths?" "Oh, yes. Some of

us are very good tinsmiths," they told her. "Then bring them to me," she said. And when the tinsmiths came, bringing with them all their tools in baskets, she inquired, "Can

you straighten out those dents in the Tin Woodman, and bend him back into shape again, and solder him together where he is broken?" The tinsmiths looked the Woodman

over carefully and then answered that they thought they could mend him so he would be as good as ever. So they set to work in one of the big yellow rooms of the castle and

worked for three days and four nights, hammering and twisting and bending and soldering and polishing and pounding at the legs and body and head of the Tin Woodman,

until at last he was straightened out into his old form, and his joints worked as well as ever. To be sure, there were several patches on him, but the tinsmiths did a good job,

and as the Woodman was not a vain man he did not mind the patches at all. When, at last, he walked into Dorothy's room and thanked her for rescuing him, he was so pleased

that he wept tears of joy, and Dorothy had to wipe every tear carefully from his face with her apron, so his joints would not be rusted. At the same time her own tears fell thick and fast at the joy of meeting her old friend again, and these tears did not need to be wiped away. As for the Lion, he wiped his eyes so often with the tip of his tail that

it became quite wet, and he was obliged to go out into the courtyard and hold it in the sun till it dried. "If we only had the Scarecrow with us again," said the Tin Woodman,

when Dorothy had finished telling him everything that had happened, "I should be quite happy." "We must try to find him," said the girl. So she called the Winkies to help

her, and they walked all that day and part of the next until they came to the tall tree in the branches of which the Winged Monkeys had tossed the Scarecrow's clothes. It was

a very tall tree, and the trunk was so smooth that no one could climb it; but the Woodman said at once, "I'll chop it down, and then we can get the Scarecrow's clothes." Now

while the tinsmiths had been at work mending the Woodman himself, another of the Winkies, who was a goldsmith, had made an axe-handle of solid gold and fitted it to the

Woodman's axe, instead of the old broken handle. Others polished the blade until all the rust was removed and it glistened like burnished silver. As soon as he had spoken,

the Tin Woodman began to chop, and in a short time the tree fell over with a crash, whereupon the Scarecrow's clothes fell out of the branches and rolled off on the ground.

Dorothy picked them up and had the Winkies carry them back to the castle, where they were stuffed with nice, clean straw; and behold! here was the Scarecrow, as good as

ever, thanking them over and over again for saving him. Now that they were reunited, Dorothy and her friends spent a few happy days at the Yellow Castle, where they found

everything they needed to make them comfortable. But one day the girl thought of Aunt Em, and said, "We must go back to Oz, and claim his promise." "Yes," said the

Woodman, "at last I shall get my heart." "And I shall get my brains," added the Scarecrow joyfully. "And I shall get my courage," said the Lion thoughtfully. "And I shall

get back to Kansas," cried Dorothy, clapping her hands. "Oh, let us start for the Emerald City tomorrow!" This they decided to do. The next day they called the Winkies

together and bade them good-bye. The Winkies were sorry to have them go, and they had grown so fond of the Tin Woodman that they begged him to stay and rule over

them and the Yellow Land of the West. Finding they were determined to go, the Winkies gave Toto and the Lion each a golden collar; and to Dorothy they presented a

beautiful bracelet studded with diamonds; and to the Scarecrow they gave a gold-headed walking stick, to keep him from stumbling; and to the Tin Woodman they offered

a silver oilcan, inlaid with gold and set with precious jewels. Every one of the travelers made the Winkies a pretty speech in return, and all shook hands with them until their

arms ached. Dorothy went to the Witch's cupboard to fill her basket with food for the journey, and there she saw the Golden Cap. She tried it on her own head and found

that it fitted her exactly. She did not know anything about the charm of the Golden Cap, but she saw that it was pretty, so she made up her mind to wear it and carry her

sunbonnet in the basket. Then, being prepared for the journey, they all started for the Emerald City; and the Winkies gave them three cheers and many good wishes to carry

with them. CHAPTER XIV The Winged Monkeys You will remember there was no road—not even a pathway—between the castle of the Wicked Witch and the Emerald

City. When the four travelers went in search of the Witch she had seen them coming, and so sent the Winged Monkeys to bring them to her. It was much harder to find their

way back through the big fields of buttercups and yellow daisies than it was being carried. They knew, of course, they must go straight east, toward the rising sun; and they started off in the right way. But at noon, when the sun was over their heads, they did not know which was east and which was west, and that was the reason they were lost in the great fields. They kept on walking, however, and at night the moon came out and shone brightly. So they lay down among the sweet-smelling yellow flowers and slept soundly until morning—all but the Scarecrow and the Tin Woodman. The next morning the sun was behind a cloud, but they started on, as if they were quite sure which way they were going. "If we walk far enough," said Dorothy, "I am sure we shall sometime come to some place." But day by day passed away, and they still saw nothing before them but the scarlet fields. The Scarecrow began to grumble a bit. "We have surely lost our way," he said, "and unless we find it again in time to reach the Emerald City, I shall never get my brains." "Nor I my heart," declared the Tin Woodman. "It seems to me I can scarcely wait till I get to Oz, and you must admit this is a very long journey." "You see," said the Cowardly Lion, with a whimper, "I haven't the courage to keep tramping forever, without getting anywhere at all." Then Dorothy lost heart. She sat down on the grass and looked at her companions, and they sat down and looked at her, and Toto found that for the first time in his life he was too tired to chase a butterfly that flew past his head. So he put out his tongue and panted and looked at Dorothy as if to ask what they should do next. "Suppose we call the field mice," she suggested. "They could probably tell us the way to the Emerald City." "To be sure they could," cried the Scarecrow. "Why didn't we think of that before?" Dorothy blew the little whistle she had always carried about her neck since the Queen of the Mice had given it to her. In a few minutes they heard the pattering of tiny feet, and many of the small gray mice came running up to her. Among them was the Queen herself, who asked, in her squeaky little voice: "What can I do for my friends?" "We have lost our way," said Dorothy. "Can you tell us where the Emerald City is?" "Certainly," answered the Queen; "but it is a great way off, for you have had it at your backs all this time." Then she noticed Dorothy's Golden Cap, and said, "Why don't you use the charm of the Cap, and call the Winged Monkeys to you? They will carry you to the City of Oz in less than an hour." "I didn't know there was a charm," answered Dorothy, in surprise. "What is it?" "It is written inside the Golden Cap," replied the Queen of the Mice. "But if you are going to call the Winged Monkeys we must run away, for they are full of mischief and think it great fun to plague us." "Won't they hurt me?" asked the girl anxiously. "Oh, no. They must obey the wearer of the Cap. Good-bye!" And she scampered out of sight, with all the mice hurrying after her. Dorothy looked inside the Golden Cap and saw some words written upon the lining. These, she thought, must be the charm, so she read the directions carefully and put the Cap upon her head. "Ep-pe, pep-pe, kak-ke!" she said, standing on her left foot. "What did you say?" asked the Scarecrow, who did not know what she was doing. "Hil-lo, hol-lo, hel-lo!" Dorothy went on, standing this time on her right foot. "Hello!" replied the Tin Woodman calmly. "Ziz-zy, zuz-zy, zik!" said Dorothy, who was now standing on both feet. This ended the saying of the charm, and they heard a great chattering and flapping of wings, as the band of Winged Monkeys flew up to them. The King bowed low before Dorothy, and asked, "What is your command?" "We wish to go to the Emerald City," said the child, "and we have lost our way." "We will carry you," replied the King, and no sooner had he spoken than two of the Monkeys caught Dorothy in their arms and flew away with her. Others took the Scarecrow and the Woodman and the Lion, and one little

Monkey seized Toto and flew after them, although the dog tried hard to bite him. The Scarecrow and the Tin Woodman were rather frightened at first, for they remembered

how badly the Winged Monkeys had treated them before; but they saw that no harm was intended, so they rode through the air quite cheerfully, and had a fine time looking

at the pretty gardens and woods far below them. Dorothy found herself riding easily between two of the biggest Monkeys, one of them the King himself. They had made a

chair of their hands and were careful not to hurt her. "Why do you have to obey the charm of the Golden Cap?" she asked. "That is a long story," answered the King, with

a laugh; "but as we have a long journey before us, I will pass the time by telling you about it, if you wish." "I shall be glad to hear it," she replied. "Once," began the leader,

"we were a free people, living happily in the great forest, flying from tree to tree, eating nuts and fruit, and doing just as we pleased without calling anybody master. Perhaps

some of us were rather too full of mischief at times, flying down to pull the tails of the animals that had no wings, chasing birds, and throwing nuts at the people who walked

in the forest. But we were careless and happy and full of fun, and enjoyed every minute of the day. This was many years ago, long before Oz came out of the clouds to rule

over this land. "There lived here then, away at the North, a beautiful princess, who was also a powerful sorceress. All her magic was used to help the people, and she was

never known to hurt anyone who was good. Her name was Gayelette, and she lived in a handsome palace built from great blocks of ruby. Everyone loved her, but her greatest

sorrow was that she could find no one to love in return, since all the men were much too stupid and ugly to mate with one so beautiful and wise. At last, however, she found

a boy who was handsome and manly and wise beyond his years. Gayelette made up her mind that when he grew to be a man she would make him her husband, so she took

him to her ruby palace and used all her magic powers to make him as strong and good and lovely as any woman could wish. When he grew to manhood, Quelala, as he was

called, was said to be the best and wisest man in all the land, while his manly beauty was so great that Gayelette loved him dearly, and hastened to make everything ready for

the wedding. "My grandfather was at that time the King of the Winged Monkeys which lived in the forest near Gayelette's palace, and the old fellow loved a joke better than

a good dinner. One day, just before the wedding, my grandfather was flying out with his band when he saw Quelala walking beside the river. He was dressed in a rich costume

of pink silk and purple velvet, and my grandfather thought he would see what he could do. At his word the band flew down and seized Quelala, carried him in their arms

until they were over the middle of the river, and then dropped him into the water. "'Swim out, my fine fellow,' cried my grandfather, 'and see if the water has spotted your

clothes.' Quelala was much too wise not to swim, and he was not in the least spoiled by all his good fortune. He laughed, when he came to the top of the water, and swam in

to shore. But when Gayelette came running out to him she found his silks and velvet all ruined by the river. "The princess was angry, and she knew, of course, who did it.

She had all the Winged Monkeys brought before her, and she said at first that their wings should be tied and they should be treated as they had treated Quelala, and dropped

in the river. But my grandfather pleaded hard, for he knew the Monkeys would drown in the river with their wings tied, and Quelala said a kind word for them also; so that

Gayelette finally spared them, on condition that the Winged Monkeys should ever after do three times the bidding of the owner of the Golden Cap. This Cap had been made for a wedding present to Quelala, and it is said to have cost the princess half her kingdom. Of course my grandfather and all the other Monkeys at once agreed to the

condition, and that is how it happens that we are three times the slaves of the owner of the Golden Cap, whosoever he may be." "And what became of them?" asked Dorothy,

who had been greatly interested in the story. "Quelala being the first owner of the Golden Cap," replied the Monkey, "he was the first to lay his wishes upon us. As his bride

could not bear the sight of us, he called us all to him in the forest after he had married her and ordered us always to keep where she could never again set eyes on a Winged

Monkey, which we were glad to do, for we were all afraid of her. "This was all we ever had to do until the Golden Cap fell into the hands of the Wicked Witch of the West,

who made us enslave the Winkies, and afterward drive Oz himself out of the Land of the West. Now the Golden Cap is yours, and three times you have the right to lay your

wishes upon us." As the Monkey King finished his story Dorothy looked down and saw the green, shining walls of the Emerald City before them. She wondered at the rapid

flight of the Monkeys, but was glad the journey was over. The strange creatures set the travelers down carefully before the gate of the City, the King bowed low to Dorothy,

and then flew swiftly away, followed by all his band. "That was a good ride," said the little girl. "Yes, and a quick way out of our troubles," replied the Lion. "How lucky it

was you brought away that wonderful Cap!" CHAPTER XV The Discovery of Oz, the Terrible The four travelers walked up to the great gate of Emerald City and rang

the bell. After ringing several times, it was opened by the same Guardian of the Gates they had met before. "What! are you back again?" he asked, in surprise. "Do you not

see us?" answered the Scarecrow. "But I thought you had gone to visit the Wicked Witch of the West." "We did visit her," said the Scarecrow. "And she let you go again?"

asked the man, in wonder. "She could not help it, for she is melted," explained the Scarecrow. "Melted! Well, that is good news, indeed," said the man. "Who melted her?"

"It was Dorothy," said the Lion gravely. "Good gracious!" exclaimed the man, and he bowed very low indeed before her. Then he led them into his little room and locked

the spectacles from the great box on all their eyes, just as he had done before. Afterward they passed on through the gate into the Emerald City. When the people heard from

the Guardian of the Gates that Dorothy had melted the Wicked Witch of the West, they all gathered around the travelers and followed them in a great crowd to the Palace

of Oz. The soldier with the green whiskers was still on guard before the door, but he let them in at once, and they were again met by the beautiful green girl, who showed

each of them to their old rooms at once, so they might rest until the Great Oz was ready to receive them. The soldier had the news carried straight to Oz that Dorothy and

the other travelers had come back again, after destroying the Wicked Witch; but Oz made no reply. They thought the Great Wizard would send for them at once, but he did

not. They had no word from him the next day, nor the next, nor the next. The waiting was tiresome and wearing, and at last they grew vexed that Oz should treat them in so

poor a fashion, after sending them to undergo hardships and slavery. So the Scarecrow at last asked the green girl to take another message to Oz, saying if he did not let them

in to see him at once they would call the Winged Monkeys to help them, and find out whether he kept his promises or not. When the Wizard was given this message he was

so frightened that he sent word for them to come to the Throne Room at four minutes after nine o'clock the next morning. He had once met the Winged Monkeys in the Land of the West, and he did not wish to meet them again. The four travelers passed a sleepless night, each thinking of the gift Oz had promised to bestow on him. Dorothy fell asleep only once, and then she dreamed she was in Kansas, where Aunt Em was telling her how glad she was to have her little girl at home again. Promptly at nine o'clock the next morning the green-whiskered soldier came to them, and four minutes later they all went into the Throne Room of the Great Oz. Of course each one of them expected to see the Wizard in the shape he had taken before, and all were greatly surprised when they looked about and saw no one at all in the room. They kept close to the door and closer to one another, for the stillness of the empty room was more dreadful than any of the forms they had seen Oz take. Presently they heard a solemn Voice, that seemed to come from somewhere near the top of the great dome, and it said: "I am Oz, the Great and Terrible. Why do you seek me?" They looked again in every part of the room, and then, seeing no one, Dorothy asked, "Where are you?" "I am everywhere," answered the Voice, "but to the eyes of common mortals I am invisible. I will now seat myself upon my throne, that you may converse with me." Indeed, the Voice seemed just then to come straight from the throne itself; so they walked toward it and stood in a row while Dorothy said: "We have come to claim our promise, O Oz." "What promise?" asked Oz. "You promised to send me back to Kansas when the Wicked Witch was destroyed," said the girl. "And you promised to give me brains," said the Scarecrow. "And you promised to give me a heart," said the Tin Woodman. "And you promised to give me courage," said the Cowardly Lion. "Is the Wicked Witch really destroyed?" asked the Voice, and Dorothy thought it trembled a little. "Yes," she answered, "I melted her with a bucket of water." "Dear me," said the Voice, "how sudden! Well, come to me tomorrow, for I must have time to think it over." "You've had plenty of time already," said the Tin Woodman angrily. "We shan't wait a day longer," said the Scarecrow. "You must keep your promises to us!" exclaimed Dorothy. The Lion thought it might be as well to frighten the Wizard, so he gave a large, loud roar, which was so fierce and dreadful that Toto jumped away from him in alarm and tipped over the screen that stood in a corner. As it fell with a crash they looked that way, and the next moment all of them were filled with wonder. For they saw, standing in just the spot the screen had hidden, a little old man, with a bald head and a wrinkled face, who seemed to be as much surprised as they were. The Tin Woodman, raising his axe, rushed toward the little man and cried out, "Who are you?" "I am Oz, the Great and Terrible," said the little man, in a trembling voice. "But don't strike me—please don't—and I'll do anything you want me to." Our friends looked at him in surprise and dismay. "I thought Oz was a great Head," said Dorothy. "And I thought Oz was a lovely Lady," said the Scarecrow. "And I thought Oz was a terrible Beast," said the Tin Woodman. "And I thought Oz was a Ball of Fire," exclaimed the Lion. "No, you are all wrong," said the little man meekly. "I have been making believe." "Making believe!" cried Dorothy. "Are you not a Great Wizard?" "Hush, my dear," he said. "Don't speak so loud, or you will be overheard—and I should be ruined. I'm supposed to be a Great Wizard." "And aren't you?" she asked. "Not a bit of it, my dear; I'm just a common man." "You're more than that," said the Scarecrow, in a grieved tone; "you're a humbug." "Exactly so!" declared the little man, rubbing his hands together as if it pleased him. "I am a humbug." "But this is terrible," said the Tin Woodman. "How shall I ever get my heart?" "Or I my courage?" asked the Lion. "Or I my brains?" wailed the Scarecrow, wiping the tears from his eyes with his coat sleeve. "My dear friends," said Oz, "I pray you not to speak of these little things. Think of me, and the terrible trouble I'm in at being found out." "Doesn't anyone else know you're a humbug?" asked Dorothy. "No one knows it but you four—and myself," replied Oz. "I have fooled everyone so long that I thought I should never be found out. It was a great mistake my ever letting you into the Throne Room. Usually I will not see even my subjects, and so they believe I am something terrible." "But, I don't understand," said Dorothy, in bewilderment. "How was it that you appeared to me as a great Head?" "That was one of my tricks," answered Oz. "Step this way, please, and I will tell you all about it." He led the way to a small chamber in the rear of the Throne Room, and they all followed him. He pointed to one corner, in which lay the great Head, made out of many thicknesses of paper, and with a carefully painted face. "This I hung from the ceiling by a wire," said Oz. "I stood behind the screen and pulled a thread, to make the eyes move and the mouth open." "But how about the voice?" she inquired. "Oh, I am a ventriloquist," said the little man. "I can throw the sound of my voice wherever I wish, so that you thought it was coming out of the Head. Here are the other things I used to deceive you." He showed the Scarecrow the dress and the mask he had worn when he seemed to be the lovely Lady. And the Tin Woodman saw that his terrible Beast was nothing but a lot of skins, sewn together, with slats to keep their sides out. As for the Ball of Fire, the false Wizard had hung that also from the ceiling. It was really a ball of cotton, but when oil was poured upon it the ball burned fiercely. "Really," said the Scarecrow, "you ought to be ashamed of yourself for being such a humbug." "I am—I certainly am," answered the little man sorrowfully; "but it was the only thing I could do. Sit down, please, there are plenty of chairs; and I will tell you my story." So they sat down and listened while he told the following tale. "I was born in Omaha—" "Why, that isn't very far from Kansas!" cried Dorothy. "No, but it's farther from here," he said, shaking his head at her sadly. "When I grew up I became a ventriloquist, and at that I was very well trained by a great master. I can imitate any kind of a bird or beast." Here he mewed so like a kitten that Toto pricked up his ears and looked everywhere to see where she was. "After a time," continued Oz, "I tired of that, and became a balloonist." "What is that?" asked Dorothy. "A man who goes up in a balloon on circus day, so as to draw a crowd of people together and get them to pay to see the circus," he explained. "Oh," she said, "I know." "Well, one day I went up in a balloon and the ropes got twisted, so that I couldn't come down again. It went way up above the clouds, so far that a current of air struck it and carried it many, many miles away. For a day and a night I traveled through the air, and on the morning of the second day I awoke and found the balloon floating over a strange and beautiful country. "It came down gradually, and I was not hurt a bit. But I found myself in the midst of a strange people, who, seeing me come from the clouds, thought I was a great Wizard. Of course I let them think so, because they were afraid of me, and promised to do anything I wished them to. "Just to amuse myself, and keep the good people busy, I ordered them to build this City, and my Palace; and they did it all willingly and well. Then I thought, as the country was so green and beautiful, I would call it the Emerald City; and to make the name fit better I put green spectacles on all the people, so that everything they saw was green." "But isn't everything here green?" asked Dorothy. "No more than in any other city," replied Oz; "but when you wear green spectacles, why of course everything you see looks green to you. The Emerald City was built a great many years ago, for I was a young man when the balloon brought me here, and I am a very old man now. But my people have worn green glasses on their eyes so long that most of them think it really is an Emerald City, and it certainly is a beautiful place, abounding in jewels and precious metals, and every good thing that is needed to make one happy. I have been good to the people, and they like me; but ever since this Palace was built, I have shut myself up and would not see any of them. "One of my greatest fears was the Witches, for while I had no magical powers at all I soon found out that the Witches were really able to do wonderful things. There were four of them in this country, and they ruled the people who live in the North and South and East and West. Fortunately, the Witches of the North and South were good, and I knew they would do me no harm; but the Witches of the East and West were terribly wicked, and had they not thought I was more powerful than they themselves, they would surely have destroyed me. As it was, I lived in deadly fear of them for many years; so you can imagine how pleased I was when I heard your house had fallen on the Wicked Witch of the East. When you came to me, I was willing to promise anything if you would only do away with the other Witch; but, now that you have melted her, I am ashamed to say that I cannot keep my promises." "I think you are a very bad man," said Dorothy. "Oh, no, my dear; I'm really a very good man, but I'm a very bad Wizard, I must admit." "Can't you give me brains?" asked the Scarecrow. "You don't need them. You are learning something every day. A baby has brains, but it doesn't know much. Experience is the only thing that brings knowledge, and the longer you are on earth the more experience you are sure to get." "That may all be true," said the Scarecrow, "but I shall be very unhappy unless you give me brains." The false Wizard looked at him carefully. "Well," he said with a sigh, "I'm not much of a magician, as I said; but if you will come to me tomorrow morning, I will stuff your head with brains. I cannot tell you how to use them, however; you must find that out for yourself." "Oh, thank you—thank you!" cried the Scarecrow. "I'll find a way to use them, never fear!" "But how about my courage?" asked the Lion anxiously. "You have plenty of courage, I am sure," answered Oz. "All you need is confidence in yourself. There is no living thing that is not afraid when it faces danger. True courage is in facing danger when you are afraid, and that kind of courage you have in plenty." "Perhaps I have, but I'm scared just the same," said the Lion. "I shall really be very unhappy unless you give me the sort of courage that makes one forget he is afraid." "Very well, I will give you that sort of courage tomorrow," replied Oz. "How about my heart?" asked the Tin Woodman. "Why, as for that," answered Oz, "I think you are wrong to want a heart. It makes most people unhappy. If you only knew it, you are in luck not to have a heart." "That must be a matter of opinion," said the Tin Woodman. "For my part, I will bear all the unhappiness without a murmur, if you will give me the heart." "Very well," answered Oz meekly. "Come to me tomorrow and you shall have a heart. I have played Wizard for so many years that I may as well continue the part a little longer." "And now," said Dorothy, "how am I to get back to Kansas?" "We shall have to think about that," replied the little man. "Give me two or three days to consider the matter and I'll try to find a way to carry you over the desert. In the meantime you shall all be treated as my guests, and while you live in the Palace my people will wait upon you and obey your slightest wish. There is only one thing I ask in return for my help—such as it is. You must keep my secret and tell no one I am a humbug." They agreed to say nothing of what they had learned, and went back to their rooms in high spirits. Even Dorothy had hope that "The Great and Terrible Humbug," as she called him, would find a way to send her back to Kansas, and if he did she was willing to forgive him everything. CHAPTER XVI The Magic Art of the Great Humbug Next morning the Scarecrow said to his friends: "Congratulate me. I am going to Oz to get my brains at last. When I return I shall be as other men are." "I have always liked you as you were," said Dorothy simply. "It is kind of you to like a Scarecrow," he replied. "But surely you will think more of me when you hear the splendid thoughts my new brain is going to turn out." Then he said good-bye to them all in a cheerful voice and went to the Throne Room, where he rapped upon the door. "Come in," said Oz. The Scarecrow went in and found the little man sitting down by the window, engaged in deep thought. "I have come for my brains," remarked the Scarecrow, a little uneasily. "Oh, yes; sit down in that chair, please," replied Oz. "You must excuse me for taking your head off, but I shall have to do it in order to put your brains in their proper place." "That's all right," said the Scarecrow. "You are quite welcome to take my head off, as long as it will be a better one when you put it on again." So the Wizard unfastened his head and emptied out the straw. Then he entered the back room and took up a measure of bran, which he mixed with a great many pins and needles. Having shaken them together thoroughly, he filled the top of the Scarecrow's head with the mixture and stuffed the rest of the space with straw, to hold it in place. When he had fastened the Scarecrow's head on his body again he said to him, "Hereafter you will be a great man, for I have given you a lot of bran-new brains." The Scarecrow was both pleased and proud at the fulfillment of his greatest wish, and having thanked Oz warmly he went back to his friends. Dorothy looked at him curiously. His head was quite bulged out at the top with brains. "How do you feel?" she asked. "I feel wise indeed," he answered earnestly. "When I get used to my brains I shall know everything." "Why are those needles and pins sticking out of your head?" asked the Tin Woodman. "That is proof that he is sharp," remarked the Lion. "Well, I must go to Oz and get my heart," said the Woodman. So he walked to the Throne Room and knocked at the door. "Come in," called Oz, and the Woodman entered and said, "I have come for my heart." "Very well," answered the little man. "But I shall have to cut a hole in your breast, so I can put your heart in the right place. I hope it won't hurt you." "Oh, no," answered the Woodman. "I shall not feel it at all." So Oz brought a pair of tinsmith's shears and cut a small, square hole in the left side of the Tin Woodman's breast. Then, going to a chest of drawers, he took out a pretty heart, made entirely of silk and stuffed with sawdust. "Isn't it a beauty?" he asked. "It is, indeed!" replied the Woodman, who was greatly pleased. "But is it a kind heart?" "Oh, very!" answered Oz. He put the heart in the Woodman's breast and then replaced the square of tin, soldering it neatly together where it had been cut. "There," said he; "now you have a heart that any man might be proud of. I'm sorry I had to put a patch on your breast, but it really couldn't be helped." "Never mind the patch," exclaimed the happy Woodman. "I am very grateful to you, and shall never forget your kindness." "Don't speak of it," replied Oz. Then the Tin Woodman went back to his friends, who wished him every joy on account of his good fortune. The Lion now walked to the Throne Room and knocked at the door. "Come in," said Oz. "I have come for my courage," announced the Lion, entering the room. "Very well," answered the little man; "I will get it for you." He went to a cupboard and reaching up to a high shelf took down a square green bottle, the contents of which he poured into a green-gold dish, beautifully carved. Placing this before the Cowardly Lion, who sniffed

at it as if he did not like it, the Wizard said: "Drink." "What is it?" asked the Lion. "Well," answered Oz, "if it were inside of you, it would be courage. You know, of course,

that courage is always inside one; so that this really cannot be called courage until you have swallowed it. Therefore I advise you to drink it as soon as possible." The Lion

hesitated no longer, but drank till the dish was empty. "How do you feel now?" asked Oz. "Full of courage," replied the Lion, who went joyfully back to his friends to tell

them of his good fortune. Oz, left to himself, smiled to think of his success in giving the Scarecrow and the Tin Woodman and the Lion exactly what they thought they

wanted. "How can I help being a humbug," he said, "when all these people make me do things that everybody knows can't be done? It was easy to make the Scarecrow and

the Lion and the Woodman happy, because they imagined I could do anything. But it will take more than imagination to carry Dorothy back to Kansas, and I'm sure I don't

know how it can be done." CHAPTER XVII How the Balloon Was Launched For three days Dorothy heard nothing from Oz. These were sad days for the little girl,

although her friends were all quite happy and contented. The Scarecrow told them there were wonderful thoughts in his head; but he would not say what they were because

he knew no one could understand them but himself. When the Tin Woodman walked about he felt his heart rattling around in his breast; and he told Dorothy he had

discovered it to be a kinder and more tender heart than the one he had owned when he was made of flesh. The Lion declared he was afraid of nothing on earth, and would

gladly face an army or a dozen of the fierce Kalidahs. Thus each of the little party was satisfied except Dorothy, who longed more than ever to get back to Kansas. On the

fourth day, to her great joy, Oz sent for her, and when she entered the Throne Room he greeted her pleasantly: "Sit down, my dear; I think I have found the way to get you

out of this country." "And back to Kansas?" she asked eagerly. "Well, I'm not sure about Kansas," said Oz, "for I haven't the faintest notion which way it lies. But the first

thing to do is to cross the desert, and then it should be easy to find your way home." "How can I cross the desert?" she inquired. "Well, I'll tell you what I think," said the

little man. "You see, when I came to this country it was in a balloon. You also came through the air, being carried by a cyclone. So I believe the best way to get across the

desert will be through the air. Now, it is quite beyond my powers to make a cyclone; but I've been thinking the matter over, and I believe I can make a balloon." "How?"

asked Dorothy. "A balloon," said Oz, "is made of silk, which is coated with glue to keep the gas in it. I have plenty of silk in the Palace, so it will be no trouble to make the

balloon. But in all this country there is no gas to fill the balloon with, to make it float." "If it won't float," remarked Dorothy, "it will be of no use to us." "True," answered

Oz. "But there is another way to make it float, which is to fill it with hot air. Hot air isn't as good as gas, for if the air should get cold the balloon would come down in the

desert, and we should be lost." "We!" exclaimed the girl. "Are you going with me?" "Yes, of course," replied Oz. "I am tired of being such a humbug. If I should go out of

this Palace my people would soon discover I am not a Wizard, and then they would be vexed with me for having deceived them. So I have to stay shut up in these rooms all

day, and it gets tiresome. I'd much rather go back to Kansas with you and be in a circus again." "I shall be glad to have your company," said Dorothy. "Thank you," he answered. "Now, if you will help me sew the silk together, we will begin to work on our balloon." So Dorothy took a needle and thread, and as fast as Oz cut the strips of

silk into proper shape the girl sewed them neatly together. First there was a strip of light green silk, then a strip of dark green and then a strip of emerald green; for Oz had

a fancy to make the balloon in different shades of the color about them. It took three days to sew all the strips together, but when it was finished they had a big bag of green

silk more than twenty feet long. Then Oz painted it on the inside with a coat of thin glue, to make it airtight, after which he announced that the balloon was ready. "But we

must have a basket to ride in," he said. So he sent the soldier with the green whiskers for a big clothes basket, which he fastened with many ropes to the bottom of the balloon.

When it was all ready, Oz sent word to his people that he was going to make a visit to a great brother Wizard who lived in the clouds. The news spread rapidly throughout

the city and everyone came to see the wonderful sight. Oz ordered the balloon carried out in front of the Palace, and the people gazed upon it with much curiosity. The Tin

Woodman had chopped a big pile of wood, and now he made a fire of it, and Oz held the bottom of the balloon over the fire so that the hot air that arose from it would be

caught in the silken bag. Gradually the balloon swelled out and rose into the air, until finally the basket just touched the ground. Then Oz got into the basket and said to all

the people in a loud voice: "I am now going away to make a visit. While I am gone the Scarecrow will rule over you. I command you to obey him as you would me." The

balloon was by this time tugging hard at the rope that held it to the ground, for the air within it was hot, and this made it so much lighter in weight than the air without that

it pulled hard to rise into the sky. "Come, Dorothy!" cried the Wizard. "Hurry up, or the balloon will fly away." "I can't find Toto anywhere," replied Dorothy, who did not

wish to leave her little dog behind. Toto had run into the crowd to bark at a kitten, and Dorothy at last found him. She picked him up and ran toward the balloon. She was

within a few steps of it, and Oz was holding out his hands to help her into the basket, when, crack! went the ropes, and the balloon rose into the air without her. "Come back!"

she screamed. "I want to go, too!" "I can't come back, my dear," called Oz from the basket. "Good-bye!" "Good-bye!" shouted everyone, and all eyes were turned upward

to where the Wizard was riding in the basket, rising every moment farther and farther into the sky. And that was the last any of them ever saw of Oz, the Wonderful Wizard,

though he may have reached Omaha safely, and be there now, for all we know. But the people remembered him lovingly, and said to one another: "Oz was always our friend.

When he was here he built for us this beautiful Emerald City, and now he is gone he has left the Wise Scarecrow to rule over us." Still, for many days they grieved over the

loss of the Wonderful Wizard, and would not be comforted. CHAPTER XVIII Away to the South Dorothy wept bitterly at the passing of her hope to get home to Kansas

again; but when she thought it all over she was glad she had not gone up in a balloon. And she also felt sorry at losing Oz, and so did her companions. The Tin Woodman

came to her and said: "Truly I should be ungrateful if I failed to mourn for the man who gave me my lovely heart. I should like to cry a little because Oz is gone, if you will

kindly wipe away my tears, so that I shall not rust." "With pleasure," she answered, and brought a towel at once. Then the Tin Woodman wept for several minutes, and she

watched the tears carefully and wiped them away with the towel. When he had finished, he thanked her kindly and oiled himself thoroughly with his jeweled oilcan, to guard against mishap. The Scarecrow was now the ruler of the Emerald City, and although he was not a Wizard the people were proud of him. "For," they said, "there is not another city in all the world that is ruled by a stuffed man." And, so far as they knew, they were quite right. The morning after the balloon had gone up with Oz, the four travelers met in the Throne Room and talked matters over. The Scarecrow sat in the big throne and the others stood respectfully before him. "We are not so unlucky," said the new ruler, "for this Palace and the Emerald City belong to us, and we can do just as we please. When I remember that a short time ago I was up on a pole in a farmer's cornfield, and that now I am the ruler of this beautiful City, I am quite satisfied with my lot." "I also," said the Tin Woodman, "am well-pleased with my new heart; and, really, that was the only thing I wished in all the world." "For my part, I am content in knowing I am as brave as any beast that ever lived, if not braver," said the Lion modestly. "If Dorothy would only be contented to live in the Emerald City," continued the Scarecrow, "we might all be happy together." "But I don't want to live here," cried Dorothy. "I want to go to Kansas, and live with Aunt Em and Uncle Henry." "Well, then, what can be done?" inquired the Woodman. The Scarecrow decided to think, and he thought so hard that the pins and needles began to stick out of his brains. Finally he said: "Why not call the Winged Monkeys, and ask them to carry you over the desert?" "I never thought of that!" said Dorothy joyfully. "It's just the thing. I'll go at once for the Golden Cap." When she brought it into the Throne Room she spoke the magic words, and soon the band of Winged Monkeys flew in through the open window and stood beside her. "This is the second time you have called us," said the Monkey King, bowing before the little girl. "What do you wish?" "I want you to fly with me to Kansas," said Dorothy. But the Monkey King shook his head. "That cannot be done," he said. "We belong to this country alone, and cannot leave it. There has never been a Winged Monkey in Kansas yet, and I suppose there never will be, for they don't belong there. We shall be glad to serve you in any way in our power, but we cannot cross the desert. Good-bye." And with another bow, the Monkey King spread his wings and flew away through the window, followed by all his band. Dorothy was ready to cry with disappointment. "I have wasted the charm of the Golden Cap to no purpose," she said, "for the Winged Monkeys cannot help me." "It is certainly too bad!" said the tender-hearted Woodman. The Scarecrow was thinking again, and his head bulged out so horribly that Dorothy feared it would burst. "Let us call in the soldier with the green whiskers," he said, "and ask his advice." So the soldier was summoned and entered the Throne Room timidly, for while Oz was alive he never was allowed to come farther than the door. "This little girl," said the Scarecrow to the soldier, "wishes to cross the desert. How can she do so?" "I cannot tell," answered the soldier, "for nobody has ever crossed the desert, unless it is Oz himself." "Is there no one who can help me?" asked Dorothy earnestly. "Glinda might," he suggested. "Who is Glinda?" inquired the Scarecrow. "The Witch of the South. She is the most powerful of all the Witches, and rules over the Quadlings. Besides, her castle stands on the edge of the desert, so she may know a way to cross it." "Glinda is a Good Witch, isn't she?" asked the child. "The Quadlings think she is good," said the soldier, "and she is kind to everyone. I have heard that Glinda is a beautiful woman, who knows how to keep young in spite of the many years she has lived." "How can I get to her castle?" asked Dorothy. "The road is straight to the South," he answered, "but it is said to be full of dangers to travelers.

There are wild beasts in the woods, and a race of queer men who do not like strangers to cross their country. For this reason none of the Quadlings ever come to the Emerald City." The soldier then left them and the Scarecrow said: "It seems, in spite of dangers, that the best thing Dorothy can do is to travel to the Land of the South and ask Glinda to help her. For, of course, if Dorothy stays here she will never get back to Kansas." "You must have been thinking again," remarked the Tin Woodman. "I have," said the Scarecrow. "I shall go with Dorothy," declared the Lion, "for I am tired of your city and long for the woods and the country again. I am really a wild beast, you know. Besides, Dorothy will need someone to protect her." "That is true," agreed the Woodman. "My axe may be of service to her; so I also will go with her to the Land of the South." "When shall we start?" asked the Scarecrow. "Are you going?" they asked, in surprise. "Certainly. If it wasn't for Dorothy I should never have had brains. She lifted me from the pole in the cornfield and brought me to the Emerald City. So my good luck is all due to her, and I shall never leave her until she starts back to Kansas for good and all." "Thank you," said Dorothy gratefully. "You are all very kind to me. But I should like to start as soon as possible." "We shall go tomorrow morning," returned the Scarecrow. "So now let us all get ready, for it will be a long journey." CHAPTER XIX Attacked by the Fighting Trees The next morning Dorothy kissed the pretty green girl good-bye, and they all shook hands with the soldier with the green whiskers, who had walked with them as far as the gate. When the Guardian of the Gates saw them again he wondered greatly that they could leave the beautiful City to get into new trouble. But he at once unlocked their spectacles, which he put back into the green box, and gave them many good wishes to carry with them. "You are now our ruler," he said to the Scarecrow; "so you must come back to us as soon as possible." "I certainly shall if I am able," the Scarecrow replied; "but I must help Dorothy to get home, first." As Dorothy bade the good-natured Guardian a last farewell she said: "I have been very kindly treated in your lovely City; everyone has been good to me. I cannot tell you how grateful I am." "Don't try, my dear," he answered. "We should like to keep you with us, but if it is your wish to return to Kansas, I hope you will find a way." He then opened the gate of the outer wall, and they walked forth and started upon their journey. The sun shone brightly as our friends turned their faces toward the Land of the South. They were all in the best of spirits, and laughed and chatted together. Dorothy was once more filled with the hope of getting home, and the Scarecrow and the Tin Woodman were glad to be of use to her. As for the Lion, he sniffed the fresh air with delight and whisked his tail from side to side in pure joy at being in the country again, while Toto ran around them and chased the moths and butterflies, barking merrily all the time. "City life does not agree with me at all," remarked the Lion, as they walked along at a brisk pace. "I have lost much flesh since I lived there, and now I am anxious for a chance to show the other beasts how courageous I have grown." They now turned and took a last look at the Emerald City. All they could see was a mass of towers and steeples behind the green walls, and high up above everything the spires and dome of the Palace of Oz. "Oz was not such a bad Wizard, after all," said the Tin Woodman, as he felt his heart rattling around in his breast. "He knew how to give me brains, and very good brains, too," said the Scarecrow. "If Oz had taken a dose of the same courage he gave me," added the Lion, "he would have been a brave man." Dorothy said nothing. Oz had not kept the promise he made her, but he had done his best, so she forgave him. As he said, he was a good man, even if he was a bad Wizard. The first day's journey was through the green fields and bright flowers that stretched about the Emerald City on every side. They slept that night on the grass, with nothing but the stars over them; and they rested very well indeed. In the morning they traveled on until they came to a thick wood. There was no way of going around it, for it seemed to extend to the right and left as far as they could see; and, besides, they did not dare change the direction of their journey for fear of getting lost. So they looked for the place where it would be easiest to get into the forest. The Scarecrow, who was in the lead, finally discovered a big tree with such wide-spreading branches that there was room for the party to pass underneath. So he walked forward to the tree, but just as he came under the first branches they bent down and twined around him, and the next minute he was raised from the ground and flung headlong among his fellow travelers. This did not hurt the Scarecrow, but it surprised him, and he looked rather dizzy when Dorothy picked him up. "Here is another space between the trees," called the Lion. "Let me try it first," said the Scarecrow, "for it doesn't hurt me to get thrown about." He walked up to another tree, as he spoke, but its branches immediately seized him and tossed him back again. "This is strange," exclaimed Dorothy. "What shall we do?" "The trees seem to have made up their minds to fight us, and stop our journey," remarked the Lion. "I believe I will try it myself," said the Woodman, and shouldering his axe, he marched up to the first tree that had handled the Scarecrow so roughly. When a big branch bent down to seize him the Woodman chopped at it so fiercely that he cut it in two. At once the tree began shaking all its branches as if in pain, and the Tin Woodman passed safely under it. "Come on!" he shouted to the others. "Be quick!" They all ran forward and passed under the tree without injury, except Toto, who was caught by a small branch and shaken until he howled. But the Woodman promptly chopped off the branch and set the little dog free. The other trees of the forest did nothing to keep them back, so they made up their minds that only the first row of trees could bend down their branches, and that probably these were the policemen of the forest, and given this wonderful power in order to keep strangers out of it. The four travelers walked with ease through the trees until they came to the farther edge of the wood. Then, to their surprise, they found before them a high wall which seemed to be made of white china. It was smooth, like the surface of a dish, and higher than their heads. "What shall we do now?" asked Dorothy. "I will make a ladder," said the Tin Woodman, "for we certainly must climb over the wall." CHAPTER XX The Dainty China Country While the Woodman was making a ladder from wood which he found in the forest Dorothy lay down and slept, for she was tired by the long walk. The Lion also curled himself up to sleep and Toto lay beside him. The Scarecrow watched the Woodman while he worked, and said to him: "I cannot think why this wall is here, nor what it is made of." "Rest your brains and do not worry about the wall," replied the Woodman. "When we have climbed over it, we shall know what is on the other side." After a time the ladder was finished. It looked clumsy, but the Tin Woodman was sure it was strong and would answer their purpose. The Scarecrow waked Dorothy and the Lion and Toto, and told them that the ladder was ready. The Scarecrow climbed up the ladder first, but he was so awkward that Dorothy had to follow close behind and keep him from falling off. When he got his head over the top of the wall the Scarecrow said, "Oh, my!" "Go on," exclaimed Dorothy. So the Scarecrow climbed farther up and sat down on the top of the wall, and Dorothy put her head over and cried, "Oh, my!" just as the Scarecrow had done. Then Toto came up, and immediately began to bark, but Dorothy made him be still. The Lion climbed the ladder next, and the Tin Woodman came last; but both of them cried, "Oh, my!" as soon as they looked over the wall. When they were all sitting in a row on the top of the wall, they looked down and saw a strange sight. Before them was a great stretch of country having a floor as smooth and shining and white as the bottom of a big platter. Scattered around were many houses made entirely of china and painted in the brightest colors. These houses were quite small, the biggest of them reaching only as high as Dorothy's waist. There were also pretty little barns, with china fences around them; and many cows and sheep and horses and pigs and chickens, all made of china, were standing about in groups. But the strangest of all were the people who lived in this queer country. There were milkmaids and shepherdesses, with brightly colored bodices and golden spots all over their gowns; and princesses with most gorgeous frocks of silver and gold and purple; and shepherds dressed in knee breeches with pink and yellow and blue stripes down them, and golden buckles on their shoes; and princes with jeweled crowns upon their heads, wearing ermine robes and satin doublets; and funny clowns in ruffled gowns, with round red spots upon their cheeks and tall, pointed caps. And, strangest of all, these people were all made of china, even to their clothes, and were so small that the tallest of them was no higher than Dorothy's knee. No one did so much as look at the travelers at first, except one little purple china dog with an extra-large head, which came to the wall and barked at them in a tiny voice, afterwards running away again. "How shall we get down?" asked Dorothy. They found the ladder so heavy they could not pull it up, so the Scarecrow fell off the wall and the others jumped down upon him so that the hard floor would not hurt their feet. Of course they took pains not to light on his head and get the pins in their feet. When all were safely down they picked up the Scarecrow, whose body was quite flattened out, and patted his straw into shape again. "We must cross this strange place in order to get to the other side," said Dorothy, "for it would be unwise for us to go any other way except due South." They began walking through the country of the china people, and the first thing they came to was a china milkmaid milking a china cow. As they drew near, the cow suddenly gave a kick and kicked over the stool, the pail, and even the milkmaid herself, and all fell on the china ground with a great clatter. Dorothy was shocked to see that the cow had broken her leg off, and that the pail was lying in several small pieces, while the poor milkmaid had a nick in her left elbow. "There!" cried the milkmaid angrily. "See what you have done! My cow has broken her leg, and I must take her to the mender's shop and have it glued on again. What do you mean by coming here and frightening my cow?" "I'm very sorry," returned Dorothy. "Please forgive us." But the pretty milkmaid was much too vexed to make any answer. She picked up the leg sulkily and led her cow away, the poor animal limping on three legs. As she left them the milkmaid cast many reproachful glances over her shoulder at the clumsy strangers, holding her nicked elbow close to her side. Dorothy was quite grieved at this mishap. "We must be very careful here," said the kindhearted Woodman, "or we may hurt these pretty little people so they will never get over it." A little farther on Dorothy met a most beautifully dressed young Princess, who stopped short as she saw the strangers and started to run away. Dorothy wanted to see more of the Princess, so she ran after her. But the china girl cried out: "Don't chase me! Don't chase me!" She had such a frightened little voice that

Dorothy stopped and said, "Why not?" "Because," answered the Princess, also stopping, a safe distance away, "if I run I may fall down and break myself." "But could you not be mended?" asked the girl. "Oh, yes; but one is never so pretty after being mended, you know," replied the Princess. "I suppose not," said Dorothy. "Now there is Mr. Joker, one of our clowns," continued the china lady, "who is always trying to stand upon his head. He has broken himself so often that he is mended in a hundred places, and doesn't look at all pretty. Here he comes now, so you can see for yourself." Indeed, a jolly little clown came walking toward them, and Dorothy could see that in spite of his pretty clothes of red and yellow and green he was completely covered with cracks, running every which way and showing plainly that he had been mended in many places.

The Clown put his hands in his pockets, and after puffing out his cheeks and nodding his head at them saucily, he said, *"My lady fair, Why do you stare At poor old Mr. Joker? You're quite as stiff And prim as if You'd eaten up a poker!"* "Be quiet, sir!" said the Princess. "Can't you see these are strangers, and should be treated with respect?" "Well, that's respect, I expect," declared the Clown, and immediately stood upon his head. "Don't mind Mr. Joker," said the Princess to Dorothy. "He is considerably cracked in his head, and that makes him foolish." "Oh, I don't mind him a bit," said Dorothy. "But you are so beautiful," she continued, "that I am sure I could love you dearly. Won't you let me carry you back to Kansas, and stand you on Aunt Em's mantel? I could carry you in my basket." "That would make me very unhappy," answered the china Princess. "You see, here in our country we live contentedly, and can talk and move around as we please. But whenever any of us are taken away our joints at once stiffen, and we can only stand straight and look pretty. Of course that is all that is expected of us when we are on mantels and cabinets and drawing-room tables, but our lives are much pleasanter here in our own country." "I would not make you unhappy for all the world!" exclaimed Dorothy. "So I'll just say good-bye." "Good-bye," replied the Princess.

They walked carefully through the china country. The little animals and all the people scampered out of their way, fearing the strangers would break them, and after an hour or so the travelers reached the other side of the country and came to another china wall. It was not so high as the first, however, and by standing upon the Lion's back they all managed to scramble to the top. Then the Lion gathered his legs under him and jumped on the wall; but just as he jumped, he upset a china church with his tail and smashed it all to pieces. "That was too bad," said Dorothy, "but really I think we were lucky in not doing these little people more harm than breaking a cow's leg and a church. They are all so brittle!" "They are, indeed," said the Scarecrow, "and I am thankful I am made of straw and cannot be easily damaged. There are worse things in the world than being a Scarecrow." CHAPTER XXI The Lion Becomes the King of Beasts After climbing down from the china wall the travelers found themselves in a disagreeable country, full of bogs and marshes and covered with tall, rank grass. It was difficult to walk without falling into muddy holes, for the grass was so thick that it hid them from sight. However, by carefully picking their way, they got safely along until they reached solid ground. But here the country seemed wilder than ever, and after a long and tiresome walk through the underbrush they entered another forest, where the trees were bigger and older than any they had ever seen. "This forest is perfectly delightful," declared the Lion, looking around him with joy. "Never have I seen a more beautiful place." "It seems gloomy," said the Scarecrow. "Not a bit of it," answered the Lion. "I should like to live here all my life. See how soft the dried leaves are under your feet and how rich and green the moss is that clings to these old trees. Surely no wild beast could wish a pleasanter home." "Perhaps there are wild beasts in the forest now," said Dorothy. "I suppose there are," returned the Lion, "but I do not see any of them about." They walked through the forest until it became too dark to go any farther. Dorothy and Toto and the Lion lay down to sleep, while the Woodman and the Scarecrow kept watch over them as usual. When morning came, they started again. Before they had gone far they heard a low rumble, as of the growling of many wild animals. Toto whimpered a little, but none of the others was frightened, and they kept along the well-trodden path until they came to an opening in the wood, in which were gathered hundreds of beasts of every variety. There were tigers and elephants and bears and wolves and foxes and all the others in the natural history, and for a moment Dorothy was afraid. But the Lion explained that the animals were holding a meeting, and he judged by their snarling and growling that they were in great trouble. As he spoke several of the beasts caught sight of him, and at once the great assemblage hushed as if by magic. The biggest of the tigers came up to the Lion and bowed, saying: "Welcome, O King of Beasts! You have come in good time to fight our enemy and bring peace to all the animals of the forest once more." "What is your trouble?" asked the Lion quietly. "We are all threatened," answered the tiger, "by a fierce enemy which has lately come into this forest. It is a most tremendous monster, like a great spider, with a body as big as an elephant and legs as long as a tree trunk. It has eight of these long legs, and as the monster crawls through the forest he seizes an animal with a leg and drags it to his mouth, where he eats it as a spider does a fly. Not one of us is safe while this fierce creature is alive, and we had called a meeting to decide how to take care of ourselves when you came among us." The Lion thought for a moment. "Are there any other lions in this forest?" he asked. "No; there were some, but the monster has eaten them all. And, besides, they were none of them nearly so large and brave as you." "If I put an end to your enemy, will you bow down to me and obey me as King of the Forest?" inquired the Lion. "We will do that gladly," returned the tiger; and all the other beasts roared with a mighty roar: "We will!" "Where is this great spider of yours now?" asked the Lion. "Yonder, among the oak trees," said the tiger, pointing with his forefoot. "Take good care of these friends of mine," said the Lion, "and I will go at once to fight the monster." He bade his comrades good-bye and marched proudly away to do battle with the enemy. The great spider was lying asleep when the Lion found him, and it looked so ugly that its foe turned up his nose in disgust. Its legs were quite as long as the tiger had said, and its body covered with coarse black hair. It had a great mouth, with a row of sharp teeth a foot long; but its head was joined to the pudgy body by a neck as slender as a wasp's waist. This gave the Lion a hint of the best way to attack the creature, and as he knew it was easier to fight it asleep than awake, he gave a great spring and landed directly upon the monster's back. Then, with one blow of his heavy paw, all armed with sharp claws, he knocked the spider's head from its body. Jumping down, he watched it until the long legs stopped wiggling, when he knew it was quite dead. The Lion went back to the opening where the beasts of the forest were waiting for him and said proudly: "You need fear your enemy no longer." Then the beasts bowed down to the Lion as their King, and he promised to come back and rule over them as soon as Dorothy was safely on her way to Kansas. CHAPTER XXII The Country of the Quadlings

The four travelers passed through the rest of the forest in safety, and when they came out from its gloom saw before them a steep hill, covered from top to bottom with great pieces of rock. "That will be a hard climb," said the Scarecrow, "but we must get over the hill, nevertheless." So he led the way and the others followed. They had nearly reached the first rock when they heard a rough voice cry out, "Keep back!" "Who are you?" asked the Scarecrow. Then a head showed itself over the rock and the same voice said, "This hill belongs to us, and we don't allow anyone to cross it." "But we must cross it," said the Scarecrow. "We're going to the country of the Quadlings." "But you shall not!" replied the voice, and there stepped from behind the rock the strangest man the travelers had ever seen. He was quite short and stout and had a big head, which was flat at the top and supported by a thick neck full of wrinkles. But he had no arms at all, and, seeing this, the Scarecrow did not fear that so helpless a creature could prevent them from climbing the hill. So he said, "I'm sorry not to do as you wish, but we must pass over your hill whether you like it or not," and he walked boldly forward. As quick as lightning the man's head shot forward and his neck stretched out until the top of the head, where it was flat, struck the Scarecrow in the middle and sent him tumbling, over and over, down the hill. Almost as quickly as it came the head went back to the body, and the man laughed harshly as he said, "It isn't as easy as you think!" A chorus of boisterous laughter came from the other rocks, and Dorothy saw hundreds of the armless Hammer-Heads upon the hillside, one behind every rock. The Lion became quite angry at the laughter caused by the Scarecrow's mishap, and giving a loud roar that echoed like thunder, he dashed up the hill. Again a head shot swiftly out, and the great Lion went rolling down the hill as if he had been struck by a cannonball. Dorothy ran down and helped the Scarecrow to his feet, and the Lion came up to her, feeling rather bruised and sore, and said, "It is useless to fight people with shooting heads; no one can withstand them." "What can we do, then?" she asked. "Call the Winged Monkeys," suggested the Tin Woodman. "You have still the right to command them once more." "Very well," she answered, and putting on the Golden Cap she uttered the magic words. The Monkeys were as prompt as ever, and in a few moments the entire band stood before her. "What are your commands?" inquired the King of the Monkeys, bowing low. "Carry us over the hill to the country of the Quadlings," answered the girl. "It shall be done," said the King, and at once the Winged Monkeys caught the four travelers and Toto up in their arms and flew away with them. As they passed over the hill the Hammer-Heads yelled with vexation, and shot their heads high in the air, but they could not reach the Winged Monkeys, which carried Dorothy and her comrades safely over the hill and set them down in the beautiful country of the Quadlings. "This is the last time you can summon us," said the leader to Dorothy; "so good-bye and good luck to you." "Good-bye, and thank you very much," returned the girl; and the Monkeys rose into the air and were out of sight in a twinkling. The country of the Quadlings seemed rich and happy. There was field upon field of ripening grain, with well-paved roads running between, and pretty rippling brooks with strong bridges across them. The fences and houses and bridges were all painted bright red, just as they had been painted yellow in the country of the Winkies and blue in the country of the Munchkins. The Quadlings themselves, who were short and fat and looked chubby and good-natured, were dressed all in red, which showed bright against the green grass and the yellowing grain. The Monkeys had set them down near a farmhouse, and the four travelers walked up to it and knocked at the door. It was opened by the farmer's wife, and when Dorothy asked for something to eat the woman gave them all a good dinner,

with three kinds of cake and four kinds of cookies, and a bowl of milk for Toto. "How far is it to the Castle of Glinda?" asked the child. "It is not a great way," answered the

farmer's wife. "Take the road to the South and you will soon reach it." Thanking the good woman, they started afresh and walked by the fields and across the pretty bridges

until they saw before them a very beautiful Castle. Before the gates were three young girls, dressed in handsome red uniforms trimmed with gold braid; and as Dorothy

approached, one of them said to her: "Why have you come to the South Country?" "To see the Good Witch who rules here," she answered. "Will you take me to her?" "Let

me have your name, and I will ask Glinda if she will receive you." They told who they were, and the girl soldier went into the Castle. After a few moments she came back

to say that Dorothy and the others were to be admitted at once. CHAPTER XXIII Glinda The Good Witch Grants Dorothy's Wish Before they went to see Glinda,

however, they were taken to a room of the Castle, where Dorothy washed her face and combed her hair, and the Lion shook the dust out of his mane, and the Scarecrow

patted himself into his best shape, and the Woodman polished his tin and oiled his joints. When they were all quite presentable they followed the soldier girl into a big room

where the Witch Glinda sat upon a throne of rubies. She was both beautiful and young to their eyes. Her hair was a rich red in color and fell in flowing ringlets over her

shoulders. Her dress was pure white but her eyes were blue, and they looked kindly upon the little girl. "What can I do for you, my child?" she asked. Dorothy told the Witch

all her story: how the cyclone had brought her to the Land of Oz, how she had found her companions, and of the wonderful adventures they had met with. "My greatest

wish now," she added, "is to get back to Kansas, for Aunt Em will surely think something dreadful has happened to me, and that will make her put on mourning; and unless

the crops are better this year than they were last, I am sure Uncle Henry cannot afford it." Glinda leaned forward and kissed the sweet, upturned face of the loving little girl.

"Bless your dear heart," she said, "I am sure I can tell you of a way to get back to Kansas." Then she added, "But, if I do, you must give me the Golden Cap." "Willingly!"

exclaimed Dorothy; "indeed, it is of no use to me now, and when you have it you can command the Winged Monkeys three times." "And I think I shall need their service

just those three times," answered Glinda, smiling. Dorothy then gave her the Golden Cap, and the Witch said to the Scarecrow, "What will you do when Dorothy has left

us?" "I will return to the Emerald City," he replied, "for Oz has made me its ruler and the people like me. The only thing that worries me is how to cross the hill of the

Hammer-Heads." "By means of the Golden Cap I shall command the Winged Monkeys to carry you to the gates of the Emerald City," said Glinda, "for it would be a shame

to deprive the people of so wonderful a ruler." "Am I really wonderful?" asked the Scarecrow. "You are unusual," replied Glinda. Turning to the Tin Woodman, she asked,

"What will become of you when Dorothy leaves this country?" He leaned on his axe and thought a moment. Then he said, "The Winkies were very kind to me, and wanted

me to rule over them after the Wicked Witch died. I am fond of the Winkies, and if I could get back again to the Country of the West, I should like nothing better than to

rule over them forever." "My second command to the Winged Monkeys," said Glinda "will be that they carry you safely to the land of the Winkies. Your brain may not be so large to look at as those of the Scarecrow, but you are really brighter than he is—when you are well polished—and I am sure you will rule the Winkies wisely and well."

Then the Witch looked at the big, shaggy Lion and asked, "When Dorothy has returned to her own home, what will become of you?" "Over the hill of the Hammer-Heads,"

he answered, "lies a grand old forest, and all the beasts that live there have made me their King. If I could only get back to this forest, I would pass my life very happily there."

"My third command to the Winged Monkeys," said Glinda, "shall be to carry you to your forest. Then, having used up the powers of the Golden Cap, I shall give it to the

King of the Monkeys, that he and his band may thereafter be free for evermore." The Scarecrow and the Tin Woodman and the Lion now thanked the Good Witch earnestly

for her kindness; and Dorothy exclaimed: "You are certainly as good as you are beautiful! But you have not yet told me how to get back to Kansas." "Your Silver Shoes will

carry you over the desert," replied Glinda. "If you had known their power you could have gone back to your Aunt Em the very first day you came to this country." "But then

I should not have had my wonderful brains!" cried the Scarecrow. "I might have passed my whole life in the farmer's cornfield." "And I should not have had my lovely heart,"

said the Tin Woodman. "I might have stood and rusted in the forest till the end of the world." "And I should have lived a coward forever," declared the Lion, "and no beast

in all the forest would have had a good word to say to me." "This is all true," said Dorothy, "and I am glad I was of use to these good friends. But now that each of them has

had what he most desired, and each is happy in having a kingdom to rule besides, I think I should like to go back to Kansas." "The Silver Shoes," said the Good Witch, "have

wonderful powers. And one of the most curious things about them is that they can carry you to any place in the world in three steps, and each step will be made in the wink

of an eye. All you have to do is to knock the heels together three times and command the shoes to carry you wherever you wish to go." "If that is so," said the child joyfully,

"I will ask them to carry me back to Kansas at once." She threw her arms around the Lion's neck and kissed him, patting his big head tenderly. Then she kissed the Tin

Woodman, who was weeping in a way most dangerous to his joints. But she hugged the soft, stuffed body of the Scarecrow in her arms instead of kissing his painted face,

and found she was crying herself at this sorrowful parting from her loving comrades. Glinda the Good stepped down from her ruby throne to give the little girl a good-bye

kiss, and Dorothy thanked her for all the kindness she had shown to her friends and herself. Dorothy now took Toto up solemnly in her arms, and having said one last good-

bye she clapped the heels of her shoes together three times, saying: "Take me home to Aunt Em!" Instantly she was whirling through the air, so swiftly that all she could see

or feel was the wind whistling past her ears. The Silver Shoes took but three steps, and then she stopped so suddenly that she rolled over upon the grass several times before

she knew where she was. At length, however, she sat up and looked about her. "Good gracious!" she cried. For she was sitting on the broad Kansas prairie, and just before

her was the new farmhouse Uncle Henry built after the cyclone had carried away the old one. Uncle Henry was milking the cows in the barnyard, and Toto had jumped out

of her arms and was running toward the barn, barking furiously. Dorothy stood up and found she was in her stocking feet. For the Silver Shoes had fallen off in her flight

through the air, and were lost forever in the desert. CHAPTER XXIV Home Again Aunt Em had just come out of the house to water the cabbages when she looked up and saw Dorothy running toward her. "My darling child!" she cried, folding the little girl in her arms and covering her face with kisses. "Where in the world did you come from?"

"From the Land of Oz," said Dorothy gravely. "And here is Toto, too. And oh, Aunt Em! I'm so glad to be at home again!" LITTLE WIZARD STORIES OF OZ The

Cowardly Lion and the Hungry Tiger In the splendid palace of the Emerald City, which is in the center of the fairy Land of Oz, is a great Throne Room, where Princess

Ozma, the Ruler, for an hour each day sits in a throne of glistening emeralds and listens to all the troubles of her people, which they are sure to tell her about. Around Ozma's

throne, on such occasions, are grouped all the important personages of Oz, such as the Scarecrow, Jack Pumpkinhead, Tiktok the Clockwork Man, the Tin Woodman, the

Wizard of Oz, the Shaggy Man and other famous fairy people. Little Dorothy usually has a seat at Ozma's feet, and crouched on either side the throne are two enormous

beasts known as the Hungry Tiger and the Cowardly Lion. These two beasts are Ozma's chief guardians, but as everyone loves the beautiful girl Princess there has never

been any disturbance in the great Throne Room, or anything for the guardians to do but look fierce and solemn and keep quiet until the Royal Audience is over and the people

go away to their homes. Of course no one would dare be naughty while the huge Lion and Tiger crouched beside the throne; but the fact is, the people of Oz are very seldom

naughty. So Ozma's big guards are more ornamental than useful, and no one realizes that better than the beasts themselves. One day, after everybody had left the Throne

Room except the Cowardly Lion and the Hungry Tiger, the Lion yawned and said to his friend: "I'm getting tired of this job. No one is afraid of us and no one pays any

attention to us." "That is true," replied the big Tiger, purring softly. "We might as well be in the thick jungles where we were born, as trying to protect Ozma when she needs

no protection. And I'm dreadfully hungry all the time." "You have enough to eat, I'm sure," said the Lion, swaying his tail slowly back and forth. "Enough, perhaps; but not

the kind of food I long for," answered the Tiger. "What I'm hungry for is fat babies. I have a great desire to eat a few fat babies. Then, perhaps, the people of Oz would fear

me and I'd become more important." "True," agreed the Lion. "It would stir up quite a rumpus if you ate but *one* fat baby. As for myself; my claws are sharp as needles and

strong as crowbars, while my teeth are powerful enough to tear a person to pieces in a few seconds. If I should spring upon a man and make chop suey of him, there would

be wild excitement in the Emerald City and the people would fall upon their knees and beg me for mercy. That, in my opinion, would render me of considerable importance."

"After you had torn the person to pieces, what would you do next?" asked the Tiger sleepily. "Then I would roar so loudly it would shake the earth and stalk away to the

jungle to hide myself, before anyone could attack me or kill me for what I had done." "I see," nodded the Tiger. "You are really cowardly." "To be sure. That is why I am

named the Cowardly Lion. That is why I have always been so tame and peaceable. But I'm awfully tired of being tame," added the Lion, with a sigh, "and it would be fun

to raise a row and show people what a terrible beast I really am." The Tiger remained silent for several minutes, thinking deeply as he slowly washed his face with his left

paw. Then he said: "I'm getting old, and it would please me to eat at least one fat baby before I die. Suppose we surprise these people of Oz and prove our power. What do

you say? We will walk out of here just as usual and the first baby we meet I'll eat in a jiffy, and the first man or woman you meet you will tear to pieces. Then we will both run out of the city gates and gallop across the country and hide in the jungle before anyone can stop us." "All right; I'm game," said the Lion, yawning again so that he showed

two rows of dreadfully sharp teeth. The Tiger got up and stretched his great, sleek body. "Come on," he said. The Lion stood up and proved he was the larger of the two,

for he was almost as big as a small horse. Out of the palace they walked, and met no one. They passed through the beautiful grounds, past fountains and beds of lovely

flowers, and met no one. Then they unlatched a gate and entered a street of the city, and met no one. "I wonder how a fat baby will taste," remarked the Tiger, as they stalked

majestically along, side by side. "I imagine it will taste like nutmegs," said the Lion. "No," said the Tiger, "I've an idea it will taste like gumdrops." They turned a corner,

but met no one, for the people of the Emerald City were accustomed to take their naps at this hour of the afternoon. "I wonder how many pieces I ought to tear a person

into," said the Lion, in a thoughtful voice. "Sixty would be about right," suggested the Tiger. "Would that hurt any more than to tear one into about a dozen pieces?" inquired

the Lion, with a little shudder. "Who cares whether it hurts or not?" growled the Tiger. The Lion did not reply. They entered a side street, but met no one. Suddenly they

heard a child crying. "Aha!" exclaimed the Tiger. "There is my meat." He rushed around a corner, the Lion following, and came upon a nice fat baby sitting in the middle

of the street and crying as if in great distress. "What's the matter?" asked the Tiger, crouching before the baby. "I—I—I—lost my m—m—mama!" wailed the baby. "Why,

you poor little thing," said the great beast, softly stroking the child's head with its paw. "Don't cry, my dear, for mama can't be far away and I'll help you to find her." "Go

on," said the Lion, who stood by. "Go on where?" asked the Tiger, looking up. "Go on and eat your fat baby." "Why, you dreadful creature!" said the Tiger reproachfully;

"would you want me to eat a poor little lost baby, that doesn't know where its mother is?" And the beast gathered the little one into its strong, hairy arms and tried to comfort

it by rocking it gently back and forth. The Lion growled low in his throat and seemed very much disappointed; but at that moment a scream reached their ears and a woman

came bounding out of a house and into the street. Seeing her baby in the embrace of the monster Tiger the woman screamed again and rushed forward to rescue it, but in

her haste she caught her foot in her skirt and tumbled head over heels and heels over head, stopping with such a bump that she saw many stars in the heavens, although it was

broad daylight. And there she lay, in a helpless manner, all tangled up and unable to stir. With one bound and a roar like thunder the huge Lion was beside her. With his strong

jaws he grasped her dress and raised her into an upright position. "Poor thing! Are you hurt?" he gently asked. Gasping for breath the woman struggled to free herself and

tried to walk, but she limped badly and tumbled down again. "My baby!" she said pleadingly. "The baby is all right; don't worry," replied the Lion; and then he added: "Keep

quiet, now, and I'll carry you back to your house, and the Hungry Tiger will carry your baby." The Tiger, who had approached the place with the child in its arms, asked in

astonishment: "Aren't you going to tear her into sixty pieces?" "No, nor into six pieces," answered the Lion indignantly. "I'm not such a brute as to destroy a poor woman

who has hurt herself trying to save her lost baby. If you are so ferocious and cruel and bloodthirsty, you may leave me and go away, for I do not care to associate with you."

"That's all right," answered the Tiger. "I'm not cruel—not in the least—I'm only hungry. But I thought *you* were cruel." "Thank heaven I'm respectable," said the Lion, with dignity. He then raised the woman and with much gentleness carried her into her house, where he laid her upon a sofa. The Tiger followed with the baby, which he safely deposited beside its mother. The little one liked the Hungry Tiger and grasping the enormous beast by both ears the baby kissed the beast's nose to show he was grateful and happy. "Thank you very much," said the woman. "I've often heard what good beasts you are, in spite of your power to do mischief to mankind, and now I know that the stories are true. I do not think either of you have ever had an evil thought." The Hungry Tiger and the Cowardly Lion hung their heads and did not look into each other's eyes, for both were shamed and humbled. They crept away and stalked back through the streets until they again entered the palace grounds, where they retreated to the pretty, comfortable rooms they occupied at the back of the palace. There they silently crouched in their usual corners to think over their adventure. After a while the Tiger said sleepily: "I don't believe fat babies taste like gumdrops. I'm quite sure they have the flavor of raspberry tarts. My, how hungry I am for fat babies!" The Lion grunted disdainfully. "You're a humbug," said he. "Am I?" retorted the Tiger, with a sneer. "Tell me, then, into how many pieces you usually tear your victims, my bold Lion?" The Lion impatiently thumped the floor with his tail. "To tear anyone into pieces would soil my claws and blunt my teeth," he said. "I'm glad I didn't muss myself up this afternoon by hurting that poor mother." The Tiger looked at him steadily and then yawned a wide, wide yawn. "You're a coward," he remarked. "Well," said the Lion, "it's better to be a coward than to do wrong." "To be sure," answered the other. "And that reminds me that I nearly lost my own reputation. For, had I eaten that fat baby I would not now be the Hungry Tiger. It's better to go hungry, seems to me, than to be cruel to a little child." And then they dropped their heads on their paws and went to sleep.

LITTLE DOROTHY AND TOTO Dorothy was a little Kansas girl who once accidentally found the beautiful Land of Oz and was invited to live there always. Toto was Dorothy's small black dog, with fuzzy, curly hair and bright black eyes. Together, when they tired of the grandeur of the Emerald City of Oz, they would wander out into the country and all through the land, peering into queer nooks and corners and having a good time in their own simple way. There was a little Wizard living in Oz who was a faithful friend of Dorothy and did not approve of her traveling alone in this way, but the girl always laughed at the little man's fears for her and said she was not afraid of anything that might happen. One day while on such a journey, Dorothy and Toto found themselves among the wild wooded hills at the southeast of Oz—a place usually avoided by travelers because so many magical things abounded there. And, as they entered a forest path, the little girl noticed a sign tacked to a tree, which said: "Look out for Crinklink." Toto could not talk, as many of the animals of Oz can, for he was just a common Kansas dog; but he looked at the sign so seriously that Dorothy almost believed he could read it, and she knew quite well that Toto understood every word she said to him. "Never mind Crinklink," said she. "I don't believe anything in Oz will try to hurt us, Toto, and if I get into trouble you must take care of me." "Bow-wow!" said Toto, and Dorothy knew that meant a promise. The path was narrow and wound here and there between the trees, but they could not lose their way, because thick vines and creepers shut them in on both sides. They had walked a long time when, suddenly turning a curve of the pathway, they came upon a lake of black water, so big and so deep that they were forced to stop. "Well, Toto," said Dorothy, looking at the lake, "we must turn back, I guess, for there is neither a bridge nor a boat to take us across the black water." "Here's the ferryman, though," cried a tiny voice beside them, and the girl gave a start and looked down at her feet, where a man no taller than three inches sat at the edge of the path with his legs dangling over the lake. "Oh!" said Dorothy; "I didn't see you before." Toto growled fiercely and made his ears stand up straight, but the little man did not seem in the least afraid of the dog. He merely repeated: "I'm the ferryman, and it's my business to carry people across the lake." Dorothy couldn't help feeling surprised, for she could have picked the little man up with one hand, and the lake was big and broad. Looking at the ferryman more closely she saw that he had small eyes, a big nose, and a sharp chin. His hair was blue and his clothes scarlet, and Dorothy noticed that every button on his jacket was the head of some animal. The top button was a bear's head and the next button a wolf's head; the next was a cat's head and the next a weasel's head, while the last button of all was the head of a field mouse. When Dorothy looked into the eyes of these animals' heads, they all nodded and said in a chorus: "Don't believe all you hear, little girl!" "Silence!" said the small ferryman, slapping each button head in turn, but not hard enough to hurt them. Then he turned to Dorothy and asked: "Do you wish to cross over the lake?" "Why, I'd like to," she answered, hesitating; "but I can't see how you will manage to carry us, without any boat." "If you can't see, you mustn't see," he answered with a laugh. "All you need do is shut your eyes, say the word, and—over you go!" Dorothy wanted to get across, in order that she might continue her journey. "All right," she said, closing her eyes; "I'm ready." Instantly she was seized in a pair of strong arms—arms so big and powerful that she was startled and cried out in fear. "Silence!" roared a great voice, and the girl opened her eyes to find that the tiny man had suddenly grown to a giant and was holding both her and Toto in a tight embrace while in one step he spanned the lake and reached the other shore. Dorothy became frightened, then, especially as the giant did not stop but continued tramping in great steps over the wooded hills, crushing bushes and trees beneath his broad feet. She struggled in vain to free herself, while Toto whined and trembled beside her, for the little dog was frightened, too. "Stop!" screamed the girl. "Let me down!" But the giant paid no attention. "Who are you, and where are you taking me?" she continued; but the giant said not a word. Close to Dorothy's ear, however, a voice answered her, saying: "This is the terrible Crinklink, and he has you in his power." Dorothy managed to twist her head around and found it was the second button on the jacket—the wolf's head—which had spoken to her. "What will Crinklink do with me?" she asked anxiously. "No one knows. You must wait and see," replied the wolf. "Some of his captives he whips," squeaked the weasel's head. "Some he transforms into bugs and other things," growled the bear's head. "Some he enchants, so that they become doorknobs," sighed the cat's head. "Some he makes his slaves—even as we are—and that is the most dreadful fate of all," added the field mouse. "As long as Crinklink exists we shall remain buttons, but as there are no more buttonholes on his jacket he will probably make you a slave." Dorothy began to wish she had not met Crinklink. Meantime, the giant took such big steps that he soon reached the heart of the hills, where, perched upon the highest peak, stood a log castle. Before this castle he paused to set down Dorothy and Toto, for Crinklink was at present far too large to enter his own doorway. So he made himself grow smaller, until he was about the size of an ordinary man. Then he said to Dorothy, in stern, commanding tones: "Enter, girl!"

Dorothy obeyed and entered the castle, with Toto at her heels. She found the place to be merely one big room. There was a table and chair of ordinary size near the center, and at one side a wee bed that seemed scarcely big enough for a doll. Everywhere else were dishes—dishes—dishes! They were all soiled, and were piled upon the floor, in all the corners and upon every shelf. Evidently Crinklink had not washed a dish for years, but had cast them aside as he used them. Dorothy's captor sat down in the chair and frowned at her. "You are young and strong, and will make a good dishwasher," said he. "Do you mean me to wash all those dishes?" she asked, feeling both indignant and fearful, for such a task would take weeks to accomplish. "That's just what I mean," he retorted. "I need clean dishes, for all I have are soiled, and you're going to make 'em clean or get trounced. So get to work and be careful not to break anything. If you smash a dish, the penalty is one lash from my dreadful cat-o'-nine-tails for every piece the dish breaks into," and here Crinklink displayed a terrible whip that made the little girl shudder. Dorothy knew how to wash dishes, but she remembered that often she carelessly broke one. In this case, however, a good deal depended on being careful, so she handled the dishes very cautiously. While she worked, Toto sat by the hearth and growled low at Crinklink, and Crinklink sat in his chair and growled at Dorothy because she moved so slowly. He expected her to break a dish any minute, but as the hours passed away and this did not happen Crinklink began to grow sleepy. It was tiresome watching the girl wash dishes and often he glanced longingly at the tiny bed. Now he began to yawn, and he yawned and yawned until finally he said: "I'm going to take a nap. But the buttons on my jacket will be wide awake and whenever you break a dish the crash will waken me. As I'm rather sleepy I hope you won't interrupt my nap by breaking anything for a long time." Then Crinklink made himself grow smaller and smaller until he was three inches high and of a size to fit the tiny bed. At once he lay down and fell fast asleep. Dorothy came close to the buttons and whispered: "Would you really warn Crinklink if I tried to escape?" "You can't escape," growled the bear. "Crinklink would become a giant, and soon overtake you." "But you might kill him while he sleeps," suggested the cat, in a soft voice. "Oh!" cried Dorothy, drawing back; "I couldn't poss'bly *kill* anything—even to save my life." But Toto had heard this conversation and was not so particular about killing monsters. Also the little dog knew he must try to save his mistress. In an instant he sprang upon the wee bed and was about to seize the sleeping Crinklink in his jaws when Dorothy heard a loud crash and a heap of dishes fell from the table to the floor. Then the girl saw Toto and the little man rolling on the floor together, like a fuzzy ball, and when the ball stopped rolling, behold! there was Toto wagging his tail joyfully and there sat the little Wizard of Oz, laughing merrily at the expression of surprise on Dorothy's face. "Yes, my dear, it's me," said he, "and I've been playing tricks on you—for your own good. I wanted to prove to you that it is really dangerous for a little girl to wander alone in a fairy country; so I took the form of Crinklink to teach you a lesson. There isn't any Crinklink, to be sure; but if there had been you'd be severely whipped for breaking all those dishes." The Wizard now rose, took off the coat with the button heads, and spread it on the floor, wrong side up.

At once there crept from beneath it a bear, a wolf, a cat, a weasel, and a field mouse, who all rushed from the room and escaped into the mountains. "Come on, Toto," said Dorothy; "let's go back to the Emerald City. You've given me a good scare, Wizard," she added, with dignity, "and p'raps I'll forgive you, by-n-by; but just now I'm mad to think how easily you fooled me." TIKTOK AND THE NOME KING The Nome King was unpleasantly angry. He had carelessly bitten his tongue at breakfast and it still hurt; so he roared and raved and stamped around in his underground palace in a way that rendered him very disagreeable. It so happened that on this unfortunate day Tiktok, the Clockwork Man, visited the Nome King to ask a favor. Tiktok lived in the Land of Oz, and although he was an active and important person, he was made entirely of metal. Machinery within him, something like the works of a clock, made him move; other machinery made him talk; still other machinery made him think. Although so cleverly constructed, the Clockwork Man was far from perfect. Three separate keys wound up his motion machinery, his speech works, and his thoughts. One or more of these contrivances was likely to run down at a critical moment, leaving poor Tiktok helpless. Also some of his parts were wearing out, through much use, and just now his thought machinery needed repair. The skillful little Wizard of Oz had tinkered with Tiktok's thoughts without being able to get them properly regulated, so he had advised the Clockwork Man to go to the Nome King and secure a new set of springs, which would render his thoughts more elastic and responsive. "Be careful what you say to the Nome King," warned the Wizard. "He has a bad temper and the least little thing makes him angry." Tiktok promised, and the Wizard wound his machinery and set him walking in the direction of the Nome King's dominions, just across the desert from the Land of Oz. He ran down just as he reached the entrance to the underground palace, and there Kaliko, the Nome King's Chief Steward, found him and wound him up again. "I want to see the King," said Tiktok, in his jerky voice. "Well," remarked Kaliko, "it may be safe for a cast-iron person like you to face his Majesty this morning; but you must announce yourself, for should I show my face inside the jewel-studded cavern where the King is now raving, I'd soon look like a dish of mashed potatoes, and be of no further use to anyone." "I'm not a-fraid," said Tiktok. "Then walk in and make yourself at home," answered Kaliko, and threw open the door of the King's cavern. Tiktok promptly walked in and faced the astonished Nome King, to whom he said: "Good morn-ing. I want two new steel springs for my thought-works and a new cog-wheel for my speech-pro-du-cer. How a-bout it, your Maj-es-ty?" The Nome King growled a menacing growl and his eyes were red with rage. "How dare you enter my presence?" he shouted. "I dare an-y-thing," said Tiktok. "I'm not a-fraid of a fat Nome." This was true, yet an unwise speech. Had Tiktok's thoughts been in good working order he would have said something else. The angry Nome King quickly caught up his heavy mace and hurled it straight at Tiktok. When it struck the metal man's breast, the force of the blow burst the bolts which held the plates of his body together and they clattered to the floor in a score of pieces. Hundreds and hundreds of wheels, pins, cogs and springs filled the air like a cloud and then rattled like hail upon the floor. Where Tiktok had stood was now only a scrap heap and the Nome King was so amazed by the terrible effect of his blow that he stared in wonder. His Majesty's anger quickly cooled. He remembered that the Clockwork Man was a favorite subject of the powerful Princess, Ozma of Oz, who would be sure to resent Tiktok's ruin. "Too bad! too bad!" he muttered, regretfully. "I'm really sorry I made junk of the fellow. I didn't know he'd break." "You'd better be," remarked Kaliko, who now ventured to enter the room. "You'll have a war on your hands when Ozma hears of this, and the chances are you will lose your throne and your kingdom." The Nome King turned pale, for he loved to rule the Nomes and did not know of any other way to earn a living in case Ozma fought and conquered him. "Do—do you think Ozma will be angry?" he asked

anxiously. "I'm sure of it," said Kaliko. "And she has the right to be. You've made scrap-iron of her favorite." The King groaned. "Sweep him up and throw the rubbish into

the black pit," he commanded; and then he shut himself up in his private den and for days would see no one, because he was so ashamed of his unreasoning anger and so

feared the results of his rash act. Kaliko swept up the pieces, but he did not throw them into the black pit. Being a clever and skillful mechanic he determined to fit the pieces

together again. No man ever faced a greater puzzle; but it was interesting work and Kaliko succeeded. When he found a spring or wheel worn or imperfect, he made a new

one. Within two weeks, by working steadily night and day, the Chief Steward completed his task and put the three sets of clockworks and the last rivet into Tiktok's body.

He then wound up the motion machinery, and the Clockwork Man walked up and down the room as naturally as ever. Then Kaliko wound up the thought works and the

speech regulator and said to Tiktok: "How do you feel now?" "Fine," said the Clockwork Man. "You have done a ve-ry good job, Kal-i-ko, and saved me from de-struc-tion.

Much o-bliged." "Don't mention it," replied the Chief Steward. "I quite enjoyed the work." Just then the Nome King's gong sounded, and Kaliko rushed away through the

jewel-studded cavern and into the den where the King had hidden, leaving the doors ajar. "Kaliko," said the King, in a meek voice, "I've been shut up here long enough to

repent bitterly the destruction of Tiktok. Of course Ozma will have revenge, and send an army to fight us, but we must take our medicine. One thing comforts me: Tiktok

wasn't really a live person; he was only a machine man, and so it wasn't very wicked to stop his clockworks. I couldn't sleep nights, at first, for worry; but there's no more

harm in smashing a machine man than in breaking a wax doll. Don't you think so?" "I am too humble to think in the presence of your Majesty," said Kaliko. "Then get me

something to eat," commanded the King, "for I'm nearly starved. Two roasted goats, a barrel of cakes and nine mince pies will do me until dinnertime." Kaliko bowed and

hurried away to the royal kitchen, forgetting Tiktok, who was wandering around in the outer cavern. Suddenly the Nome King looked up and saw the Clockwork Man

standing before him, and at the sight the monarch's eyes grew big and round and he fell a-trembling in every limb. "Away, grim Shadow!" he cried. "You're not here, you

know; you're only a hash of cogwheels and springs, lying at the bottom of the black pit. Vanish, thou Vision of the demolished Tiktok, and leave me in peace—for I have

bitterly repented!" "Then beg my pardon," said Tiktok in a gruff voice, for Kaliko had forgotten to oil the speech works. But the sound of a voice coming from what he

thought a mere vision was too much for the Nome King's shaken nerves. He gave a yell of fear and rushed from the room. Tiktok followed, so the King bolted through the

corridors on a swift run and bumped against Kaliko, who was returning with a tray of things to eat. The sound of the breaking dishes, as they struck the floor, added to the

King's terror and he yelled again and dashed into a great cavern where a thousand Nomes were at work hammering metal. "Look out! Here comes a phantom clockwork

man!" screamed the terrified monarch, and every Nome dropped his tools and made a rush from the cavern, knocking over their King in their mad flight and recklessly

trampling upon his prostrate fat body. So, when Tiktok came into the cavern, there was only the Nome King left, and he was rolling upon the rocky floor and howling for mercy, with his eyes fast shut so that he could not see what he was sure was a dreadful phantom that was coming straight toward him. "It oc-curs to me," said Tiktok calmly,

"that your Maj-es-ty is act-ing like a ba-by. I am not a phan-tom. A phan-tom is unreal, while I am the real thing." The King rolled over, sat up and opened his eyes. "Didn't

I smash you to pieces?" he asked in trembling tones. "Yes," said Tiktok. "Then you are nothing but a junk heap, and this form in which you now appear cannot be real." "It

is, though," declared Tiktok. "Kal-i-ko picked up my piec-es and put me to-geth-er a-gain. I'm as good as new, and perhaps bet-ter." "That is true, your Majesty," added

Kaliko, who now made his appearance, "and I hope you will forgive me for mending Tiktok. He was quite broken up, after you smashed him, and I found it almost as hard

a job to match his pieces as to pick turnips from gooseberry bushes. But I did it," he added proudly. "You are forgiven," announced the Nome King, rising to his feet and

drawing a long breath. "I will raise your wages one specto a year, and Tiktok shall return to the Land of Oz loaded with jewels for the Princess Ozma." "That is all right,"

said Tiktok. "But what I want to know is, why did you hit me with your mace?" "Because I was angry," admitted the King. "When I am angry I always do something that I

am sorry for afterward. So I have firmly resolved never to get angry again; unless—unless—" "Unless what, your Majesty?" inquired Kaliko. "Unless something annoys

me," said the Nome King. And then he went to his treasure chamber to get the jewels for Princess Ozma of Oz. OZMA AND THE LITTLE WIZARD Once upon a time

there lived in the beautiful Emerald City, which lies in the center of the fairy Land of Oz, a lovely girl called Princess Ozma, who was ruler of all that country. And among

those who served this girlish Ruler and lived in a cozy suite of rooms in her splendid palace, was a little, withered old man known as the Wizard of Oz. This little Wizard

could do a good many queer things in magic; but he was a kind man, with merry, twinkling eyes and a sweet smile; so, instead of fearing him because of his magic, everybody

loved him. Now, Ozma was very anxious that all her people who inhabited the pleasant Land of Oz should be happy and contented, and therefore she decided one morning

to make a journey to all parts of the country, that she might discover if anything was amiss, or anyone discontented, or if there was any wrong that ought to be righted. She

asked the little Wizard to accompany her and he was glad to go. "Shall I take my bag of magic tools with me?" he asked. "Of course," said Ozma. "We may need a lot of

magic before we return, for we are going into strange corners of the land, where we may meet with unknown creatures and dangerous adventures." So the Wizard took his

bag of magic tools and the two left the Emerald City and wandered over the country for many days, at last reaching a place far up in the mountains which neither of them

had ever visited before. Stopping one morning at a cottage, built beside the rocky path which led into a pretty valley beyond, Ozma asked a man: "Are you happy? Have you

any complaint to make of your lot?" And the man replied: "We are happy except for three mischievous Imps that live in yonder valley and often come here to annoy us. If

your Highness would only drive away those Imps, I and my family would be very happy and very grateful to you." "Who are these bad Imps?" inquired the girl Ruler. "One

is named Olite, and one Udent and one Ertinent, and they have no respect for anyone or anything. If strangers pass through the valley the Imps jeer at them and make horrid

faces and call names, and often they push travelers out of the path or throw stones at them. Whenever Imp Olite or Imp Udent or Imp Ertinent comes here to bother us, I and my family run into the house and lock all the doors and windows, and we dare not venture out again until the Imps have gone away." Princess Ozma was grieved to hear this report and the little Wizard shook his head gravely and said the naughty Imps deserved to be punished. They told the good man they would see what could be done to protect him and at once entered the valley to seek the dwelling place of the three mischievous creatures. Before long they came upon three caves, hollowed from the rocks, and in front of each cave squatted a queer little dwarf. Ozma and the Wizard paused to examine them and found them well-shaped, strong and lively. They had big round ears, flat noses and wide grinning mouths, and their jet-black hair came to points on top of their heads, much resembling horns. Their clothing fitted snugly to their bodies and limbs and the Imps were so small in size that at first Ozma did not consider them at all dangerous. But one of them suddenly reached out a hand and caught the dress of the Princess, jerking it so sharply that she nearly fell down, and a moment later another Imp pushed the little Wizard so hard that he bumped against Ozma and both unexpectedly sat down upon the ground. At this the Imps laughed boisterously and began running around in a circle and kicking dust upon the Royal Princess, who cried in a sharp voice: "Wizard, do your duty!" The Wizard promptly obeyed. Without rising from the ground he opened his bag, got the tools he required and muttered a magic spell. Instantly the three Imps became three bushes—of a thorny stubby kind—with their roots in the ground. As the bushes were at first motionless, perhaps through surprise at their sudden transformation, the Wizard and the Princess found time to rise from the ground and brush the dust off their pretty clothes. Then Ozma turned to the bushes and said: "The unhappy lot you now endure, my poor Imps, is due entirely to your naughty actions. You can no longer annoy harmless travelers and you must remain ugly bushes, covered with sharp thorns, until you repent of your bad ways and promise to be good Imps." "They can't help being good now, your Highness," said the Wizard, who was much pleased with his work, "and the safest plan will be to allow them always to remain bushes." But something must have been wrong with the Wizard's magic, or the creatures had magic of their own, for no sooner were the words spoken than the bushes began to move. At first they only waved their branches at the girl and little man, but pretty soon they began to slide over the ground, their roots dragging through the earth, and one pushed itself against the Wizard and pricked him so sharply with its thorns that he cried out: "Ouch!" and started to run away. Ozma followed, for the other bushes were trying to stick their thorns into her legs and one actually got so near her that it tore a great rent in her beautiful dress. The girl Princess could run, however, and she followed the fleeing Wizard until he tumbled headfirst over a log and rolled upon the ground. Then she sprang behind a tree and shouted: "Quick! Transform them into something else." The Wizard heard, but he was much confused by his fall. Grabbing from his bag the first magical tool he could find he transformed the bushes into three white pigs. That astonished the Imps. In the shape of pigs—fat, roly-poly and cute—they scampered off a little distance and sat down to think about their new condition. Ozma drew a long breath and coming from behind the tree she said: "That is much better, Wiz, for such pigs as these must be quite harmless. No one need now fear the mischievous Imps." "I intended to transform them into mice," replied the Wizard, "but in my excitement I worked the wrong magic. However, unless the horrid creatures behave themselves hereafter, they are liable to be killed and eaten. They would make good chops, sausages or roasts." But the Imps were now angry and had no intention of behaving. As Ozma and the little Wizard turned to resume their journey,

the three pigs rushed forward, dashed between their legs, and tripped them up, so that both lost their balance and toppled over, clinging to one another. As the Wizard tried

to get up he was tripped again and fell across the back of the third pig, which carried him on a run far down the valley until it dumped the little man in the river. Ozma had

been sprawled upon the ground but found she was not hurt, so she picked herself up and ran to the assistance of the Wizard, reaching him just as he was crawling out of the

river, gasping for breath and dripping with water. The girl could not help laughing at his woeful appearance. But he had no sooner wiped the wet from his eyes than one of

the impish pigs tripped him again and sent him into the river for a second bath. The pigs tried to trip Ozma, too, but she ran around a stump and so managed to keep out of

their way. So the Wizard scrambled out of the water again and picked up a sharp stick to defend himself. Then he mumbled a magic mutter which instantly dried his clothes,

after which he hurried to assist Ozma. The pigs were afraid of the sharp stick and kept away from it. "This won't do," said the Princess. "We have accomplished nothing,

for the pig Imps would annoy travelers as much as the real Imps. Transform them into something else, Wiz." The Wizard took time to think. Then he transformed the white

pigs into three blue doves. "Doves," said he, "are the most harmless things in the world." But scarcely had he spoken when the doves flew at them and tried to peck out their

eyes. When they endeavored to shield their eyes with their hands, two of the doves bit the Wizard's fingers and another caught the pretty pink ear of the Princess in its bill

and gave it such a cruel tweak that she cried out in pain and threw her skirt over her head. "These birds are worse than pigs, Wizard," she called to her companion. "Nothing

is harmless that is animated by impudent anger or impertinent mischief. You must transform the Imps into something that is not alive." The Wizard was pretty busy, just

then, driving off the birds, but he managed to open his bag of magic and find a charm which instantly transformed the doves into three buttons. As they fell to the ground

he picked them up and smiled with satisfaction. The tin button was Imp Olite, the brass button was Imp Udent and the lead button was Imp Ertinent. These buttons the

Wizard placed in a little box which he put in his jacket pocket. "Now," said he, "the Imps cannot annoy travelers, for we shall carry them back with us to the Emerald City."

"But we dare not use the buttons," said Ozma, smiling once more now that the danger was over. "Why not?" asked the Wizard. "I intend to sew them upon my coat and

watch them carefully. The spirits of the Imps are still in the buttons, and after a time they will repent and be sorry for their naughtiness. Then they will decide to be very good

in the future. When they feel that way, the tin button will turn to silver and the brass to gold, while the lead button will become aluminum. I shall then restore them to their

proper forms, changing their names to pretty names instead of the ugly ones they used to bear. Thereafter the three Imps will become good citizens of the Land of Oz and

I think you will find they will prove faithful subjects of our beloved Princess Ozma." "Ah, that is magic well worthwhile," exclaimed Ozma, well pleased. "There is no doubt,

my friend, but that you are a very clever Wizard." JACK PUMPKINHEAD AND THE SAWHORSE In a room of the Royal Palace of the Emerald City of Oz hangs a

Magic Picture, in which are shown all the important scenes that transpire in those fairy dominions. The scenes shift constantly and by watching them, Ozma, the girl Ruler, is able to discover events taking place in any part of her kingdom. One day she saw in her Magic Picture that a little girl and a little boy had wandered together into a great, gloomy forest at the far west of Oz and had become hopelessly lost. Their friends were seeking them in the wrong direction and unless Ozma came to their rescue the little ones would never be found in time to save them from starving. So the Princess sent a message to Jack Pumpkinhead and asked him to come to the palace. This personage, one of the queerest of the queer inhabitants of Oz, was an old friend and companion of Ozma. His form was made of rough sticks fitted together and dressed in ordinary clothes. His head was a pumpkin with a face carved upon it, and was set on top a sharp stake which formed his neck. Jack was active, good-natured and a general favorite; but his pumpkin head was likely to spoil with age, so in order to secure a good supply of heads he grew a big field of pumpkins and lived in the middle of it, his house being a huge pumpkin hollowed out. Whenever he needed a new head he picked a pumpkin, carved a face on it and stuck it upon the stake of his neck, throwing away the old head as of no further use. The day Ozma sent for him Jack was in prime condition and was glad to be of service in rescuing the lost children. Ozma made him a map, showing just where the forest was and how to get to it and the paths he must take to reach the little ones. Then she said: "You'd better ride the Sawhorse, for he is swift and intelligent and will help you accomplish your task." "All right," answered Jack, and went to the royal stable to tell the Sawhorse to be ready for the trip. This remarkable animal was not unlike Jack Pumpkinhead in form, although so different in shape. Its body was a log, with four sticks stuck into it for legs. A branch at one end of the log served as a tail, while in the other end was chopped a gash that formed a mouth. Above this were two small knots that did nicely for eyes. The Sawhorse was the favorite steed of Ozma and to prevent its wooden legs from wearing out she had them shod with plates of gold. Jack said "Good morning" to the Sawhorse and placed upon the creature's back a saddle of purple leather, studded with jewels. "Where now?" asked the horse, blinking its knot eyes at Jack. "We're going to rescue two babes in the wood," was the reply. Then he climbed into the saddle and the wooden animal pranced out of the stable, through the streets of the Emerald City and out upon the highway leading to the western forest where the children were lost. Small though he was, the Sawhorse was swift and untiring. By nightfall they were in the far west and quite close to the forest they sought. They passed the night standing quietly by the roadside. They needed no food, for their wooden bodies never became hungry; nor did they sleep, because they never tired. At daybreak they continued their journey and soon reached the forest. Jack now examined the map Ozma had given him and found the right path to take, which the Sawhorse obediently followed. Underneath the trees all was silent and gloomy and Jack beguiled the way by whistling gayly as the Sawhorse trotted along. The paths branched so many times and in so many different ways that the Pumpkinhead was often obliged to consult Ozma's map, and finally the Sawhorse became suspicious. "Are you sure you are right?" it asked. "Of course," answered Jack. "Even a Pumpkinhead whose brains are seeds can follow so clear a map as this. Every path is plainly marked, and here is a cross where the children are." Finally they reached a place, in the very heart of the forest, where they came upon the lost boy and girl. But they found the two children bound fast to the trunk of a big tree, at the foot of which they were sitting. When the rescuers arrived, the little girl was sobbing bitterly and the boy was trying to comfort her, though he was probably frightened as much as she. "Cheer up, my dears," said Jack, getting out of the saddle. "I have come to take you back to your parents. But why are

you bound to that tree?" "Because," cried a small, sharp voice, "they are thieves and robbers. That's why!" "Dear me!" said Jack, looking around to see who had spoken.

The voice seemed to come from above. A big grey squirrel was sitting upon a low branch of the tree. Upon the squirrel's head was a circle of gold, with a diamond set in the

center of it. He was running up and down the limbs and chattering excitedly. "These children," continued the squirrel, angrily, "robbed our storehouse of all the nuts we had

saved up for winter. Therefore, being King of all the Squirrels in this forest, I ordered them arrested and put in prison, as you now see them. They had no right to steal our

provisions and we are going to punish them." "We were hungry," said the boy, pleadingly, "and we found a hollow tree full of nuts, and ate them to keep alive. We didn't

want to starve when there was food right in front of us." "Quite right," remarked Jack, nodding his pumpkin head. "I don't blame you one bit, under the circumstances. Not

a bit." Then he began to untie the ropes that bound the children to the tree. "Stop that!" cried the King Squirrel, chattering and whisking about. "You mustn't release our

prisoners. You have no right to." But Jack paid no attention to the protest. His wooden fingers were awkward and it took him some time to untie the ropes. When at last he

succeeded, the tree was full of squirrels, called together by their King, and they were furious at losing their prisoners. From the tree they began to hurl nuts at the

Pumpkinhead, who laughed at them as he helped the two children to their feet. Now, at the top of this tree was a big dead limb, and so many squirrels gathered upon it that

suddenly it broke away and fell to the ground. Poor Jack was standing directly under it and when the limb struck him it smashed his pumpkin head into a pulpy mass and sent

Jack's wooden form tumbling, to stop with a bump against a tree a dozen feet away. He sat up, a moment afterward, but when he felt for his head it was gone. He could not

see; neither could he speak. It was perhaps the greatest misfortune that could have happened to Jack Pumpkinhead, and the squirrels were delighted. They danced around in

the tree in great glee as they saw Jack's plight. The boy and girl were indeed free, but their protector was ruined. The Sawhorse was there, however, and in his way he was

wise. He had seen the accident and knew that the smashed pumpkin would never again serve Jack as a head. So he said to the children, who were frightened at this accident

to their newfound friend: "Pick up the Pumpkinhead's body and set it on my saddle. Then mount behind it and hold on. We must get out of this forest as soon as we can, or

the squirrels may capture you again. I must guess at the right path, for Jack's map is no longer of any use to him since that limb destroyed his head." The two children lifted

Jack's body, which was not at all heavy, and placed it upon the saddle. Then they climbed up behind it and the Sawhorse immediately turned and trotted back along the path

he had come, bearing all three with ease. However, when the path began to branch into many paths, all following different directions, the wooden animal became puzzled

and soon was wandering aimlessly about, without any hope of finding the right way. Toward evening they came upon a fine fruit tree, which furnished the children a supper,

and at night the little ones lay upon a bed of leaves while the Sawhorse stood watch, with the limp, headless form of poor Jack Pumpkinhead lying helpless across the saddle.

Now, Ozma had seen in her Magic Picture all that had happened in the forest, so she sent the little Wizard, mounted upon the Cowardly Lion, to save the unfortunates. The

Lion knew the forest well and when he reached it he bounded straight through the tangled paths to where the Sawhorse was wandering, with Jack and the two children on his back. The Wizard was grieved at the sight of the headless Jack, but believed he could save him. He first led the Sawhorse out of the forest and restored the boy and girl to the arms of their anxious friends, and then he sent the Lion back to Ozma to tell her what had happened. The Wizard now mounted the Sawhorse and supported Jack's form on the long ride to the pumpkin field. When they arrived at Jack's house the Wizard selected a fine pumpkin—not too ripe—and very neatly carved a face on it. Then he stuck the pumpkin solidly on Jack's neck and asked him: "Well, old friend, how do you feel?" "Fine!" replied Jack, and shook the hand of the little Wizard gratefully.

"You have really saved my life, for without your assistance I could not have found my way home to get a new head. But I'm all right, now, and I shall be very careful not to get this beautiful head smashed." And he shook the Wizard's hand again. "Are the brains in the new head any better than the old ones?" inquired the Sawhorse, who had watched Jack's restoration. "Why, these seeds are quite tender," replied the Wizard, "so they will give our friend tender thoughts. But, to speak truly, my dear Sawhorse, Jack Pumpkinhead, with all his good qualities, will never be noted for his wisdom." THE SCARECROW AND THE TIN WOODMAN There lived in the Land of Oz two queerly made men who were the best of friends. They were so much happier when together that they were seldom apart; yet they liked to separate, once in a while, that they might enjoy the pleasure of meeting again. One was a Scarecrow. That means he was a suit of blue Munchkin clothes, stuffed with straw, on top of which was fastened a round cloth head, filled with bran to hold it in shape. On the head were painted two eyes, two ears, a nose and a mouth. The Scarecrow had never been much of a success in scaring crows, but he prided himself on being a superior man, because he could feel no pain, was never tired and did not have to eat or drink. His brains were sharp, for the Wizard of Oz had put pins and needles in the Scarecrow's brains. The other man was made all of tin, his arms and legs and head being cleverly jointed so that he could move them freely. He was known as the Tin Woodman, having at one time been a woodchopper, and everyone loved him because the Wizard had given him an excellent heart of red plush. The Tin Woodman lived in a magnificent tin castle, built on his country estate in the Winkie Land, not far from the Emerald City of Oz. It had pretty tin furniture and was surrounded by lovely gardens in which were many tin trees and beds of tin flowers. The palace of the Scarecrow was not far distant, on the banks of a river, and this palace was in the shape of an immense ear of corn. One morning the Tin Woodman went to visit his friend the Scarecrow, and as they had nothing better to do they decided to take a boat ride on the river. So they got into the Scarecrow's boat, which was formed from a big corncob, hollowed out and pointed at both ends and decorated around the edges with brilliant jewels. The sail was of purple silk and glittered gayly in the sunshine. There was a good breeze that day, so the boat glided swiftly over the water. By and by they came to a smaller river that flowed from out a deep forest, and the Tin Woodman proposed they sail up this stream, as it would be cool and shady beneath the trees of the forest. So the Scarecrow, who was steering, turned the boat up the stream and the friends continued talking together of old times and the wonderful adventures they had met with while traveling with Dorothy, the little Kansas girl. They became so much interested in this talk that they forgot to notice that the boat was now sailing through the forest, or that the stream was growing more narrow and crooked. Suddenly the Scarecrow glanced up and saw a big rock just ahead of

them. "Look out!" he cried; but the warning came too late. The Tin Woodman sprang to his feet just as the boat bumped into the rock, and the jar made him lose his balance.

He toppled and fell overboard and being made of tin he sank to the bottom of the water in an instant and lay there at full length, face up. Immediately the Scarecrow threw

out the anchor, so as to hold the boat in that place, and then he leaned over the side and through the clear water looked at his friend sorrowfully. "Dear me!" he exclaimed;

"what a misfortune!" "It is, indeed," replied the Tin Woodman, speaking in muffled tones because so much water covered him. "I cannot drown, of course, but I must lie

here until you find a way to get me out. Meantime, the water is soaking into all my joints and I shall become badly rusted before I am rescued." "Very true," agreed the

Scarecrow; "but be patient, my friend, and I'll dive down and get you. My straw will not rust, and is easily replaced, if damaged, so I'm not afraid of the water." The

Scarecrow now took off his hat and made a dive from the boat into the water; but he was so light in weight that he barely dented the surface of the stream, nor could he reach

the Tin Woodman with his outstretched straw arms. So he floated to the boat and climbed into it, saying the while: "Do not despair, my friend. We have an extra anchor

aboard, and I will tie it around my waist, to make me sink, and dive again." "Don't do that!" called the tin man. "That would anchor you also to the bottom, where I am, and

we'd both be helpless." "True enough," sighed the Scarecrow, wiping his wet face with a handkerchief; and then he gave a cry of astonishment, for he found he had wiped

off one painted eye and now had but one eye to see with. "How dreadful!" said the poor Scarecrow. "That eye must have been painted in watercolor, instead of oil. I must

be careful not to wipe off the other eye, for then I could not see to help you at all." A shriek of elfish laughter greeted this speech and looking up the Scarecrow found the

trees full of black crows, who seemed much amused by the straw man's one-eyed countenance. He knew the crows well, however, and they had usually been friendly to him

because he had never deceived them into thinking he was a meat man—the sort of man they really feared. "Don't laugh," said he; "you may lose an eye yourselves someday."

"We couldn't look as funny as you, if we did," replied one old crow, the king of them. "But what has gone wrong with you?" "The Tin Woodman, my dear friend and

companion, has fallen overboard and is now on the bottom of the river," said the Scarecrow. "I'm trying to get him out again, but I fear I shall not succeed." "Why, it's easy

enough," declared the old crow. "Tie a string to him and all of my crows will fly down, take hold of the string, and pull him up out of the water. There are hundreds of us

here, so our united strength could lift much more than that." "But I can't tie a string to him," replied the Scarecrow. "My straw is so light that I am unable to dive through

the water. I've tried it, and knocked one eye out." "Can't you fish for him?" "Ah, that is a good idea," said the Scarecrow. "I'll make the attempt." He found a fishline in the

boat, with a stout hook at the end of it. No bait was needed, so the Scarecrow dropped the hook into the water till it touched the Woodman. "Hook it into a joint," advised

the crow, who was now perched upon a branch that stuck far out and bent down over the water. The Scarecrow tried to do this, but having only one eye he could not see the

joints very clearly. "Hurry up, please," begged the Tin Woodman; "you've no idea how damp it is down here." "Can't you help?" asked the crow. "How?" inquired the tin man. "Catch the line and hook it around your neck." The Tin Woodman made the attempt and after several trials wound the line around his neck and hooked it securely.

"Good!" cried the King Crow, a mischievous old fellow. "Now, then, we'll all grab the line and pull you out." At once the air was filled with black crows, each of whom

seized the cord with beak or talons. The Scarecrow watched them with much interest and forgot that he had tied the other end of the line around his own waist, so he would

not lose it while fishing for his friend. "All together for the good caws!" shrieked the King Crow, and with a great flapping of wings the birds rose into the air. The Scarecrow

clapped his stuffed hands in glee as he saw his friend drawn from the water into the air; but the next moment the straw man was himself in the air, his stuffed legs kicking

wildly; for the crows had flown straight up through the trees. On one end of the line dangled the Tin Woodman, hung by the neck, and on the other dangled the Scarecrow,

hung by the waist and clinging fast to the spare anchor of the boat, which he had seized hoping to save himself. "Hi, there—be careful!" shouted the Scarecrow to the crows.

"Don't take us so high. Land us on the riverbank." But the crows were bent on mischief. They thought it a good joke to bother the two, now that they held them captive.

"Here's where the crows scare the Scarecrow!" chuckled the naughty King Crow, and at his command the birds flew over the forest to where a tall dead tree stood higher

than all the other trees. At the very top was a crotch, formed by two dead limbs, and into the crotch the crows dropped the center of the line. Then, letting go their hold, they

flew away, chattering with laughter, and left the two friends suspended high in the air—one on each side of the tree. Now the Tin Woodman was much heavier than the

Scarecrow, but the reason they balanced so nicely was because the straw man still clung fast to the iron anchor. There they hung, not ten feet apart, yet unable to reach the

bare tree trunk. "For goodness sake don't drop that anchor," said the Tin Woodman anxiously. "Why not?" inquired the Scarecrow. "If you did I'd tumble to the ground,

where my tin would be badly dented by the fall. Also you would shoot into the air and alight somewhere among the treetops." "Then," said the Scarecrow, earnestly, "I shall

hold fast to the anchor." For a time they both dangled in silence, the breeze swaying them gently to and fro. Finally the tin man said: "Here is an emergency, friend, where

only brains can help us. We must think of some way to escape." "I'll do the thinking," replied the Scarecrow. "My brains are the sharpest." He thought so long that the tin

man grew tired and tried to change his position, but found his joints had already rusted so badly that he could not move them. And his oilcan was back in the boat. "Do you

suppose your brains are rusted, friend Scarecrow?" he asked in a weak voice, for his jaws would scarcely move. "No, indeed. Ah, here's an idea at last!" And with this the

Scarecrow clapped his hands to his head, forgetting the anchor, which tumbled to the ground. The result was astonishing; for, just as the tin man had said, the light Scarecrow

flew into the air, sailed over the top of the tree and landed in a bramblebush, while the tin man fell plump to the ground, and landing on a bed of dry leaves was not dented

at all. The Tin Woodman's joints were so rusted, however, that he was unable to move, while the thorns held the Scarecrow a fast prisoner. While they were in this sad plight

the sound of hoofs was heard and along the forest path rode the little Wizard of Oz, seated on a wooden Sawhorse. He smiled when he saw the one-eyed head of the

Scarecrow sticking out of the bramblebush, but he helped the poor straw man out of his prison. "Thank you, dear Wiz," said the grateful Scarecrow. "Now we must get the oilcan and rescue the Tin Woodman." Together they ran to the riverbank, but the boat was floating in midstream and the Wizard was obliged to mumble some magic words to draw it to the bank, so the Scarecrow could get the oilcan. Then back they flew to the tin man, and while the Scarecrow carefully oiled each joint the little Wizard moved the joints gently back and forth until they worked freely. After an hour of this labor the Tin Woodman was again on his feet, and although still a little stiff he managed to walk to the boat. The Wizard and the Sawhorse also got aboard the corncob craft and together they returned to the Scarecrow's palace. But the Tin Woodman was very careful not to stand up in the boat again. THE END. CHAPTER I The Cyclone Dorothy lived in the midst of the great Kansas prairies, with Uncle Henry, who was a farmer, and Aunt Em, who was the farmer's wife. Their house was small, for the lumber to build it had to be carried by wagon many miles. There were four walls, a floor and a roof, which made one room; and this room contained a rusty-looking cookstove, a cupboard for the dishes, a table, three or four chairs, and the beds. Uncle Henry and Aunt Em had a big bed in one corner, and Dorothy a little bed in another corner. There was no garret at all, and no cellar—except a small hole dug in the ground, called a cyclone cellar, where the family could go in case one of those great whirlwinds arose, mighty enough to crush any building in its path. It was reached by a trapdoor in the middle of the floor, from which a ladder led down into the small, dark hole. When Dorothy stood in the doorway and looked around, she could see nothing but the great gray prairie on every side. Not a tree nor a house broke the broad sweep of flat country that reached to the edge of the sky in all directions. The sun had baked the plowed land into a gray mass, with little cracks running through it. Even the grass was not green, for the sun had burned the tops of the long blades until they were the same gray color to be seen everywhere. Once the house had been painted, but the sun blistered the paint and the rains washed it away, and now the house was as dull and gray as everything else. When Aunt Em came there to live she was a young, pretty wife. The sun and wind had changed her, too. They had taken the sparkle from her eyes and left them a sober gray; they had taken the red from her cheeks and lips, and they were gray also. She was thin and gaunt, and never smiled now. When Dorothy, who was an orphan, first came to her, Aunt Em had been so startled by the child's laughter that she would scream and press her hand upon her heart whenever Dorothy's merry voice reached her ears; and she still looked at the little girl with wonder that she could find anything to laugh at. Uncle Henry never laughed. He worked hard from morning till night and did not know what joy was. He was gray also, from his long beard to his rough boots, and he looked stern and solemn, and rarely spoke. It was Toto that made Dorothy laugh, and saved her from growing as gray as her other surroundings. Toto was not gray; he was a little black dog, with long silky hair and small black eyes that twinkled merrily on either side of his funny, wee nose. Toto played all day long, and Dorothy played with him, and loved him dearly. Today, however, they were not playing. Uncle Henry sat upon the doorstep and looked anxiously at the sky, which was even grayer than usual. Dorothy stood in the door with Toto in her arms, and looked at the sky too. Aunt Em was washing the dishes. From the far north they heard a low wail of the wind, and Uncle Henry and Dorothy could see where the long grass bowed in waves before the coming storm. There now came a sharp whistling in the air from the south, and as they turned their eyes that way they saw ripples in the grass coming from that direction also.

Suddenly Uncle Henry stood up. "There's a cyclone coming, Em," he called to his wife. "I'll go look after the stock." Then he ran toward the sheds where the cows and horses were kept. Aunt Em dropped her work and came to the door. One glance told her of the danger close at hand. "Quick, Dorothy!" she screamed. "Run for the cellar!"

Toto jumped out of Dorothy's arms and hid under the bed, and the girl started to get him. Aunt Em, badly frightened, threw open the trapdoor in the floor and climbed down the ladder into the small, dark hole. Dorothy caught Toto at last and started to follow her aunt. When she was halfway across the room there came a great shriek from the wind, and the house shook so hard that she lost her footing and sat down suddenly upon the floor. Then a strange thing happened. The house whirled around two or three times and rose slowly through the air. Dorothy felt as if she were going up in a balloon. The north and south winds met where the house stood, and made it the exact center of the cyclone. In the middle of a cyclone the air is generally still, but the great pressure of the wind on every side of the house raised it up higher and higher, until it was at the very top of the cyclone; and there it remained and was carried miles and miles away as easily as you could carry a feather. It was very dark, and the wind howled horribly around her, but Dorothy found she was riding quite easily. After the first few whirls around, and one other time when the house tipped badly, she felt as if she were being rocked gently, like a baby in a cradle. Toto did not like it. He ran about the room, now here, now there, barking loudly; but Dorothy sat quite still on the floor and waited to see what would happen. Once Toto got too near the open trapdoor, and fell in; and at first the little girl thought she had lost him. But soon she saw one of his ears sticking up through the hole, for the strong pressure of the air was keeping him up so that he could not fall. She crept to the hole, caught Toto by the ear, and dragged him into the room again, afterward closing the trapdoor so that no more accidents could happen. Hour after hour passed away, and slowly Dorothy got over her fright; but she felt quite lonely, and the wind shrieked so loudly all about her that she nearly became deaf. At first she had wondered if she would be dashed to pieces when the house fell again; but as the hours passed and nothing terrible happened, she stopped worrying and resolved to wait calmly and see what the future would bring. At last she crawled over the swaying floor to her bed, and lay down upon it; and Toto followed and lay down beside her. In spite of the swaying of the house and the wailing of the wind, Dorothy soon closed her eyes and fell fast asleep. CHAPTER II The Council with the Munchkins She was awakened by a shock, so sudden and severe that if Dorothy had not been lying on the soft bed she might have been hurt. As it was, the jar made her catch her breath and wonder what had happened; and Toto put his cold little nose into her face and whined dismally. Dorothy sat up and noticed that the house was not moving; nor was it dark, for the bright sunshine came in at the window, flooding the little room. She sprang from her bed and with Toto at her heels ran and opened the door. The little girl gave a cry of amazement and looked about her, her eyes growing bigger and bigger at the wonderful sights she saw. The cyclone had set the house down very gently—for a cyclone—in the midst of a country of marvelous beauty. There were lovely patches of greensward all about, with stately trees bearing rich and luscious fruits. Banks of gorgeous flowers were on every hand, and birds with rare and brilliant plumage sang and fluttered in the trees and bushes. A little way off was a small brook, rushing and sparkling along between green banks, and murmuring in a voice very grateful to a little girl who had lived so long on the dry, gray prairies. While she stood looking eagerly at the strange and beautiful sights, she noticed coming toward her a group of the queerest

people she had ever seen. They were not as big as the grown folk she had always been used to; but neither were they very small. In fact, they seemed about as tall as Dorothy,

who was a well-grown child for her age, although they were, so far as looks go, many years older. Three were men and one a woman, and all were oddly dressed. They wore

round hats that rose to a small point a foot above their heads, with little bells around the brims that tinkled sweetly as they moved. The hats of the men were blue; the little

woman's hat was white, and she wore a white gown that hung in pleats from her shoulders. Over it were sprinkled little stars that glistened in the sun like diamonds. The men

were dressed in blue, of the same shade as their hats, and wore well-polished boots with a deep roll of blue at the tops. The men, Dorothy thought, were about as old as Uncle

Henry, for two of them had beards. But the little woman was doubtless much older. Her face was covered with wrinkles, her hair was nearly white, and she walked rather

stiffly. When these people drew near the house where Dorothy was standing in the doorway, they paused and whispered among themselves, as if afraid to come farther. But

the little old woman walked up to Dorothy, made a low bow and said, in a sweet voice: "You are welcome, most noble Sorceress, to the land of the Munchkins. We are so

grateful to you for having killed the Wicked Witch of the East, and for setting our people free from bondage." Dorothy listened to this speech with wonder. What could the

little woman possibly mean by calling her a sorceress, and saying she had killed the Wicked Witch of the East? Dorothy was an innocent, harmless little girl, who had been

carried by a cyclone many miles from home; and she had never killed anything in all her life. But the little woman evidently expected her to answer; so Dorothy said, with

hesitation, "You are very kind, but there must be some mistake. I have not killed anything." "Your house did, anyway," replied the little old woman, with a laugh, "and that

is the same thing. See!" she continued, pointing to the corner of the house. "There are her two feet, still sticking out from under a block of wood." Dorothy looked, and gave

a little cry of fright. There, indeed, just under the corner of the great beam the house rested on, two feet were sticking out, shod in Silver Shoes with pointed toes. "Oh, dear!

Oh, dear!" cried Dorothy, clasping her hands together in dismay. "The house must have fallen on her. Whatever shall we do?" "There is nothing to be done," said the little

woman calmly. "But who was she?" asked Dorothy. "She was the Wicked Witch of the East, as I said," answered the little woman. "She has held all the Munchkins in

bondage for many years, making them slave for her night and day. Now they are all set free, and are grateful to you for the favor." "Who are the Munchkins?" inquired

Dorothy. "They are the people who live in this land of the East where the Wicked Witch ruled." "Are you a Munchkin?" asked Dorothy. "No, but I am their friend, although

I live in the land of the North. When they saw the Witch of the East was dead the Munchkins sent a swift messenger to me, and I came at once. I am the Witch of the North."

"Oh, gracious!" cried Dorothy. "Are you a real witch?" "Yes, indeed," answered the little woman. "But I am a good witch, and the people love me. I am not as powerful as

the Wicked Witch was who ruled here, or I should have set the people free myself." "But I thought all witches were wicked," said the girl, who was half frightened at facing

a real witch. "Oh, no, that is a great mistake. There were only four witches in all the Land of Oz, and two of them, those who live in the North and the South, are good witches. I know this is true, for I am one of them myself, and cannot be mistaken. Those who dwelt in the East and the West were, indeed, wicked witches; but now that you

have killed one of them, there is but one Wicked Witch in all the Land of Oz—the one who lives in the West." "But," said Dorothy, after a moment's thought, "Aunt Em

has told me that the witches were all dead—years and years ago." "Who is Aunt Em?" inquired the little old woman. "She is my aunt who lives in Kansas, where I came

from." The Witch of the North seemed to think for a time, with her head bowed and her eyes upon the ground. Then she looked up and said, "I do not know where Kansas

is, for I have never heard that country mentioned before. But tell me, is it a civilized country?" "Oh, yes," replied Dorothy. "Then that accounts for it. In the civilized

countries I believe there are no witches left, nor wizards, nor sorceresses, nor magicians. But, you see, the Land of Oz has never been civilized, for we are cut off from all the

rest of the world. Therefore we still have witches and wizards amongst us." "Who are the wizards?" asked Dorothy. "Oz himself is the Great Wizard," answered the Witch,

sinking her voice to a whisper. "He is more powerful than all the rest of us together. He lives in the City of Emeralds." Dorothy was going to ask another question, but just

then the Munchkins, who had been standing silently by, gave a loud shout and pointed to the corner of the house where the Wicked Witch had been lying. "What is it?" asked

the little old woman, and looked, and began to laugh. The feet of the dead Witch had disappeared entirely, and nothing was left but the Silver Shoes. "She was so old,"

explained the Witch of the North, "that she dried up quickly in the sun. That is the end of her. But the Silver Shoes are yours, and you shall have them to wear." She reached

down and picked up the shoes, and after shaking the dust out of them handed them to Dorothy. "The Witch of the East was proud of those Silver Shoes," said one of the

Munchkins, "and there is some charm connected with them; but what it is we never knew." Dorothy carried the shoes into the house and placed them on the table. Then she

came out again to the Munchkins and said: "I am anxious to get back to my aunt and uncle, for I am sure they will worry about me. Can you help me find my way?" The

Munchkins and the Witch first looked at one another, and then at Dorothy, and then shook their heads. "At the East, not far from here," said one, "there is a great desert, and

none could live to cross it." "It is the same at the South," said another, "for I have been there and seen it. The South is the country of the Quadlings." "I am told," said the

third man, "that it is the same at the West. And that country, where the Winkies live, is ruled by the Wicked Witch of the West, who would make you her slave if you passed

her way." "The North is my home," said the old lady, "and at its edge is the same great desert that surrounds this Land of Oz. I'm afraid, my dear, you will have to live with

us." Dorothy began to sob at this, for she felt lonely among all these strange people. Her tears seemed to grieve the kindhearted Munchkins, for they immediately took out

their handkerchiefs and began to weep also. As for the little old woman, she took off her cap and balanced the point on the end of her nose, while she counted "One, two,

three" in a solemn voice. At once the cap changed to a slate, on which was written in big, white chalk marks: "LET DOROTHY GO TO THE CITY OF EMERALDS."

The little old woman took the slate from her nose, and having read the words on it, asked, "Is your name Dorothy, my dear?" "Yes," answered the child, looking up and

drying her tears. "Then you must go to the City of Emeralds. Perhaps Oz will help you." "Where is this city?" asked Dorothy. "It is exactly in the center of the country, and is ruled by Oz, the Great Wizard I told you of." "Is he a good man?" inquired the girl anxiously. "He is a good Wizard. Whether he is a man or not I cannot tell, for I have never seen him." "How can I get there?" asked Dorothy. "You must walk. It is a long journey, through a country that is sometimes pleasant and sometimes dark and terrible. However, I will use all the magic arts I know of to keep you from harm." "Won't you go with me?" pleaded the girl, who had begun to look upon the little old woman as her only friend. "No, I cannot do that," she replied, "but I will give you my kiss, and no one will dare injure a person who has been kissed by the Witch of the North." She came close to Dorothy and kissed her gently on the forehead. Where her lips touched the girl they left a round, shining mark, as Dorothy found out soon after. "The road to the City of Emeralds is paved with yellow brick," said the Witch, "so you cannot miss it. When you get to Oz do not be afraid of him, but tell your story and ask him to help you. Good-bye, my dear." The three Munchkins bowed low to her and wished her a pleasant journey, after which they walked away through the trees. The Witch gave Dorothy a friendly little nod, whirled around on her left heel three times, and straightway disappeared, much to the surprise of little Toto, who barked after her loudly enough when she had gone, because he had been afraid even to growl while she stood by. But Dorothy, knowing her to be a witch, had expected her to disappear in just that way, and was not surprised in the least. CHAPTER III How Dorothy Saved the Scarecrow When Dorothy was left alone she began to feel hungry. So she went to the cupboard and cut herself some bread, which she spread with butter. She gave some to Toto, and taking a pail from the shelf she carried it down to the little brook and filled it with clear, sparkling water. Toto ran over to the trees and began to bark at the birds sitting there. Dorothy went to get him, and saw such delicious fruit hanging from the branches that she gathered some of it, finding it just what she wanted to help out her breakfast. Then she went back to the house, and having helped herself and Toto to a good drink of the cool, clear water, she set about making ready for the journey to the City of Emeralds. Dorothy had only one other dress, but that happened to be clean and was hanging on a peg beside her bed. It was gingham, with checks of white and blue; and although the blue was somewhat faded with many washings, it was still a pretty frock. The girl washed herself carefully, dressed herself in the clean gingham, and tied her pink sunbonnet on her head. She took a little basket and filled it with bread from the cupboard, laying a white cloth over the top. Then she looked down at her feet and noticed how old and worn her shoes were. "They surely will never do for a long journey, Toto," she said. And Toto looked up into her face with his little black eyes and wagged his tail to show he knew what she meant. At that moment Dorothy saw lying on the table the Silver Shoes that had belonged to the Witch of the East. "I wonder if they will fit me," she said to Toto. "They would be just the thing to take a long walk in, for they could not wear out." She took off her old leather shoes and tried on the silver ones, which fitted her as well as if they had been made for her. Finally she picked up her basket. "Come along, Toto," she said. "We will go to the Emerald City and ask the Great Oz how to get back to Kansas again." She closed the door, locked it, and put the key carefully in the pocket of her dress. And so, with Toto trotting along soberly behind her, she started on her journey. There were several roads near by, but it did not take her long to find the one paved with yellow bricks. Within a short time she was walking briskly toward the Emerald City, her Silver Shoes tinkling merrily on the hard, yellow road-bed. The sun shone bright and the birds sang sweetly, and Dorothy did not feel nearly so bad as you might think a little girl would who had been suddenly whisked away from her own country and set down in the midst of a strange land. She was surprised, as she walked along, to see how pretty the country was about her. There were neat fences at the sides of the road, painted a dainty blue color, and beyond them were fields of grain and vegetables in abundance. Evidently the Munchkins were good farmers and able to raise large crops. Once in a while she would pass a house, and the people came out to look at her and bow low as she went by; for everyone knew she had been the means of destroying the Wicked Witch and setting them free from bondage. The houses of the Munchkins were odd-looking dwellings, for each was round, with a big dome for a roof. All were painted blue, for in this country of the East blue was the favorite color. Toward evening, when Dorothy was tired with her long walk and began to wonder where she should pass the night, she came to a house rather larger than the rest. On the green lawn before it many men and women were dancing. Five little fiddlers played as loudly as possible, and the people were laughing and singing, while a big table near by was loaded with delicious fruits and nuts, pies and cakes, and many other good things to eat. The people greeted Dorothy kindly, and invited her to supper and to pass the night with them; for this was the home of one of the richest Munchkins in the land, and his friends were gathered with him to celebrate their freedom from the bondage of the Wicked Witch. Dorothy ate a hearty supper and was waited upon by the rich Munchkin himself, whose name was Boq. Then she sat upon a settee and watched the people dance. When Boq saw her Silver Shoes he said, "You must be a great sorceress." "Why?" asked the girl. "Because you wear Silver Shoes and have killed the Wicked Witch. Besides, you have white in your frock, and only witches and sorceresses wear white." "My dress is blue and white checked," said Dorothy, smoothing out the wrinkles in it. "It is kind of you to wear that," said Boq. "Blue is the color of the Munchkins, and white is the witch color. So we know you are a friendly witch." Dorothy did not know what to say to this, for all the people seemed to think her a witch, and she knew very well she was only an ordinary little girl who had come by the chance of a cyclone into a strange land. When she had tired watching the dancing, Boq led her into the house, where he gave her a room with a pretty bed in it. The sheets were made of blue cloth, and Dorothy slept soundly in them till morning, with Toto curled up on the blue rug beside her. She ate a hearty breakfast, and watched a wee Munchkin baby, who played with Toto and pulled his tail and crowed and laughed in a way that greatly amused Dorothy. Toto was a fine curiosity to all the people, for they had never seen a dog before. "How far is it to the Emerald City?" the girl asked. "I do not know," answered Boq gravely, "for I have never been there. It is better for people to keep away from Oz, unless they have business with him. But it is a long way to the Emerald City, and it will take you many days. The country here is rich and pleasant, but you must pass through rough and dangerous places before you reach the end of your journey." This worried Dorothy a little, but she knew that only the Great Oz could help her get to Kansas again, so she bravely resolved not to turn back. She bade her friends good-bye, and again started along the road of yellow brick. When she had gone several miles she thought she would stop to rest, and so climbed to the top of the fence beside the road and sat down. There was a great cornfield beyond the fence, and not far away she saw a Scarecrow, placed high on a pole to keep the birds from the ripe corn. Dorothy leaned her chin upon her hand

and gazed thoughtfully at the Scarecrow. Its head was a small sack stuffed with straw, with eyes, nose, and mouth painted on it to represent a face. An old, pointed blue hat,

that had belonged to some Munchkin, was perched on his head, and the rest of the figure was a blue suit of clothes, worn and faded, which had also been stuffed with straw.

On the feet were some old boots with blue tops, such as every man wore in this country, and the figure was raised above the stalks of corn by means of the pole stuck up its

back. While Dorothy was looking earnestly into the queer, painted face of the Scarecrow, she was surprised to see one of the eyes slowly wink at her. She thought she must

have been mistaken at first, for none of the scarecrows in Kansas ever wink; but presently the figure nodded its head to her in a friendly way. Then she climbed down from

the fence and walked up to it, while Toto ran around the pole and barked. "Good day," said the Scarecrow, in a rather husky voice. "Did you speak?" asked the girl, in

wonder. "Certainly," answered the Scarecrow. "How do you do?" "I'm pretty well, thank you," replied Dorothy politely. "How do you do?" "I'm not feeling well," said the

Scarecrow, with a smile, "for it is very tedious being perched up here night and day to scare away crows." "Can't you get down?" asked Dorothy. "No, for this pole is stuck

up my back. If you will please take away the pole I shall be greatly obliged to you." Dorothy reached up both arms and lifted the figure off the pole, for, being stuffed with

straw, it was quite light. "Thank you very much," said the Scarecrow, when he had been set down on the ground. "I feel like a new man." Dorothy was puzzled at this, for it

sounded queer to hear a stuffed man speak, and to see him bow and walk along beside her. "Who are you?" asked the Scarecrow when he had stretched himself and yawned.

"And where are you going?" "My name is Dorothy," said the girl, "and I am going to the Emerald City, to ask the Great Oz to send me back to Kansas." "Where is the

Emerald City?" he inquired. "And who is Oz?" "Why, don't you know?" she returned, in surprise. "No, indeed. I don't know anything. You see, I am stuffed, so I have no

brains at all," he answered sadly. "Oh," said Dorothy, "I'm awfully sorry for you." "Do you think," he asked, "if I go to the Emerald City with you, that Oz would give me

some brains?" "I cannot tell," she returned, "but you may come with me, if you like. If Oz will not give you any brains you will be no worse off than you are now." "That

is true," said the Scarecrow. "You see," he continued confidentially, "I don't mind my legs and arms and body being stuffed, because I cannot get hurt. If anyone treads on

my toes or sticks a pin into me, it doesn't matter, for I can't feel it. But I do not want people to call me a fool, and if my head stays stuffed with straw instead of with brains,

as yours is, how am I ever to know anything?" "I understand how you feel," said the little girl, who was truly sorry for him. "If you will come with me I'll ask Oz to do all

he can for you." "Thank you," he answered gratefully. They walked back to the road. Dorothy helped him over the fence, and they started along the path of yellow brick

for the Emerald City. Toto did not like this addition to the party at first. He smelled around the stuffed man as if he suspected there might be a nest of rats in the straw, and

he often growled in an unfriendly way at the Scarecrow. "Don't mind Toto," said Dorothy to her new friend. "He never bites." "Oh, I'm not afraid," replied the Scarecrow.

"He can't hurt the straw. Do let me carry that basket for you. I shall not mind it, for I can't get tired. I'll tell you a secret," he continued, as he walked along. "There is only

one thing in the world I am afraid of." "What is that?" asked Dorothy; "the Munchkin farmer who made you?" "No," answered the Scarecrow; "it's a lighted match."

CHAPTER IV The Road Through the Forest After a few hours the road began to be rough, and the walking grew so difficult that the Scarecrow often stumbled over the yellow bricks, which were here very uneven. Sometimes, indeed, they were broken or missing altogether, leaving holes that Toto jumped across and Dorothy walked around. As for the Scarecrow, having no brains, he walked straight ahead, and so stepped into the holes and fell at full length on the hard bricks. It never hurt him, however, and Dorothy would pick him up and set him upon his feet again, while he joined her in laughing merrily at his own mishap. The farms were not nearly so well cared for here as they were farther back. There were fewer houses and fewer fruit trees, and the farther they went the more dismal and lonesome the country became. At noon they sat down by the roadside, near a little brook, and Dorothy opened her basket and got out some bread. She offered a piece to the Scarecrow, but he refused. "I am never hungry," he said, "and it is a lucky thing I am not, for my mouth is only painted, and if I should cut a hole in it so I could eat, the straw I am stuffed with would come out, and that would spoil the shape of my head." Dorothy saw at once that this was true, so she only nodded and went on eating her bread. "Tell me something about yourself and the country you came from," said the Scarecrow, when she had finished her dinner. So she told him all about Kansas, and how gray everything was there, and how the cyclone had carried her to this queer Land of Oz. The Scarecrow listened carefully, and said, "I cannot understand why you should wish to leave this beautiful country and go back to the dry, gray place you call Kansas." "That is because you have no brains" answered the girl. "No matter how dreary and gray our homes are, we people of flesh and blood would rather live there than in any other country, be it ever so beautiful. There is no place like home." The Scarecrow sighed. "Of course I cannot understand it," he said. "If your heads were stuffed with straw, like mine, you would probably all live in the beautiful places, and then Kansas would have no people at all. It is fortunate for Kansas that you have brains." "Won't you tell me a story, while we are resting?" asked the child. The Scarecrow looked at her reproachfully, and answered: "My life has been so short that I really know nothing whatever. I was only made day before yesterday. What happened in the world before that time is all unknown to me. Luckily, when the farmer made my head, one of the first things he did was to paint my ears, so that I heard what was going on. There was another Munchkin with him, and the first thing I heard was the farmer saying, 'How do you like those ears?' "'They aren't straight,' answered the other. "'Never mind,' said the farmer. 'They are ears just the same,' which was true enough. "'Now I'll make the eyes,' said the farmer. So he painted my right eye, and as soon as it was finished I found myself looking at him and at everything around me with a great deal of curiosity, for this was my first glimpse of the world. "'That's a rather pretty eye,' remarked the Munchkin who was watching the farmer. 'Blue paint is just the color for eyes.' "'I think I'll make the other a little bigger,' said the farmer. And when the second eye was done I could see much better than before. Then he made my nose and my mouth. But I did not speak, because at that time I didn't know what a mouth was for. I had the fun of watching them make my body and my arms and legs; and when they fastened on my head, at last, I felt very proud, for I thought I was just as good a man as anyone. "'This fellow will scare the crows fast enough,' said the farmer. 'He looks just like a man.' "'Why, he is a man,' said the other, and I quite agreed with him. The farmer carried me under his arm to the cornfield, and set me up on a tall stick, where you found me. He and his friend soon after walked away and left me alone. "I did not like to be deserted this way. So I tried to walk after them. But my feet would not touch

the ground, and I was forced to stay on that pole. It was a lonely life to lead, for I had nothing to think of, having been made such a little while before. Many crows and other

birds flew into the cornfield, but as soon as they saw me they flew away again, thinking I was a Munchkin; and this pleased me and made me feel that I was quite an important

person. By and by an old crow flew near me, and after looking at me carefully he perched upon my shoulder and said: "'I wonder if that farmer thought to fool me in this

clumsy manner. Any crow of sense could see that you are only stuffed with straw.' Then he hopped down at my feet and ate all the corn he wanted. The other birds, seeing

he was not harmed by me, came to eat the corn too, so in a short time there was a great flock of them about me. "I felt sad at this, for it showed I was not such a good Scarecrow

after all; but the old crow comforted me, saying, 'If you only had brains in your head you would be as good a man as any of them, and a better man than some of them. Brains

are the only things worth having in this world, no matter whether one is a crow or a man.' "After the crows had gone I thought this over, and decided I would try hard to get

some brains. By good luck you came along and pulled me off the stake, and from what you say I am sure the Great Oz will give me brains as soon as we get to the Emerald

City." "I hope so," said Dorothy earnestly, "since you seem anxious to have them." "Oh, yes; I am anxious," returned the Scarecrow. "It is such an uncomfortable feeling to

know one is a fool." "Well," said the girl, "let us go." And she handed the basket to the Scarecrow. There were no fences at all by the roadside now, and the land was rough

and untilled. Toward evening they came to a great forest, where the trees grew so big and close together that their branches met over the road of yellow brick. It was almost

dark under the trees, for the branches shut out the daylight; but the travelers did not stop, and went on into the forest. "If this road goes in, it must come out," said the

Scarecrow, "and as the Emerald City is at the other end of the road, we must go wherever it leads us." "Anyone would know that," said Dorothy. "Certainly; that is why I

know it," returned the Scarecrow. "If it required brains to figure it out, I never should have said it." After an hour or so the light faded away, and they found themselves

stumbling along in the darkness. Dorothy could not see at all, but Toto could, for some dogs see very well in the dark; and the Scarecrow declared he could see as well as by

day. So she took hold of his arm and managed to get along fairly well. "If you see any house, or any place where we can pass the night," she said, "you must tell me; for it is

very uncomfortable walking in the dark." Soon after the Scarecrow stopped. "I see a little cottage at the right of us," he said, "built of logs and branches. Shall we go there?"

"Yes, indeed," answered the child. "I am all tired out." So the Scarecrow led her through the trees until they reached the cottage, and Dorothy entered and found a bed of

dried leaves in one corner. She lay down at once, and with Toto beside her soon fell into a sound sleep. The Scarecrow, who was never tired, stood up in another corner and

waited patiently until morning came. CHAPTER V The Rescue of the Tin Woodman When Dorothy awoke the sun was shining through the trees and Toto had long been

out chasing birds around him and squirrels. She sat up and looked around her. There was the Scarecrow, still standing patiently in his corner, waiting for her. "We must go

and search for water," she said to him. "Why do you want water?" he asked. "To wash my face clean after the dust of the road, and to drink, so the dry bread will not stick in my throat." "It must be inconvenient to be made of flesh," said the Scarecrow thoughtfully, "for you must sleep, and eat and drink. However, you have brains, and it is worth a lot of bother to be able to think properly." They left the cottage and walked through the trees until they found a little spring of clear water, where Dorothy drank and bathed and ate her breakfast. She saw there was not much bread left in the basket, and the girl was thankful the Scarecrow did not have to eat anything, for there was scarcely enough for herself and Toto for the day. When she had finished her meal, and was about to go back to the road of yellow brick, she was startled to hear a deep groan near by. "What was that?" she asked timidly. "I cannot imagine," replied the Scarecrow; "but we can go and see." Just then another groan reached their ears, and the sound seemed to come from behind them. They turned and walked through the forest a few steps, when Dorothy discovered something shining in a ray of sunshine that fell between the trees. She ran to the place and then stopped short, with a little cry of surprise. One of the big trees had been partly chopped through, and standing beside it, with an uplifted axe in his hands, was a man made entirely of tin. His head and arms and legs were jointed upon his body, but he stood perfectly motionless, as if he could not stir at all. Dorothy looked at him in amazement, and so did the Scarecrow, while Toto barked sharply and made a snap at the tin legs, which hurt his teeth. "Did you groan?" asked Dorothy. "Yes," answered the tin man, "I did. I've been groaning for more than a year, and no one has ever heard me before or come to help me." "What can I do for you?" she inquired softly, for she was moved by the sad voice in which the man spoke. "Get an oilcan and oil my joints," he answered. "They are rusted so badly that I cannot move them at all; if I am well oiled I shall soon be all right again. You will find an oilcan on a shelf in my cottage." Dorothy at once ran back to the cottage and found the oilcan, and then she returned and asked anxiously, "Where are your joints?" "Oil my neck, first," replied the Tin Woodman. So she oiled it, and as it was quite badly rusted the Scarecrow took hold of the tin head and moved it gently from side to side until it worked freely, and then the man could turn it himself. "Now oil the joints in my arms," he said. And Dorothy oiled them and the Scarecrow bent them carefully until they were quite free from rust and as good as new. The Tin Woodman gave a sigh of satisfaction and lowered his axe, which he leaned against the tree. "This is a great comfort," he said. "I have been holding that axe in the air ever since I rusted, and I'm glad to be able to put it down at last. Now, if you will oil the joints of my legs, I shall be all right once more." So they oiled his legs until he could move them freely; and he thanked them again and again for his release, for he seemed a very polite creature, and very grateful. "I might have stood there always if you had not come along," he said; "so you have certainly saved my life. How did you happen to be here?" "We are on our way to the Emerald City to see the Great Oz," she answered, "and we stopped at your cottage to pass the night." "Why do you wish to see Oz?" he asked. "I want him to send me back to Kansas, and the Scarecrow wants him to put a few brains into his head," she replied. The Tin Woodman appeared to think deeply for a moment. Then he said: "Do you suppose Oz could give me a heart?" "Why, I guess so," Dorothy answered. "It would be as easy as to give the Scarecrow brains." "True," the Tin Woodman returned. "So, if you will allow me to join your party, I will also go to the Emerald City and ask Oz to help me." "Come along," said the Scarecrow heartily, and Dorothy added that she would be pleased to have his company. So the Tin Woodman shouldered his axe and they all passed through the forest until they came to the road that was paved with yellow brick. The Tin Woodman had asked Dorothy to put the oilcan in her basket. "For,"

he said, "if I should get caught in the rain, and rust again, I would need the oilcan badly." It was a bit of good luck to have their new comrade join the party, for soon after

they had begun their journey again they came to a place where the trees and branches grew so thick over the road that the travelers could not pass. But the Tin Woodman set

to work with his axe and chopped so well that soon he cleared a passage for the entire party. Dorothy was thinking so earnestly as they walked along that she did not notice

when the Scarecrow stumbled into a hole and rolled over to the side of the road. Indeed he was obliged to call to her to help him up again. "Why didn't you walk around the

hole?" asked the Tin Woodman. "I don't know enough," replied the Scarecrow cheerfully. "My head is stuffed with straw, you know, and that is why I am going to Oz to

ask him for some brains." "Oh, I see," said the Tin Woodman. "But, after all, brains are not the best things in the world." "Have you any?" inquired the Scarecrow. "No, my

head is quite empty," answered the Woodman. "But once I had brains, and a heart also; so, having tried them both, I should much rather have a heart." "And why is that?"

asked the Scarecrow. "I will tell you my story, and then you will know." So, while they were walking through the forest, the Tin Woodman told the following story: "I was

born the son of a woodman who chopped down trees in the forest and sold the wood for a living. When I grew up, I too became a woodchopper, and after my father died I

took care of my old mother as long as she lived. Then I made up my mind that instead of living alone I would marry, so that I might not become lonely. "There was one of

the Munchkin girls who was so beautiful that I soon grew to love her with all my heart. She, on her part, promised to marry me as soon as I could earn enough money to build

a better house for her; so I set to work harder than ever. But the girl lived with an old woman who did not want her to marry anyone, for she was so lazy she wished the girl

to remain with her and do the cooking and the housework. So the old woman went to the Wicked Witch of the East, and promised her two sheep and a cow if she would

prevent the marriage. Thereupon the Wicked Witch enchanted my axe, and when I was chopping away at my best one day, for I was anxious to get the new house and my

wife as soon as possible, the axe slipped all at once and cut off my left leg. "This at first seemed a great misfortune, for I knew a one-legged man could not do very well as a

woodchopper. So I went to a tinsmith and had him make me a new leg out of tin. The leg worked very well, once I was used to it. But my action angered the Wicked Witch

of the East, for she had promised the old woman I should not marry the pretty Munchkin girl. When I began chopping again, my axe slipped and cut off my right leg. Again

I went to the tinsmith, and again he made me a leg out of tin. After this the enchanted axe cut off my arms, one after the other; but, nothing daunted, I had them replaced

with tin ones. The Wicked Witch then made the axe slip and cut off my head, and at first I thought that was the end of me. But the tinsmith happened to come along, and he

made me a new head out of tin. "I thought I had beaten the Wicked Witch then, and I worked harder than ever; but I little knew how cruel my enemy could be. She thought

of a new way to kill my love for the beautiful Munchkin maiden, and made my axe slip again, so that it cut right through my body, splitting me into two halves. Once more

the tinsmith came to my help and made me a body of tin, fastening my tin arms and legs and head to it, by means of joints, so that I could move around as well as ever. But, alas! I had now no heart, so that I lost all my love for the Munchkin girl, and did not care whether I married her or not. I suppose she is still living with the old woman, waiting

for me to come after her. "My body shone so brightly in the sun that I felt very proud of it and it did not matter now if my axe slipped, for it could not cut me. There was

only one danger—that my joints would rust; but I kept an oilcan in my cottage and took care to oil myself whenever I needed it. However, there came a day when I forgot

to do this, and, being caught in a rainstorm, before I thought of the danger my joints had rusted, and I was left to stand in the woods until you came to help me. It was a

terrible thing to undergo, but during the year I stood there I had time to think that the greatest loss I had known was the loss of my heart. While I was in love I was the happiest

man on earth; but no one can love who has not a heart, and so I am resolved to ask Oz to give me one. If he does, I will go back to the Munchkin maiden and marry her."

Both Dorothy and the Scarecrow had been greatly interested in the story of the Tin Woodman, and now they knew why he was so anxious to get a new heart. "All the same,"

said the Scarecrow, "I shall ask for brains instead of a heart; for a fool would not know what to do with a heart if he had one." "I shall take the heart," returned the Tin

Woodman; "for brains do not make one happy, and happiness is the best thing in the world." Dorothy did not say anything, for she was puzzled to know which of her two

friends was right, and she decided if she could only get back to Kansas and Aunt Em, it did not matter so much whether the Woodman had no brains and the Scarecrow no

heart, or each got what he wanted. What worried her most was that the bread was nearly gone, and another meal for herself and Toto would empty the basket. To be sure

neither the Woodman nor the Scarecrow ever ate anything, but she was not made of tin nor straw, and could not live unless she was fed. CHAPTER VI The Cowardly Lion

All this time Dorothy and her companions had been walking through the thick woods. The road was still paved with yellow brick, but these were much covered by dried

branches and dead leaves from the trees, and the walking was not at all good. There were few birds in this part of the forest, for birds love the open country where there is

plenty of sunshine. But now and then there came a deep growl from some wild animal hidden among the trees. These sounds made the little girl's heart beat fast, for she did

not know what made them; but Toto knew, and he walked close to Dorothy's side, and did not even bark in return. "How long will it be," the child asked of the Tin

Woodman, "before we are out of the forest?" "I cannot tell," was the answer, "for I have never been to the Emerald City. But my father went there once, when I was a boy,

and he said it was a long journey through a dangerous country, although nearer to the city where Oz dwells the country is beautiful. But I am not afraid so long as I have my

oilcan, and nothing can hurt the Scarecrow, while you bear upon your forehead the mark of the Good Witch's kiss, and that will protect you from harm." "But Toto!" said

the girl anxiously. "What will protect him?" "We must protect him ourselves if he is in danger," replied the Tin Woodman. Just as he spoke there came from the forest a

terrible roar, and the next moment a great Lion bounded into the road. With one blow of his paw he sent the Scarecrow spinning over and over to the edge of the road, and

then he struck at the Tin Woodman with his sharp claws. But, to the Lion's surprise, he could make no impression on the tin, although the Woodman fell over in the road

and lay still. Little Toto, now that he had an enemy to face, ran barking toward the Lion, and the great beast had opened his mouth to bite the dog, when Dorothy, fearing

Toto would be killed, and heedless of danger, rushed forward and slapped the Lion upon his nose as hard as she could, while she cried out: "Don't you dare to bite Toto! You ought to be ashamed of yourself, a big beast like you, to bite a poor little dog!" "I didn't bite him," said the Lion, as he rubbed his nose with his paw where Dorothy had hit it. "No, but you tried to," she retorted. "You are nothing but a big coward." "I know it," said the Lion, hanging his head in shame. "I've always known it. But how can I help it?" "I don't know, I'm sure. To think of your striking a stuffed man, like the poor Scarecrow!" "Is he stuffed?" asked the Lion in surprise, as he watched her pick up the Scarecrow and set him upon his feet, while she patted him into shape again. "Of course he's stuffed," replied Dorothy, who was still angry. "That's why he went over so easily," remarked the Lion. "It astonished me to see him whirl around so. Is the other one stuffed also?" "No," said Dorothy, "he's made of tin." And she helped the Woodman up again. "That's why he nearly blunted my claws," said the Lion. "When they scratched against the tin it made a cold shiver run down my back. What is that little animal you are so tender of?" "He is my dog, Toto," answered Dorothy. "Is he made of tin, or stuffed?" asked the Lion. "Neither. He's a—a—a meat dog," said the girl. "Oh! He's a curious animal and seems remarkably small, now that I look at him. No one would think of biting such a little thing, except a coward like me," continued the Lion sadly. "What makes you a coward?" asked Dorothy, looking at the great beast in wonder, for he was as big as a small horse. "It's a mystery," replied the Lion. "I suppose I was born that way. All the other animals in the forest naturally expect me to be brave, for the Lion is everywhere thought to be the King of Beasts. I learned that if I roared very loudly every living thing was frightened and got out of my way. Whenever I've met a man I've been awfully scared; but I just roared at him, and he has always run away as fast as he could go. If the elephants and the tigers and the bears had ever tried to fight me, I should have run myself—I'm such a coward; but just as soon as they hear me roar they all try to get away from me, and of course I let them go." "But that isn't right. The King of Beasts shouldn't be a coward," said the Scarecrow. "I know it," returned the Lion, wiping a tear from his eye with the tip of his tail. "It is my great sorrow, and makes my life very unhappy. But whenever there is danger, my heart begins to beat fast." "Perhaps you have heart disease," said the Tin Woodman. "It may be," said the Lion. "If you have," continued the Tin Woodman, "you ought to be glad, for it proves you have a heart. For my part, I have no heart; so I cannot have heart disease." "Perhaps," said the Lion thoughtfully, "if I had no heart I should not be a coward." "Have you brains?" asked the Scarecrow. "I suppose so. I've never looked to see," replied the Lion. "I am going to the Great Oz to ask him to give me some," remarked the Scarecrow, "for my head is stuffed with straw." "And I am going to ask him to give me a heart," said the Woodman. "And I am going to ask him to send Toto and me back to Kansas," added Dorothy. "Do you think Oz could give me courage?" asked the Cowardly Lion. "Just as easily as he could give me brains," said the Scarecrow. "Or give me a heart," said the Tin Woodman. "Or send me back to Kansas," said Dorothy. "Then, if you don't mind, I'll go with you," said the Lion, "for my life is simply unbearable without a bit of courage." "You will be very welcome," answered Dorothy, "for you will help to keep away the other wild beasts. It seems to me they must be more cowardly than you are if they allow you to scare them so easily." "They really are," said the Lion, "but that doesn't make me any braver, and as long as I know myself to be a coward I shall be unhappy." So once more the little company set off upon the journey, the Lion walking with stately strides at Dorothy's side. Toto did not approve this new comrade at first, for he could not forget how nearly he had been crushed between the Lion's great jaws. But after a time he became more at ease, and presently Toto and the Cowardly Lion had grown to be good friends. During the rest of that day there was no other adventure to mar the peace of their journey. Once, indeed, the Tin Woodman stepped upon a beetle that was crawling along the road, and killed the poor little thing. This made the Tin Woodman very unhappy, for he was always careful not to hurt any living creature; and as he walked along he wept several tears of sorrow and regret. These tears ran slowly down his face and over the hinges of his jaw, and there they rusted. When Dorothy presently asked him a question the Tin Woodman could not open his mouth, for his jaws were tightly rusted together. He became greatly frightened at this and made many motions to Dorothy to relieve him, but she could not understand. The Lion was also puzzled to know what was wrong. But the Scarecrow seized the oilcan from Dorothy's basket and oiled the Woodman's jaws, so that after a few moments he could talk as well as before. "This will serve me a lesson," said he, "to look where I step. For if I should kill another bug or beetle I should surely cry again, and crying rusts my jaws so that I cannot speak." Thereafter he walked very carefully, with his eyes on the road, and when he saw a tiny ant toiling by he would step over it, so as not to harm it. The Tin Woodman knew very well he had no heart, and therefore he took great care never to be cruel or unkind to anything. "You people with hearts," he said, "have something to guide you, and need never do wrong; but I have no heart, and so I must be very careful. When Oz gives me a heart of course I needn't mind so much." CHAPTER VII The Journey to the Great Oz They were obliged to camp out that night under a large tree in the forest, for there were no houses near. The tree made a good, thick covering to protect them from the dew, and the Tin Woodman chopped a great pile of wood with his axe and Dorothy built a splendid fire that warmed her and made her feel less lonely. She and Toto ate the last of their bread, and now she did not know what they would do for breakfast. "If you wish," said the Lion, "I will go into the forest and kill a deer for you. You can roast it by the fire, since your tastes are so peculiar that you prefer cooked food, and then you will have a very good breakfast." "Don't! Please don't," begged the Tin Woodman. "I should certainly weep if you killed a poor deer, and then my jaws would rust again." But the Lion went away into the forest and found his own supper, and no one ever knew what it was, for he didn't mention it. And the Scarecrow found a tree full of nuts and filled Dorothy's basket with them, so that she would not be hungry for a long time. She thought this was very kind and thoughtful of the Scarecrow, but she laughed heartily at the awkward way in which the poor creature picked up the nuts. His padded hands were so clumsy and the nuts were so small that he dropped almost as many as he put in the basket. But the Scarecrow did not mind how long it took him to fill the basket, for it enabled him to keep away from the fire, as he feared a spark might get into his straw and burn him up. So he kept a good distance away from the flames, and only came near to cover Dorothy with dry leaves when she lay down to sleep. These kept her very snug and warm, and she slept soundly until morning. When it was daylight, the girl bathed her face in a little rippling brook, and soon after they all started toward the Emerald City. This was to be an eventful day for the travelers. They had hardly been walking an hour when they saw before them a great ditch that crossed the road and divided the forest as far as they could see on either side. It was a very wide ditch, and when they crept

up to the edge and looked into it they could see it was also very deep, and there were many big, jagged rocks at the bottom. The sides were so steep that none of them could

climb down, and for a moment it seemed that their journey must end. "What shall we do?" asked Dorothy despairingly. "I haven't the faintest idea," said the Tin Woodman,

and the Lion shook his shaggy mane and looked thoughtful. But the Scarecrow said, "We cannot fly, that is certain. Neither can we climb down into this great ditch.

Therefore, if we cannot jump over it, we must stop where we are." "I think I could jump over it," said the Cowardly Lion, after measuring the distance carefully in his mind.

"Then we are all right," answered the Scarecrow, "for you can carry us all over on your back, one at a time." "Well, I'll try it," said the Lion. "Who will go first?" "I will,"

declared the Scarecrow, "for, if you found that you could not jump over the gulf, Dorothy would be killed, or the Tin Woodman badly dented on the rocks below. But if I

am on your back it will not matter so much, for the fall would not hurt me at all." "I am terribly afraid of falling, myself," said the Cowardly Lion, "but I suppose there is

nothing to do but try it. So get on my back and we will make the attempt." The Scarecrow sat upon the Lion's back, and the big beast walked to the edge of the gulf and

crouched down. "Why don't you run and jump?" asked the Scarecrow. "Because that isn't the way we Lions do these things," he replied. Then giving a great spring, he shot

through the air and landed safely on the other side. They were all greatly pleased to see how easily he did it, and after the Scarecrow had got down from his back the Lion

sprang across the ditch again. Dorothy thought she would go next; so she took Toto in her arms and climbed on the Lion's back, holding tightly to his mane with one hand.

The next moment it seemed as if she were flying through the air; and then, before she had time to think about it, she was safe on the other side. The Lion went back a third

time and got the Tin Woodman, and then they all sat down for a few moments to give the beast a chance to rest, for his great leaps had made his breath short, and he panted

like a big dog that has been running too long. They found the forest very thick on this side, and it looked dark and gloomy. After the Lion had rested they started along the

road of yellow brick, silently wondering, each in his own mind, if ever they would come to the end of the woods and reach the bright sunshine again. To add to their

discomfort, they soon heard strange noises in the depths of the forest, and the Lion whispered to them that it was in this part of the country that the Kalidahs lived. "What

are the Kalidahs?" asked the girl. "They are monstrous beasts with bodies like bears and heads like tigers," replied the Lion, "and with claws so long and sharp that they could

tear me in two as easily as I could kill Toto. I'm terribly afraid of the Kalidahs." "I'm not surprised that you are," returned Dorothy. "They must be dreadful beasts." The

Lion was about to reply when suddenly they came to another gulf across the road. But this one was so broad and deep that the Lion knew at once he could not leap across it.

So they sat down to consider what they should do, and after serious thought the Scarecrow said: "Here is a great tree, standing close to the ditch. If the Tin Woodman can

chop it down, so that it will fall to the other side, we can walk across it easily." "That is a first-rate idea," said the Lion. "One would almost suspect you had brains in your

head, instead of straw." The Woodman set to work at once, and so sharp was his axe that the tree was soon chopped nearly through. Then the Lion put his strong front legs against the tree and pushed with all his might, and slowly the big tree tipped and fell with a crash across the ditch, with its top branches on the other side. They had just started

to cross this queer bridge when a sharp growl made them all look up, and to their horror they saw running toward them two great beasts with bodies like bears and heads like

tigers. "They are the Kalidahs!" said the Cowardly Lion, beginning to tremble. "Quick!" cried the Scarecrow. "Let us cross over." So Dorothy went first, holding Toto in

her arms, the Tin Woodman followed, and the Scarecrow came next. The Lion, although he was certainly afraid, turned to face the Kalidahs, and then he gave so loud and

terrible a roar that Dorothy screamed and the Scarecrow fell over backward, while even the fierce beasts stopped short and looked at him in surprise. But, seeing they were

bigger than the Lion, and remembering that there were two of them and only one of him, the Kalidahs again rushed forward, and the Lion crossed over the tree and turned

to see what they would do next. Without stopping an instant the fierce beasts also began to cross the tree. And the Lion said to Dorothy: "We are lost, for they will surely

tear us to pieces with their sharp claws. But stand close behind me, and I will fight them as long as I am alive." "Wait a minute!" called the Scarecrow. He had been thinking

what was best to be done, and now he asked the Woodman to chop away the end of the tree that rested on their side of the ditch. The Tin Woodman began to use his axe at

once, and, just as the two Kalidahs were nearly across, the tree fell with a crash into the gulf, carrying the ugly, snarling brutes with it, and both were dashed to pieces on the

sharp rocks at the bottom. "Well," said the Cowardly Lion, drawing a long breath of relief, "I see we are going to live a little while longer, and I am glad of it, for it must be

a very uncomfortable thing not to be alive. Those creatures frightened me so badly that my heart is beating yet." "Ah," said the Tin Woodman sadly, "I wish I had a heart to

beat." This adventure made the travelers more anxious than ever to get out of the forest, and they walked so fast that Dorothy became tired, and had to ride on the Lion's

back. To their great joy the trees became thinner the farther they advanced, and in the afternoon they suddenly came upon a broad river, flowing swiftly just before them.

On the other side of the water they could see the road of yellow brick running through a beautiful country, with green meadows dotted with bright flowers and all the road

bordered with trees hanging full of delicious fruits. They were greatly pleased to see this delightful country before them. "How shall we cross the river?" asked Dorothy.

"That is easily done," replied the Scarecrow. "The Tin Woodman must build us a raft, so we can float to the other side." So the Woodman took his axe and began to chop

down small trees to make a raft, and while he was busy at this the Scarecrow found on the riverbank a tree full of fine fruit. This pleased Dorothy, who had eaten nothing but

nuts all day, and she made a hearty meal of the ripe fruit. But it takes time to make a raft, even when one is as industrious and untiring as the Tin Woodman, and when night

came the work was not done. So they found a cozy place under the trees where they slept well until the morning; and Dorothy dreamed of the Emerald City, and of the good

Wizard Oz, who would soon send her back to her own home again. CHAPTER VIII The Deadly Poppy Field Our little party of travelers awakened the next morning

refreshed and full of hope, and Dorothy breakfasted like a princess off peaches and plums from the trees beside the river. Behind them was the dark forest they had passed

safely through, although they had suffered many discouragements; but before them was a lovely, sunny country that seemed to beckon them on to the Emerald City. To be sure, the broad river now cut them off from this beautiful land. But the raft was nearly done, and after the Tin Woodman had cut a few more logs and fastened them together with wooden pins, they were ready to start. Dorothy sat down in the middle of the raft and held Toto in her arms. When the Cowardly Lion stepped upon the raft it tipped badly, for he was big and heavy; but the Scarecrow and the Tin Woodman stood upon the other end to steady it, and they had long poles in their hands to push the raft through the water. They got along quite well at first, but when they reached the middle of the river the swift current swept the raft downstream, farther and farther away from the road of yellow brick. And the water grew so deep that the long poles would not touch the bottom. "This is bad," said the Tin Woodman, "for if we cannot get to the land we shall be carried into the country of the Wicked Witch of the West, and she will enchant us and make us her slaves." "And then I should get no brains," said the Scarecrow. "And I should get no courage," said the Cowardly Lion. "And I should get no heart," said the Tin Woodman. "And I should never get back to Kansas," said Dorothy. "We must certainly get to the Emerald City if we can," the Scarecrow continued, and he pushed so hard on his long pole that it stuck fast in the mud at the bottom of the river. Then, before he could pull it out again—or let go—the raft was swept away, and the poor Scarecrow left clinging to the pole in the middle of the river. "Good-bye!" he called after them, and they were very sorry to leave him. Indeed, the Tin Woodman began to cry, but fortunately remembered that he might rust, and so dried his tears on Dorothy's apron. Of course this was a bad thing for the Scarecrow. "I am now worse off than when I first met Dorothy," he thought. "Then, I was stuck on a pole in a cornfield, where I could make-believe scare the crows, at any rate. But surely there is no use for a Scarecrow stuck on a pole in the middle of a river. I am afraid I shall never have any brains, after all!" Down the stream the raft floated, and the poor Scarecrow was left far behind. Then the Lion said: "Something must be done to save us. I think I can swim to the shore and pull the raft after me, if you will only hold fast to the tip of my tail." So he sprang into the water, and the Tin Woodman caught fast hold of his tail. Then the Lion began to swim with all his might toward the shore. It was hard work, although he was so big; but by and by they were drawn out of the current, and then Dorothy took the Tin Woodman's long pole and helped push the raft to the land. They were all tired out when they reached the shore at last and stepped off upon the pretty green grass, and they also knew that the stream had carried them a long way past the road of yellow brick that led to the Emerald City. "What shall we do now?" asked the Tin Woodman, as the Lion lay down on the grass to let the sun dry him. "We must get back to the road, in some way," said Dorothy. "The best plan will be to walk along the riverbank until we come to the road again," remarked the Lion. So, when they were rested, Dorothy picked up her basket and they started along the grassy bank, to the road from which the river had carried them. It was a lovely country, with plenty of flowers and fruit trees and sunshine to cheer them, and had they not felt so sorry for the poor Scarecrow, they could have been very happy. They walked along as fast as they could, Dorothy only stopping once to pick a beautiful flower; and after a time the Tin Woodman cried out: "Look!" Then they all looked at the river and saw the Scarecrow perched upon his pole in the middle of the water, looking very lonely and sad. "What can we do to save him?" asked Dorothy. The Lion and the Woodman both shook their heads, for they did not know. So they sat down upon the bank and gazed wistfully at the Scarecrow until a Stork flew by, who, upon seeing them, stopped to rest at the water's edge. "Who are you and where are you going?" asked the Stork. "I am Dorothy," answered the girl,

"and these are my friends, the Tin Woodman and the Cowardly Lion; and we are going to the Emerald City." "This isn't the road," said the Stork, as she twisted her long

neck and looked sharply at the queer party. "I know it," returned Dorothy, "but we have lost the Scarecrow, and are wondering how we shall get him again." "Where is he?"

asked the Stork. "Over there in the river," answered the little girl. "If he wasn't so big and heavy I would get him for you," remarked the Stork. "He isn't heavy a bit," said

Dorothy eagerly, "for he is stuffed with straw; and if you will bring him back to us, we shall thank you ever and ever so much." "Well, I'll try," said the Stork, "but if I find

he is too heavy to carry I shall have to drop him in the river again." So the big bird flew into the air and over the water till she came to where the Scarecrow was perched upon

his pole. Then the Stork with her great claws grabbed the Scarecrow by the arm and carried him up into the air and back to the bank, where Dorothy and the Lion and the

Tin Woodman and Toto were sitting. When the Scarecrow found himself among his friends again, he was so happy that he hugged them all, even the Lion and Toto; and as

they walked along he sang "Tol-de-ri-de-oh!" at every step, he felt so gay. "I was afraid I should have to stay in the river forever," he said, "but the kind Stork saved me, and

if I ever get any brains I shall find the Stork again and do her some kindness in return." "That's all right," said the Stork, who was flying along beside them. "I always like

to help anyone in trouble. But I must go now, for my babies are waiting in the nest for me. I hope you will find the Emerald City and that Oz will help you." "Thank you,"

replied Dorothy, and then the kind Stork flew into the air and was soon out of sight. They walked along listening to the singing of the brightly colored birds and looking at

the lovely flowers which now became so thick that the ground was carpeted with them. There were big yellow and white and blue and purple blossoms, besides great clusters

of scarlet poppies, which were so brilliant in color they almost dazzled Dorothy's eyes. "Aren't they beautiful?" the girl asked, as she breathed in the spicy scent of the bright

flowers. "I suppose so," answered the Scarecrow. "When I have brains, I shall probably like them better." "If I only had a heart, I should love them," added the Tin

Woodman. "I always did like flowers," said the Lion. "They seem so helpless and frail. But there are none in the forest so bright as these." They now came upon more and

more of the big scarlet poppies, and fewer and fewer of the other flowers; and soon they found themselves in the midst of a great meadow of poppies. Now it is well known

that when there are many of these flowers together their odor is so powerful that anyone who breathes it falls asleep, and if the sleeper is not carried away from the scent of

the flowers, he sleeps on and on forever. But Dorothy did not know this, nor could she get away from the bright red flowers that were everywhere about; so presently her

eyes grew heavy and she felt she must sit down to rest and to sleep. But the Tin Woodman would not let her do this. "We must hurry and get back to the road of yellow brick

before dark," he said; and the Scarecrow agreed with him. So they kept walking until Dorothy could stand no longer. Her eyes closed in spite of herself and she forgot where

she was and fell among the poppies, fast asleep. "What shall we do?" asked the Tin Woodman. "If we leave her here she will die," said the Lion. "The smell of the flowers

is killing us all. I myself can scarcely keep my eyes open, and the dog is asleep already." It was true; Toto had fallen down beside his little mistress. But the Scarecrow and the

Tin Woodman, not being made of flesh, were not troubled by the scent of the flowers. "Run fast," said the Scarecrow to the Lion, "and get out of this deadly flower bed as soon as you can. We will bring the little girl with us, but if you should fall asleep you are too big to be carried." So the Lion aroused himself and bounded forward as fast as he could go. In a moment he was out of sight. "Let us make a chair with our hands and carry her," said the Scarecrow. So they picked up Toto and put the dog in Dorothy's lap, and then they made a chair with their hands for the seat and their arms for the arms and carried the sleeping girl between them through the flowers. On and on they walked, and it seemed that the great carpet of deadly flowers that surrounded them would never end. They followed the bend of the river, and at last came upon their friend the Lion, lying fast asleep among the poppies. The flowers had been too strong for the huge beast and he had given up at last, and fallen only a short distance from the end of the poppy bed, where the sweet grass spread in beautiful green fields before them. "We can do nothing for him," said the Tin Woodman, sadly; "for he is much too heavy to lift. We must leave him here to sleep on forever, and perhaps he will dream that he has found courage at last." "I'm sorry," said the Scarecrow. "The Lion was a very good comrade for one so cowardly. But let us go on." They carried the sleeping girl to a pretty spot beside the river, far enough from the poppy field to prevent her breathing any more of the poison of the flowers, and here they laid her gently on the soft grass and waited for the fresh breeze to waken her. CHAPTER IX The Queen of the Field Mice "We cannot be far from the road of yellow brick, now," remarked the Scarecrow, as he stood beside the girl, "for we have come nearly as far as the river carried us away." The Tin Woodman was about to reply when he heard a low growl, and turning his head (which worked beautifully on hinges) he saw a strange beast come bounding over the grass toward them. It was, indeed, a great yellow Wildcat, and the Woodman thought it must be chasing something, for its ears were lying close to its head and its mouth was wide open, showing two rows of ugly teeth, while its red eyes glowed like balls of fire. As it came nearer the Tin Woodman saw that running before the beast was a little gray field mouse, and although he had no heart he knew it was wrong for the Wildcat to try to kill such a pretty, harmless creature. So the Woodman raised his axe, and as the Wildcat ran by he gave it a quick blow that cut the beast's head clean off from its body, and it rolled over at his feet in two pieces. The field mouse, now that it was freed from its enemy, stopped short; and coming slowly up to the Woodman it said, in a squeaky little voice: "Oh, thank you! Thank you ever so much for saving my life." "Don't speak of it, I beg of you," replied the Woodman. "I have no heart, you know, so I am careful to help all those who may need a friend, even if it happens to be only a mouse." "Only a mouse!" cried the little animal, indignantly. "Why, I am a Queen—the Queen of all the Field Mice!" "Oh, indeed," said the Woodman, making a bow. "Therefore you have done a great deed, as well as a brave one, in saving my life," added the Queen. At that moment several mice were seen running up as fast as their little legs could carry them, and when they saw their Queen they exclaimed: "Oh, your Majesty, we thought you would be killed! How did you manage to escape the great Wildcat?" They all bowed so low to the little Queen that they almost stood upon their heads. "This funny tin man," she answered, "killed the Wildcat and saved my life. So hereafter you must all serve him, and obey his slightest wish." "We will!" cried all the mice, in a shrill chorus. And then they scampered in all directions, for Toto had awakened from his sleep, and seeing all these mice around him he gave one bark of delight and jumped right into the middle of the group. Toto had always loved to chase mice when he lived in Kansas,

and he saw no harm in it. But the Tin Woodman caught the dog in his arms and held him tight, while he called to the mice, "Come back! Come back! Toto shall not hurt

you." At this the Queen of the Mice stuck her head out from underneath a clump of grass and asked, in a timid voice, "Are you sure he will not bite us?" "I will not let him,"

said the Woodman; "so do not be afraid." One by one the mice came creeping back, and Toto did not bark again, although he tried to get out of the Woodman's arms, and

would have bitten him had he not known very well he was made of tin. Finally one of the biggest mice spoke. "Is there anything we can do," it asked, "to repay you for saving

the life of our Queen?" "Nothing that I know of," answered the Woodman; but the Scarecrow, who had been trying to think, but could not because his head was stuffed with

straw, said, quickly, "Oh, yes; you can save our friend, the Cowardly Lion, who is asleep in the poppy bed." "A Lion!" cried the little Queen. "Why, he would eat us all up."

"Oh, no," declared the Scarecrow; "this Lion is a coward." "Really?" asked the Mouse. "He says so himself," answered the Scarecrow, "and he would never hurt anyone

who is our friend. If you will help us to save him I promise that he shall treat you all with kindness." "Very well," said the Queen, "we trust you. But what shall we do?" "Are

there many of these mice which call you Queen and are willing to obey you?" "Oh, yes; there are thousands," she replied. "Then send for them all to come here as soon as

possible, and let each one bring a long piece of string." The Queen turned to the mice that attended her and told them to go at once and get all her people. As soon as they

heard her orders they ran away in every direction as fast as possible. "Now," said the Scarecrow to the Tin Woodman, "you must go to those trees by the riverside and make

a truck that will carry the Lion." So the Woodman went at once to the trees and began to work; and he soon made a truck out of the limbs of trees, from which he chopped

away all the leaves and branches. He fastened it together with wooden pegs and made the four wheels out of short pieces of a big tree trunk. So fast and so well did he work

that by the time the mice began to arrive the truck was all ready for them. They came from all directions, and there were thousands of them: big mice and little mice and

middle-sized mice; and each one brought a piece of string in his mouth. It was about this time that Dorothy woke from her long sleep and opened her eyes. She was greatly

astonished to find herself lying upon the grass, with thousands of mice standing around and looking at her timidly. But the Scarecrow told her about everything, and turning

to the dignified little Mouse, he said: "Permit me to introduce to you her Majesty, the Queen." Dorothy nodded gravely and the Queen made a curtsy, after which she became

quite friendly with the little girl. The Scarecrow and the Woodman now began to fasten the mice to the truck, using the strings they had brought. One end of a string was

tied around the neck of each mouse and the other end to the truck. Of course the truck was a thousand times bigger than any of the mice who were to draw it; but when all

the mice had been harnessed, they were able to pull it quite easily. Even the Scarecrow and the Tin Woodman could sit on it, and were drawn swiftly by their queer little

horses to the place where the Lion lay asleep. After a great deal of hard work, for the Lion was heavy, they managed to get him up on the truck. Then the Queen hurriedly

gave her people the order to start, for she feared if the mice stayed among the poppies too long they also would fall asleep. At first the little creatures, many though they were, could hardly stir the heavily loaded truck; but the Woodman and the Scarecrow both pushed from behind, and they got along better. Soon they rolled the Lion out of the poppy bed to the green fields, where he could breathe the sweet, fresh air again, instead of the poisonous scent of the flowers. Dorothy came to meet them and thanked the little mice warmly for saving her companion from death. She had grown so fond of the big Lion she was glad he had been rescued. Then the mice were unharnessed from the truck and scampered away through the grass to their homes. The Queen of the Mice was the last to leave. "If ever you need us again," she said, "come out into the field and call, and we shall hear you and come to your assistance. Good-bye!" "Good-bye!" they all answered, and away the Queen ran, while Dorothy held Toto tightly lest he should run after her and frighten her. After this they sat down beside the Lion until he should awaken; and the Scarecrow brought Dorothy some fruit from a tree near by, which she ate for her dinner. CHAPTER X The Guardian of the Gates It was some time before the Cowardly Lion awakened, for he had lain among the poppies a long while, breathing in their deadly fragrance; but when he did open his eyes and roll off the truck he was very glad to find himself still alive. "I ran as fast as I could," he said, sitting down and yawning, "but the flowers were too strong for me. How did you get me out?" Then they told him of the field mice, and how they had generously saved him from death; and the Cowardly Lion laughed, and said: "I have always thought myself very big and terrible; yet such little things as flowers came near to killing me, and such small animals as mice have saved my life. How strange it all is! But, comrades, what shall we do now?" "We must journey on until we find the road of yellow brick again," said Dorothy, "and then we can keep on to the Emerald City." So, the Lion being fully refreshed, and feeling quite himself again, they all started upon the journey, greatly enjoying the walk through the soft, fresh grass; and it was not long before they reached the road of yellow brick and turned again toward the Emerald City where the Great Oz dwelt. The road was smooth and well paved, now, and the country about was beautiful, so that the travelers rejoiced in leaving the forest far behind, and with it the many dangers they had met in its gloomy shades. Once more they could see fences built beside the road; but these were painted green, and when they came to a small house, in which a farmer evidently lived, that also was painted green. They passed by several of these houses during the afternoon, and sometimes people came to the doors and looked at them as if they would like to ask questions; but no one came near them nor spoke to them because of the great Lion, of which they were very much afraid. The people were all dressed in clothing of a lovely emerald-green color and wore peaked hats like those of the Munchkins. "This must be the Land of Oz," said Dorothy, "and we are surely getting near the Emerald City." "Yes," answered the Scarecrow. "Everything is green here, while in the country of the Munchkins blue was the favorite color. But the people do not seem to be as friendly as the Munchkins, and I'm afraid we shall be unable to find a place to pass the night." "I should like something to eat besides fruit," said the girl, "and I'm sure Toto is nearly starved. Let us stop at the next house and talk to the people." So, when they came to a good-sized farmhouse, Dorothy walked boldly up to the door and knocked. A woman opened it just far enough to look out, and said, "What do you want, child, and why is that great Lion with you?" "We wish to pass the night with you, if you will allow us," answered Dorothy; "and the Lion is my friend and comrade, and would not hurt you for the world." "Is he tame?" asked the woman, opening the door a little wider. "Oh, yes," said the girl, "and he is a great coward, too. He will be more afraid of you than you are of him." "Well," said the woman, after

thinking it over and taking another peep at the Lion, "if that is the case you may come in, and I will give you some supper and a place to sleep." So they all entered the house,

where there were, besides the woman, two children and a man. The man had hurt his leg, and was lying on the couch in a corner. They seemed greatly surprised to see so

strange a company, and while the woman was busy laying the table the man asked: "Where are you all going?" "To the Emerald City," said Dorothy, "to see the Great Oz."

"Oh, indeed!" exclaimed the man. "Are you sure that Oz will see you?" "Why not?" she replied. "Why, it is said that he never lets anyone come into his presence. I have

been to the Emerald City many times, and it is a beautiful and wonderful place; but I have never been permitted to see the Great Oz, nor do I know of any living person who

has seen him." "Does he never go out?" asked the Scarecrow. "Never. He sits day after day in the great Throne Room of his Palace, and even those who wait upon him do

not see him face-to-face." "What is he like?" asked the girl. "That is hard to tell," said the man thoughtfully. "You see, Oz is a Great Wizard, and can take on any form he

wishes. So that some say he looks like a bird; and some say he looks like an elephant; and some say he looks like a cat. To others he appears as a beautiful fairy, or a brownie,

or in any other form that pleases him. But who the real Oz is, when he is in his own form, no living person can tell." "That is very strange," said Dorothy, "but we must try,

in some way, to see him, or we shall have made our journey for nothing." "Why do you wish to see the terrible Oz?" asked the man. "I want him to give me some brains,"

said the Scarecrow eagerly. "Oh, Oz could do that easily enough," declared the man. "He has more brains than he needs." "And I want him to give me a heart," said the Tin

Woodman. "That will not trouble him," continued the man, "for Oz has a large collection of hearts, of all sizes and shapes." "And I want him to give me courage," said the

Cowardly Lion. "Oz keeps a great pot of courage in his Throne Room," said the man, "which he has covered with a golden plate, to keep it from running over. He will be

glad to give you some." "And I want him to send me back to Kansas," said Dorothy. "Where is Kansas?" asked the man, with surprise. "I don't know," replied Dorothy

sorrowfully, "but it is my home, and I'm sure it's somewhere." "Very likely. Well, Oz can do anything; so I suppose he will find Kansas for you. But first you must get to see

him, and that will be a hard task; for the Great Wizard does not like to see anyone, and he usually has his own way. But what do *you* want?" he continued, speaking to Toto.

Toto only wagged his tail; for, strange to say, he could not speak. The woman now called to them that supper was ready, so they gathered around the table and Dorothy ate

some delicious porridge and a dish of scrambled eggs and a plate of nice white bread, and enjoyed her meal. The Lion ate some of the porridge, but did not care for it, saying

it was made from oats and oats were food for horses, not for lions. The Scarecrow and the Tin Woodman ate nothing at all. Toto ate a little of everything, and was glad to

get a good supper again. The woman now gave Dorothy a bed to sleep in, and Toto lay down beside her, while the Lion guarded the door of her room so she might not be

disturbed. The Scarecrow and the Tin Woodman stood up in a corner and kept quiet all night, although of course they could not sleep. The next morning, as soon as the sun

was up, they started on their way, and soon saw a beautiful green glow in the sky just before them. "That must be the Emerald City," said Dorothy. As they walked on, the green glow became brighter and brighter, and it seemed that at last they were nearing the end of their travels. Yet it was afternoon before they came to the great wall that surrounded the City. It was high and thick and of a bright green color. In front of them, and at the end of the road of yellow brick, was a big gate, all studded with emeralds that glittered so in the sun that even the painted eyes of the Scarecrow were dazzled by their brilliancy. There was a bell beside the gate, and Dorothy pushed the button and heard a silvery tinkle sound within. Then the big gate swung slowly open, and they all passed through and found themselves in a high arched room, the walls of which glistened with countless emeralds. Before them stood a little man about the same size as the Munchkins. He was clothed all in green, from his head to his feet, and even his skin was of a greenish tint. At his side was a large green box. When he saw Dorothy and her companions the man asked, "What do you wish in the Emerald City?" "We came here to see the Great Oz," said Dorothy. The man was so surprised at this answer that he sat down to think it over. "It has been many years since anyone asked me to see Oz," he said, shaking his head in perplexity. "He is powerful and terrible, and if you come on an idle or foolish errand to bother the wise reflections of the Great Wizard, he might be angry and destroy you all in an instant." "But it is not a foolish errand, nor an idle one," replied the Scarecrow; "it is important. And we have been told that Oz is a good Wizard." "So he is," said the green man, "and he rules the Emerald City wisely and well. But to those who are not honest, or who approach him from curiosity, he is most terrible, and few have ever dared ask to see his face. I am the Guardian of the Gates, and since you demand to see the Great Oz I must take you to his Palace. But first you must put on the spectacles." "Why?" asked Dorothy. "Because if you did not wear spectacles the brightness and glory of the Emerald City would blind you. Even those who live in the City must wear spectacles night and day. They are all locked on, for Oz so ordered it when the City was first built, and I have the only key that will unlock them." He opened the big box, and Dorothy saw that it was filled with spectacles of every size and shape. All of them had green glasses in them. The Guardian of the Gates found a pair that would just fit Dorothy and put them over her eyes. There were two golden bands fastened to them that passed around the back of her head, where they were locked together by a little key that was at the end of a chain the Guardian of the Gates wore around his neck. When they were on, Dorothy could not take them off had she wished, but of course she did not wish to be blinded by the glare of the Emerald City, so she said nothing. Then the green man fitted spectacles for the Scarecrow and the Tin Woodman and the Lion, and even on little Toto; and all were locked fast with the key. Then the Guardian of the Gates put on his own glasses and told them he was ready to show them to the Palace. Taking a big golden key from a peg on the wall, he opened another gate, and they all followed him through the portal into the streets of the Emerald City. CHAPTER XI The Wonderful Emerald City of Oz Even with eyes protected by the green spectacles, Dorothy and her friends were at first dazzled by the brilliancy of the wonderful City. The streets were lined with beautiful houses all built of green marble and studded everywhere with sparkling emeralds. They walked over a pavement of the same green marble, and where the blocks were joined together were rows of emeralds, set closely, and glittering in the brightness of the sun. The windowpanes were of green glass; even the sky above the City had a green tint, and the rays of the sun were green. There were many people—men, women, and children—

walking about, and these were all dressed in green clothes and had greenish skins. They looked at Dorothy and her strangely assorted company with wondering eyes, and the children all ran away and hid behind their mothers when they saw the Lion; but no one spoke to them. Many shops stood in the street, and Dorothy saw that everything in them was green. Green candy and green popcorn were offered for sale, as well as green shoes, green hats, and green clothes of all sorts. At one place a man was selling green lemonade, and when the children bought it Dorothy could see that they paid for it with green pennies. There seemed to be no horses nor animals of any kind; the men carried things around in little green carts, which they pushed before them. Everyone seemed happy and contented and prosperous. The Guardian of the Gates led them through the streets until they came to a big building, exactly in the middle of the City, which was the Palace of Oz, the Great Wizard. There was a soldier before the door, dressed in a green uniform and wearing a long green beard. "Here are strangers," said the Guardian of the Gates to him, "and they demand to see the Great Oz." "Step inside," answered the soldier, "and I will carry your message to him." So they passed through the Palace Gates and were led into a big room with a green carpet and lovely green furniture set with emeralds. The soldier made them all wipe their feet upon a green mat before entering this room, and when they were seated he said politely: "Please make yourselves comfortable while I go to the door of the Throne Room and tell Oz you are here." They had to wait a long time before the soldier returned. When, at last, he came back, Dorothy asked: "Have you seen Oz?" "Oh, no," returned the soldier; "I have never seen him. But I spoke to him as he sat behind his screen and gave him your message. He said he will grant you an audience, if you so desire; but each one of you must enter his presence alone, and he will admit but one each day. Therefore, as you must remain in the Palace for several days, I will have you shown to rooms where you may rest in comfort after your journey." "Thank you," replied the girl; "that is very kind of Oz." The soldier now blew upon a green whistle, and at once a young girl, dressed in a pretty green silk gown, entered the room. She had lovely green hair and green eyes, and she bowed low before Dorothy as she said, "Follow me and I will show you your room." So Dorothy said good-bye to all her friends except Toto, and taking the dog in her arms followed the green girl through seven passages and up three flights of stairs until they came to a room at the front of the Palace. It was the sweetest little room in the world, with a soft comfortable bed that had sheets of green silk and a green velvet counterpane. There was a tiny fountain in the middle of the room, that shot a spray of green perfume into the air, to fall back into a beautifully carved green marble basin. Beautiful green flowers stood in the windows, and there was a shelf with a row of little green books. When Dorothy had time to open these books she found them full of queer green pictures that made her laugh, they were so funny. In a wardrobe were many green dresses, made of silk and satin and velvet; and all of them fitted Dorothy exactly. "Make yourself perfectly at home," said the green girl, "and if you wish for anything ring the bell. Oz will send for you tomorrow morning." She left Dorothy alone and went back to the others. These she also led to rooms, and each one of them found himself lodged in a very pleasant part of the Palace. Of course this politeness was wasted on the Scarecrow; for when he found himself alone in his room he stood stupidly in one spot, just within the doorway, to wait till morning. It would not rest him to lie down, and he could not close his eyes; so he remained all night staring at a little spider which was weaving its web in a corner of the room, just as if it were not one of the most wonderful rooms in the world. The Tin Woodman lay down on his bed from force of habit, for he remembered when he was made of flesh; but not being able to sleep, he passed the night moving his joints up and down to make sure they kept in good working order. The Lion would have preferred a bed of dried leaves in the forest, and did not like being shut up in a room; but he had too much sense to let this worry him, so he sprang upon the bed and rolled himself up like a cat and purred himself asleep in a minute. The next morning, after breakfast, the green maiden came to fetch Dorothy, and she dressed her in one of the prettiest gowns, made of green brocaded satin. Dorothy put on a green silk apron and tied a green ribbon around Toto's neck, and they started for the Throne Room of the Great Oz. First they came to a great hall in which were many ladies and gentlemen of the court, all dressed in rich costumes. These people had nothing to do but talk to each other, but they always came to wait outside the Throne Room every morning, although they were never permitted to see Oz. As Dorothy entered they looked at her curiously, and one of them whispered: "Are you really going to look upon the face of Oz the Terrible?" "Of course," answered the girl, "if he will see me." "Oh, he will see you," said the soldier who had taken her message to the Wizard, "although he does not like to have people ask to see him. Indeed, at first he was angry and said I should send you back where you came from. Then he asked me what you looked like, and when I mentioned your Silver Shoes he was very much interested. At last I told him about the mark upon your forehead, and he decided he would admit you to his presence." Just then a bell rang, and the green girl said to Dorothy, "That is the signal. You must go into the Throne Room alone." She opened a little door and Dorothy walked boldly through and found herself in a wonderful place. It was a big, round room with a high arched roof, and the walls and ceiling and floor were covered with large emeralds set closely together. In the center of the roof was a great light, as bright as the sun, which made the emeralds sparkle in a wonderful manner. But what interested Dorothy most was the big throne of green marble that stood in the middle of the room. It was shaped like a chair and sparkled with gems, as did everything else. In the center of the chair was an enormous Head, without a body to support it or any arms or legs whatever. There was no hair upon this head, but it had eyes and a nose and mouth, and was much bigger than the head of the biggest giant. As Dorothy gazed upon this in wonder and fear, the eyes turned slowly and looked at her sharply and steadily. Then the mouth moved, and Dorothy heard a voice say: "I am Oz, the Great and Terrible. Who are you, and why do you seek me?" It was not such an awful voice as she had expected to come from the big Head; so she took courage and answered: "I am Dorothy, the Small and Meek. I have come to you for help." The eyes looked at her thoughtfully for a full minute. Then said the voice: "Where did you get the Silver Shoes?" "I got them from the Wicked Witch of the East, when my house fell on her and killed her," she replied. "Where did you get the mark upon your forehead?" continued the voice. "That is where the Good Witch of the North kissed me when she bade me good-bye and sent me to you," said the girl. Again the eyes looked at her sharply, and they saw she was telling the truth. Then Oz asked, "What do you wish me to do?" "Send me back to Kansas, where my Aunt Em and Uncle Henry are," she answered earnestly. "I don't like your country, although it is so beautiful. And I am sure Aunt Em will be dreadfully worried over my being away so long." The eyes winked three times, and then they turned up to the ceiling and down to the floor and rolled around so queerly that they seemed to see every part of the room. And at last they looked

at Dorothy again. "Why should I do this for you?" asked Oz. "Because you are strong and I am weak; because you are a Great Wizard and I am only a little girl." "But you

were strong enough to kill the Wicked Witch of the East," said Oz. "That just happened," returned Dorothy simply; "I could not help it." "Well," said the Head, "I will give

you my answer. You have no right to expect me to send you back to Kansas unless you do something for me in return. In this country everyone must pay for everything he

gets. If you wish me to use my magic power to send you home again you must do something for me first. Help me and I will help you." "What must I do?" asked the girl.

"Kill the Wicked Witch of the West," answered Oz. "But I cannot!" exclaimed Dorothy, greatly surprised. "You killed the Witch of the East and you wear the Silver Shoes,

which bear a powerful charm. There is now but one Wicked Witch left in all this land, and when you can tell me she is dead I will send you back to Kansas—but not before."

The little girl began to weep, she was so much disappointed; and the eyes winked again and looked upon her anxiously, as if the Great Oz felt that she could help him if she

would. "I never killed anything, willingly," she sobbed. "Even if I wanted to, how could I kill the Wicked Witch? If you, who are Great and Terrible, cannot kill her yourself,

how do you expect me to do it?" "I do not know," said the Head; "but that is my answer, and until the Wicked Witch dies you will not see your uncle and aunt again.

Remember that the Witch is Wicked—tremendously Wicked—and ought to be killed. Now go, and do not ask to see me again until you have done your task." Sorrowfully

Dorothy left the Throne Room and went back where the Lion and the Scarecrow and the Tin Woodman were waiting to hear what Oz had said to her. "There is no hope

for me," she said sadly, "for Oz will not send me home until I have killed the Wicked Witch of the West; and that I can never do." Her friends were sorry, but could do nothing

to help her; so Dorothy went to her own room and lay down on the bed and cried herself to sleep. The next morning the soldier with the green whiskers came to the

Scarecrow and said: "Come with me, for Oz has sent for you." So the Scarecrow followed him and was admitted into the great Throne Room, where he saw, sitting in the

emerald throne, a most lovely Lady. She was dressed in green silk gauze and wore upon her flowing green locks a crown of jewels. Growing from her shoulders were wings,

gorgeous in color and so light that they fluttered if the slightest breath of air reached them. When the Scarecrow had bowed, as prettily as his straw stuffing would let him,

before this beautiful creature, she looked upon him sweetly, and said: "I am Oz, the Great and Terrible. Who are you, and why do you seek me?" Now the Scarecrow, who

had expected to see the great Head Dorothy had told him of, was much astonished; but he answered her bravely. "I am only a Scarecrow, stuffed with straw. Therefore I have

no brains, and I come to you praying that you will put brains in my head instead of straw, so that I may become as much a man as any other in your dominions." "Why should

I do this for you?" asked the Lady. "Because you are wise and powerful, and no one else can help me," answered the Scarecrow. "I never grant favors without some return,"

said Oz; "but this much I will promise. If you will kill for me the Wicked Witch of the West, I will bestow upon you a great many brains, and such good brains that you will

be the wisest man in all the Land of Oz." "I thought you asked Dorothy to kill the Witch," said the Scarecrow, in surprise. "So I did. I don't care who kills her. But until she is dead I will not grant your wish. Now go, and do not seek me again until you have earned the brains you so greatly desire." The Scarecrow went sorrowfully back to his friends and told them what Oz had said; and Dorothy was surprised to find that the Great Wizard was not a Head, as she had seen him, but a lovely Lady. "All the same," said the Scarecrow, "she needs a heart as much as the Tin Woodman." On the next morning the soldier with the green whiskers came to the Tin Woodman and said: "Oz has sent for you. Follow me." So the Tin Woodman followed him and came to the great Throne Room. He did not know whether he would find Oz a lovely Lady or a Head, but he hoped it would be the lovely Lady. "For," he said to himself, "if it is the head, I am sure I shall not be given a heart, since a head has no heart of its own and therefore cannot feel for me. But if it is the lovely Lady I shall beg hard for a heart, for all ladies are themselves said to be kindly hearted." But when the Woodman entered the great Throne Room he saw neither the Head nor the Lady, for Oz had taken the shape of a most terrible Beast. It was nearly as big as an elephant, and the green throne seemed hardly strong enough to hold its weight. The Beast had a head like that of a rhinoceros, only there were five eyes in its face. There were five long arms growing out of its body, and it also had five long, slim legs. Thick, woolly hair covered every part of it, and a more dreadful-looking monster could not be imagined. It was fortunate the Tin Woodman had no heart at that moment, for it would have beat loud and fast from terror. But being only tin, the Woodman was not at all afraid, although he was much disappointed. "I am Oz, the Great and Terrible," spoke the Beast, in a voice that was one great roar. "Who are you, and why do you seek me?" "I am a Woodman, and made of tin. Therefore I have no heart, and cannot love. I pray you to give me a heart that I may be as other men are." "Why should I do this?" demanded the Beast. "Because I ask it, and you alone can grant my request," answered the Woodman. Oz gave a low growl at this, but said, gruffly: "If you indeed desire a heart, you must earn it." "How?" asked the Woodman. "Help Dorothy to kill the Wicked Witch of the West," replied the Beast. "When the Witch is dead, come to me, and I will then give you the biggest and kindest and most loving heart in all the Land of Oz." So the Tin Woodman was forced to return sorrowfully to his friends and tell them of the terrible Beast he had seen. They all wondered greatly at the many forms the Great Wizard could take upon himself, and the Lion said: "If he is a Beast when I go to see him, I shall roar my loudest, and so frighten him that he will grant all I ask. And if he is the lovely Lady, I shall pretend to spring upon her, and so compel her to do my bidding. And if he is the great Head, he will be at my mercy; for I will roll this head all about the room until he promises to give us what we desire. So be of good cheer, my friends, for all will yet be well." The next morning the soldier with the green whiskers led the Lion to the great Throne Room and bade him enter the presence of Oz. The Lion at once passed through the door, and glancing around saw, to his surprise, that before the throne was a Ball of Fire, so fierce and glowing he could scarcely bear to gaze upon it. His first thought was that Oz had by accident caught on fire and was burning up; but when he tried to go nearer, the heat was so intense that it singed his whiskers, and he crept back tremblingly to a spot nearer the door. Then a low, quiet voice came from the Ball of Fire, and these were the words it spoke: "I am Oz, the Great and Terrible. Who are you, and why do you seek me?" And the Lion answered, "I am a Cowardly Lion, afraid of everything. I came to you to beg that you give me courage, so that in reality I may become the King of Beasts, as men call me." "Why should I give you courage?" demanded Oz. "Because of all Wizards you are the greatest, and alone have power to grant my request,"

answered the Lion. The Ball of Fire burned fiercely for a time, and the voice said, "Bring me proof that the Wicked Witch is dead, and that moment I will give you courage.

But as long as the Witch lives, you must remain a coward." The Lion was angry at this speech, but could say nothing in reply, and while he stood silently gazing at the Ball

of Fire it became so furiously hot that he turned tail and rushed from the room. He was glad to find his friends waiting for him, and told them of his terrible interview with

the Wizard. "What shall we do now?" asked Dorothy sadly. "There is only one thing we can do," returned the Lion, "and that is to go to the land of the Winkies, seek out

the Wicked Witch, and destroy her." "But suppose we cannot?" said the girl. "Then I shall never have courage," declared the Lion. "And I shall never have brains," added

the Scarecrow. "And I shall never have a heart," spoke the Tin Woodman. "And I shall never see Aunt Em and Uncle Henry," said Dorothy, beginning to cry. "Be careful!"

cried the green girl. "The tears will fall on your green silk gown and spot it." So Dorothy dried her eyes and said, "I suppose we must try it; but I am sure I do not want to

kill anybody, even to see Aunt Em again." "I will go with you; but I'm too much of a coward to kill the Witch," said the Lion. "I will go too," declared the Scarecrow; "but

I shall not be of much help to you, I am such a fool." "I haven't the heart to harm even a Witch," remarked the Tin Woodman; "but if you go I certainly shall go with you."

Therefore it was decided to start upon their journey the next morning, and the Woodman sharpened his axe on a green grindstone and had all his joints properly oiled. The

Scarecrow stuffed himself with fresh straw and Dorothy put new paint on his eyes that he might see better. The green girl, who was very kind to them, filled Dorothy's basket

with good things to eat, and fastened a little bell around Toto's neck with a green ribbon. They went to bed quite early and slept soundly until daylight, when they were

awakened by the crowing of a green cock that lived in the backyard of the Palace, and the cackling of a hen that had laid a green egg. CHAPTER XII The Search for the

Wicked Witch The soldier with the green whiskers led them through the streets of the Emerald City until they reached the room where the Guardian of the Gates lived.

This officer unlocked their spectacles to put them back in his great box, and then he politely opened the gate for our friends. "Which road leads to the Wicked Witch of the

West?" asked Dorothy. "There is no road," answered the Guardian of the Gates. "No one ever wishes to go that way." "How, then, are we to find her?" inquired the girl.

"That will be easy," replied the man, "for when she knows you are in the country of the Winkies she will find you, and make you all her slaves." "Perhaps not," said the

Scarecrow, "for we mean to destroy her." "Oh, that is different," said the Guardian of the Gates. "No one has ever destroyed her before, so I naturally thought she would

make slaves of you, as she has of the rest. But take care; for she is wicked and fierce, and may not allow you to destroy her. Keep to the West, where the sun sets, and you

cannot fail to find her." They thanked him and bade him good-bye, and turned toward the West, walking over fields of soft grass dotted here and there with daisies and

buttercups. Dorothy still wore the pretty silk dress she had put on in the palace, but now, to her surprise, she found it was no longer green, but pure white. The ribbon around

Toto's neck had also lost its green color and was as white as Dorothy's dress. The Emerald City was soon left far behind. As they advanced the ground became rougher and hillier, for there were no farms nor houses in this country of the West, and the ground was untilled. In the afternoon the sun shone hot in their faces, for there were no trees

to offer them shade; so that before night Dorothy and Toto and the Lion were tired, and lay down upon the grass and fell asleep, with the Woodman and the Scarecrow

keeping watch. Now the Wicked Witch of the West had but one eye, yet that was as powerful as a telescope, and could see everywhere. So, as she sat in the door of her castle,

she happened to look around and saw Dorothy lying asleep, with her friends all about her. They were a long distance off, but the Wicked Witch was angry to find them in

her country; so she blew upon a silver whistle that hung around her neck. At once there came running to her from all directions a pack of great wolves. They had long legs

and fierce eyes and sharp teeth. "Go to those people," said the Witch, "and tear them to pieces." "Are you not going to make them your slaves?" asked the leader of the

wolves. "No," she answered, "one is of tin, and one of straw; one is a girl and another a Lion. None of them is fit to work, so you may tear them into small pieces." "Very

well," said the wolf, and he dashed away at full speed, followed by the others. It was lucky the Scarecrow and the Woodman were wide awake and heard the wolves coming.

"This is my fight," said the Woodman, "so get behind me and I will meet them as they come." He seized his axe, which he had made very sharp, and as the leader of the

wolves came on the Tin Woodman swung his arm and chopped the wolf's head from its body, so that it immediately died. As soon as he could raise his axe another wolf

came up, and he also fell under the sharp edge of the Tin Woodman's weapon. There were forty wolves, and forty times a wolf was killed, so that at last they all lay dead in

a heap before the Woodman. Then he put down his axe and sat beside the Scarecrow, who said, "It was a good fight, friend." They waited until Dorothy awoke the next

morning. The little girl was quite frightened when she saw the great pile of shaggy wolves, but the Tin Woodman told her all. She thanked him for saving them and sat down

to breakfast, after which they started again upon their journey. Now this same morning the Wicked Witch came to the door of her castle and looked out with her one eye

that could see far off. She saw all her wolves lying dead, and the strangers still traveling through her country. This made her angrier than before, and she blew her silver

whistle twice. Straightway a great flock of wild crows came flying toward her, enough to darken the sky. And the Wicked Witch said to the King Crow, "Fly at once to the

strangers; peck out their eyes and tear them to pieces." The wild crows flew in one great flock toward Dorothy and her companions. When the little girl saw them coming

she was afraid. But the Scarecrow said, "This is my battle, so lie down beside me and you will not be harmed." So they all lay upon the ground except the Scarecrow, and he

stood up and stretched out his arms. And when the crows saw him they were frightened, as these birds always are by scarecrows, and did not dare to come any nearer. But

the King Crow said: "It is only a stuffed man. I will peck his eyes out." The King Crow flew at the Scarecrow, who caught it by the head and twisted its neck until it died.

And then another crow flew at him, and the Scarecrow twisted its neck also. There were forty crows, and forty times the Scarecrow twisted a neck, until at last all were lying

dead beside him. Then he called to his companions to rise, and again they went upon their journey. When the Wicked Witch looked out again and saw all her crows lying in

a heap, she got into a terrible rage, and blew three times upon her silver whistle. Forthwith there was heard a great buzzing in the air, and a swarm of black bees came flying toward her. "Go to the strangers and sting them to death!" commanded the Witch, and the bees turned and flew rapidly until they came to where Dorothy and her friends were walking. But the Woodman had seen them coming, and the Scarecrow had decided what to do. "Take out my straw and scatter it over the little girl and the dog and the Lion," he said to the Woodman, "and the bees cannot sting them." This the Woodman did, and as Dorothy lay close beside the Lion and held Toto in her arms, the straw covered them entirely. The bees came and found no one but the Woodman to sting, so they flew at him and broke off all their stings against the tin, without hurting the Woodman at all. And as bees cannot live when their stings are broken that was the end of the black bees, and they lay scattered thick about the Woodman, like little heaps of fine coal. Then Dorothy and the Lion got up, and the girl helped the Tin Woodman put the straw back into the Scarecrow again, until he was as good as ever. So they started upon their journey once more. The Wicked Witch was so angry when she saw her black bees in little heaps like fine coal that she stamped her foot and tore her hair and gnashed her teeth. And then she called a dozen of her slaves, who were the Winkies, and gave them sharp spears, telling them to go to the strangers and destroy them. The Winkies were not a brave people, but they had to do as they were told. So they marched away until they came near to Dorothy. Then the Lion gave a great roar and sprang towards them, and the poor Winkies were so frightened that they ran back as fast as they could. When they returned to the castle the Wicked Witch beat them well with a strap, and sent them back to their work, after which she sat down to think what she should do next. She could not understand how all her plans to destroy these strangers had failed; but she was a powerful Witch, as well as a wicked one, and she soon made up her mind how to act. There was, in her cupboard, a Golden Cap, with a circle of diamonds and rubies running round it. This Golden Cap had a charm. Whoever owned it could call three times upon the Winged Monkeys, who would obey any order they were given. But no person could command these strange creatures more than three times. Twice already the Wicked Witch had used the charm of the Cap. Once was when she had made the Winkies her slaves, and set herself to rule over their country. The Winged Monkeys had helped her do this. The second time was when she had fought against the Great Oz himself, and driven him out of the land of the West. The Winged Monkeys had also helped her in doing this. Only once more could she use this Golden Cap, for which reason she did not like to do so until all her other powers were exhausted. But now that her fierce wolves and her wild crows and her stinging bees were gone, and her slaves had been scared away by the Cowardly Lion, she saw there was only one way left to destroy Dorothy and her friends. So the Wicked Witch took the Golden Cap from her cupboard and placed it upon her head. Then she stood upon her left foot and said slowly: "Ep-pe, pep-pe, kak-ke!" Next she stood upon her right foot and said: "Hil-lo, hol-lo, hel-lo!" After this she stood upon both feet and cried in a loud voice: "Ziz-zy, zuz-zy, zik!" Now the charm began to work. The sky was darkened, and a low rumbling sound was heard in the air. There was a rushing of many wings, a great chattering and laughing, and the sun came out of the dark sky to show the Wicked Witch surrounded by a crowd of monkeys, each with a pair of immense and powerful wings on his shoulders. One, much bigger than the others, seemed to be their leader. He flew close to the Witch and said, "You have called us for the third and last time. What do you command?" "Go to the strangers who are within my land and destroy them all except the Lion," said the Wicked Witch. "Bring that beast to me, for I have a mind to harness him like a horse, and make him work." "Your commands shall be obeyed," said the leader. Then, with a great deal of chattering and noise, the Winged Monkeys flew away to the place where Dorothy and her friends were walking. Some of the Monkeys seized the Tin Woodman and carried him through the air until they were over a country thickly covered with sharp rocks. Here they dropped the poor Woodman, who fell a great distance to the rocks, where he lay so battered and dented that he could neither move nor groan. Others of the Monkeys caught the Scarecrow, and with their long fingers pulled all of the straw out of his clothes and head. They made his hat and boots and clothes into a small bundle and threw it into the top branches of a tall tree. The remaining Monkeys threw pieces of stout rope around the Lion and wound many coils about his body and head and legs, until he was unable to bite or scratch or struggle in any way. Then they lifted him up and flew away with him to the Witch's castle, where he was placed in a small yard with a high iron fence around it, so that he could not escape. But Dorothy they did not harm at all. She stood, with Toto in her arms, watching the sad fate of her comrades and thinking it would soon be her turn. The leader of the Winged Monkeys flew up to her, his long, hairy arms stretched out and his ugly face grinning terribly; but he saw the mark of the Good Witch's kiss upon her forehead and stopped short, motioning the others not to touch her. "We dare not harm this little girl," he said to them, "for she is protected by the Power of Good, and that is greater than the Power of Evil. All we can do is to carry her to the castle of the Wicked Witch and leave her there." So, carefully and gently, they lifted Dorothy in their arms and carried her swiftly through the air until they came to the castle, where they set her down upon the front doorstep. Then the leader said to the Witch: "We have obeyed you as far as we were able. The Tin Woodman and the Scarecrow are destroyed, and the Lion is tied up in your yard. The little girl we dare not harm, nor the dog she carries in her arms. Your power over our band is now ended, and you will never see us again." Then all the Winged Monkeys, with much laughing and chattering and noise, flew into the air and were soon out of sight. The Wicked Witch was both surprised and worried when she saw the mark on Dorothy's forehead, for she knew well that neither the Winged Monkeys nor she, herself, dare hurt the girl in any way. She looked down at Dorothy's feet, and seeing the Silver Shoes, began to tremble with fear, for she knew what a powerful charm belonged to them. At first the Witch was tempted to run away from Dorothy; but she happened to look into the child's eyes and saw how simple the soul behind them was, and that the little girl did not know of the wonderful power the Silver Shoes gave her. So the Wicked Witch laughed to herself, and thought, "I can still make her my slave, for she does not know how to use her power." Then she said to Dorothy, harshly and severely: "Come with me; and see that you mind everything I tell you, for if you do not I will make an end of you, as I did of the Tin Woodman and the Scarecrow." Dorothy followed her through many of the beautiful rooms in her castle until they came to the kitchen, where the Witch bade her clean the pots and kettles and sweep the floor and keep the fire fed with wood. Dorothy went to work meekly, with her mind made up to work as hard as she could; for she was glad the Wicked Witch had decided not to kill her. With Dorothy hard at work, the Witch thought she would go into the courtyard and harness the Cowardly Lion like a horse; it would amuse her, she was sure, to make him draw her chariot whenever she wished to go to drive. But as she opened the gate the Lion gave a loud roar and bounded at her so fiercely that the Witch was afraid, and ran out and shut the gate again. "If I cannot harness you," said the Witch to

the Lion, speaking through the bars of the gate, "I can starve you. You shall have nothing to eat until you do as I wish." So after that she took no food to the imprisoned Lion;

but every day she came to the gate at noon and asked, "Are you ready to be harnessed like a horse?" And the Lion would answer, "No. If you come in this yard, I will bite

you." The reason the Lion did not have to do as the Witch wished was that every night, while the woman was asleep, Dorothy carried him food from the cupboard. After he

had eaten he would lie down on his bed of straw, and Dorothy would lie beside him and put her head on his soft, shaggy mane, while they talked of their troubles and tried

to plan some way to escape. But they could find no way to get out of the castle, for it was constantly guarded by the yellow Winkies, who were the slaves of the Wicked Witch

and too afraid of her not to do as she told them. The girl had to work hard during the day, and often the Witch threatened to beat her with the same old umbrella she always

carried in her hand. But, in truth, she did not dare to strike Dorothy, because of the mark upon her forehead. The child did not know this, and was full of fear for herself and

Toto. Once the Witch struck Toto a blow with her umbrella and the brave little dog flew at her and bit her leg in return. The Witch did not bleed where she was bitten, for

she was so wicked that the blood in her had dried up many years before. Dorothy's life became very sad as she grew to understand that it would be harder than ever to get

back to Kansas and Aunt Em again. Sometimes she would cry bitterly for hours, with Toto sitting at her feet and looking into her face, whining dismally to show how sorry

he was for his little mistress. Toto did not really care whether he was in Kansas or the Land of Oz so long as Dorothy was with him; but he knew the little girl was unhappy,

and that made him unhappy too. Now the Wicked Witch had a great longing to have for her own the Silver Shoes which the girl always wore. Her bees and her crows and

her wolves were lying in heaps and drying up, and she had used up all the power of the Golden Cap; but if she could only get hold of the Silver Shoes, they would give her

more power than all the other things she had lost. She watched Dorothy carefully, to see if she ever took off her shoes, thinking she might steal them. But the child was so

proud of her pretty shoes that she never took them off except at night and when she took her bath. The Witch was too much afraid of the dark to dare go in Dorothy's room

at night to take the shoes, and her dread of water was greater than her fear of the dark, so she never came near when Dorothy was bathing. Indeed, the old Witch never

touched water, nor ever let water touch her in any way. But the wicked creature was very cunning, and she finally thought of a trick that would give her what she wanted.

She placed a bar of iron in the middle of the kitchen floor, and then by her magic arts made the iron invisible to human eyes. So that when Dorothy walked across the floor

she stumbled over the bar, not being able to see it, and fell at full length. She was not much hurt, but in her fall one of the Silver Shoes came off; and before she could reach

it, the Witch had snatched it away and put it on her own skinny foot. The wicked woman was greatly pleased with the success of her trick, for as long as she had one of the

shoes she owned half the power of their charm, and Dorothy could not use it against her, even had she known how to do so. The little girl, seeing she had lost one of her

pretty shoes, grew angry, and said to the Witch, "Give me back my shoe!" "I will not," retorted the Witch, "for it is now my shoe, and not yours." "You are a wicked creature!" cried Dorothy. "You have no right to take my shoe from me." "I shall keep it, just the same," said the Witch, laughing at her, "and someday I shall get the other

one from you, too." This made Dorothy so very angry that she picked up the bucket of water that stood near and dashed it over the Witch, wetting her from head to foot.

Instantly the wicked woman gave a loud cry of fear, and then, as Dorothy looked at her in wonder, the Witch began to shrink and fall away. "See what you have done!" she

screamed. "In a minute I shall melt away." "I'm very sorry, indeed," said Dorothy, who was truly frightened to see the Witch actually melting away like brown sugar before

her very eyes. "Didn't you know water would be the end of me?" asked the Witch, in a wailing, despairing voice. "Of course not," answered Dorothy. "How should I?"

"Well, in a few minutes I shall be all melted, and you will have the castle to yourself. I have been wicked in my day, but I never thought a little girl like you would ever be able

to melt me and end my wicked deeds. Look out—here I go!" With these words the Witch fell down in a brown, melted, shapeless mass and began to spread over the clean

boards of the kitchen floor. Seeing that she had really melted away to nothing, Dorothy drew another bucket of water and threw it over the mess. She then swept it all out

the door. After picking out the silver shoe, which was all that was left of the old woman, she cleaned and dried it with a cloth, and put it on her foot again. Then, being at last

free to do as she chose, she ran out to the courtyard to tell the Lion that the Wicked Witch of the West had come to an end, and that they were no longer prisoners in a strange

land. CHAPTER XIII The Rescue The Cowardly Lion was much pleased to hear that the Wicked Witch had been melted by a bucket of water, and Dorothy at once

unlocked the gate of his prison and set him free. They went in together to the castle, where Dorothy's first act was to call all the Winkies together and tell them that they were

no longer slaves. There was great rejoicing among the yellow Winkies, for they had been made to work hard during many years for the Wicked Witch, who had always

treated them with great cruelty. They kept this day as a holiday, then and ever after, and spent the time in feasting and dancing. "If our friends, the Scarecrow and the Tin

Woodman, were only with us," said the Lion, "I should be quite happy." "Don't you suppose we could rescue them?" asked the girl anxiously. "We can try," answered the

Lion. So they called the yellow Winkies and asked them if they would help to rescue their friends, and the Winkies said that they would be delighted to do all in their power

for Dorothy, who had set them free from bondage. So she chose a number of the Winkies who looked as if they knew the most, and they all started away. They traveled that

day and part of the next until they came to the rocky plain where the Tin Woodman lay, all battered and bent. His axe was near him, but the blade was rusted and the handle

broken off short. The Winkies lifted him tenderly in their arms, and carried him back to the Yellow Castle again, Dorothy shedding a few tears by the way at the sad plight

of her old friend, and the Lion looking sober and sorry. When they reached the castle Dorothy said to the Winkies: "Are any of your people tinsmiths?" "Oh, yes. Some of

us are very good tinsmiths," they told her. "Then bring them to me," she said. And when the tinsmiths came, bringing with them all their tools in baskets, she inquired, "Can

you straighten out those dents in the Tin Woodman, and bend him back into shape again, and solder him together where he is broken?" The tinsmiths looked the Woodman

over carefully and then answered that they thought they could mend him so he would be as good as ever. So they set to work in one of the big yellow rooms of the castle and worked for three days and four nights, hammering and twisting and bending and soldering and polishing and pounding at the legs and body and head of the Tin Woodman,

until at last he was straightened out into his old form, and his joints worked as well as ever. To be sure, there were several patches on him, but the tinsmiths did a good job,

and as the Woodman was not a vain man he did not mind the patches at all. When, at last, he walked into Dorothy's room and thanked her for rescuing him, he was so pleased

that he wept tears of joy, and Dorothy had to wipe every tear carefully from his face with her apron, so his joints would not be rusted. At the same time her own tears fell

thick and fast at the joy of meeting her old friend again, and these tears did not need to be wiped away. As for the Lion, he wiped his eyes so often with the tip of his tail that

it became quite wet, and he was obliged to go out into the courtyard and hold it in the sun till it dried. "If we only had the Scarecrow with us again," said the Tin Woodman,

when Dorothy had finished telling him everything that had happened, "I should be quite happy." "We must try to find him," said the girl. So she called the Winkies to help

her, and they walked all that day and part of the next until they came to the tall tree in the branches of which the Winged Monkeys had tossed the Scarecrow's clothes. It was

a very tall tree, and the trunk was so smooth that no one could climb it; but the Woodman said at once, "I'll chop it down, and then we can get the Scarecrow's clothes." Now

while the tinsmiths had been at work mending the Woodman himself, another of the Winkies, who was a goldsmith, had made an axe-handle of solid gold and fitted it to the

Woodman's axe, instead of the old broken handle. Others polished the blade until all the rust was removed and it glistened like burnished silver. As soon as he had spoken,

the Tin Woodman began to chop, and in a short time the tree fell over with a crash, whereupon the Scarecrow's clothes fell out of the branches and rolled off on the ground.

Dorothy picked them up and had the Winkies carry them back to the castle, where they were stuffed with nice, clean straw; and behold! here was the Scarecrow, as good as

ever, thanking them over and over again for saving him. Now that they were reunited, Dorothy and her friends spent a few happy days at the Yellow Castle, where they found

everything they needed to make them comfortable. But one day the girl thought of Aunt Em, and said, "We must go back to Oz, and claim his promise." "Yes," said the

Woodman, "at last I shall get my heart." "And I shall get my brains," added the Scarecrow joyfully. "And I shall get my courage," said the Lion thoughtfully. "And I shall

get back to Kansas," cried Dorothy, clapping her hands. "Oh, let us start for the Emerald City tomorrow!" This they decided to do. The next day they called the Winkies

together and bade them good-bye. The Winkies were sorry to have them go, and they had grown so fond of the Tin Woodman that they begged him to stay and rule over

them and the Yellow Land of the West. Finding they were determined to go, the Winkies gave Toto and the Lion each a golden collar; and to Dorothy they presented a

beautiful bracelet studded with diamonds; and to the Scarecrow they gave a gold-headed walking stick, to keep him from stumbling; and to the Tin Woodman they offered

a silver oilcan, inlaid with gold and set with precious jewels. Every one of the travelers made the Winkies a pretty speech in return, and all shook hands with them until their

arms ached. Dorothy went to the Witch's cupboard to fill her basket with food for the journey, and there she saw the Golden Cap. She tried it on her own head and found

that it fitted her exactly. She did not know anything about the charm of the Golden Cap, but she saw that it was pretty, so she made up her mind to wear it and carry her sunbonnet in the basket. Then, being prepared for the journey, they all started for the Emerald City; and the Winkies gave them three cheers and many good wishes to carry with them. CHAPTER XIV The Winged Monkeys You will remember there was no road—not even a pathway—between the castle of the Wicked Witch and the Emerald City. When the four travelers went in search of the Witch she had seen them coming, and so sent the Winged Monkeys to bring them to her. It was much harder to find their way back through the big fields of buttercups and yellow daisies than it was being carried. They knew, of course, they must go straight east, toward the rising sun; and they started off in the right way. But at noon, when the sun was over their heads, they did not know which was east and which was west, and that was the reason they were lost in the great fields. They kept on walking, however, and at night the moon came out and shone brightly. So they lay down among the sweet-smelling yellow flowers and slept soundly until morning—all but the Scarecrow and the Tin Woodman. The next morning the sun was behind a cloud, but they started on, as if they were quite sure which way they were going. "If we walk far enough," said Dorothy, "I am sure we shall sometime come to some place." But day by day passed away, and they still saw nothing before them but the scarlet fields. The Scarecrow began to grumble a bit. "We have surely lost our way," he said, "and unless we find it again in time to reach the Emerald City, I shall never get my brains." "Nor I my heart," declared the Tin Woodman. "It seems to me I can scarcely wait till I get to Oz, and you must admit this is a very long journey." "You see," said the Cowardly Lion, with a whimper, "I haven't the courage to keep tramping forever, without getting anywhere at all." Then Dorothy lost heart. She sat down on the grass and looked at her companions, and they sat down and looked at her, and Toto found that for the first time in his life he was too tired to chase a butterfly that flew past his head. So he put out his tongue and panted and looked at Dorothy as if to ask what they should do next. "Suppose we call the field mice," she suggested. "They could probably tell us the way to the Emerald City." "To be sure they could," cried the Scarecrow. "Why didn't we think of that before?" Dorothy blew the little whistle she had always carried about her neck since the Queen of the Mice had given it to her. In a few minutes they heard the pattering of tiny feet, and many of the small gray mice came running up to her. Among them was the Queen herself, who asked, in her squeaky little voice: "What can I do for my friends?" "We have lost our way," said Dorothy. "Can you tell us where the Emerald City is?" "Certainly," answered the Queen; "but it is a great way off, for you have had it at your backs all this time." Then she noticed Dorothy's Golden Cap, and said, "Why don't you use the charm of the Cap, and call the Winged Monkeys to you? They will carry you to the City of Oz in less than an hour." "I didn't know there was a charm," answered Dorothy, in surprise. "What is it?" "It is written inside the Golden Cap," replied the Queen of the Mice. "But if you are going to call the Winged Monkeys we must run away, for they are full of mischief and think it great fun to plague us." "Won't they hurt me?" asked the girl anxiously. "Oh, no. They must obey the wearer of the Cap. Good-bye!" And she scampered out of sight, with all the mice hurrying after her. Dorothy looked inside the Golden Cap and saw some words written upon the lining. These, she thought, must be the charm, so she read the directions carefully and put the Cap upon her head. "Ep-pe, pep-pe, kak-ke!" she said, standing on her left foot. "What did you say?" asked the Scarecrow, who did not know what she was doing. "Hil-lo, hol-lo, hel-lo!" Dorothy went on, standing this time on her right foot. "Hello!" replied the Tin Woodman calmly. "Ziz-zy, zuz-zy, zik!" said Dorothy, who was now standing on both feet. This ended the

saying of the charm, and they heard a great chattering and flapping of wings, as the band of Winged Monkeys flew up to them. The King bowed low before Dorothy, and

asked, "What is your command?" "We wish to go to the Emerald City," said the child, "and we have lost our way." "We will carry you," replied the King, and no sooner

had he spoken than two of the Monkeys caught Dorothy in their arms and flew away with her. Others took the Scarecrow and the Woodman and the Lion, and one little

Monkey seized Toto and flew after them, although the dog tried hard to bite him. The Scarecrow and the Tin Woodman were rather frightened at first, for they remembered

how badly the Winged Monkeys had treated them before; but they saw that no harm was intended, so they rode through the air quite cheerfully, and had a fine time looking

at the pretty gardens and woods far below them. Dorothy found herself riding easily between two of the biggest Monkeys, one of them the King himself. They had made a

chair of their hands and were careful not to hurt her. "Why do you have to obey the charm of the Golden Cap?" she asked. "That is a long story," answered the King, with

a laugh; "but as we have a long journey before us, I will pass the time by telling you about it, if you wish." "I shall be glad to hear it," she replied. **"Once," began the leader,**

"we were a free people, living happily in the great forest, flying from tree to tree, eating nuts and fruit, and doing just as we pleased without calling anybody master. Perhaps

some of us were rather too full of mischief at times, flying down to pull the tails of the animals that had no wings, chasing birds, and throwing nuts at the people who walked

in the forest. But we were careless and happy and full of fun, and enjoyed every minute of the day. This was many years ago, long before Oz came out of the clouds to rule

over this land. "There lived here then, away at the North, a beautiful princess, who was also a powerful sorceress. All her magic was used to help the people, and she was

never known to hurt anyone who was good. Her name was Gayelette, and she lived in a handsome palace built from great blocks of ruby. Everyone loved her, but her greatest

sorrow was that she could find no one to love in return, since all the men were much too stupid and ugly to mate with one so beautiful and wise. At last, however, she found

a boy who was handsome and manly and wise beyond his years. Gayelette made up her mind that when he grew to be a man she would make him her husband, so she took

him to her ruby palace and used all her magic powers to make him as strong and good and lovely as any woman could wish. When he grew to manhood, Quelala, as he was

called, was said to be the best and wisest man in all the land, while his manly beauty was so great that Gayelette loved him dearly, and hastened to make everything ready for

the wedding. "My grandfather was at that time the King of the Winged Monkeys which lived in the forest near Gayelette's palace, and the old fellow loved a joke better than

a good dinner. One day, just before the wedding, my grandfather was flying out with his band when he saw Quelala walking beside the river. He was dressed in a rich costume

of pink silk and purple velvet, and my grandfather thought he would see what he could do. At his word the band flew down and seized Quelala, carried him in their arms

until they were over the middle of the river, and then dropped him into the water. "'Swim out, my fine fellow,' cried my grandfather, 'and see if the water has spotted your

clothes.' Quelala was much too wise not to swim, and he was not in the least spoiled by all his good fortune. He laughed, when he came to the top of the water, and swam in to shore. But when Gayelette came running out to him she found his silks and velvet all ruined by the river. "The princess was angry, and she knew, of course, who did it.

She had all the Winged Monkeys brought before her, and she said at first that their wings should be tied and they should be treated as they had treated Quelala, and dropped

in the river. But my grandfather pleaded hard, for he knew the Monkeys would drown in the river with their wings tied, and Quelala said a kind word for them also; so that

Gayelette finally spared them, on condition that the Winged Monkeys should ever after do three times the bidding of the owner of the Golden Cap. This Cap had been made

for a wedding present to Quelala, and it is said to have cost the princess half her kingdom. Of course my grandfather and all the other Monkeys at once agreed to the

condition, and that is how it happens that we are three times the slaves of the owner of the Golden Cap, whosoever he may be." "And what became of them?" asked Dorothy,

who had been greatly interested in the story. "Quelala being the first owner of the Golden Cap," replied the Monkey, "he was the first to lay his wishes upon us. As his bride

could not bear the sight of us, he called us all to him in the forest after he had married her and ordered us always to keep where she could never again set eyes on a Winged

Monkey, which we were glad to do, for we were all afraid of her. "This was all we ever had to do until the Golden Cap fell into the hands of the Wicked Witch of the West,

who made us enslave the Winkies, and afterward drive Oz himself out of the Land of the West. Now the Golden Cap is yours, and three times you have the right to lay your

wishes upon us." As the Monkey King finished his story Dorothy looked down and saw the green, shining walls of the Emerald City before them. She wondered at the rapid

flight of the Monkeys, but was glad the journey was over. The strange creatures set the travelers down carefully before the gate of the City, the King bowed low to Dorothy,

and then flew swiftly away, followed by all his band. "That was a good ride," said the little girl. "Yes, and a quick way out of our troubles," replied the Lion. "How lucky it

was you brought away that wonderful Cap!" CHAPTER XV The Discovery of Oz, the Terrible The four travelers walked up to the great gate of Emerald City and rang

the bell. After ringing several times, it was opened by the same Guardian of the Gates they had met before. "What! are you back again?" he asked, in surprise. "Do you not

see us?" answered the Scarecrow. "But I thought you had gone to visit the Wicked Witch of the West." "We did visit her," said the Scarecrow. "And she let you go again?"

asked the man, in wonder. "She could not help it, for she is melted," explained the Scarecrow. "Melted! Well, that is good news, indeed," said the man. "Who melted her?"

"It was Dorothy," said the Lion gravely. "Good gracious!" exclaimed the man, and he bowed very low indeed before her. Then he led them into his little room and locked

the spectacles from the great box on all their eyes, just as he had done before. Afterward they passed on through the gate into the Emerald City. When the people heard from

the Guardian of the Gates that Dorothy had melted the Wicked Witch of the West, they all gathered around the travelers and followed them in a great crowd to the Palace

of Oz. The soldier with the green whiskers was still on guard before the door, but he let them in at once, and they were again met by the beautiful green girl, who showed

each of them to their old rooms at once, so they might rest until the Great Oz was ready to receive them. The soldier had the news carried straight to Oz that Dorothy and

the other travelers had come back again, after destroying the Wicked Witch; but Oz made no reply. They thought the Great Wizard would send for them at once, but he did not. They had no word from him the next day, nor the next, nor the next. The waiting was tiresome and wearing, and at last they grew vexed that Oz should treat them in so

poor a fashion, after sending them to undergo hardships and slavery. So the Scarecrow at last asked the green girl to take another message to Oz, saying if he did not let them

in to see him at once they would call the Winged Monkeys to help them, and find out whether he kept his promises or not. When the Wizard was given this message he was

so frightened that he sent word for them to come to the Throne Room at four minutes after nine o'clock the next morning. He had once met the Winged Monkeys in the Land

of the West, and he did not wish to meet them again. The four travelers passed a sleepless night, each thinking of the gift Oz had promised to bestow on him. Dorothy fell

asleep only once, and then she dreamed she was in Kansas, where Aunt Em was telling her how glad she was to have her little girl at home again. Promptly at nine o'clock

the next morning the green-whiskered soldier came to them, and four minutes later they all went into the Throne Room of the Great Oz. Of course each one of them

expected to see the Wizard in the shape he had taken before, and all were greatly surprised when they looked about and saw no one at all in the room. They kept close to the

door and closer to one another, for the stillness of the empty room was more dreadful than any of the forms they had seen Oz take. Presently they heard a solemn Voice, that

seemed to come from somewhere near the top of the great dome, and it said: "I am Oz, the Great and Terrible. Why do you seek me?" They looked again in every part of

the room, and then, seeing no one, Dorothy asked, "Where are you?" "I am everywhere," answered the Voice, "but to the eyes of common mortals I am invisible. I will now

seat myself upon my throne, that you may converse with me." Indeed, the Voice seemed just then to come straight from the throne itself; so they walked toward it and stood

in a row while Dorothy said: "We have come to claim our promise, O Oz." "What promise?" asked Oz. "You promised to send me back to Kansas when the Wicked Witch

was destroyed," said the girl. "And you promised to give me brains," said the Scarecrow. "And you promised to give me a heart," said the Tin Woodman. "And you promised

to give me courage," said the Cowardly Lion. "Is the Wicked Witch really destroyed?" asked the Voice, and Dorothy thought it trembled a little. "Yes," she answered, "I

melted her with a bucket of water." "Dear me," said the Voice, "how sudden! Well, come to me tomorrow, for I must have time to think it over." "You've had plenty of time

already," said the Tin Woodman angrily. "We shan't wait a day longer," said the Scarecrow. "You must keep your promises to us!" exclaimed Dorothy. The Lion thought it

might be as well to frighten the Wizard, so he gave a large, loud roar, which was so fierce and dreadful that Toto jumped away from him in alarm and tipped over the screen

that stood in a corner. As it fell with a crash they looked that way, and the next moment all of them were filled with wonder. For they saw, standing in just the spot the screen

had hidden, a little old man, with a bald head and a wrinkled face, who seemed to be as much surprised as they were. The Tin Woodman, raising his axe, rushed toward the

little man and cried out, "Who are you?" "I am Oz, the Great and Terrible," said the little man, in a trembling voice. "But don't strike me—please don't—and I'll do

anything you want me to." Our friends looked at him in surprise and dismay. "I thought Oz was a great Head," said Dorothy. "And I thought Oz was a lovely Lady," said

the Scarecrow. "And I thought Oz was a terrible Beast," said the Tin Woodman. "And I thought Oz was a Ball of Fire," exclaimed the Lion. "No, you are all wrong," said the little man meekly. "I have been making believe." "Making believe!" cried Dorothy. "Are you not a Great Wizard?" "Hush, my dear," he said. "Don't speak so loud, or you will be overheard—and I should be ruined. I'm supposed to be a Great Wizard." "And aren't you?" she asked. "Not a bit of it, my dear; I'm just a common man." "You're more than that," said the Scarecrow, in a grieved tone; "you're a humbug." "Exactly so!" declared the little man, rubbing his hands together as if it pleased him. "I am a humbug." "But this is terrible," said the Tin Woodman. "How shall I ever get my heart?" "Or I my courage?" asked the Lion. "Or I my brains?" wailed the Scarecrow, wiping the tears from his eyes with his coat sleeve. "My dear friends," said Oz, "I pray you not to speak of these little things. Think of me, and the terrible trouble I'm in at being found out." "Doesn't anyone else know you're a humbug?" asked Dorothy. "No one knows it but you four—and myself," replied Oz. "I have fooled everyone so long that I thought I should never be found out. It was a great mistake my ever letting you into the Throne Room. Usually I will not see even my subjects, and so they believe I am something terrible." "But, I don't understand," said Dorothy, in bewilderment. "How was it that you appeared to me as a great Head?" "That was one of my tricks," answered Oz. "Step this way, please, and I will tell you all about it." He led the way to a small chamber in the rear of the Throne Room, and they all followed him. He pointed to one corner, in which lay the great Head, made out of many thicknesses of paper, and with a carefully painted face. "This I hung from the ceiling by a wire," said Oz. "I stood behind the screen and pulled a thread, to make the eyes move and the mouth open." "But how about the voice?" she inquired. "Oh, I am a ventriloquist," said the little man. "I can throw the sound of my voice wherever I wish, so that you thought it was coming out of the Head. Here are the other things I used to deceive you." He showed the Scarecrow the dress and the mask he had worn when he seemed to be the lovely Lady. And the Tin Woodman saw that his terrible Beast was nothing but a lot of skins, sewn together, with slats to keep their sides out. As for the Ball of Fire, the false Wizard had hung that also from the ceiling. It was really a ball of cotton, but when oil was poured upon it the ball burned fiercely. "Really," said the Scarecrow, "you ought to be ashamed of yourself for being such a humbug." "I am—I certainly am," answered the little man sorrowfully; "but it was the only thing I could do. Sit down, please, there are plenty of chairs; and I will tell you my story." So they sat down and listened while he told the following tale. "I was born in Omaha—" "Why, that isn't very far from Kansas!" cried Dorothy. "No, but it's farther from here," he said, shaking his head at her sadly. "When I grew up I became a ventriloquist, and at that I was very well trained by a great master. I can imitate any kind of a bird or beast." Here he mewed so like a kitten that Toto pricked up his ears and looked everywhere to see where she was. "After a time," continued Oz, "I tired of that, and became a balloonist." "What is that?" asked Dorothy. "A man who goes up in a balloon on circus day, so as to draw a crowd of people together and get them to pay to see the circus," he explained. "Oh," she said, "I know." "Well, one day I went up in a balloon and the ropes got twisted, so that I couldn't come down again. It went way up above the clouds, so far that a current of air struck it and carried it many, many miles away. For a day and a night I traveled through the air, and on the morning of the second day I awoke and found the balloon floating over a strange and beautiful country. "It came down gradually, and I was not hurt a bit. But I found myself in the midst of a strange people, who, seeing me come from the clouds, thought I was a great Wizard. Of course I let them think so, because they were afraid of me, and promised to do anything I wished them to. "Just to amuse myself,

and keep the good people busy, I ordered them to build this City, and my Palace; and they did it all willingly and well. Then I thought, as the country was so green and

beautiful, I would call it the Emerald City; and to make the name fit better I put green spectacles on all the people, so that everything they saw was green." "But isn't

everything here green?" asked Dorothy. "No more than in any other city," replied Oz; "but when you wear green spectacles, why of course everything you see looks green

to you. The Emerald City was built a great many years ago, for I was a young man when the balloon brought me here, and I am a very old man now. But my people have

worn green glasses on their eyes so long that most of them think it really is an Emerald City, and it certainly is a beautiful place, abounding in jewels and precious metals,

and every good thing that is needed to make one happy. I have been good to the people, and they like me; but ever since this Palace was built, I have shut myself up and would

not see any of them. "One of my greatest fears was the Witches, for while I had no magical powers at all I soon found out that the Witches were really able to do wonderful

things. There were four of them in this country, and they ruled the people who live in the North and South and East and West. Fortunately, the Witches of the North and

South were good, and I knew they would do me no harm; but the Witches of the East and West were terribly wicked, and had they not thought I was more powerful than

they themselves, they would surely have destroyed me. As it was, I lived in deadly fear of them for many years; so you can imagine how pleased I was when I heard your

house had fallen on the Wicked Witch of the East. When you came to me, I was willing to promise anything if you would only do away with the other Witch; but, now that

you have melted her, I am ashamed to say that I cannot keep my promises." "I think you are a very bad man," said Dorothy. "Oh, no, my dear; I'm really a very good man,

but I'm a very bad Wizard, I must admit." "Can't you give me brains?" asked the Scarecrow. "You don't need them. You are learning something every day. A baby has brains,

but it doesn't know much. Experience is the only thing that brings knowledge, and the longer you are on earth the more experience you are sure to get." "That may all be

true," said the Scarecrow, "but I shall be very unhappy unless you give me brains." The false Wizard looked at him carefully. "Well," he said with a sigh, "I'm not much of

a magician, as I said; but if you will come to me tomorrow morning, I will stuff your head with brains. I cannot tell you how to use them, however; you must find that out

for yourself." "Oh, thank you—thank you!" cried the Scarecrow. "I'll find a way to use them, never fear!" "But how about my courage?" asked the Lion anxiously. "You

have plenty of courage, I am sure," answered Oz. "All you need is confidence in yourself. There is no living thing that is not afraid when it faces danger. True courage is in

facing danger when you are afraid, and that kind of courage you have in plenty." "Perhaps I have, but I'm scared just the same," said the Lion. "I shall really be very unhappy

unless you give me the sort of courage that makes one forget he is afraid." "Very well, I will give you that sort of courage tomorrow," replied Oz. "How about my heart?"

asked the Tin Woodman. "Why, as for that," answered Oz, "I think you are wrong to want a heart. It makes most people unhappy. If you only knew it, you are in luck not

to have a heart." "That must be a matter of opinion," said the Tin Woodman. "For my part, I will bear all the unhappiness without a murmur, if you will give me the heart."

"Very well," answered Oz meekly. "Come to me tomorrow and you shall have a heart. I have played Wizard for so many years that I may as well continue the part a little longer." "And now," said Dorothy, "how am I to get back to Kansas?" "We shall have to think about that," replied the little man. "Give me two or three days to consider the matter and I'll try to find a way to carry you over the desert. In the meantime you shall all be treated as my guests, and while you live in the Palace my people will wait upon you and obey your slightest wish. There is only one thing I ask in return for my help—such as it is. You must keep my secret and tell no one I am a humbug." They agreed to say nothing of what they had learned, and went back to their rooms in high spirits. Even Dorothy had hope that "The Great and Terrible Humbug," as she called him, would find a way to send her back to Kansas, and if he did she was willing to forgive him everything. CHAPTER XVI The Magic Art of the Great Humbug Next morning the Scarecrow said to his friends: "Congratulate me. I am going to Oz to get my brains at last. When I return I shall be as other men are." "I have always liked you as you were," said Dorothy simply. "It is kind of you to like a Scarecrow," he replied. "But surely you will think more of me when you hear the splendid thoughts my new brain is going to turn out." Then he said good-bye to them all in a cheerful voice and went to the Throne Room, where he rapped upon the door. "Come in," said Oz. The Scarecrow went in and found the little man sitting down by the window, engaged in deep thought. "I have come for my brains," remarked the Scarecrow, a little uneasily. "Oh, yes; sit down in that chair, please," replied Oz. "You must excuse me for taking your head off, but I shall have to do it in order to put your brains in their proper place." "That's all right," said the Scarecrow. "You are quite welcome to take my head off, as long as it will be a better one when you put it on again." So the Wizard unfastened his head and emptied out the straw. Then he entered the back room and took up a measure of bran, which he mixed with a great many pins and needles. Having shaken them together thoroughly, he filled the top of the Scarecrow's head with the mixture and stuffed the rest of the space with straw, to hold it in place. When he had fastened the Scarecrow's head on his body again he said to him, "Hereafter you will be a great man, for I have given you a lot of bran-new brains." The Scarecrow was both pleased and proud at the fulfillment of his greatest wish, and having thanked Oz warmly he went back to his friends. Dorothy looked at him curiously. His head was quite bulged out at the top with brains. "How do you feel?" she asked. "I feel wise indeed," he answered earnestly. "When I get used to my brains I shall know everything." "Why are those needles and pins sticking out of your head?" asked the Tin Woodman. "That is proof that he is sharp," remarked the Lion. "Well, I must go to Oz and get my heart," said the Woodman. So he walked to the Throne Room and knocked at the door. "Come in," called Oz, and the Woodman entered and said, "I have come for my heart." "Very well," answered the little man. "But I shall have to cut a hole in your breast, so I can put your heart in the right place. I hope it won't hurt you." "Oh, no," answered the Woodman. "I shall not feel it at all." So Oz brought a pair of tinsmith's shears and cut a small, square hole in the left side of the Tin Woodman's breast. Then, going to a chest of drawers, he took out a pretty heart, made entirely of silk and stuffed with sawdust. "Isn't it a beauty?" he asked. "It is, indeed!" replied the Woodman, who was greatly pleased. "But is it a kind heart?" "Oh, very!" answered Oz. He put the heart in the Woodman's breast and then replaced the square of tin, soldering it neatly together where it had been cut.

"There," said he; "now you have a heart that any man might be proud of. I'm sorry I had to put a patch on your breast, but it really couldn't be helped." "Never mind the patch," exclaimed the happy Woodman. "I am very grateful to you, and shall never forget your kindness." "Don't speak of it," replied Oz. Then the Tin Woodman went back to his friends, who wished him every joy on account of his good fortune. The Lion now walked to the Throne Room and knocked at the door. "Come in," said Oz. "I have come for my courage," announced the Lion, entering the room. "Very well," answered the little man; "I will get it for you." He went to a cupboard and reaching up to a high shelf took down a square green bottle, the contents of which he poured into a green-gold dish, beautifully carved. Placing this before the Cowardly Lion, who sniffed at it as if he did not like it, the Wizard said: "Drink." "What is it?" asked the Lion. "Well," answered Oz, "if it were inside of you, it would be courage. You know, of course, that courage is always inside one; so that this really cannot be called courage until you have swallowed it. Therefore I advise you to drink it as soon as possible." The Lion hesitated no longer, but drank till the dish was empty. "How do you feel now?" asked Oz. "Full of courage," replied the Lion, who went joyfully back to his friends to tell them of his good fortune. Oz, left to himself, smiled to think of his success in giving the Scarecrow and the Tin Woodman and the Lion exactly what they thought they wanted. "How can I help being a humbug," he said, "when all these people make me do things that everybody knows can't be done? It was easy to make the Scarecrow and the Lion and the Woodman happy, because they imagined I could do anything. But it will take more than imagination to carry Dorothy back to Kansas, and I'm sure I don't know how it can be done." CHAPTER XVII How the Balloon Was Launched For three days Dorothy heard nothing from Oz. These were sad days for the little girl, although her friends were all quite happy and contented. The Scarecrow told them there were wonderful thoughts in his head; but he would not say what they were because he knew no one could understand them but himself. When the Tin Woodman walked about he felt his heart rattling around in his breast; and he told Dorothy he had discovered it to be a kinder and more tender heart than the one he had owned when he was made of flesh. The Lion declared he was afraid of nothing on earth, and would gladly face an army or a dozen of the fierce Kalidahs. Thus each of the little party was satisfied except Dorothy, who longed more than ever to get back to Kansas. On the fourth day, to her great joy, Oz sent for her, and when she entered the Throne Room he greeted her pleasantly: "Sit down, my dear; I think I have found the way to get you out of this country." "And back to Kansas?" she asked eagerly. "Well, I'm not sure about Kansas," said Oz, "for I haven't the faintest notion which way it lies. But the first thing to do is to cross the desert, and then it should be easy to find your way home." "How can I cross the desert?" she inquired. "Well, I'll tell you what I think," said the little man. "You see, when I came to this country it was in a balloon. You also came through the air, being carried by a cyclone. So I believe the best way to get across the desert will be through the air. Now, it is quite beyond my powers to make a cyclone; but I've been thinking the matter over, and I believe I can make a balloon." "How?" asked Dorothy. "A balloon," said Oz, "is made of silk, which is coated with glue to keep the gas in it. I have plenty of silk in the Palace, so it will be no trouble to make the balloon. But in all this country there is no gas to fill the balloon with, to make it float." "If it won't float," remarked Dorothy, "it will be of no use to us." "True," answered

Oz. "But there is another way to make it float, which is to fill it with hot air. Hot air isn't as good as gas, for if the air should get cold the balloon would come down in the

desert, and we should be lost." "We!" exclaimed the girl. "Are you going with me?" "Yes, of course," replied Oz. "I am tired of being such a humbug. If I should go out of

this Palace my people would soon discover I am not a Wizard, and then they would be vexed with me for having deceived them. So I have to stay shut up in these rooms all

day, and it gets tiresome. I'd much rather go back to Kansas with you and be in a circus again." "I shall be glad to have your company," said Dorothy. "Thank you," he

answered. "Now, if you will help me sew the silk together, we will begin to work on our balloon." So Dorothy took a needle and thread, and as fast as Oz cut the strips of

silk into proper shape the girl sewed them neatly together. First there was a strip of light green silk, then a strip of dark green and then a strip of emerald green; for Oz had

a fancy to make the balloon in different shades of the color about them. It took three days to sew all the strips together, but when it was finished they had a big bag of green

silk more than twenty feet long. Then Oz painted it on the inside with a coat of thin glue, to make it airtight, after which he announced that the balloon was ready. "But we

must have a basket to ride in," he said. So he sent the soldier with the green whiskers for a big clothes basket, which he fastened with many ropes to the bottom of the balloon.

When it was all ready, Oz sent word to his people that he was going to make a visit to a great brother Wizard who lived in the clouds. The news spread rapidly throughout

the city and everyone came to see the wonderful sight. Oz ordered the balloon carried out in front of the Palace, and the people gazed upon it with much curiosity. The Tin

Woodman had chopped a big pile of wood, and now he made a fire of it, and Oz held the bottom of the balloon over the fire so that the hot air that arose from it would be

caught in the silken bag. Gradually the balloon swelled out and rose into the air, until finally the basket just touched the ground. Then Oz got into the basket and said to all

the people in a loud voice: "I am now going away to make a visit. While I am gone the Scarecrow will rule over you. I command you to obey him as you would me." The

balloon was by this time tugging hard at the rope that held it to the ground, for the air within it was hot, and this made it so much lighter in weight than the air without that

it pulled hard to rise into the sky. "Come, Dorothy!" cried the Wizard. "Hurry up, or the balloon will fly away." "I can't find Toto anywhere," replied Dorothy, who did not

wish to leave her little dog behind. Toto had run into the crowd to bark at a kitten, and Dorothy at last found him. She picked him up and ran toward the balloon. She was

within a few steps of it, and Oz was holding out his hands to help her into the basket, when, crack! went the ropes, and the balloon rose into the air without her. "Come back!"

she screamed. "I want to go, too!" "I can't come back, my dear," called Oz from the basket. "Good-bye!" "Good-bye!" shouted everyone, and all eyes were turned upward

to where the Wizard was riding in the basket, rising every moment farther and farther into the sky. And that was the last any of them ever saw of Oz, the Wonderful Wizard,

though he may have reached Omaha safely, and be there now, for all we know. But the people remembered him lovingly, and said to one another: "Oz was always our friend.

When he was here he built for us this beautiful Emerald City, and now he is gone he has left the Wise Scarecrow to rule over us." Still, for many days they grieved over the

loss of the Wonderful Wizard, and would not be comforted. CHAPTER XVIII Away to the South Dorothy wept bitterly at the passing of her hope to get home to Kansas again; but when she thought it all over she was glad she had not gone up in a balloon. And she also felt sorry at losing Oz, and so did her companions. The Tin Woodman came to her and said: "Truly I should be ungrateful if I failed to mourn for the man who gave me my lovely heart. I should like to cry a little because Oz is gone, if you will kindly wipe away my tears, so that I shall not rust." "With pleasure," she answered, and brought a towel at once. Then the Tin Woodman wept for several minutes, and she watched the tears carefully and wiped them away with the towel. When he had finished, he thanked her kindly and oiled himself thoroughly with his jeweled oilcan, to guard against mishap. The Scarecrow was now the ruler of the Emerald City, and although he was not a Wizard the people were proud of him. "For," they said, "there is not another city in all the world that is ruled by a stuffed man." And, so far as they knew, they were quite right. The morning after the balloon had gone up with Oz, the four travelers met in the Throne Room and talked matters over. The Scarecrow sat in the big throne and the others stood respectfully before him. "We are not so unlucky," said the new ruler, "for this Palace and the Emerald City belong to us, and we can do just as we please. When I remember that a short time ago I was up on a pole in a farmer's cornfield, and that now I am the ruler of this beautiful City, I am quite satisfied with my lot." "I also," said the Tin Woodman, "am well-pleased with my new heart; and, really, that was the only thing I wished in all the world." "For my part, I am content in knowing I am as brave as any beast that ever lived, if not braver," said the Lion modestly. "If Dorothy would only be contented to live in the Emerald City," continued the Scarecrow, "we might all be happy together." "But I don't want to live here," cried Dorothy. "I want to go to Kansas, and live with Aunt Em and Uncle Henry." "Well, then, what can be done?" inquired the Woodman. The Scarecrow decided to think, and he thought so hard that the pins and needles began to stick out of his brains. Finally he said: "Why not call the Winged Monkeys, and ask them to carry you over the desert?" "I never thought of that!" said Dorothy joyfully. "It's just the thing. I'll go at once for the Golden Cap." When she brought it into the Throne Room she spoke the magic words, and soon the band of Winged Monkeys flew in through the open window and stood beside her. "This is the second time you have called us," said the Monkey King, bowing before the little girl. "What do you wish?" "I want you to fly with me to Kansas," said Dorothy. But the Monkey King shook his head. "That cannot be done," he said. "We belong to this country alone, and cannot leave it. There has never been a Winged Monkey in Kansas yet, and I suppose there never will be, for they don't belong there. We shall be glad to serve you in any way in our power, but we cannot cross the desert. Good-bye." And with another bow, the Monkey King spread his wings and flew away through the window, followed by all his band. Dorothy was ready to cry with disappointment. "I have wasted the charm of the Golden Cap to no purpose," she said, "for the Winged Monkeys cannot help me." "It is certainly too bad!" said the tender-hearted Woodman. The Scarecrow was thinking again, and his head bulged out so horribly that Dorothy feared it would burst. "Let us call in the soldier with the green whiskers," he said, "and ask his advice." So the soldier was summoned and entered the Throne Room timidly, for while Oz was alive he never was allowed to come farther than the door. "This little girl," said the Scarecrow to the soldier, "wishes to cross the desert. How can she do so?" "I cannot tell," answered the soldier, "for nobody has ever crossed the desert, unless it is Oz himself." "Is there no one who can help me?" asked

Dorothy earnestly. "Glinda might," he suggested. "Who is Glinda?" inquired the Scarecrow. "The Witch of the South. She is the most powerful of all the Witches, and rules over the Quadlings. Besides, her castle stands on the edge of the desert, so she may know a way to cross it." "Glinda is a Good Witch, isn't she?" asked the child. "The Quadlings think she is good," said the soldier, "and she is kind to everyone. I have heard that Glinda is a beautiful woman, who knows how to keep young in spite of the many years she has lived." "How can I get to her castle?" asked Dorothy. "The road is straight to the South," he answered, "but it is said to be full of dangers to travelers. There are wild beasts in the woods, and a race of queer men who do not like strangers to cross their country. For this reason none of the Quadlings ever come to the Emerald City." The soldier then left them and the Scarecrow said: "It seems, in spite of dangers, that the best thing Dorothy can do is to travel to the Land of the South and ask Glinda to help her. For, of course, if Dorothy stays here she will never get back to Kansas." "You must have been thinking again," remarked the Tin Woodman. "I have," said the Scarecrow. "I shall go with Dorothy," declared the Lion, "for I am tired of your city and long for the woods and the country again. I am really a wild beast, you know. Besides, Dorothy will need someone to protect her." "That is true," agreed the Woodman. "My axe may be of service to her; so I also will go with her to the Land of the South." "When shall we start?" asked the Scarecrow. "Are you going?" they asked, in surprise. "Certainly. If it wasn't for Dorothy I should never have had brains. She lifted me from the pole in the cornfield and brought me to the Emerald City. So my good luck is all due to her, and I shall never leave her until she starts back to Kansas for good and all." "Thank you," said Dorothy gratefully. "You are all very kind to me. But I should like to start as soon as possible." "We shall go tomorrow morning," returned the Scarecrow. "So now let us all get ready, for it will be a long journey." CHAPTER XIX Attacked by the Fighting Trees The next morning Dorothy kissed the pretty green girl good-bye, and they all shook hands with the soldier with the green whiskers, who had walked with them as far as the gate. When the Guardian of the Gates saw them again he wondered greatly that they could leave the beautiful City to get into new trouble. But he at once unlocked their spectacles, which he put back into the green box, and gave them many good wishes to carry with them. "You are now our ruler," he said to the Scarecrow; "so you must come back to us as soon as possible." "I certainly shall if I am able," the Scarecrow replied; "but I must help Dorothy to get home, first." As Dorothy bade the good-natured Guardian a last farewell she said: "I have been very kindly treated in your lovely City; everyone has been good to me. I cannot tell you how grateful I am." "Don't try, my dear," he answered. "We should like to keep you with us, but if it is your wish to return to Kansas, I hope you will find a way." He then opened the gate of the outer wall, and they walked forth and started upon their journey. The sun shone brightly as our friends turned their faces toward the Land of the South. They were all in the best of spirits, and laughed and chatted together. Dorothy was once more filled with the hope of getting home, and the Scarecrow and the Tin Woodman were glad to be of use to her. As for the Lion, he sniffed the fresh air with delight and whisked his tail from side to side in pure joy at being in the country again, while Toto ran around them and chased the moths and butterflies, barking merrily all the time. "City life does not agree with me at all," remarked the Lion, as they walked along at a brisk pace. "I have lost much flesh since I lived there, and now I am anxious for a chance to show the other beasts how courageous I have grown." They now turned and took a last look at the Emerald City. All they could see was a mass of towers and steeples behind the green walls, and high up above everything the spires and dome of the Palace of Oz. "Oz was not such a bad Wizard, after all," said the Tin Woodman, as he felt his heart rattling around in his breast. "He knew how to give me brains, and very good brains, too," said the Scarecrow. "If Oz had taken a dose of the same courage he gave me," added the Lion, "he would have been a brave man." Dorothy said nothing. Oz had not kept the promise he made her, but he had done his best, so she forgave him. As he said, he was a good man, even if he was a bad Wizard. The first day's journey was through the green fields and bright flowers that stretched about the Emerald City on every side. They slept that night on the grass, with nothing but the stars over them; and they rested very well indeed. In the morning they traveled on until they came to a thick wood. There was no way of going around it, for it seemed to extend to the right and left as far as they could see; and, besides, they did not dare change the direction of their journey for fear of getting lost. So they looked for the place where it would be easiest to get into the forest. The Scarecrow, who was in the lead, finally discovered a big tree with such wide-spreading branches that there was room for the party to pass underneath. So he walked forward to the tree, but just as he came under the first branches they bent down and twined around him, and the next minute he was raised from the ground and flung headlong among his fellow travelers. This did not hurt the Scarecrow, but it surprised him, and he looked rather dizzy when Dorothy picked him up. "Here is another space between the trees," called the Lion. "Let me try it first," said the Scarecrow, "for it doesn't hurt me to get thrown about." He walked up to another tree, as he spoke, but its branches immediately seized him and tossed him back again. "This is strange," exclaimed Dorothy. "What shall we do?" "The trees seem to have made up their minds to fight us, and stop our journey," remarked the Lion. "I believe I will try it myself," said the Woodman, and shouldering his axe, he marched up to the first tree that had handled the Scarecrow so roughly. When a big branch bent down to seize him the Woodman chopped at it so fiercely that he cut it in two. At once the tree began shaking all its branches as if in pain, and the Tin Woodman passed safely under it. "Come on!" he shouted to the others. "Be quick!" They all ran forward and passed under the tree without injury, except Toto, who was caught by a small branch and shaken until he howled. But the Woodman promptly chopped off the branch and set the little dog free. The other trees of the forest did nothing to keep them back, so they made up their minds that only the first row of trees could bend down their branches, and that probably these were the policemen of the forest, and given this wonderful power in order to keep strangers out of it. The four travelers walked with ease through the trees until they came to the farther edge of the wood. Then, to their surprise, they found before them a high wall which seemed to be made of white china. It was smooth, like the surface of a dish, and higher than their heads. "What shall we do now?" asked Dorothy. "I will make a ladder," said the Tin Woodman, "for we certainly must climb over the wall." CHAPTER XX The Dainty China Country While the Woodman was making a ladder from wood which he found in the forest Dorothy lay down and slept, for she was tired by the long walk. The Lion also curled himself up to sleep and Toto lay beside him. The Scarecrow watched the Woodman while he worked, and said to him: "I cannot think why this wall is here, nor what it is made of." "Rest your brains and do not worry about the wall," replied the Woodman. "When we have climbed over it, we shall know what is on the other side." After a time the ladder was finished. It looked clumsy, but the Tin Woodman was sure it was strong and would answer their purpose. The Scarecrow waked Dorothy and the Lion and Toto, and told them that the ladder was ready. The Scarecrow climbed up the ladder first, but he was so awkward that Dorothy had to follow close behind and keep him from falling off. When he got his head over the top of the wall the Scarecrow said, "Oh, my!" "Go on," exclaimed Dorothy. So the Scarecrow climbed farther up and sat down on the top of the wall, and Dorothy put her head over and cried, "Oh, my!" just as the Scarecrow had done. Then Toto came up, and immediately began to bark, but Dorothy made him be still. The Lion climbed the ladder next, and the Tin Woodman came last; but both of them cried, "Oh, my!" as soon as they looked over the wall. When they were all sitting in a row on the top of the wall, they looked down and saw a strange sight. Before them was a great stretch of country having a floor as smooth and shining and white as the bottom of a big platter. Scattered around were many houses made entirely of china and painted in the brightest colors. These houses were quite small, the biggest of them reaching only as high as Dorothy's waist. There were also pretty little barns, with china fences around them; and many cows and sheep and horses and pigs and chickens, all made of china, were standing about in groups. But the strangest of all were the people who lived in this queer country. There were milkmaids and shepherdesses, with brightly colored bodices and golden spots all over their gowns; and princesses with most gorgeous frocks of silver and gold and purple; and shepherds dressed in knee breeches with pink and yellow and blue stripes down them, and golden buckles on their shoes; and princes with jeweled crowns upon their heads, wearing ermine robes and satin doublets; and funny clowns in ruffled gowns, with round red spots upon their cheeks and tall, pointed caps. And, strangest of all, these people were all made of china, even to their clothes, and were so small that the tallest of them was no higher than Dorothy's knee. No one did so much as look at the travelers at first, except one little purple china dog with an extra-large head, which came to the wall and barked at them in a tiny voice, afterwards running away again. "How shall we get down?" asked Dorothy. They found the ladder so heavy they could not pull it up, so the Scarecrow fell off the wall and the others jumped down upon him so that the hard floor would not hurt their feet. Of course they took pains not to light on his head and get the pins in their feet. When all were safely down they picked up the Scarecrow, whose body was quite flattened out, and patted his straw into shape again. "We must cross this strange place in order to get to the other side," said Dorothy, "for it would be unwise for us to go any other way except due South." They began walking through the country of the china people, and the first thing they came to was a china milkmaid milking a china cow. As they drew near, the cow suddenly gave a kick and kicked over the stool, the pail, and even the milkmaid herself, and all fell on the china ground with a great clatter. Dorothy was shocked to see that the cow had broken her leg off, and that the pail was lying in several small pieces, while the poor milkmaid had a nick in her left elbow. "There!" cried the milkmaid angrily. "See what you have done! My cow has broken her leg, and I must take her to the mender's shop and have it glued on again. What do you mean by coming here and frightening my cow?" "I'm very sorry," returned Dorothy. "Please forgive us." But the pretty milkmaid was much too vexed to make any answer. She picked up the leg sulkily and led her cow away, the poor animal limping on three legs. As she left them the milkmaid cast many reproachful glances over her shoulder at the clumsy strangers, holding her nicked elbow close to her side. Dorothy was quite grieved at this mishap. "We must be very careful here," said the kindhearted Woodman, "or we may hurt these pretty little people so they will never get over it." A little farther on Dorothy met a most beautifully dressed young Princess, who stopped short as she saw the strangers and started to run away.

Dorothy wanted to see more of the Princess, so she ran after her. But the china girl cried out: "Don't chase me! Don't chase me!" She had such a frightened little voice that Dorothy stopped and said, "Why not?" "Because," answered the Princess, also stopping, a safe distance away, "if I run I may fall down and break myself." "But could you not be mended?" asked the girl. "Oh, yes; but one is never so pretty after being mended, you know," replied the Princess. "I suppose not," said Dorothy. "Now there is Mr. Joker, one of our clowns," continued the china lady, "who is always trying to stand upon his head. He has broken himself so often that he is mended in a hundred places, and doesn't look at all pretty. Here he comes now, so you can see for yourself." Indeed, a jolly little clown came walking toward them, and Dorothy could see that in spite of his pretty clothes of red and yellow and green he was completely covered with cracks, running every which way and showing plainly that he had been mended in many places.

The Clown put his hands in his pockets, and after puffing out his cheeks and nodding his head at them saucily, he said, *"My lady fair, Why do you stare At poor old Mr. Joker? You're quite as stiff And prim as if You'd eaten up a poker!"* "Be quiet, sir!" said the Princess. "Can't you see these are strangers, and should be treated with respect?" "Well, that's respect, I expect," declared the Clown, and immediately stood upon his head. "Don't mind Mr. Joker," said the Princess to Dorothy. "He is considerably cracked in his head, and that makes him foolish." "Oh, I don't mind him a bit," said Dorothy. "But you are so beautiful," she continued, "that I am sure I could love you dearly. Won't you let me carry you back to Kansas, and stand you on Aunt Em's mantel? I could carry you in my basket." "That would make me very unhappy," answered the china Princess. "You see, here in our country we live contentedly, and can talk and move around as we please. But whenever any of us are taken away our joints at once stiffen, and we can only stand straight and look pretty. Of course that is all that is expected of us when we are on mantels and cabinets and drawing-room tables, but our lives are much pleasanter here in our own country." "I would not make you unhappy for all the world!" exclaimed Dorothy. "So I'll just say good-bye." "Good-bye," replied the Princess.

They walked carefully through the china country. The little animals and all the people scampered out of their way, fearing the strangers would break them, and after an hour or so the travelers reached the other side of the country and came to another china wall. It was not so high as the first, however, and by standing upon the Lion's back they all managed to scramble to the top. Then the Lion gathered his legs under him and jumped on the wall; but just as he jumped, he upset a china church with his tail and smashed it all to pieces. "That was too bad," said Dorothy, "but really I think we were lucky in not doing these little people more harm than breaking a cow's leg and a church. They are all so brittle!" "They are, indeed," said the Scarecrow, "and I am thankful I am made of straw and cannot be easily damaged. There are worse things in the world than being a Scarecrow." CHAPTER XXI The Lion Becomes the King of Beasts After climbing down from the china wall the travelers found themselves in a disagreeable country, full of bogs and marshes and covered with tall, rank grass. It was difficult to walk without falling into muddy holes, for the grass was so thick that it hid them from sight. However, by carefully picking their way, they got safely along until they reached solid ground. But here the country seemed wilder than ever, and after a long and tiresome walk through the underbrush they entered another forest, where the trees were bigger and older than any they had ever seen. "This forest is perfectly delightful," declared the Lion, looking around him with joy. "Never have I seen a more beautiful place." "It seems gloomy," said the Scarecrow. "Not a bit of it," answered the Lion. "I should like to live here all my life. See how soft the dried leaves are under your feet and how rich and green the moss is that clings to these old trees. Surely no wild beast could wish a pleasanter home." "Perhaps there are wild beasts in the forest now," said Dorothy. "I suppose there are," returned the Lion, "but I do not see any of them about." They walked through the forest until it became too dark to go any farther. Dorothy and Toto and the Lion lay down to sleep, while the Woodman and the Scarecrow kept watch over them as usual. When morning came, they started again. Before they had gone far they heard a low rumble, as of the growling of many wild animals. Toto whimpered a little, but none of the others was frightened, and they kept along the well-trodden path until they came to an opening in the wood, in which were gathered hundreds of beasts of every variety. There were tigers and elephants and bears and wolves and foxes and all the others in the natural history, and for a moment Dorothy was afraid. But the Lion explained that the animals were holding a meeting, and he judged by their snarling and growling that they were in great trouble. As he spoke several of the beasts caught sight of him, and at once the great assemblage hushed as if by magic. The biggest of the tigers came up to the Lion and bowed, saying: "Welcome, O King of Beasts! You have come in good time to fight our enemy and bring peace to all the animals of the forest once more." "What is your trouble?" asked the Lion quietly. "We are all threatened," answered the tiger, "by a fierce enemy which has lately come into this forest. It is a most tremendous monster, like a great spider, with a body as big as an elephant and legs as long as a tree trunk. It has eight of these long legs, and as the monster crawls through the forest he seizes an animal with a leg and drags it to his mouth, where he eats it as a spider does a fly. Not one of us is safe while this fierce creature is alive, and we had called a meeting to decide how to take care of ourselves when you came among us." The Lion thought for a moment. "Are there any other lions in this forest?" he asked. "No; there were some, but the monster has eaten them all. And, besides, they were none of them nearly so large and brave as you." "If I put an end to your enemy, will you bow down to me and obey me as King of the Forest?" inquired the Lion. "We will do that gladly," returned the tiger; and all the other beasts roared with a mighty roar: "We will!" "Where is this great spider of yours now?" asked the Lion. "Yonder, among the oak trees," said the tiger, pointing with his forefoot. "Take good care of these friends of mine," said the Lion, "and I will go at once to fight the monster." He bade his comrades good-bye and marched proudly away to do battle with the enemy. The great spider was lying asleep when the Lion found him, and it looked so ugly that its foe turned up his nose in disgust. Its legs were quite as long as the tiger had said, and its body covered with coarse black hair. It had a great mouth, with a row of sharp teeth a foot long; but its head was joined to the pudgy body by a neck as slender as a wasp's waist. This gave the Lion a hint of the best way to attack the creature, and as he knew it was easier to fight it asleep than awake, he gave a great spring and landed directly upon the monster's back. Then, with one blow of his heavy paw, all armed with sharp claws, he knocked the spider's head from its body. Jumping down, he watched it until the long legs stopped wiggling, when he knew it was quite dead. The Lion went back to the opening where the beasts of the forest were waiting for him and said proudly: "You need fear your enemy no longer." Then the beasts bowed down to the Lion as their King, and he promised to come back and rule over them as soon as Dorothy was safely on her way to Kansas. CHAPTER XXII The Country of the Quadlings

The four travelers passed through the rest of the forest in safety, and when they came out from its gloom saw before them a steep hill, covered from top to bottom with great pieces of rock. "That will be a hard climb," said the Scarecrow, "but we must get over the hill, nevertheless." So he led the way and the others followed. They had nearly reached the first rock when they heard a rough voice cry out, "Keep back!" "Who are you?" asked the Scarecrow. Then a head showed itself over the rock and the same voice said, "This hill belongs to us, and we don't allow anyone to cross it." "But we must cross it," said the Scarecrow. "We're going to the country of the Quadlings." "But you shall not!" replied the voice, and there stepped from behind the rock the strangest man the travelers had ever seen. He was quite short and stout and had a big head, which was flat at the top and supported by a thick neck full of wrinkles. But he had no arms at all, and, seeing this, the Scarecrow did not fear that so helpless a creature could prevent them from climbing the hill. So he said, "I'm sorry not to do as you wish, but we must pass over your hill whether you like it or not," and he walked boldly forward. As quick as lightning the man's head shot forward and his neck stretched out until the top of the head, where it was flat, struck the Scarecrow in the middle and sent him tumbling, over and over, down the hill. Almost as quickly as it came the head went back to the body, and the man laughed harshly as he said, "It isn't as easy as you think!" A chorus of boisterous laughter came from the other rocks, and Dorothy saw hundreds of the armless Hammer-Heads upon the hillside, one behind every rock. The Lion became quite angry at the laughter caused by the Scarecrow's mishap, and giving a loud roar that echoed like thunder, he dashed up the hill. Again a head shot swiftly out, and the great Lion went rolling down the hill as if he had been struck by a cannonball. Dorothy ran down and helped the Scarecrow to his feet, and the Lion came up to her, feeling rather bruised and sore, and said, "It is useless to fight people with shooting heads; no one can withstand them." "What can we do, then?" she asked. "Call the Winged Monkeys," suggested the Tin Woodman. "You have still the right to command them once more." "Very well," she answered, and putting on the Golden Cap she uttered the magic words. The Monkeys were as prompt as ever, and in a few moments the entire band stood before her. "What are your commands?" inquired the King of the Monkeys, bowing low. "Carry us over the hill to the country of the Quadlings," answered the girl. "It shall be done," said the King, and at once the Winged Monkeys caught the four travelers and Toto up in their arms and flew away with them. As they passed over the hill the Hammer-Heads yelled with vexation, and shot their heads high in the air, but they could not reach the Winged Monkeys, which carried Dorothy and her comrades safely over the hill and set them down in the beautiful country of the Quadlings. "This is the last time you can summon us," said the leader to Dorothy; "so good-bye and good luck to you." "Good-bye, and thank you very much," returned the girl; and the

Monkeys rose into the air and were out of sight in a twinkling. The country of the Quadlings seemed rich and happy. There was field upon field of ripening grain, with well-paved roads running between, and pretty rippling brooks with strong bridges across them. The fences and houses and bridges were all painted bright red, just as they had been painted yellow in the country of the Winkies and blue in the country of the Munchkins. The Quadlings themselves, who were short and fat and looked chubby and good-natured, were dressed all in red, which showed bright against the green grass and the yellowing grain. The Monkeys had set them down near a farmhouse, and the four travelers walked up to it and knocked at the door. It was opened by the farmer's wife, and when Dorothy asked for something to eat the woman gave them all a good dinner, with three kinds of cake and four kinds of cookies, and a bowl of milk for Toto. "How far is it to the Castle of Glinda?" asked the child. "It is not a great way," answered the farmer's wife. "Take the road to the South and you will soon reach it." Thanking the good woman, they started afresh and walked by the fields and across the pretty bridges until they saw before them a very beautiful Castle. Before the gates were three young girls, dressed in handsome red uniforms trimmed with gold braid; and as Dorothy approached, one of them said to her: "Why have you come to the South Country?" "To see the Good Witch who rules here," she answered. "Will you take me to her?" "Let me have your name, and I will ask Glinda if she will receive you." They told who they were, and the girl soldier went into the Castle. After a few moments she came back to say that Dorothy and the others were to be admitted at once. CHAPTER XXIII Glinda The Good Witch Grants Dorothy's Wish Before they went to see Glinda, however, they were taken to a room of the Castle, where Dorothy washed her face and combed her hair, and the Lion shook the dust out of his mane, and the Scarecrow patted himself into his best shape, and the Woodman polished his tin and oiled his joints. When they were all quite presentable they followed the soldier girl into a big room where the Witch Glinda sat upon a throne of rubies. She was both beautiful and young to their eyes. Her hair was a rich red in color and fell in flowing ringlets over her shoulders. Her dress was pure white but her eyes were blue, and they looked kindly upon the little girl. "What can I do for you, my child?" she asked. Dorothy told the Witch all her story: how the cyclone had brought her to the Land of Oz, how she had found her companions, and of the wonderful adventures they had met with. "My greatest wish now," she added, "is to get back to Kansas, for Aunt Em will surely think something dreadful has happened to me, and that will make her put on mourning; and unless the crops are better this year than they were last, I am sure Uncle Henry cannot afford it." Glinda leaned forward and kissed the sweet, upturned face of the loving little girl. "Bless your dear heart," she said, "I am sure I can tell you of a way to get back to Kansas." Then she added, "But, if I do, you must give me the Golden Cap." "Willingly!" exclaimed Dorothy; "indeed, it is of no use to me now, and when you have it you can command the Winged Monkeys three times." "And I think I shall need their service just those three times," answered Glinda, smiling. Dorothy then gave her the Golden Cap, and the Witch said to the Scarecrow, "What will you do when Dorothy has left us?" "I will return to the Emerald City," he replied, "for Oz has made me its ruler and the people like me. The only thing that worries me is how to cross the hill of the Hammer-Heads." "By means of the Golden Cap I shall command the Winged Monkeys to carry you to the gates of the Emerald City," said Glinda, "for it would be a shame to deprive the people of so wonderful a ruler." "Am I really wonderful?" asked the Scarecrow. "You are unusual," replied Glinda. Turning to the Tin Woodman, she asked,

"What will become of you when Dorothy leaves this country?" He leaned on his axe and thought a moment. Then he said, "The Winkies were very kind to me, and wanted

me to rule over them after the Wicked Witch died. I am fond of the Winkies, and if I could get back again to the Country of the West, I should like nothing better than to

rule over them forever." "My second command to the Winged Monkeys," said Glinda "will be that they carry you safely to the land of the Winkies. Your brain may not be

so large to look at as those of the Scarecrow, but you are really brighter than he is—when you are well polished—and I am sure you will rule the Winkies wisely and well."

Then the Witch looked at the big, shaggy Lion and asked, "When Dorothy has returned to her own home, what will become of you?" "Over the hill of the Hammer-Heads,"

he answered, "lies a grand old forest, and all the beasts that live there have made me their King. If I could only get back to this forest, I would pass my life very happily there."

"My third command to the Winged Monkeys," said Glinda, "shall be to carry you to your forest. Then, having used up the powers of the Golden Cap, I shall give it to the

King of the Monkeys, that he and his band may thereafter be free for evermore." The Scarecrow and the Tin Woodman and the Lion now thanked the Good Witch earnestly

for her kindness; and Dorothy exclaimed: "You are certainly as good as you are beautiful! But you have not yet told me how to get back to Kansas." "Your Silver Shoes will

carry you over the desert," replied Glinda. "If you had known their power you could have gone back to your Aunt Em the very first day you came to this country." "But then

I should not have had my wonderful brains!" cried the Scarecrow. "I might have passed my whole life in the farmer's cornfield." "And I should not have had my lovely heart,"

said the Tin Woodman. "I might have stood and rusted in the forest till the end of the world." "And I should have lived a coward forever," declared the Lion, "and no beast

in all the forest would have had a good word to say to me." "This is all true," said Dorothy, "and I am glad I was of use to these good friends. But now that each of them has

had what he most desired, and each is happy in having a kingdom to rule besides, I think I should like to go back to Kansas." "The Silver Shoes," said the Good Witch, "have

wonderful powers. And one of the most curious things about them is that they can carry you to any place in the world in three steps, and each step will be made in the wink

of an eye. All you have to do is to knock the heels together three times and command the shoes to carry you wherever you wish to go." "If that is so," said the child joyfully,

"I will ask them to carry me back to Kansas at once." She threw her arms around the Lion's neck and kissed him, patting his big head tenderly. Then she kissed the Tin

Woodman, who was weeping in a way most dangerous to his joints. But she hugged the soft, stuffed body of the Scarecrow in her arms instead of kissing his painted face,

and found she was crying herself at this sorrowful parting from her loving comrades. Glinda the Good stepped down from her ruby throne to give the little girl a good-bye

kiss, and Dorothy thanked her for all the kindness she had shown to her friends and herself. Dorothy now took Toto up solemnly in her arms, and having said one last good-

bye she clapped the heels of her shoes together three times, saying: "Take me home to Aunt Em!" Instantly she was whirling through the air, so swiftly that all she could see

or feel was the wind whistling past her ears. The Silver Shoes took but three steps, and then she stopped so suddenly that she rolled over upon the grass several times before she knew where she was. At length, however, she sat up and looked about her. "Good gracious!" she cried. For she was sitting on the broad Kansas prairie, and just before her was the new farmhouse Uncle Henry built after the cyclone had carried away the old one. Uncle Henry was milking the cows in the barnyard, and Toto had jumped out of her arms and was running toward the barn, barking furiously. Dorothy stood up and found she was in her stocking feet. For the Silver Shoes had fallen off in her flight through the air, and were lost forever in the desert. CHAPTER XXIV Home Again Aunt Em had just come out of the house to water the cabbages when she looked up and saw Dorothy running toward her. "My darling child!" she cried, folding the little girl in her arms and covering her face with kisses. "Where in the world did you come from?" "From the Land of Oz," said Dorothy gravely. "And here is Toto, too. And oh, Aunt Em! I'm so glad to be at home again!" LITTLE WIZARD STORIES OF OZ The Cowardly Lion and the Hungry Tiger In the splendid palace of the Emerald City, which is in the center of the fairy Land of Oz, is a great Throne Room, where Princess Ozma, the Ruler, for an hour each day sits in a throne of glistening emeralds and listens to all the troubles of her people, which they are sure to tell her about. Around Ozma's throne, on such occasions, are grouped all the important personages of Oz, such as the Scarecrow, Jack Pumpkinhead, Tiktok the Clockwork Man, the Tin Woodman, the Wizard of Oz, the Shaggy Man and other famous fairy people. Little Dorothy usually has a seat at Ozma's feet, and crouched on either side the throne are two enormous beasts known as the Hungry Tiger and the Cowardly Lion. These two beasts are Ozma's chief guardians, but as everyone loves the beautiful girl Princess there has never been any disturbance in the great Throne Room, or anything for the guardians to do but look fierce and solemn and keep quiet until the Royal Audience is over and the people go away to their homes. Of course no one would dare be naughty while the huge Lion and Tiger crouched beside the throne; but the fact is, the people of Oz are very seldom naughty. So Ozma's big guards are more ornamental than useful, and no one realizes that better than the beasts themselves. One day, after everybody had left the Throne Room except the Cowardly Lion and the Hungry Tiger, the Lion yawned and said to his friend: "I'm getting tired of this job. No one is afraid of us and no one pays any attention to us." "That is true," replied the big Tiger, purring softly. "We might as well be in the thick jungles where we were born, as trying to protect Ozma when she needs no protection. And I'm dreadfully hungry all the time." "You have enough to eat, I'm sure," said the Lion, swaying his tail slowly back and forth. "Enough, perhaps; but not the kind of food I long for," answered the Tiger. "What I'm hungry for is fat babies. I have a great desire to eat a few fat babies. Then, perhaps, the people of Oz would fear me and I'd become more important." "True," agreed the Lion. "It would stir up quite a rumpus if you ate but *one* fat baby. As for myself; my claws are sharp as needles and strong as crowbars, while my teeth are powerful enough to tear a person to pieces in a few seconds. If I should spring upon a man and make chop suey of him, there would be wild excitement in the Emerald City and the people would fall upon their knees and beg me for mercy. That, in my opinion, would render me of considerable importance." "After you had torn the person to pieces, what would you do next?" asked the Tiger sleepily. "Then I would roar so loudly it would shake the earth and stalk away to the jungle to hide myself, before anyone could attack me or kill me for what I had done." "I see," nodded the Tiger. "You are really cowardly." "To be sure. That is why I am named the Cowardly Lion. That is why I have always been so tame and peaceable. But I'm awfully tired of being tame," added the Lion, with a sigh, "and it would be fun

to raise a row and show people what a terrible beast I really am." The Tiger remained silent for several minutes, thinking deeply as he slowly washed his face with his left

paw. Then he said: "I'm getting old, and it would please me to eat at least one fat baby before I die. Suppose we surprise these people of Oz and prove our power. What do

you say? We will walk out of here just as usual and the first baby we meet I'll eat in a jiffy, and the first man or woman you meet you will tear to pieces. Then we will both

run out of the city gates and gallop across the country and hide in the jungle before anyone can stop us." "All right; I'm game," said the Lion, yawning again so that he showed

two rows of dreadfully sharp teeth. The Tiger got up and stretched his great, sleek body. "Come on," he said. The Lion stood up and proved he was the larger of the two,

for he was almost as big as a small horse. Out of the palace they walked, and met no one. They passed through the beautiful grounds, past fountains and beds of lovely

flowers, and met no one. Then they unlatched a gate and entered a street of the city, and met no one. "I wonder how a fat baby will taste," remarked the Tiger, as they stalked

majestically along, side by side. "I imagine it will taste like nutmegs," said the Lion. "No," said the Tiger, "I've an idea it will taste like gumdrops." They turned a corner,

but met no one, for the people of the Emerald City were accustomed to take their naps at this hour of the afternoon. "I wonder how many pieces I ought to tear a person

into," said the Lion, in a thoughtful voice. "Sixty would be about right," suggested the Tiger. "Would that hurt any more than to tear one into about a dozen pieces?" inquired

the Lion, with a little shudder. "Who cares whether it hurts or not?" growled the Tiger. The Lion did not reply. They entered a side street, but met no one. Suddenly they

heard a child crying. "Aha!" exclaimed the Tiger. "There is my meat." He rushed around a corner, the Lion following, and came upon a nice fat baby sitting in the middle

of the street and crying as if in great distress. "What's the matter?" asked the Tiger, crouching before the baby. "I—I—I—lost my m—m—mama!" wailed the baby. "Why,

you poor little thing," said the great beast, softly stroking the child's head with its paw. "Don't cry, my dear, for mama can't be far away and I'll help you to find her." "Go

on," said the Lion, who stood by. "Go on where?" asked the Tiger, looking up. "Go on and eat your fat baby." "Why, you dreadful creature!" said the Tiger reproachfully;

"would you want me to eat a poor little lost baby, that doesn't know where its mother is?" And the beast gathered the little one into its strong, hairy arms and tried to comfort

it by rocking it gently back and forth. The Lion growled low in his throat and seemed very much disappointed; but at that moment a scream reached their ears and a woman

came bounding out of a house and into the street. Seeing her baby in the embrace of the monster Tiger the woman screamed again and rushed forward to rescue it, but in

her haste she caught her foot in her skirt and tumbled head over heels and heels over head, stopping with such a bump that she saw many stars in the heavens, although it was

broad daylight. And there she lay, in a helpless manner, all tangled up and unable to stir. With one bound and a roar like thunder the huge Lion was beside her. With his strong

jaws he grasped her dress and raised her into an upright position. "Poor thing! Are you hurt?" he gently asked. Gasping for breath the woman struggled to free herself and

tried to walk, but she limped badly and tumbled down again. "My baby!" she said pleadingly. "The baby is all right; don't worry," replied the Lion; and then he added: "Keep quiet, now, and I'll carry you back to your house, and the Hungry Tiger will carry your baby." The Tiger, who had approached the place with the child in its arms, asked in astonishment: "Aren't you going to tear her into sixty pieces?" "No, nor into six pieces," answered the Lion indignantly. "I'm not such a brute as to destroy a poor woman who has hurt herself trying to save her lost baby. If you are so ferocious and cruel and bloodthirsty, you may leave me and go away, for I do not care to associate with you."

"That's all right," answered the Tiger. "I'm not cruel—not in the least—I'm only hungry. But I thought *you* were cruel." "Thank heaven I'm respectable," said the Lion, with dignity. He then raised the woman and with much gentleness carried her into her house, where he laid her upon a sofa. The Tiger followed with the baby, which he safely deposited beside its mother. The little one liked the Hungry Tiger and grasping the enormous beast by both ears the baby kissed the beast's nose to show he was grateful and happy. "Thank you very much," said the woman. "I've often heard what good beasts you are, in spite of your power to do mischief to mankind, and now I know that the stories are true. I do not think either of you have ever had an evil thought." The Hungry Tiger and the Cowardly Lion hung their heads and did not look into each other's eyes, for both were shamed and humbled. They crept away and stalked back through the streets until they again entered the palace grounds, where they retreated to the pretty, comfortable rooms they occupied at the back of the palace. There they silently crouched in their usual corners to think over their adventure. After a while the Tiger said sleepily: "I don't believe fat babies taste like gumdrops. I'm quite sure they have the flavor of raspberry tarts. My, how hungry I am for fat babies!" The Lion grunted disdainfully. "You're a humbug," said he. "Am I?" retorted the Tiger, with a sneer. "Tell me, then, into how many pieces you usually tear your victims, my bold Lion?" The Lion impatiently thumped the floor with his tail. "To tear anyone into pieces would soil my claws and blunt my teeth," he said. "I'm glad I didn't muss myself up this afternoon by hurting that poor mother." The Tiger looked at him steadily and then yawned a wide, wide yawn. "You're a coward," he remarked. "Well," said the Lion, "it's better to be a coward than to do wrong." "To be sure," answered the other. "And that reminds me that I nearly lost my own reputation. For, had I eaten that fat baby I would not now be the Hungry Tiger. It's better to go hungry, seems to me, than to be cruel to a little child." And then they dropped their heads on their paws and went to sleep.

LITTLE DOROTHY AND TOTO Dorothy was a little Kansas girl who once accidentally found the beautiful Land of Oz and was invited to live there always. Toto was Dorothy's small black dog, with fuzzy, curly hair and bright black eyes. Together, when they tired of the grandeur of the Emerald City of Oz, they would wander out into the country and all through the land, peering into queer nooks and corners and having a good time in their own simple way. There was a little Wizard living in Oz who was a faithful friend of Dorothy and did not approve of her traveling alone in this way, but the girl always laughed at the little man's fears for her and said she was not afraid of anything that might happen. One day while on such a journey, Dorothy and Toto found themselves among the wild wooded hills at the southeast of Oz—a place usually avoided by travelers because so many magical things abounded there. And, as they entered a forest path, the little girl noticed a sign tacked to a tree, which said: "Look out for Crinklink." Toto could not talk, as many of the animals of Oz can, for he was just a common Kansas dog; but he looked at the sign so seriously that Dorothy almost believed he could read it, and she knew quite well that Toto understood every word she said to him. "Never mind Crinklink," said she. "I don't believe anything in Oz will try to hurt us, Toto, and if I get into trouble you must take care of me." "Bow-wow!" said Toto, and Dorothy knew that meant a promise. The path was narrow and wound here and there between the trees, but they could not lose their way, because thick vines and creepers shut them in on both sides. They had walked a long time when, suddenly turning a curve of the pathway, they came upon a lake of black water, so big and so deep that they were forced to stop. "Well, Toto," said Dorothy, looking at the lake, "we must turn back, I guess, for there is neither a bridge nor a boat to take us across the black water." "Here's the ferryman, though," cried a tiny voice beside them, and the girl gave a start and looked down at her feet, where a man no taller than three inches sat at the edge of the path with his legs dangling over the lake. "Oh!" said Dorothy; "I didn't see you before." Toto growled fiercely and made his ears stand up straight, but the little man did not seem in the least afraid of the dog. He merely repeated: "I'm the ferryman, and it's my business to carry people across the lake." Dorothy couldn't help feeling surprised, for she could have picked the little man up with one hand, and the lake was big and broad. Looking at the ferryman more closely she saw that he had small eyes, a big nose, and a sharp chin. His hair was blue and his clothes scarlet, and Dorothy noticed that every button on his jacket was the head of some animal. The top button was a bear's head and the next button a wolf's head; the next was a cat's head and the next a weasel's head, while the last button of all was the head of a field mouse. When Dorothy looked into the eyes of these animals' heads, they all nodded and said in a chorus: "Don't believe all you hear, little girl!" "Silence!" said the small ferryman, slapping each button head in turn, but not hard enough to hurt them. Then he turned to Dorothy and asked: "Do you wish to cross over the lake?" "Why, I'd like to," she answered, hesitating; "but I can't see how you will manage to carry us, without any boat." "If you can't see, you mustn't see," he answered with a laugh. "All you need do is shut your eyes, say the word, and—over you go!" Dorothy wanted to get across, in order that she might continue her journey. "All right," she said, closing her eyes; "I'm ready." Instantly she was seized in a pair of strong arms—arms so big and powerful that she was startled and cried out in fear. "Silence!" roared a great voice, and the girl opened her eyes to find that the tiny man had suddenly grown to a giant and was holding both her and Toto in a tight embrace while in one step he spanned the lake and reached the other shore. Dorothy became frightened, then, especially as the giant did not stop but continued tramping in great steps over the wooded hills, crushing bushes and trees beneath his broad feet. She struggled in vain to free herself, while Toto whined and trembled beside her, for the little dog was frightened, too. "Stop!" screamed the girl. "Let me down!" But the giant paid no attention. "Who are you, and where are you taking me?" she continued; but the giant said not a word. Close to Dorothy's ear, however, a voice answered her, saying: "This is the terrible Crinklink, and he has you in his power." Dorothy managed to twist her head around and found it was the second button on the jacket—the wolf's head—which had spoken to her. "What will Crinklink do with me?" she asked anxiously. "No one knows. You must wait and see," replied the wolf. "Some of his captives he whips," squeaked the weasel's head. "Some he transforms into bugs and other things," growled the bear's head. "Some he enchants, so that they become doorknobs," sighed the cat's head. "Some he makes his slaves—even as we are—and that is the most dreadful fate of all," added the field mouse. "As long as Crinklink exists we shall remain buttons, but as there are no more buttonholes on his jacket he will probably make you a slave." Dorothy began to wish she had not met Crinklink. Meantime, the giant took such big steps that he soon reached the heart of the hills, where, perched upon the highest peak, stood a log castle. Before this castle he paused to set down Dorothy and Toto, for Crinklink was at present far too large to enter his own doorway. So he made himself grow smaller, until he was about the size of an ordinary man. Then he said to Dorothy, in stern, commanding tones: "Enter, girl!" Dorothy obeyed and entered the castle, with Toto at her heels. She found the place to be merely one big room. There was a table and chair of ordinary size near the center, and at one side a wee bed that seemed scarcely big enough for a doll. Everywhere else were dishes—dishes—dishes! They were all soiled, and were piled upon the floor, in all the corners and upon every shelf. Evidently Crinklink had not washed a dish for years, but had cast them aside as he used them. Dorothy's captor sat down in the chair and frowned at her. "You are young and strong, and will make a good dishwasher," said he. "Do you mean me to wash all those dishes?" she asked, feeling both indignant and fearful, for such a task would take weeks to accomplish. "That's just what I mean," he retorted. "I need clean dishes, for all I have are soiled, and you're going to make 'em clean or get trounced. So get to work and be careful not to break anything. If you smash a dish, the penalty is one lash from my dreadful cat-o'-nine-tails for every piece the dish breaks into," and here Crinklink displayed a terrible whip that made the little girl shudder. Dorothy knew how to wash dishes, but she remembered that often she carelessly broke one. In this case, however, a good deal depended on being careful, so she handled the dishes very cautiously. While she worked, Toto sat by the hearth and growled low at Crinklink, and Crinklink sat in his chair and growled at Dorothy because she moved so slowly. He expected her to break a dish any minute, but as the hours passed away and this did not happen Crinklink began to grow sleepy. It was tiresome watching the girl wash dishes and often he glanced longingly at the tiny bed. Now he began to yawn, and he yawned and yawned until finally he said: "I'm going to take a nap. But the buttons on my jacket will be wide awake and whenever you break a dish the crash will waken me. As I'm rather sleepy I hope you won't interrupt my nap by breaking anything for a long time." Then Crinklink made himself grow smaller and smaller until he was three inches high and of a size to fit the tiny bed. At once he lay down and fell fast asleep. Dorothy came close to the buttons and whispered: "Would you really warn Crinklink if I tried to escape?" "You can't escape," growled the bear. "Crinklink would become a giant, and soon overtake you." "But you might kill him while he sleeps," suggested the cat, in a soft voice. "Oh!" cried Dorothy, drawing back; "I couldn't poss'bly *kill* anything—even to save my life." But Toto had heard this conversation and was not so particular about killing monsters. Also the little dog knew he must try to save his mistress. In an instant he sprang upon the wee bed and was about to seize the sleeping Crinklink in his jaws when Dorothy heard a loud crash and a heap of dishes fell from the table to the floor. Then the girl saw Toto and the little man rolling on the floor together, like a fuzzy ball, and when the ball stopped rolling, behold! there was Toto wagging his tail joyfully and there sat the little Wizard of Oz, laughing merrily at the expression of surprise on Dorothy's face. "Yes, my dear, it's me," said he, "and I've been playing tricks on you—for your own good. I wanted to prove to you that it is really dangerous for a little girl to wander alone in a fairy country; so I took the form of Crinklink to teach you a lesson. There isn't any Crinklink, to be sure; but if there had been you'd be severely whipped for breaking all those dishes." The Wizard now rose, took off the coat with the button heads, and spread it on the floor, wrong side up. At once there crept from beneath it a bear, a wolf, a cat, a weasel, and a field mouse, who all rushed from the room and escaped into the mountains. "Come on, Toto," said Dorothy; "let's go back to the Emerald City. You've given me a good scare, Wizard," she added, with dignity, "and p'raps I'll forgive you, by-n-by; but just now I'm mad to think how easily you fooled me." TIKTOK AND THE NOME KING The Nome King was unpleasantly angry. He had carelessly bitten his tongue at breakfast and it still hurt; so he roared and raved and stamped around in his underground palace in a way that rendered him very disagreeable. It so happened that on this unfortunate day Tiktok, the Clockwork Man, visited the Nome King to ask a favor. Tiktok lived in the Land of Oz, and although he was an active and important person, he was made entirely of metal. Machinery within him, something like the works of a clock, made him move; other machinery made him talk; still other machinery made him think. Although so cleverly constructed, the Clockwork Man was far from perfect. Three separate keys wound up his motion machinery, his speech works, and his thoughts. One or more of these contrivances was likely to run down at a critical moment, leaving poor Tiktok helpless. Also some of his parts were wearing out, through much use, and just now his thought machinery needed repair. The skillful little Wizard of Oz had tinkered with Tiktok's thoughts without being able to get them properly regulated, so he had advised the Clockwork Man to go to the Nome King and secure a new set of springs, which would render his thoughts more elastic and responsive. "Be careful what you say to the Nome King," warned the Wizard. "He has a bad temper and the least little thing makes him angry." Tiktok promised, and the Wizard wound his machinery and set him walking in the direction of the Nome King's dominions, just across the desert from the Land of Oz. He ran down just as he reached the entrance to the underground palace, and there Kaliko, the Nome King's Chief Steward, found him and wound him up again. "I want to see the King," said Tiktok, in his jerky voice. "Well," remarked Kaliko, "it may be safe for a cast-iron person like you to face his Majesty this morning; but you must announce yourself, for should I show my face inside the jewel-studded cavern where the King is now raving, I'd soon look like a dish of mashed potatoes, and be of no further use to anyone." "I'm not a-fraid," said Tiktok. "Then walk in and make yourself at home," answered Kaliko, and threw open the door of the King's cavern. Tiktok promptly walked in and faced the astonished Nome King, to whom he said: "Good morn-ing. I want two new steel springs for my thought-works and a new cog-wheel for my speech-pro-du-cer. How a-bout it, your Maj-es-ty?" The Nome King growled a menacing growl and his eyes were red with rage. "How dare you enter my presence?" he shouted. "I dare an-y-thing," said Tiktok. "I'm not a-fraid of a fat Nome." This was true, yet an unwise speech. Had Tiktok's thoughts been in good working order he would have said something else. The angry Nome King quickly caught up his heavy mace and hurled it straight at Tiktok. When it struck the metal man's breast, the force of the blow burst the bolts which held the plates of his body together and they clattered to the floor in a score of pieces. Hundreds and hundreds of wheels, pins, cogs and springs filled the air like a cloud and then rattled like hail upon the floor.

Where Tiktok had stood was now only a scrap heap and the Nome King was so amazed by the terrible effect of his blow that he stared in wonder. His Majesty's anger quickly cooled. He remembered that the Clockwork Man was a favorite subject of the powerful Princess, Ozma of Oz, who would be sure to resent Tiktok's ruin. "Too bad! too bad!" he muttered, regretfully. "I'm really sorry I made junk of the fellow. I didn't know he'd break." "You'd better be," remarked Kaliko, who now ventured to enter the room. "You'll have a war on your hands when Ozma hears of this, and the chances are you will lose your throne and your kingdom." The Nome King turned pale, for he loved to rule the Nomes and did not know of any other way to earn a living in case Ozma fought and conquered him. "Do—do you think Ozma will be angry?" he asked anxiously. "I'm sure of it," said Kaliko. "And she has the right to be. You've made scrap-iron of her favorite." The King groaned. "Sweep him up and throw the rubbish into the black pit," he commanded; and then he shut himself up in his private den and for days would see no one, because he was so ashamed of his unreasoning anger and so feared the results of his rash act. Kaliko swept up the pieces, but he did not throw them into the black pit. Being a clever and skillful mechanic he determined to fit the pieces together again. No man ever faced a greater puzzle; but it was interesting work and Kaliko succeeded. When he found a spring or wheel worn or imperfect, he made a new one. Within two weeks, by working steadily night and day, the Chief Steward completed his task and put the three sets of clockworks and the last rivet into Tiktok's body. He then wound up the motion machinery, and the Clockwork Man walked up and down the room as naturally as ever. Then Kaliko wound up the thought works and the speech regulator and said to Tiktok: "How do you feel now?" "Fine," said the Clockwork Man. "You have done a ve-ry good job, Kal-i-ko, and saved me from de-struc-tion. Much o-bliged." "Don't mention it," replied the Chief Steward. "I quite enjoyed the work." Just then the Nome King's gong sounded, and Kaliko rushed away through the jewel-studded cavern and into the den where the King had hidden, leaving the doors ajar. "Kaliko," said the King, in a meek voice, "I've been shut up here long enough to repent bitterly the destruction of Tiktok. Of course Ozma will have revenge, and send an army to fight us, but we must take our medicine. One thing comforts me: Tiktok wasn't really a live person; he was only a machine man, and so it wasn't very wicked to stop his clockworks. I couldn't sleep nights, at first, for worry; but there's no more harm in smashing a machine man than in breaking a wax doll. Don't you think so?" "I am too humble to think in the presence of your Majesty," said Kaliko. "Then get me something to eat," commanded the King, "for I'm nearly starved. Two roasted goats, a barrel of cakes and nine mince pies will do me until dinnertime." Kaliko bowed and hurried away to the royal kitchen, forgetting Tiktok, who was wandering around in the outer cavern. Suddenly the Nome King looked up and saw the Clockwork Man standing before him, and at the sight the monarch's eyes grew big and round and he fell a-trembling in every limb. "Away, grim Shadow!" he cried. "You're not here, you know; you're only a hash of cogwheels and springs, lying at the bottom of the black pit. Vanish, thou Vision of the demolished Tiktok, and leave me in peace—for I have bitterly repented!" "Then beg my pardon," said Tiktok in a gruff voice, for Kaliko had forgotten to oil the speech works. But the sound of a voice coming from what he thought a mere vision was too much for the Nome King's shaken nerves. He gave a yell of fear and rushed from the room. Tiktok followed, so the King bolted through the corridors on a swift run and bumped against Kaliko, who was returning with a tray of things to eat. The sound of the breaking dishes, as they struck the floor, added to the King's terror and he yelled again and dashed into a great cavern where a thousand Nomes were at work hammering metal. "Look out! Here comes a phantom clockwork man!" screamed the terrified monarch, and every Nome dropped his tools and made a rush from the cavern, knocking over their King in their mad flight and recklessly trampling upon his prostrate fat body. So, when Tiktok came into the cavern, there was only the Nome King left, and he was rolling upon the rocky floor and howling for mercy, with his eyes fast shut so that he could not see what he was sure was a dreadful phantom that was coming straight toward him. "It oc-curs to me," said Tiktok calmly, "that your Maj-es-ty is act-ing like a ba-by. I am not a phan-tom. A phan-tom is unreal, while I am the real thing." The King rolled over, sat up and opened his eyes. "Didn't I smash you to pieces?" he asked in trembling tones. "Yes," said Tiktok. "Then you are nothing but a junk heap, and this form in which you now appear cannot be real." "It is, though," declared Tiktok. "Kal-i-ko picked up my piec-es and put me to-geth-er a-gain. I'm as good as new, and perhaps bet-ter." "That is true, your Majesty," added Kaliko, who now made his appearance, "and I hope you will forgive me for mending Tiktok. He was quite broken up, after you smashed him, and I found it almost as hard a job to match his pieces as to pick turnips from gooseberry bushes. But I did it," he added proudly. "You are forgiven," announced the Nome King, rising to his feet and drawing a long breath. "I will raise your wages one specto a year, and Tiktok shall return to the Land of Oz loaded with jewels for the Princess Ozma." "That is all right," said Tiktok. "But what I want to know is, why did you hit me with your mace?" "Because I was angry," admitted the King. "When I am angry I always do something that I am sorry for afterward. So I have firmly resolved never to get angry again; unless—unless—" "Unless what, your Majesty?" inquired Kaliko. "Unless something annoys me," said the Nome King. And then he went to his treasure chamber to get the jewels for Princess Ozma of Oz. OZMA AND THE LITTLE WIZARD Once upon a time there lived in the beautiful Emerald City, which lies in the center of the fairy Land of Oz, a lovely girl called Princess Ozma, who was ruler of all that country. And among those who served this girlish Ruler and lived in a cozy suite of rooms in her splendid palace, was a little, withered old man known as the Wizard of Oz. This little Wizard could do a good many queer things in magic; but he was a kind man, with merry, twinkling eyes and a sweet smile; so, instead of fearing him because of his magic, everybody loved him. Now, Ozma was very anxious that all her people who inhabited the pleasant Land of Oz should be happy and contented, and therefore she decided one morning to make a journey to all parts of the country, that she might discover if anything was amiss, or anyone discontented, or if there was any wrong that ought to be righted. She asked the little Wizard to accompany her and he was glad to go. "Shall I take my bag of magic tools with me?" he asked. "Of course," said Ozma. "We may need a lot of magic before we return, for we are going into strange corners of the land, where we may meet with unknown creatures and dangerous adventures." So the Wizard took his bag of magic tools and the two left the Emerald City and wandered over the country for many days, at last reaching a place far up in the mountains which neither of them had ever visited before. Stopping one morning at a cottage, built beside the rocky path which led into a pretty valley beyond, Ozma asked a man: "Are you happy? Have you any complaint to make of your lot?" And the man replied: "We are happy except for three mischievous Imps that live in yonder valley and often come here to annoy us. If

your Highness would only drive away those Imps, I and my family would be very happy and very grateful to you." "Who are these bad Imps?" inquired the girl Ruler. "One

is named Olite, and one Udent and one Ertinent, and they have no respect for anyone or anything. If strangers pass through the valley the Imps jeer at them and make horrid

faces and call names, and often they push travelers out of the path or throw stones at them. Whenever Imp Olite or Imp Udent or Imp Ertinent comes here to bother us, I

and my family run into the house and lock all the doors and windows, and we dare not venture out again until the Imps have gone away." Princess Ozma was grieved to hear

this report and the little Wizard shook his head gravely and said the naughty Imps deserved to be punished. They told the good man they would see what could be done to

protect him and at once entered the valley to seek the dwelling place of the three mischievous creatures. Before long they came upon three caves, hollowed from the rocks,

and in front of each cave squatted a queer little dwarf. Ozma and the Wizard paused to examine them and found them well-shaped, strong and lively. They had big round

ears, flat noses and wide grinning mouths, and their jet-black hair came to points on top of their heads, much resembling horns. Their clothing fitted snugly to their bodies

and limbs and the Imps were so small in size that at first Ozma did not consider them at all dangerous. But one of them suddenly reached out a hand and caught the dress of

the Princess, jerking it so sharply that she nearly fell down, and a moment later another Imp pushed the little Wizard so hard that he bumped against Ozma and both

unexpectedly sat down upon the ground. At this the Imps laughed boisterously and began running around in a circle and kicking dust upon the Royal Princess, who cried in

a sharp voice: "Wizard, do your duty!" The Wizard promptly obeyed. Without rising from the ground he opened his bag, got the tools he required and muttered a magic

spell. Instantly the three Imps became three bushes—of a thorny stubby kind—with their roots in the ground. As the bushes were at first motionless, perhaps through

surprise at their sudden transformation, the Wizard and the Princess found time to rise from the ground and brush the dust off their pretty clothes. Then Ozma turned to the

bushes and said: "The unhappy lot you now endure, my poor Imps, is due entirely to your naughty actions. You can no longer annoy harmless travelers and you must remain

ugly bushes, covered with sharp thorns, until you repent of your bad ways and promise to be good Imps." "They can't help being good now, your Highness," said the

Wizard, who was much pleased with his work, "and the safest plan will be to allow them always to remain bushes." But something must have been wrong with the Wizard's

magic, or the creatures had magic of their own, for no sooner were the words spoken than the bushes began to move. At first they only waved their branches at the girl and

little man, but pretty soon they began to slide over the ground, their roots dragging through the earth, and one pushed itself against the Wizard and pricked him so sharply

with its thorns that he cried out: "Ouch!" and started to run away. Ozma followed, for the other bushes were trying to stick their thorns into her legs and one actually got so

near her that it tore a great rent in her beautiful dress. The girl Princess could run, however, and she followed the fleeing Wizard until he tumbled headfirst over a log and

rolled upon the ground. Then she sprang behind a tree and shouted: "Quick! Transform them into something else." The Wizard heard, but he was much confused by his fall. Grabbing from his bag the first magical tool he could find he transformed the bushes into three white pigs. That astonished the Imps. In the shape of pigs—fat, roly-poly

and cute—they scampered off a little distance and sat down to think about their new condition. Ozma drew a long breath and coming from behind the tree she said: "That

is much better, Wiz, for such pigs as these must be quite harmless. No one need now fear the mischievous Imps." "I intended to transform them into mice," replied the

Wizard, "but in my excitement I worked the wrong magic. However, unless the horrid creatures behave themselves hereafter, they are liable to be killed and eaten. They

would make good chops, sausages or roasts." But the Imps were now angry and had no intention of behaving. As Ozma and the little Wizard turned to resume their journey,

the three pigs rushed forward, dashed between their legs, and tripped them up, so that both lost their balance and toppled over, clinging to one another. As the Wizard tried

to get up he was tripped again and fell across the back of the third pig, which carried him on a run far down the valley until it dumped the little man in the river. Ozma had

been sprawled upon the ground but found she was not hurt, so she picked herself up and ran to the assistance of the Wizard, reaching him just as he was crawling out of the

river, gasping for breath and dripping with water. The girl could not help laughing at his woeful appearance. But he had no sooner wiped the wet from his eyes than one of

the impish pigs tripped him again and sent him into the river for a second bath. The pigs tried to trip Ozma, too, but she ran around a stump and so managed to keep out of

their way. So the Wizard scrambled out of the water again and picked up a sharp stick to defend himself. Then he mumbled a magic mutter which instantly dried his clothes,

after which he hurried to assist Ozma. The pigs were afraid of the sharp stick and kept away from it. "This won't do," said the Princess. "We have accomplished nothing,

for the pig Imps would annoy travelers as much as the real Imps. Transform them into something else, Wiz." The Wizard took time to think. Then he transformed the white

pigs into three blue doves. "Doves," said he, "are the most harmless things in the world." But scarcely had he spoken when the doves flew at them and tried to peck out their

eyes. When they endeavored to shield their eyes with their hands, two of the doves bit the Wizard's fingers and another caught the pretty pink ear of the Princess in its bill

and gave it such a cruel tweak that she cried out in pain and threw her skirt over her head. "These birds are worse than pigs, Wizard," she called to her companion. "Nothing

is harmless that is animated by impudent anger or impertinent mischief. You must transform the Imps into something that is not alive." The Wizard was pretty busy, just

then, driving off the birds, but he managed to open his bag of magic and find a charm which instantly transformed the doves into three buttons. As they fell to the ground

he picked them up and smiled with satisfaction. The tin button was Imp Olite, the brass button was Imp Udent and the lead button was Imp Ertinent. These buttons the

Wizard placed in a little box which he put in his jacket pocket. "Now," said he, "the Imps cannot annoy travelers, for we shall carry them back with us to the Emerald City."

"But we dare not use the buttons," said Ozma, smiling once more now that the danger was over. "Why not?" asked the Wizard. "I intend to sew them upon my coat and

watch them carefully. The spirits of the Imps are still in the buttons, and after a time they will repent and be sorry for their naughtiness. Then they will decide to be very good

in the future. When they feel that way, the tin button will turn to silver and the brass to gold, while the lead button will become aluminum. I shall then restore them to their proper forms, changing their names to pretty names instead of the ugly ones they used to bear. Thereafter the three Imps will become good citizens of the Land of Oz and I think you will find they will prove faithful subjects of our beloved Princess Ozma." "Ah, that is magic well worthwhile," exclaimed Ozma, well pleased. "There is no doubt, my friend, but that you are a very clever Wizard."

JACK PUMPKINHEAD AND THE SAWHORSE In a room of the Royal Palace of the Emerald City of Oz hangs a Magic Picture, in which are shown all the important scenes that transpire in those fairy dominions. The scenes shift constantly and by watching them, Ozma, the girl Ruler, is able to discover events taking place in any part of her kingdom. One day she saw in her Magic Picture that a little girl and a little boy had wandered together into a great, gloomy forest at the far west of Oz and had become hopelessly lost. Their friends were seeking them in the wrong direction and unless Ozma came to their rescue the little ones would never be found in time to save them from starving. So the Princess sent a message to Jack Pumpkinhead and asked him to come to the palace. This personage, one of the queerest of the queer inhabitants of Oz, was an old friend and companion of Ozma. His form was made of rough sticks fitted together and dressed in ordinary clothes. His head was a pumpkin with a face carved upon it, and was set on top a sharp stake which formed his neck. Jack was active, good-natured and a general favorite; but his pumpkin head was likely to spoil with age, so in order to secure a good supply of heads he grew a big field of pumpkins and lived in the middle of it, his house being a huge pumpkin hollowed out. Whenever he needed a new head he picked a pumpkin, carved a face on it and stuck it upon the stake of his neck, throwing away the old head as of no further use. The day Ozma sent for him Jack was in prime condition and was glad to be of service in rescuing the lost children. Ozma made him a map, showing just where the forest was and how to get to it and the paths he must take to reach the little ones. Then she said: "You'd better ride the Sawhorse, for he is swift and intelligent and will help you accomplish your task." "All right," answered Jack, and went to the royal stable to tell the Sawhorse to be ready for the trip. This remarkable animal was not unlike Jack Pumpkinhead in form, although so different in shape. Its body was a log, with four sticks stuck into it for legs. A branch at one end of the log served as a tail, while in the other end was chopped a gash that formed a mouth. Above this were two small knots that did nicely for eyes. The Sawhorse was the favorite steed of Ozma and to prevent its wooden legs from wearing out she had them shod with plates of gold. Jack said "Good morning" to the Sawhorse and placed upon the creature's back a saddle of purple leather, studded with jewels. "Where now?" asked the horse, blinking its knot eyes at Jack. "We're going to rescue two babes in the wood," was the reply. Then he climbed into the saddle and the wooden animal pranced out of the stable, through the streets of the Emerald City and out upon the highway leading to the western forest where the children were lost. Small though he was, the Sawhorse was swift and untiring. By nightfall they were in the far west and quite close to the forest they sought. They passed the night standing quietly by the roadside. They needed no food, for their wooden bodies never became hungry; nor did they sleep, because they never tired. At daybreak they continued their journey and soon reached the forest. Jack now examined the map Ozma had given him and found the right path to take, which the Sawhorse obediently followed. Underneath the trees all was silent and gloomy and Jack beguiled the way by whistling gayly as the Sawhorse trotted along. The paths branched so many times and in so many different ways that the Pumpkinhead was often obliged to consult Ozma's map, and finally the Sawhorse became suspicious. "Are you sure you are right?" it asked. "Of course," answered Jack. "Even a Pumpkinhead whose brains are seeds can follow so clear a map as this. Every path is plainly marked, and here is a cross where the children are." Finally they reached a place, in the very heart of the forest, where they came upon the lost boy and girl. But they found the two children bound fast to the trunk of a big tree, at the foot of which they were sitting. When the rescuers arrived, the little girl was sobbing bitterly and the boy was trying to comfort her, though he was probably frightened as much as she. "Cheer up, my dears," said Jack, getting out of the saddle. "I have come to take you back to your parents. But why are you bound to that tree?" "Because," cried a small, sharp voice, "they are thieves and robbers. That's why!" "Dear me!" said Jack, looking around to see who had spoken. The voice seemed to come from above. A big grey squirrel was sitting upon a low branch of the tree. Upon the squirrel's head was a circle of gold, with a diamond set in the center of it. He was running up and down the limbs and chattering excitedly. "These children," continued the squirrel, angrily, "robbed our storehouse of all the nuts we had saved up for winter. Therefore, being King of all the Squirrels in this forest, I ordered them arrested and put in prison, as you now see them. They had no right to steal our provisions and we are going to punish them." "We were hungry," said the boy, pleadingly, "and we found a hollow tree full of nuts, and ate them to keep alive. We didn't want to starve when there was food right in front of us." "Quite right," remarked Jack, nodding his pumpkin head. "I don't blame you one bit, under the circumstances. Not a bit." Then he began to untie the ropes that bound the children to the tree. "Stop that!" cried the King Squirrel, chattering and whisking about. "You mustn't release our prisoners. You have no right to." But Jack paid no attention to the protest. His wooden fingers were awkward and it took him some time to untie the ropes. When at last he succeeded, the tree was full of squirrels, called together by their King, and they were furious at losing their prisoners. From the tree they began to hurl nuts at the Pumpkinhead, who laughed at them as he helped the two children to their feet. Now, at the top of this tree was a big dead limb, and so many squirrels gathered upon it that suddenly it broke away and fell to the ground. Poor Jack was standing directly under it and when the limb struck him it smashed his pumpkin head into a pulpy mass and sent Jack's wooden form tumbling, to stop with a bump against a tree a dozen feet away. He sat up, a moment afterward, but when he felt for his head it was gone. He could not see; neither could he speak. It was perhaps the greatest misfortune that could have happened to Jack Pumpkinhead, and the squirrels were delighted. They danced around in the tree in great glee as they saw Jack's plight. The boy and girl were indeed free, but their protector was ruined. The Sawhorse was there, however, and in his way he was wise. He had seen the accident and knew that the smashed pumpkin would never again serve Jack as a head. So he said to the children, who were frightened at this accident to their newfound friend: "Pick up the Pumpkinhead's body and set it on my saddle. Then mount behind it and hold on. We must get out of this forest as soon as we can, or the squirrels may capture you again. I must guess at the right path, for Jack's map is no longer of any use to him since that limb destroyed his head." The two children lifted Jack's body, which was not at all heavy, and placed it upon the saddle. Then they climbed up behind it and the Sawhorse immediately turned and trotted back along the path he had come, bearing all three with ease. However, when the path began to branch into many paths, all following different directions, the wooden animal became puzzled and soon was wandering aimlessly about, without any hope of finding the right way. Toward evening they came upon a fine fruit tree, which furnished the children a supper, and at night the little ones lay upon a bed of leaves while the Sawhorse stood watch, with the limp, headless form of poor Jack Pumpkinhead lying helpless across the saddle.

Now, Ozma had seen in her Magic Picture all that had happened in the forest, so she sent the little Wizard, mounted upon the Cowardly Lion, to save the unfortunates. The Lion knew the forest well and when he reached it he bounded straight through the tangled paths to where the Sawhorse was wandering, with Jack and the two children on his back. The Wizard was grieved at the sight of the headless Jack, but believed he could save him. He first led the Sawhorse out of the forest and restored the boy and girl to the arms of their anxious friends, and then he sent the Lion back to Ozma to tell her what had happened. The Wizard now mounted the Sawhorse and supported Jack's form on the long ride to the pumpkin field. When they arrived at Jack's house the Wizard selected a fine pumpkin—not too ripe—and very neatly carved a face on it. Then he stuck the pumpkin solidly on Jack's neck and asked him: "Well, old friend, how do you feel?" "Fine!" replied Jack, and shook the hand of the little Wizard gratefully. "You have really saved my life, for without your assistance I could not have found my way home to get a new head. But I'm all right, now, and I shall be very careful not to get this beautiful head smashed." And he shook the Wizard's hand again. "Are the brains in the new head any better than the old ones?" inquired the Sawhorse, who had watched Jack's restoration. "Why, these seeds are quite tender," replied the Wizard, "so they will give our friend tender thoughts. But, to speak truly, my dear Sawhorse, Jack Pumpkinhead, with all his good qualities, will never be noted for his wisdom." THE SCARECROW AND THE TIN WOODMAN There lived in the Land of Oz two queerly made men who were the best of friends. They were so much happier when together that they were seldom apart; yet they liked to separate, once in a while, that they might enjoy the pleasure of meeting again. One was a Scarecrow. That means he was a suit of blue Munchkin clothes, stuffed with straw, on top of which was fastened a round cloth head, filled with bran to hold it in shape. On the head were painted two eyes, two ears, a nose and a mouth. The Scarecrow had never been much of a success in scaring crows, but he prided himself on being a superior man, because he could feel no pain, was never tired and did not have to eat or drink. His brains were sharp, for the Wizard of Oz had put pins and needles in the Scarecrow's brains. The other man was made all of tin, his arms and legs and head being cleverly jointed so that he could move them freely. He was known as the Tin Woodman, having at one time been a woodchopper, and everyone loved him because the Wizard had given him an excellent heart of red plush. The Tin Woodman lived in a magnificent tin castle, built on his country estate in the Winkie Land, not far from the Emerald City of Oz. It had pretty tin furniture and was surrounded by lovely gardens in which were many tin trees and beds of tin flowers. The palace of the Scarecrow was not far distant, on the banks of a river, and this palace was in the shape of an immense ear of corn. One morning the Tin Woodman went to visit his friend the Scarecrow, and as they had nothing better to do they decided to take a boat ride on the river. So they got into the Scarecrow's boat, which was formed from a big corncob, hollowed out and pointed at both ends and decorated around the edges with brilliant jewels. The sail was of purple silk and glittered gayly in the sunshine. There was a good breeze that day, so the boat glided swiftly

over the water. By and by they came to a smaller river that flowed from out a deep forest, and the Tin Woodman proposed they sail up this stream, as it would be cool and

shady beneath the trees of the forest. So the Scarecrow, who was steering, turned the boat up the stream and the friends continued talking together of old times and the

wonderful adventures they had met with while traveling with Dorothy, the little Kansas girl. They became so much interested in this talk that they forgot to notice that the

boat was now sailing through the forest, or that the stream was growing more narrow and crooked. Suddenly the Scarecrow glanced up and saw a big rock just ahead of

them. "Look out!" he cried; but the warning came too late. The Tin Woodman sprang to his feet just as the boat bumped into the rock, and the jar made him lose his balance.

He toppled and fell overboard and being made of tin he sank to the bottom of the water in an instant and lay there at full length, face up. Immediately the Scarecrow threw

out the anchor, so as to hold the boat in that place, and then he leaned over the side and through the clear water looked at his friend sorrowfully. "Dear me!" he exclaimed;

"what a misfortune!" "It is, indeed," replied the Tin Woodman, speaking in muffled tones because so much water covered him. "I cannot drown, of course, but I must lie

here until you find a way to get me out. Meantime, the water is soaking into all my joints and I shall become badly rusted before I am rescued." "Very true," agreed the

Scarecrow; "but be patient, my friend, and I'll dive down and get you. My straw will not rust, and is easily replaced, if damaged, so I'm not afraid of the water." The

Scarecrow now took off his hat and made a dive from the boat into the water; but he was so light in weight that he barely dented the surface of the stream, nor could he reach

the Tin Woodman with his outstretched straw arms. So he floated to the boat and climbed into it, saying the while: "Do not despair, my friend. We have an extra anchor

aboard, and I will tie it around my waist, to make me sink, and dive again." "Don't do that!" called the tin man. "That would anchor you also to the bottom, where I am, and

we'd both be helpless." "True enough," sighed the Scarecrow, wiping his wet face with a handkerchief; and then he gave a cry of astonishment, for he found he had wiped

off one painted eye and now had but one eye to see with. "How dreadful!" said the poor Scarecrow. "That eye must have been painted in watercolor, instead of oil. I must

be careful not to wipe off the other eye, for then I could not see to help you at all." A shriek of elfish laughter greeted this speech and looking up the Scarecrow found the

trees full of black crows, who seemed much amused by the straw man's one-eyed countenance. He knew the crows well, however, and they had usually been friendly to him

because he had never deceived them into thinking he was a meat man—the sort of man they really feared. "Don't laugh," said he; "you may lose an eye yourselves someday."

"We couldn't look as funny as you, if we did," replied one old crow, the king of them. "But what has gone wrong with you?" "The Tin Woodman, my dear friend and

companion, has fallen overboard and is now on the bottom of the river," said the Scarecrow. "I'm trying to get him out again, but I fear I shall not succeed." "Why, it's easy

enough," declared the old crow. "Tie a string to him and all of my crows will fly down, take hold of the string, and pull him up out of the water. There are hundreds of us

here, so our united strength could lift much more than that." "But I can't tie a string to him," replied the Scarecrow. "My straw is so light that I am unable to dive through the water. I've tried it, and knocked one eye out." "Can't you fish for him?" "Ah, that is a good idea," said the Scarecrow. "I'll make the attempt." He found a fishline in the

boat, with a stout hook at the end of it. No bait was needed, so the Scarecrow dropped the hook into the water till it touched the Woodman. "Hook it into a joint," advised

the crow, who was now perched upon a branch that stuck far out and bent down over the water. The Scarecrow tried to do this, but having only one eye he could not see the

joints very clearly. "Hurry up, please," begged the Tin Woodman; "you've no idea how damp it is down here." "Can't you help?" asked the crow. "How?" inquired the tin

man. "Catch the line and hook it around your neck." The Tin Woodman made the attempt and after several trials wound the line around his neck and hooked it securely.

"Good!" cried the King Crow, a mischievous old fellow. "Now, then, we'll all grab the line and pull you out." At once the air was filled with black crows, each of whom

seized the cord with beak or talons. The Scarecrow watched them with much interest and forgot that he had tied the other end of the line around his own waist, so he would

not lose it while fishing for his friend. "All together for the good caws!" shrieked the King Crow, and with a great flapping of wings the birds rose into the air. The Scarecrow

clapped his stuffed hands in glee as he saw his friend drawn from the water into the air; but the next moment the straw man was himself in the air, his stuffed legs kicking

wildly; for the crows had flown straight up through the trees. On one end of the line dangled the Tin Woodman, hung by the neck, and on the other dangled the Scarecrow,

hung by the waist and clinging fast to the spare anchor of the boat, which he had seized hoping to save himself. "Hi, there—be careful!" shouted the Scarecrow to the crows.

"Don't take us so high. Land us on the riverbank." But the crows were bent on mischief. **They thought it a good joke to bother the two, now that they held them captive.**

"Here's where the crows scare the Scarecrow!" chuckled the naughty King Crow, and at his command the birds flew over the forest to where a tall dead tree stood higher

than all the other trees. At the very top was a crotch, formed by two dead limbs, and into the crotch the crows dropped the center of the line. Then, letting go their hold, they

flew away, chattering with laughter, and left the two friends suspended high in the air—one on each side of the tree. Now the Tin Woodman was much heavier than the

Scarecrow, but the reason they balanced so nicely was because the straw man still clung fast to the iron anchor. There they hung, not ten feet apart, yet unable to reach the

bare tree trunk. "For goodness sake don't drop that anchor," said the Tin Woodman anxiously. "Why not?" inquired the Scarecrow. "If you did I'd tumble to the ground,

where my tin would be badly dented by the fall. Also you would shoot into the air and alight somewhere among the treetops." "Then," said the Scarecrow, earnestly, "I shall

hold fast to the anchor." For a time they both dangled in silence, the breeze swaying them gently to and fro. Finally the tin man said: "Here is an emergency, friend, where

only brains can help us. We must think of some way to escape." "I'll do the thinking," replied the Scarecrow. "My brains are the sharpest." He thought so long that the tin

man grew tired and tried to change his position, but found his joints had already rusted so badly that he could not move them. And his oilcan was back in the boat. "Do you

suppose your brains are rusted, friend Scarecrow?" he asked in a weak voice, for his jaws would scarcely move. "No, indeed. Ah, here's an idea at last!" And with this the

Scarecrow clapped his hands to his head, forgetting the anchor, which tumbled to the ground. The result was astonishing; for, just as the tin man had said, the light Scarecrow flew into the air, sailed over the top of the tree and landed in a bramblebush, while the tin man fell plump to the ground, and landing on a bed of dry leaves was not dented at all. The Tin Woodman's joints were so rusted, however, that he was unable to move, while the thorns held the Scarecrow a fast prisoner. While they were in this sad plight the sound of hoofs was heard and along the forest path rode the little Wizard of Oz, seated on a wooden Sawhorse. He smiled when he saw the one-eyed head of the Scarecrow sticking out of the bramblebush, but he helped the poor straw man out of his prison. "Thank you, dear Wiz," said the grateful Scarecrow. "Now we must get the oilcan and rescue the Tin Woodman." Together they ran to the riverbank, but the boat was floating in midstream and the Wizard was obliged to mumble some magic words to draw it to the bank, so the Scarecrow could get the oilcan. Then back they flew to the tin man, and while the Scarecrow carefully oiled each joint the little Wizard moved the joints gently back and forth until they worked freely. After an hour of this labor the Tin Woodman was again on his feet, and although still a little stiff he managed to walk to the boat. The Wizard and the Sawhorse also got aboard the corncob craft and together they returned to the Scarecrow's palace. But the Tin Woodman was very careful not to stand up in the boat again. THE END. CHAPTER I The Cyclone Dorothy lived in the midst of the great Kansas prairies, with Uncle Henry, who was a farmer, and Aunt Em, who was the farmer's wife. Their house was small, for the lumber to build it had to be carried by wagon many miles. There were four walls, a floor and a roof, which made one room; and this room contained a rusty-looking cookstove, a cupboard for the dishes, a table, three or four chairs, and the beds. Uncle Henry and Aunt Em had a big bed in one corner, and Dorothy a little bed in another corner. There was no garret at all, and no cellar—except a small hole dug in the ground, called a cyclone cellar, where the family could go in case one of those great whirlwinds arose, mighty enough to crush any building in its path. It was reached by a trapdoor in the middle of the floor, from which a ladder led down into the small, dark hole. When Dorothy stood in the doorway and looked around, she could see nothing but the great gray prairie on every side. Not a tree nor a house broke the broad sweep of flat country that reached to the edge of the sky in all directions. The sun had baked the plowed land into a gray mass, with little cracks running through it. Even the grass was not green, for the sun had burned the tops of the long blades until they were the same gray color to be seen everywhere. Once the house had been painted, but the sun blistered the paint and the rains washed it away, and now the house was as dull and gray as everything else. When Aunt Em came there to live she was a young, pretty wife. The sun and wind had changed her, too. They had taken the sparkle from her eyes and left them a sober gray; they had taken the red from her cheeks and lips, and they were gray also. She was thin and gaunt, and never smiled now. When Dorothy, who was an orphan, first came to her, Aunt Em had been so startled by the child's laughter that she would scream and press her hand upon her heart whenever Dorothy's merry voice reached her ears; and she still looked at the little girl with wonder that she could find anything to laugh at. Uncle Henry never laughed. He worked hard from morning till night and did not know what joy was. He was gray also, from his long beard to his rough boots, and he looked stern and solemn, and rarely spoke. It was Toto that made Dorothy laugh, and saved her from growing as gray as her other surroundings. Toto was not gray; he was a little black dog, with long silky hair and small black eyes that twinkled merrily on either side of his funny, wee nose. Toto played all day long, and Dorothy played with him, and loved him dearly. Today, however, they were not playing. Uncle Henry sat upon

the doorstep and looked anxiously at the sky, which was even grayer than usual. Dorothy stood in the door with Toto in her arms, and looked at the sky too. Aunt Em was

washing the dishes. From the far north they heard a low wail of the wind, and Uncle Henry and Dorothy could see where the long grass bowed in waves before the coming

storm. There now came a sharp whistling in the air from the south, and as they turned their eyes that way they saw ripples in the grass coming from that direction also.

Suddenly Uncle Henry stood up. "There's a cyclone coming, Em," he called to his wife. "I'll go look after the stock." Then he ran toward the sheds where the cows and

horses were kept. Aunt Em dropped her work and came to the door. One glance told her of the danger close at hand. "Quick, Dorothy!" she screamed. "Run for the cellar!"

Toto jumped out of Dorothy's arms and hid under the bed, and the girl started to get him. Aunt Em, badly frightened, threw open the trapdoor in the floor and climbed down

the ladder into the small, dark hole. Dorothy caught Toto at last and started to follow her aunt. When she was halfway across the room there came a great shriek from the

wind, and the house shook so hard that she lost her footing and sat down suddenly upon the floor. Then a strange thing happened. The house whirled around two or three

times and rose slowly through the air. Dorothy felt as if she were going up in a balloon. The north and south winds met where the house stood, and made it the exact center

of the cyclone. In the middle of a cyclone the air is generally still, but the great pressure of the wind on every side of the house raised it up higher and higher, until it was at

the very top of the cyclone; and there it remained and was carried miles and miles away as easily as you could carry a feather. It was very dark, and the wind howled horribly

around her, but Dorothy found she was riding quite easily. After the first few whirls around, and one other time when the house tipped badly, she felt as if she were being

rocked gently, like a baby in a cradle. Toto did not like it. He ran about the room, now here, now there, barking loudly; but Dorothy sat quite still on the floor and waited to

see what would happen. Once Toto got too near the open trapdoor, and fell in; and at first the little girl thought she had lost him. But soon she saw one of his ears sticking

up through the hole, for the strong pressure of the air was keeping him up so that he could not fall. She crept to the hole, caught Toto by the ear, and dragged him into the

room again, afterward closing the trapdoor so that no more accidents could happen. Hour after hour passed away, and slowly Dorothy got over her fright; but she felt quite

lonely, and the wind shrieked so loudly all about her that she nearly became deaf. At first she had wondered if she would be dashed to pieces when the house fell again; but

as the hours passed and nothing terrible happened, she stopped worrying and resolved to wait calmly and see what the future would bring. At last she crawled over the

swaying floor to her bed, and lay down upon it; and Toto followed and lay down beside her. In spite of the swaying of the house and the wailing of the wind, Dorothy soon

closed her eyes and fell fast asleep. CHAPTER II The Council with the Munchkins She was awakened by a shock, so sudden and severe that if Dorothy had not been lying

on the soft bed she might have been hurt. As it was, the jar made her catch her breath and wonder what had happened; and Toto put his cold little nose into her face and

whined dismally. Dorothy sat up and noticed that the house was not moving; nor was it dark, for the bright sunshine came in at the window, flooding the little room. She sprang from her bed and with Toto at her heels ran and opened the door. The little girl gave a cry of amazement and looked about her, her eyes growing bigger and bigger

at the wonderful sights she saw. The cyclone had set the house down very gently—for a cyclone—in the midst of a country of marvelous beauty. There were lovely patches

of greensward all about, with stately trees bearing rich and luscious fruits. Banks of gorgeous flowers were on every hand, and birds with rare and brilliant plumage sang and

fluttered in the trees and bushes. A little way off was a small brook, rushing and sparkling along between green banks, and murmuring in a voice very grateful to a little girl

who had lived so long on the dry, gray prairies. While she stood looking eagerly at the strange and beautiful sights, she noticed coming toward her a group of the queerest

people she had ever seen. They were not as big as the grown folk she had always been used to; but neither were they very small. In fact, they seemed about as tall as Dorothy,

who was a well-grown child for her age, although they were, so far as looks go, many years older. Three were men and one a woman, and all were oddly dressed. They wore

round hats that rose to a small point a foot above their heads, with little bells around the brims that tinkled sweetly as they moved. The hats of the men were blue; the little

woman's hat was white, and she wore a white gown that hung in pleats from her shoulders. Over it were sprinkled little stars that glistened in the sun like diamonds. The men

were dressed in blue, of the same shade as their hats, and wore well-polished boots with a deep roll of blue at the tops. The men, Dorothy thought, were about as old as Uncle

Henry, for two of them had beards. But the little woman was doubtless much older. Her face was covered with wrinkles, her hair was nearly white, and she walked rather

stiffly. When these people drew near the house where Dorothy was standing in the doorway, they paused and whispered among themselves, as if afraid to come farther. But

the little old woman walked up to Dorothy, made a low bow and said, in a sweet voice: "You are welcome, most noble Sorceress, to the land of the Munchkins. We are so

grateful to you for having killed the Wicked Witch of the East, and for setting our people free from bondage." Dorothy listened to this speech with wonder. What could the

little woman possibly mean by calling her a sorceress, and saying she had killed the Wicked Witch of the East? Dorothy was an innocent, harmless little girl, who had been

carried by a cyclone many miles from home; and she had never killed anything in all her life. But the little woman evidently expected her to answer; so Dorothy said, with

hesitation, "You are very kind, but there must be some mistake. I have not killed anything." "Your house did, anyway," replied the little old woman, with a laugh, "and that

is the same thing. See!" she continued, pointing to the corner of the house. "There are her two feet, still sticking out from under a block of wood." Dorothy looked, and gave

a little cry of fright. There, indeed, just under the corner of the great beam the house rested on, two feet were sticking out, shod in Silver Shoes with pointed toes. "Oh, dear!

Oh, dear!" cried Dorothy, clasping her hands together in dismay. "The house must have fallen on her. Whatever shall we do?" "There is nothing to be done," said the little

woman calmly. "But who was she?" asked Dorothy. "She was the Wicked Witch of the East, as I said," answered the little woman. "She has held all the Munchkins in

bondage for many years, making them slave for her night and day. Now they are all set free, and are grateful to you for the favor." "Who are the Munchkins?" inquired

Dorothy. "They are the people who live in this land of the East where the Wicked Witch ruled." "Are you a Munchkin?" asked Dorothy. "No, but I am their friend, although

I live in the land of the North. When they saw the Witch of the East was dead the Munchkins sent a swift messenger to me, and I came at once. I am the Witch of the North."

"Oh, gracious!" cried Dorothy. "Are you a real witch?" "Yes, indeed," answered the little woman. "But I am a good witch, and the people love me. I am not as powerful as

the Wicked Witch was who ruled here, or I should have set the people free myself." "But I thought all witches were wicked," said the girl, who was half frightened at facing

a real witch. "Oh, no, that is a great mistake. There were only four witches in all the Land of Oz, and two of them, those who live in the North and the South, are good

witches. I know this is true, for I am one of them myself, and cannot be mistaken. Those who dwelt in the East and the West were, indeed, wicked witches; but now that you

have killed one of them, there is but one Wicked Witch in all the Land of Oz—the one who lives in the West." "But," said Dorothy, after a moment's thought, "Aunt Em

has told me that the witches were all dead—years and years ago." "Who is Aunt Em?" inquired the little old woman. "She is my aunt who lives in Kansas, where I came

from." The Witch of the North seemed to think for a time, with her head bowed and her eyes upon the ground. Then she looked up and said, "I do not know where Kansas

is, for I have never heard that country mentioned before. But tell me, is it a civilized country?" "Oh, yes," replied Dorothy. "Then that accounts for it. In the civilized

countries I believe there are no witches left, nor wizards, nor sorceresses, nor magicians. But, you see, the Land of Oz has never been civilized, for we are cut off from all the

rest of the world. Therefore we still have witches and wizards amongst us." "Who are the wizards?" asked Dorothy. "Oz himself is the Great Wizard," answered the Witch,

sinking her voice to a whisper. "He is more powerful than all the rest of us together. He lives in the City of Emeralds." Dorothy was going to ask another question, but just

then the Munchkins, who had been standing silently by, gave a loud shout and pointed to the corner of the house where the Wicked Witch had been lying. "What is it?" asked

the little old woman, and looked, and began to laugh. The feet of the dead Witch had disappeared entirely, and nothing was left but the Silver Shoes. "She was so old,"

explained the Witch of the North, "that she dried up quickly in the sun. That is the end of her. But the Silver Shoes are yours, and you shall have them to wear." She reached

down and picked up the shoes, and after shaking the dust out of them handed them to Dorothy. "The Witch of the East was proud of those Silver Shoes," said one of the

Munchkins, "and there is some charm connected with them; but what it is we never knew." Dorothy carried the shoes into the house and placed them on the table. Then she

came out again to the Munchkins and said: "I am anxious to get back to my aunt and uncle, for I am sure they will worry about me. Can you help me find my way?" The

Munchkins and the Witch first looked at one another, and then at Dorothy, and then shook their heads. "At the East, not far from here," said one, "there is a great desert, and

none could live to cross it." "It is the same at the South," said another, "for I have been there and seen it. The South is the country of the Quadlings." "I am told," said the

third man, "that it is the same at the West. And that country, where the Winkies live, is ruled by the Wicked Witch of the West, who would make you her slave if you passed

her way." "The North is my home," said the old lady, "and at its edge is the same great desert that surrounds this Land of Oz. I'm afraid, my dear, you will have to live with

us." Dorothy began to sob at this, for she felt lonely among all these strange people. Her tears seemed to grieve the kindhearted Munchkins, for they immediately took out their handkerchiefs and began to weep also. As for the little old woman, she took off her cap and balanced the point on the end of her nose, while she counted "One, two, three" in a solemn voice. At once the cap changed to a slate, on which was written in big, white chalk marks: "LET DOROTHY GO TO THE CITY OF EMERALDS."

The little old woman took the slate from her nose, and having read the words on it, asked, "Is your name Dorothy, my dear?" "Yes," answered the child, looking up and drying her tears. "Then you must go to the City of Emeralds. Perhaps Oz will help you." "Where is this city?" asked Dorothy. "It is exactly in the center of the country, and is ruled by Oz, the Great Wizard I told you of." "Is he a good man?" inquired the girl anxiously. "He is a good Wizard. Whether he is a man or not I cannot tell, for I have never seen him." "How can I get there?" asked Dorothy. "You must walk. It is a long journey, through a country that is sometimes pleasant and sometimes dark and terrible. However, I will use all the magic arts I know of to keep you from harm." "Won't you go with me?" pleaded the girl, who had begun to look upon the little old woman as her only friend. "No, I cannot do that," she replied, "but I will give you my kiss, and no one will dare injure a person who has been kissed by the Witch of the North." She came close to Dorothy and kissed her gently on the forehead. Where her lips touched the girl they left a round, shining mark, as Dorothy found out soon after. "The road to the City of Emeralds is paved with yellow brick," said the Witch, "so you cannot miss it. When you get to Oz do not be afraid of him, but tell your story and ask him to help you. Good-bye, my dear." The three Munchkins bowed low to her and wished her a pleasant journey, after which they walked away through the trees. The Witch gave Dorothy a friendly little nod, whirled around on her left heel three times, and straightway disappeared, much to the surprise of little Toto, who barked after her loudly enough when she had gone, because he had been afraid even to growl while she stood by. But Dorothy, knowing her to be a witch, had expected her to disappear in just that way, and was not surprised in the least. CHAPTER III How Dorothy Saved the Scarecrow When Dorothy was left alone she began to feel hungry. So she went to the cupboard and cut herself some bread, which she spread with butter. She gave some to Toto, and taking a pail from the shelf she carried it down to the little brook and filled it with clear, sparkling water. Toto ran over to the trees and began to bark at the birds sitting there. Dorothy went to get him, and saw such delicious fruit hanging from the branches that she gathered some of it, finding it just what she wanted to help out her breakfast. Then she went back to the house, and having helped herself and Toto to a good drink of the cool, clear water, she set about making ready for the journey to the City of Emeralds. Dorothy had only one other dress, but that happened to be clean and was hanging on a peg beside her bed. It was gingham, with checks of white and blue; and although the blue was somewhat faded with many washings, it was still a pretty frock. The girl washed herself carefully, dressed herself in the clean gingham, and tied her pink sunbonnet on her head. She took a little basket and filled it with bread from the cupboard, laying a white cloth over the top. Then she looked down at her feet and noticed how old and worn her shoes were. "They surely will never do for a long journey, Toto," she said. And Toto looked up into her face with his little black eyes and wagged his tail to show he knew what she meant. At that moment Dorothy saw lying on the table the Silver Shoes that had belonged to the Witch of the East. "I wonder if they will fit me," she said to Toto. "They would be just the thing to take a long walk in, for they could not wear out." She took off her old leather shoes and tried on the silver ones, which fitted her as well as if they had been made for her. Finally she picked up her basket. "Come along, Toto," she said. "We will go to the Emerald City and ask the Great Oz how to get back to Kansas again." She closed the door, locked it, and put the key carefully in the pocket of her dress. And so, with Toto trotting along soberly behind her, she started on her journey. There were several roads near by, but it did not take her long to find the one paved with yellow bricks. Within a short time she was walking briskly toward the Emerald City, her Silver Shoes tinkling merrily on the hard, yellow road-bed. The sun shone bright and the birds sang sweetly, and Dorothy did not feel nearly so bad as you might think a little girl would who had been suddenly whisked away from her own country and set down in the midst of a strange land. She was surprised, as she walked along, to see how pretty the country was about her. There were neat fences at the sides of the road, painted a dainty blue color, and beyond them were fields of grain and vegetables in abundance. Evidently the Munchkins were good farmers and able to raise large crops. Once in a while she would pass a house, and the people came out to look at her and bow low as she went by; for everyone knew she had been the means of destroying the Wicked Witch and setting them free from bondage. The houses of the Munchkins were odd-looking dwellings, for each was round, with a big dome for a roof. All were painted blue, for in this country of the East blue was the favorite color. Toward evening, when Dorothy was tired with her long walk and began to wonder where she should pass the night, she came to a house rather larger than the rest. On the green lawn before it many men and women were dancing. Five little fiddlers played as loudly as possible, and the people were laughing and singing, while a big table near by was loaded with delicious fruits and nuts, pies and cakes, and many other good things to eat. The people greeted Dorothy kindly, and invited her to supper and to pass the night with them; for this was the home of one of the richest Munchkins in the land, and his friends were gathered with him to celebrate their freedom from the bondage of the Wicked Witch. Dorothy ate a hearty supper and was waited upon by the rich Munchkin himself, whose name was Boq. Then she sat upon a settee and watched the people dance. When Boq saw her Silver Shoes he said, "You must be a great sorceress." "Why?" asked the girl. "Because you wear Silver Shoes and have killed the Wicked Witch. Besides, you have white in your frock, and only witches and sorceresses wear white." "My dress is blue and white checked," said Dorothy, smoothing out the wrinkles in it. "It is kind of you to wear that," said Boq. "Blue is the color of the Munchkins, and white is the witch color. So we know you are a friendly witch." Dorothy did not know what to say to this, for all the people seemed to think her a witch, and she knew very well she was only an ordinary little girl who had come by the chance of a cyclone into a strange land. When she had tired watching the dancing, Boq led her into the house, where he gave her a room with a pretty bed in it. The sheets were made of blue cloth, and Dorothy slept soundly in them till morning, with Toto curled up on the blue rug beside her. She ate a hearty breakfast, and watched a wee Munchkin baby, who played with Toto and pulled his tail and crowed and laughed in a way that greatly amused Dorothy. Toto was a fine curiosity to all the people, for they had never seen a dog before. "How far is it to the Emerald City?" the girl asked. "I do not know," answered Boq gravely, "for I have never been there. It is better for people to keep away from Oz, unless they have business with him. But it is a long way to the Emerald City, and it will take you many days. The country here is rich and pleasant, but you must pass through rough and dangerous places before you reach the end of your journey." This worried Dorothy a little,

but she knew that only the Great Oz could help her get to Kansas again, so she bravely resolved not to turn back. She bade her friends good-bye, and again started along the

road of yellow brick. When she had gone several miles she thought she would stop to rest, and so climbed to the top of the fence beside the road and sat down. There was a

great cornfield beyond the fence, and not far away she saw a Scarecrow, placed high on a pole to keep the birds from the ripe corn. Dorothy leaned her chin upon her hand

and gazed thoughtfully at the Scarecrow. Its head was a small sack stuffed with straw, with eyes, nose, and mouth painted on it to represent a face. An old, pointed blue hat,

that had belonged to some Munchkin, was perched on his head, and the rest of the figure was a blue suit of clothes, worn and faded, which had also been stuffed with straw.

On the feet were some old boots with blue tops, such as every man wore in this country, and the figure was raised above the stalks of corn by means of the pole stuck up its

back. While Dorothy was looking earnestly into the queer, painted face of the Scarecrow, she was surprised to see one of the eyes slowly wink at her. She thought she must

have been mistaken at first, for none of the scarecrows in Kansas ever wink; but presently the figure nodded its head to her in a friendly way. Then she climbed down from

the fence and walked up to it, while Toto ran around the pole and barked. "Good day," said the Scarecrow, in a rather husky voice. "Did you speak?" asked the girl, in

wonder. "Certainly," answered the Scarecrow. "How do you do?" "I'm pretty well, thank you," replied Dorothy politely. "How do you do?" "I'm not feeling well," said the

Scarecrow, with a smile, "for it is very tedious being perched up here night and day to scare away crows." "Can't you get down?" asked Dorothy. "No, for this pole is stuck

up my back. If you will please take away the pole I shall be greatly obliged to you." Dorothy reached up both arms and lifted the figure off the pole, for, being stuffed with

straw, it was quite light. "Thank you very much," said the Scarecrow, when he had been set down on the ground. "I feel like a new man." Dorothy was puzzled at this, for it

sounded queer to hear a stuffed man speak, and to see him bow and walk along beside her. "Who are you?" asked the Scarecrow when he had stretched himself and yawned.

"And where are you going?" "My name is Dorothy," said the girl, "and I am going to the Emerald City, to ask the Great Oz to send me back to Kansas." "Where is the

Emerald City?" he inquired. "And who is Oz?" "Why, don't you know?" she returned, in surprise. "No, indeed. I don't know anything. You see, I am stuffed, so I have no

brains at all," he answered sadly. "Oh," said Dorothy, "I'm awfully sorry for you." "Do you think," he asked, "if I go to the Emerald City with you, that Oz would give me

some brains?" "I cannot tell," she returned, "but you may come with me, if you like. If Oz will not give you any brains you will be no worse off than you are now." "That

is true," said the Scarecrow. "You see," he continued confidentially, "I don't mind my legs and arms and body being stuffed, because I cannot get hurt. If anyone treads on

my toes or sticks a pin into me, it doesn't matter, for I can't feel it. But I do not want people to call me a fool, and if my head stays stuffed with straw instead of with brains,

as yours is, how am I ever to know anything?" "I understand how you feel," said the little girl, who was truly sorry for him. "If you will come with me I'll ask Oz to do all

he can for you." "Thank you," he answered gratefully. They walked back to the road. Dorothy helped him over the fence, and they started along the path of yellow brick for the Emerald City. Toto did not like this addition to the party at first. He smelled around the stuffed man as if he suspected there might be a nest of rats in the straw, and he often growled in an unfriendly way at the Scarecrow. "Don't mind Toto," said Dorothy to her new friend. "He never bites." "Oh, I'm not afraid," replied the Scarecrow. "He can't hurt the straw. Do let me carry that basket for you. I shall not mind it, for I can't get tired. I'll tell you a secret," he continued, as he walked along. "There is only one thing in the world I am afraid of." "What is that?" asked Dorothy; "the Munchkin farmer who made you?" "No," answered the Scarecrow; "it's a lighted match."

CHAPTER IV The Road Through the Forest After a few hours the road began to be rough, and the walking grew so difficult that the Scarecrow often stumbled over the yellow bricks, which were here very uneven. Sometimes, indeed, they were broken or missing altogether, leaving holes that Toto jumped across and Dorothy walked around. As for the Scarecrow, having no brains, he walked straight ahead, and so stepped into the holes and fell at full length on the hard bricks. It never hurt him, however, and Dorothy would pick him up and set him upon his feet again, while he joined her in laughing merrily at his own mishap. The farms were not nearly so well cared for here as they were farther back. There were fewer houses and fewer fruit trees, and the farther they went the more dismal and lonesome the country became. At noon they sat down by the roadside, near a little brook, and Dorothy opened her basket and got out some bread. She offered a piece to the Scarecrow, but he refused. "I am never hungry," he said, "and it is a lucky thing I am not, for my mouth is only painted, and if I should cut a hole in it so I could eat, the straw I am stuffed with would come out, and that would spoil the shape of my head." Dorothy saw at once that this was true, so she only nodded and went on eating her bread. "Tell me something about yourself and the country you came from," said the Scarecrow, when she had finished her dinner. So she told him all about Kansas, and how gray everything was there, and how the cyclone had carried her to this queer Land of Oz. The Scarecrow listened carefully, and said, "I cannot understand why you should wish to leave this beautiful country and go back to the dry, gray place you call Kansas." "That is because you have no brains" answered the girl. "No matter how dreary and gray our homes are, we people of flesh and blood would rather live there than in any other country, be it ever so beautiful. There is no place like home." The Scarecrow sighed. "Of course I cannot understand it," he said. "If your heads were stuffed with straw, like mine, you would probably all live in the beautiful places, and then Kansas would have no people at all. It is fortunate for Kansas that you have brains." "Won't you tell me a story, while we are resting?" asked the child. The Scarecrow looked at her reproachfully, and answered: "My life has been so short that I really know nothing whatever. I was only made day before yesterday. What happened in the world before that time is all unknown to me. Luckily, when the farmer made my head, one of the first things he did was to paint my ears, so that I heard what was going on. There was another Munchkin with him, and the first thing I heard was the farmer saying, 'How do you like those ears?' "'They aren't straight,' answered the other. "'Never mind,' said the farmer. 'They are ears just the same,' which was true enough. "'Now I'll make the eyes,' said the farmer. So he painted my right eye, and as soon as it was finished I found myself looking at him and at everything around me with a great deal of curiosity, for this was my first glimpse of the world. "'That's a rather pretty eye,' remarked the Munchkin who was watching the farmer. 'Blue paint is just the color for eyes.' "'I think I'll make the other a little bigger,' said the farmer. And when the second eye was done I could see much better than before. Then he made my nose and my mouth. But I did not speak, because at that time I didn't know what a mouth was for. I had the fun of watching them make my body and my arms and legs; and when they fastened on my head, at last, I felt very proud, for I thought I was just as good a man as anyone. "'This fellow will scare the crows fast enough,' said the farmer. 'He looks just like a man.' "'Why, he is a man,' said the other, and I quite agreed with him. The farmer carried me under his arm to the cornfield, and set me up on a tall stick, where you found me. He and his friend soon after walked away and left me alone. "I did not like to be deserted this way. So I tried to walk after them. But my feet would not touch the ground, and I was forced to stay on that pole. It was a lonely life to lead, for I had nothing to think of, having been made such a little while before. Many crows and other birds flew into the cornfield, but as soon as they saw me they flew away again, thinking I was a Munchkin; and this pleased me and made me feel that I was quite an important person. By and by an old crow flew near me, and after looking at me carefully he perched upon my shoulder and said: "'I wonder if that farmer thought to fool me in this clumsy manner. Any crow of sense could see that you are only stuffed with straw.' Then he hopped down at my feet and ate all the corn he wanted. The other birds, seeing he was not harmed by me, came to eat the corn too, so in a short time there was a great flock of them about me. "I felt sad at this, for it showed I was not such a good Scarecrow after all; but the old crow comforted me, saying, 'If you only had brains in your head you would be as good a man as any of them, and a better man than some of them. Brains are the only things worth having in this world, no matter whether one is a crow or a man.' "After the crows had gone I thought this over, and decided I would try hard to get some brains. By good luck you came along and pulled me off the stake, and from what you say I am sure the Great Oz will give me brains as soon as we get to the Emerald City." "I hope so," said Dorothy earnestly, "since you seem anxious to have them." "Oh, yes; I am anxious," returned the Scarecrow. "It is such an uncomfortable feeling to know one is a fool." "Well," said the girl, "let us go." And she handed the basket to the Scarecrow. There were no fences at all by the roadside now, and the land was rough and untilled. Toward evening they came to a great forest, where the trees grew so big and close together that their branches met over the road of yellow brick. It was almost dark under the trees, for the branches shut out the daylight; but the travelers did not stop, and went on into the forest. "If this road goes in, it must come out," said the Scarecrow, "and as the Emerald City is at the other end of the road, we must go wherever it leads us." "Anyone would know that," said Dorothy. "Certainly; that is why I know it," returned the Scarecrow. "If it required brains to figure it out, I never should have said it." After an hour or so the light faded away, and they found themselves stumbling along in the darkness. Dorothy could not see at all, but Toto could, for some dogs see very well in the dark; and the Scarecrow declared he could see as well as by day. So she took hold of his arm and managed to get along fairly well. "If you see any house, or any place where we can pass the night," she said, "you must tell me; for it is very uncomfortable walking in the dark." Soon after the Scarecrow stopped. "I see a little cottage at the right of us," he said, "built of logs and branches. Shall we go there?"

"Yes, indeed," answered the child. "I am all tired out." So the Scarecrow led her through the trees until they reached the cottage, and Dorothy entered and found a bed of dried leaves in one corner. She lay down at once, and with Toto beside her soon fell into a sound sleep. The Scarecrow, who was never tired, stood up in another corner and

waited patiently until morning came. CHAPTER V The Rescue of the Tin Woodman When Dorothy awoke the sun was shining through the trees and Toto had long been

out chasing birds around him and squirrels. She sat up and looked around her. There was the Scarecrow, still standing patiently in his corner, waiting for her. "We must go

and search for water," she said to him. "Why do you want water?" he asked. "To wash my face clean after the dust of the road, and to drink, so the dry bread will not stick

in my throat." "It must be inconvenient to be made of flesh," said the Scarecrow thoughtfully, "for you must sleep, and eat and drink. However, you have brains, and it is

worth a lot of bother to be able to think properly." They left the cottage and walked through the trees until they found a little spring of clear water, where Dorothy drank

and bathed and ate her breakfast. She saw there was not much bread left in the basket, and the girl was thankful the Scarecrow did not have to eat anything, for there was

scarcely enough for herself and Toto for the day. When she had finished her meal, and was about to go back to the road of yellow brick, she was startled to hear a deep groan

near by. "What was that?" she asked timidly. "I cannot imagine," replied the Scarecrow; "but we can go and see." Just then another groan reached their ears, and the sound

seemed to come from behind them. They turned and walked through the forest a few steps, when Dorothy discovered something shining in a ray of sunshine that fell

between the trees. She ran to the place and then stopped short, with a little cry of surprise. One of the big trees had been partly chopped through, and standing beside it, with

an uplifted axe in his hands, was a man made entirely of tin. His head and arms and legs were jointed upon his body, but he stood perfectly motionless, as if he could not stir

at all. Dorothy looked at him in amazement, and so did the Scarecrow, while Toto barked sharply and made a snap at the tin legs, which hurt his teeth. "Did you groan?"

asked Dorothy. "Yes," answered the tin man, "I did. I've been groaning for more than a year, and no one has ever heard me before or come to help me." "What can I do for

you?" she inquired softly, for she was moved by the sad voice in which the man spoke. "Get an oilcan and oil my joints," he answered. "They are rusted so badly that I cannot

move them at all; if I am well oiled I shall soon be all right again. You will find an oilcan on a shelf in my cottage." Dorothy at once ran back to the cottage and found the

oilcan, and then she returned and asked anxiously, "Where are your joints?" "Oil my neck, first," replied the Tin Woodman. So she oiled it, and as it was quite badly rusted

the Scarecrow took hold of the tin head and moved it gently from side to side until it worked freely, and then the man could turn it himself. "Now oil the joints in my arms,"

he said. And Dorothy oiled them and the Scarecrow bent them carefully until they were quite free from rust and as good as new. The Tin Woodman gave a sigh of satisfaction

and lowered his axe, which he leaned against the tree. "This is a great comfort," he said. "I have been holding that axe in the air ever since I rusted, and I'm glad to be able

to put it down at last. Now, if you will oil the joints of my legs, I shall be all right once more." So they oiled his legs until he could move them freely; and he thanked them

again and again for his release, for he seemed a very polite creature, and very grateful. "I might have stood there always if you had not come along," he said; "so you have

certainly saved my life. How did you happen to be here?" "We are on our way to the Emerald City to see the Great Oz," she answered, "and we stopped at your cottage to pass the night." "Why do you wish to see Oz?" he asked. "I want him to send me back to Kansas, and the Scarecrow wants him to put a few brains into his head," she replied.

The Tin Woodman appeared to think deeply for a moment. Then he said: "Do you suppose Oz could give me a heart?" "Why, I guess so," Dorothy answered. "It would

be as easy as to give the Scarecrow brains." "True," the Tin Woodman returned. "So, if you will allow me to join your party, I will also go to the Emerald City and ask Oz

to help me." "Come along," said the Scarecrow heartily, and Dorothy added that she would be pleased to have his company. So the Tin Woodman shouldered his axe and

they all passed through the forest until they came to the road that was paved with yellow brick. The Tin Woodman had asked Dorothy to put the oilcan in her basket. "For,"

he said, "if I should get caught in the rain, and rust again, I would need the oilcan badly." It was a bit of good luck to have their new comrade join the party, for soon after

they had begun their journey again they came to a place where the trees and branches grew so thick over the road that the travelers could not pass. But the Tin Woodman set

to work with his axe and chopped so well that soon he cleared a passage for the entire party. Dorothy was thinking so earnestly as they walked along that she did not notice

when the Scarecrow stumbled into a hole and rolled over to the side of the road. Indeed he was obliged to call to her to help him up again. "Why didn't you walk around the

hole?" asked the Tin Woodman. "I don't know enough," replied the Scarecrow cheerfully. "My head is stuffed with straw, you know, and that is why I am going to Oz to

ask him for some brains." "Oh, I see," said the Tin Woodman. "But, after all, brains are not the best things in the world." "Have you any?" inquired the Scarecrow. "No, my

head is quite empty," answered the Woodman. "But once I had brains, and a heart also; so, having tried them both, I should much rather have a heart." "And why is that?"

asked the Scarecrow. "I will tell you my story, and then you will know." So, while they were walking through the forest, the Tin Woodman told the following story: "I was

born the son of a woodman who chopped down trees in the forest and sold the wood for a living. When I grew up, I too became a woodchopper, and after my father died I

took care of my old mother as long as she lived. Then I made up my mind that instead of living alone I would marry, so that I might not become lonely. "There was one of

the Munchkin girls who was so beautiful that I soon grew to love her with all my heart. She, on her part, promised to marry me as soon as I could earn enough money to build

a better house for her; so I set to work harder than ever. But the girl lived with an old woman who did not want her to marry anyone, for she was so lazy she wished the girl

to remain with her and do the cooking and the housework. So the old woman went to the Wicked Witch of the East, and promised her two sheep and a cow if she would

prevent the marriage. Thereupon the Wicked Witch enchanted my axe, and when I was chopping away at my best one day, for I was anxious to get the new house and my

wife as soon as possible, the axe slipped all at once and cut off my left leg. "This at first seemed a great misfortune, for I knew a one-legged man could not do very well as a

woodchopper. So I went to a tinsmith and had him make me a new leg out of tin. The leg worked very well, once I was used to it. But my action angered the Wicked Witch

of the East, for she had promised the old woman I should not marry the pretty Munchkin girl. When I began chopping again, my axe slipped and cut off my right leg. Again

I went to the tinsmith, and again he made me a leg out of tin. After this the enchanted axe cut off my arms, one after the other; but, nothing daunted, I had them replaced with tin ones. The Wicked Witch then made the axe slip and cut off my head, and at first I thought that was the end of me. But the tinsmith happened to come along, and he made me a new head out of tin. "I thought I had beaten the Wicked Witch then, and I worked harder than ever; but I little knew how cruel my enemy could be. She thought of a new way to kill my love for the beautiful Munchkin maiden, and made my axe slip again, so that it cut right through my body, splitting me into two halves. Once more the tinsmith came to my help and made me a body of tin, fastening my tin arms and legs and head to it, by means of joints, so that I could move around as well as ever. But, alas! I had now no heart, so that I lost all my love for the Munchkin girl, and did not care whether I married her or not. I suppose she is still living with the old woman, waiting for me to come after her. "My body shone so brightly in the sun that I felt very proud of it and it did not matter now if my axe slipped, for it could not cut me. There was only one danger—that my joints would rust; but I kept an oilcan in my cottage and took care to oil myself whenever I needed it. However, there came a day when I forgot to do this, and, being caught in a rainstorm, before I thought of the danger my joints had rusted, and I was left to stand in the woods until you came to help me. It was a terrible thing to undergo, but during the year I stood there I had time to think that the greatest loss I had known was the loss of my heart. While I was in love I was the happiest man on earth; but no one can love who has not a heart, and so I am resolved to ask Oz to give me one. If he does, I will go back to the Munchkin maiden and marry her."

Both Dorothy and the Scarecrow had been greatly interested in the story of the Tin Woodman, and now they knew why he was so anxious to get a new heart. "All the same," said the Scarecrow, "I shall ask for brains instead of a heart; for a fool would not know what to do with a heart if he had one." "I shall take the heart," returned the Tin Woodman; "for brains do not make one happy, and happiness is the best thing in the world." Dorothy did not say anything, for she was puzzled to know which of her two friends was right, and she decided if she could only get back to Kansas and Aunt Em, it did not matter so much whether the Woodman had no brains and the Scarecrow no heart, or each got what he wanted. What worried her most was that the bread was nearly gone, and another meal for herself and Toto would empty the basket. To be sure neither the Woodman nor the Scarecrow ever ate anything, but she was not made of tin nor straw, and could not live unless she was fed. CHAPTER VI The Cowardly Lion

All this time Dorothy and her companions had been walking through the thick woods. The road was still paved with yellow brick, but these were much covered by dried branches and dead leaves from the trees, and the walking was not at all good. There were few birds in this part of the forest, for birds love the open country where there is plenty of sunshine. But now and then there came a deep growl from some wild animal hidden among the trees. These sounds made the little girl's heart beat fast, for she did not know what made them; but Toto knew, and he walked close to Dorothy's side, and did not even bark in return. "How long will it be," the child asked of the Tin Woodman, "before we are out of the forest?" "I cannot tell," was the answer, "for I have never been to the Emerald City. But my father went there once, when I was a boy, and he said it was a long journey through a dangerous country, although nearer to the city where Oz dwells the country is beautiful. But I am not afraid so long as I have my oilcan, and nothing can hurt the Scarecrow, while you bear upon your forehead the mark of the Good Witch's kiss, and that will protect you from harm." "But Toto!" said the girl anxiously. "What will protect him?" "We must protect him ourselves if he is in danger," replied the Tin Woodman. Just as he spoke there came from the forest a terrible roar, and the next moment a great Lion bounded into the road. With one blow of his paw he sent the Scarecrow spinning over and over to the edge of the road, and then he struck at the Tin Woodman with his sharp claws. But, to the Lion's surprise, he could make no impression on the tin, although the Woodman fell over in the road and lay still. Little Toto, now that he had an enemy to face, ran barking toward the Lion, and the great beast had opened his mouth to bite the dog, when Dorothy, fearing Toto would be killed, and heedless of danger, rushed forward and slapped the Lion upon his nose as hard as she could, while she cried out: "Don't you dare to bite Toto! You ought to be ashamed of yourself, a big beast like you, to bite a poor little dog!" "I didn't bite him," said the Lion, as he rubbed his nose with his paw where Dorothy had hit it. "No, but you tried to," she retorted. "You are nothing but a big coward." "I know it," said the Lion, hanging his head in shame. "I've always known it. But how can I help it?" "I don't know, I'm sure. To think of your striking a stuffed man, like the poor Scarecrow!" "Is he stuffed?" asked the Lion in surprise, as he watched her pick up the Scarecrow and set him upon his feet, while she patted him into shape again. "Of course he's stuffed," replied Dorothy, who was still angry. "That's why he went over so easily," remarked the Lion. "It astonished me to see him whirl around so. Is the other one stuffed also?" "No," said Dorothy, "he's made of tin." And she helped the Woodman up again. "That's why he nearly blunted my claws," said the Lion. "When they scratched against the tin it made a cold shiver run down my back. What is that little animal you are so tender of?" "He is my dog, Toto," answered Dorothy. "Is he made of tin, or stuffed?" asked the Lion. "Neither. He's a—a—a meat dog," said the girl. "Oh! He's a curious animal and seems remarkably small, now that I look at him. No one would think of biting such a little thing, except a coward like me," continued the Lion sadly. "What makes you a coward?" asked Dorothy, looking at the great beast in wonder, for he was as big as a small horse. "It's a mystery," replied the Lion. "I suppose I was born that way. All the other animals in the forest naturally expect me to be brave, for the Lion is everywhere thought to be the King of Beasts. I learned that if I roared very loudly every living thing was frightened and got out of my way. Whenever I've met a man I've been awfully scared; but I just roared at him, and he has always run away as fast as he could go. If the elephants and the tigers and the bears had ever tried to fight me, I should have run myself—I'm such a coward; but just as soon as they hear me roar they all try to get away from me, and of course I let them go." "But that isn't right. The King of Beasts shouldn't be a coward," said the Scarecrow. "I know it," returned the Lion, wiping a tear from his eye with the tip of his tail. "It is my great sorrow, and makes my life very unhappy. But whenever there is danger, my heart begins to beat fast." "Perhaps you have heart disease," said the Tin Woodman. "It may be," said the Lion. "If you have," continued the Tin Woodman, "you ought to be glad, for it proves you have a heart. For my part, I have no heart; so I cannot have heart disease." "Perhaps," said the Lion thoughtfully, "if I had no heart I should not be a coward." "Have you brains?" asked the Scarecrow. "I suppose so. I've never looked to see," replied the Lion. "I am going to the Great Oz to ask him to give me some," remarked the Scarecrow, "for my head is stuffed with straw." "And I am going to ask him to give me a heart," said the Woodman. "And I am going to ask him to send Toto and me back to Kansas," added Dorothy. "Do you think Oz could give me courage?" asked the Cowardly Lion. "Just as easily as he could give me brains," said the Scarecrow. "Or give me a heart," said the Tin Woodman. "Or send me back to Kansas," said Dorothy. "Then, if you don't mind, I'll go with you," said the Lion, "for my life is simply unbearable without a bit of courage." "You will be very welcome," answered Dorothy, "for you will help to keep away the other wild beasts. It seems to me they must be more cowardly than you are if they allow you to scare them so easily." "They really are," said the Lion, "but that doesn't make me any braver, and as long as I know myself to be a coward I shall be unhappy." So once more the little company set off upon the journey, the Lion walking with stately strides at Dorothy's side. Toto did not approve this new comrade at first, for he could not forget how nearly he had been crushed between the Lion's great jaws. But after a time he became more at ease, and presently Toto and the Cowardly Lion had grown to be good friends. During the rest of that day there was no other adventure to mar the peace of their journey. Once, indeed, the Tin Woodman stepped upon a beetle that was crawling along the road, and killed the poor little thing. This made the Tin Woodman very unhappy, for he was always careful not to hurt any living creature; and as he walked along he wept several tears of sorrow and regret. These tears ran slowly down his face and over the hinges of his jaw, and there they rusted. When Dorothy presently asked him a question the Tin Woodman could not open his mouth, for his jaws were tightly rusted together. He became greatly frightened at this and made many motions to Dorothy to relieve him, but she could not understand. The Lion was also puzzled to know what was wrong. But the Scarecrow seized the oilcan from Dorothy's basket and oiled the Woodman's jaws, so that after a few moments he could talk as well as before. "This will serve me a lesson," said he, "to look where I step. For if I should kill another bug or beetle I should surely cry again, and crying rusts my jaws so that I cannot speak." Thereafter he walked very carefully, with his eyes on the road, and when he saw a tiny ant toiling by he would step over it, so as not to harm it. The Tin Woodman knew very well he had no heart, and therefore he took great care never to be cruel or unkind to anything. "You people with hearts," he said, "have something to guide you, and need never do wrong; but I have no heart, and so I must be very careful. When Oz gives me a heart of course I needn't mind so much." CHAPTER VII The Journey to the Great Oz They were obliged to camp out that night under a large tree in the forest, for there were no houses near. The tree made a good, thick covering to protect them from the dew, and the Tin Woodman chopped a great pile of wood with his axe and Dorothy built a splendid fire that warmed her and made her feel less lonely. She and Toto ate the last of their bread, and now she did not know what they would do for breakfast. "If you wish," said the Lion, "I will go into the forest and kill a deer for you. You can roast it by the fire, since your tastes are so peculiar that you prefer cooked food, and then you will have a very good breakfast." "Don't! Please don't," begged the Tin Woodman. "I should certainly weep if you killed a poor deer, and then my jaws would rust again." But the Lion went away into the forest and found his own supper, and no one ever knew what it was, for he didn't mention it. And the Scarecrow found a tree full of nuts and filled Dorothy's basket with them, so that she would not be hungry for a long time. She thought this was very kind and thoughtful of the Scarecrow, but she laughed heartily at the awkward way in which the poor creature picked up the nuts. His padded hands were so clumsy and the nuts were so small that he dropped almost as many as he put in the basket. But the Scarecrow did not mind how long it took him to fill the basket, for it enabled him to keep away from the fire, as he feared a spark might get into his straw and burn him up. So he kept a good distance away from the flames, and only came near to cover Dorothy with dry leaves when she lay down to sleep. These kept her very snug and warm, and she slept soundly until morning. When it was daylight, the girl bathed her face in a little rippling brook, and soon after they all started toward the Emerald City. This was to be an eventful day for the travelers. They had hardly been walking an hour when they saw before them a great ditch that crossed the road and divided the forest as far as they could see on either side. It was a very wide ditch, and when they crept up to the edge and looked into it they could see it was also very deep, and there were many big, jagged rocks at the bottom. The sides were so steep that none of them could climb down, and for a moment it seemed that their journey must end. "What shall we do?" asked Dorothy despairingly. "I haven't the faintest idea," said the Tin Woodman, and the Lion shook his shaggy mane and looked thoughtful. But the Scarecrow said, "We cannot fly, that is certain. Neither can we climb down into this great ditch. Therefore, if we cannot jump over it, we must stop where we are." "I think I could jump over it," said the Cowardly Lion, after measuring the distance carefully in his mind.

"Then we are all right," answered the Scarecrow, "for you can carry us all over on your back, one at a time." "Well, I'll try it," said the Lion. "Who will go first?" "I will," declared the Scarecrow, "for, if you found that you could not jump over the gulf, Dorothy would be killed, or the Tin Woodman badly dented on the rocks below. But if I am on your back it will not matter so much, for the fall would not hurt me at all." "I am terribly afraid of falling, myself," said the Cowardly Lion, "but I suppose there is nothing to do but try it. So get on my back and we will make the attempt." The Scarecrow sat upon the Lion's back, and the big beast walked to the edge of the gulf and crouched down. "Why don't you run and jump?" asked the Scarecrow. "Because that isn't the way we Lions do these things," he replied. Then giving a great spring, he shot through the air and landed safely on the other side. They were all greatly pleased to see how easily he did it, and after the Scarecrow had got down from his back the Lion sprang across the ditch again. Dorothy thought she would go next; so she took Toto in her arms and climbed on the Lion's back, holding tightly to his mane with one hand. The next moment it seemed as if she were flying through the air; and then, before she had time to think about it, she was safe on the other side. The Lion went back a third time and got the Tin Woodman, and then they all sat down for a few moments to give the beast a chance to rest, for his great leaps had made his breath short, and he panted like a big dog that has been running too long. They found the forest very thick on this side, and it looked dark and gloomy. After the Lion had rested they started along the road of yellow brick, silently wondering, each in his own mind, if ever they would come to the end of the woods and reach the bright sunshine again. To add to their discomfort, they soon heard strange noises in the depths of the forest, and the Lion whispered to them that it was in this part of the country that the Kalidahs lived. "What are the Kalidahs?" asked the girl. "They are monstrous beasts with bodies like bears and heads like tigers," replied the Lion, "and with claws so long and sharp that they could tear me in two as easily as I could kill Toto. I'm terribly afraid of the Kalidahs." "I'm not surprised that you are," returned Dorothy. "They must be dreadful beasts." The

Lion was about to reply when suddenly they came to another gulf across the road. But this one was so broad and deep that the Lion knew at once he could not leap across it.

So they sat down to consider what they should do, and after serious thought the Scarecrow said: "Here is a great tree, standing close to the ditch. If the Tin Woodman can

chop it down, so that it will fall to the other side, we can walk across it easily." "That is a first-rate idea," said the Lion. "One would almost suspect you had brains in your

head, instead of straw." The Woodman set to work at once, and so sharp was his axe that the tree was soon chopped nearly through. Then the Lion put his strong front legs

against the tree and pushed with all his might, and slowly the big tree tipped and fell with a crash across the ditch, with its top branches on the other side. They had just started

to cross this queer bridge when a sharp growl made them all look up, and to their horror they saw running toward them two great beasts with bodies like bears and heads like

tigers. "They are the Kalidahs!" said the Cowardly Lion, beginning to tremble. "Quick!" cried the Scarecrow. "Let us cross over." So Dorothy went first, holding Toto in

her arms, the Tin Woodman followed, and the Scarecrow came next. The Lion, although he was certainly afraid, turned to face the Kalidahs, and then he gave so loud and

terrible a roar that Dorothy screamed and the Scarecrow fell over backward, while even the fierce beasts stopped short and looked at him in surprise. But, seeing they were

bigger than the Lion, and remembering that there were two of them and only one of him, the Kalidahs again rushed forward, and the Lion crossed over the tree and turned

to see what they would do next. Without stopping an instant the fierce beasts also began to cross the tree. And the Lion said to Dorothy: "We are lost, for they will surely

tear us to pieces with their sharp claws. But stand close behind me, and I will fight them as long as I am alive." "Wait a minute!" called the Scarecrow. He had been thinking

what was best to be done, and now he asked the Woodman to chop away the end of the tree that rested on their side of the ditch. The Tin Woodman began to use his axe at

once, and, just as the two Kalidahs were nearly across, the tree fell with a crash into the gulf, carrying the ugly, snarling brutes with it, and both were dashed to pieces on the

sharp rocks at the bottom. "Well," said the Cowardly Lion, drawing a long breath of relief, "I see we are going to live a little while longer, and I am glad of it, for it must be

a very uncomfortable thing not to be alive. Those creatures frightened me so badly that my heart is beating yet." "Ah," said the Tin Woodman sadly, "I wish I had a heart to

beat." This adventure made the travelers more anxious than ever to get out of the forest, and they walked so fast that Dorothy became tired, and had to ride on the Lion's

back. To their great joy the trees became thinner the farther they advanced, and in the afternoon they suddenly came upon a broad river, flowing swiftly just before them.

On the other side of the water they could see the road of yellow brick running through a beautiful country, with green meadows dotted with bright flowers and all the road

bordered with trees hanging full of delicious fruits. They were greatly pleased to see this delightful country before them. "How shall we cross the river?" asked Dorothy.

"That is easily done," replied the Scarecrow. "The Tin Woodman must build us a raft, so we can float to the other side." So the Woodman took his axe and began to chop

down small trees to make a raft, and while he was busy at this the Scarecrow found on the riverbank a tree full of fine fruit. This pleased Dorothy, who had eaten nothing but

nuts all day, and she made a hearty meal of the ripe fruit. But it takes time to make a raft, even when one is as industrious and untiring as the Tin Woodman, and when night came the work was not done. So they found a cozy place under the trees where they slept well until the morning; and Dorothy dreamed of the Emerald City, and of the good

Wizard Oz, who would soon send her back to her own home again. CHAPTER VIII The Deadly Poppy Field Our little party of travelers awakened the next morning

refreshed and full of hope, and Dorothy breakfasted like a princess off peaches and plums from the trees beside the river. Behind them was the dark forest they had passed

safely through, although they had suffered many discouragements; but before them was a lovely, sunny country that seemed to beckon them on to the Emerald City. To be

sure, the broad river now cut them off from this beautiful land. But the raft was nearly done, and after the Tin Woodman had cut a few more logs and fastened them together

with wooden pins, they were ready to start. Dorothy sat down in the middle of the raft and held Toto in her arms. When the Cowardly Lion stepped upon the raft it tipped

badly, for he was big and heavy; but the Scarecrow and the Tin Woodman stood upon the other end to steady it, and they had long poles in their hands to push the raft through

the water. They got along quite well at first, but when they reached the middle of the river the swift current swept the raft downstream, farther and farther away from the

road of yellow brick. And the water grew so deep that the long poles would not touch the bottom. "This is bad," said the Tin Woodman, "for if we cannot get to the land

we shall be carried into the country of the Wicked Witch of the West, and she will enchant us and make us her slaves." "And then I should get no brains," said the Scarecrow.

"And I should get no courage," said the Cowardly Lion. "And I should get no heart," said the Tin Woodman. "And I should never get back to Kansas," said Dorothy. "We

must certainly get to the Emerald City if we can," the Scarecrow continued, and he pushed so hard on his long pole that it stuck fast in the mud at the bottom of the river.

Then, before he could pull it out again—or let go—the raft was swept away, and the poor Scarecrow left clinging to the pole in the middle of the river. "Good-bye!" he called

after them, and they were very sorry to leave him. Indeed, the Tin Woodman began to cry, but fortunately remembered that he might rust, and so dried his tears on Dorothy's

apron. Of course this was a bad thing for the Scarecrow. "I am now worse off than when I first met Dorothy," he thought. "Then, I was stuck on a pole in a cornfield, where

I could make-believe scare the crows, at any rate. But surely there is no use for a Scarecrow stuck on a pole in the middle of a river. I am afraid I shall never have any brains,

after all!" Down the stream the raft floated, and the poor Scarecrow was left far behind. Then the Lion said: "Something must be done to save us. I think I can swim to the

shore and pull the raft after me, if you will only hold fast to the tip of my tail." So he sprang into the water, and the Tin Woodman caught fast hold of his tail. Then the Lion

began to swim with all his might toward the shore. It was hard work, although he was so big; but by and by they were drawn out of the current, and then Dorothy took the

Tin Woodman's long pole and helped push the raft to the land. They were all tired out when they reached the shore at last and stepped off upon the pretty green grass, and

they also knew that the stream had carried them a long way past the road of yellow brick that led to the Emerald City. "What shall we do now?" asked the Tin Woodman,

as the Lion lay down on the grass to let the sun dry him. "We must get back to the road, in some way," said Dorothy. "The best plan will be to walk along the riverbank until

we come to the road again," remarked the Lion. So, when they were rested, Dorothy picked up her basket and they started along the grassy bank, to the road from which the river had carried them. It was a lovely country, with plenty of flowers and fruit trees and sunshine to cheer them, and had they not felt so sorry for the poor Scarecrow, they could have been very happy. They walked along as fast as they could, Dorothy only stopping once to pick a beautiful flower; and after a time the Tin Woodman cried out: "Look!" Then they all looked at the river and saw the Scarecrow perched upon his pole in the middle of the water, looking very lonely and sad. "What can we do to save him?" asked Dorothy. The Lion and the Woodman both shook their heads, for they did not know. So they sat down upon the bank and gazed wistfully at the Scarecrow until a Stork flew by, who, upon seeing them, stopped to rest at the water's edge. "Who are you and where are you going?" asked the Stork. "I am Dorothy," answered the girl, "and these are my friends, the Tin Woodman and the Cowardly Lion; and we are going to the Emerald City." "This isn't the road," said the Stork, as she twisted her long neck and looked sharply at the queer party. "I know it," returned Dorothy, "but we have lost the Scarecrow, and are wondering how we shall get him again." "Where is he?" asked the Stork. "Over there in the river," answered the little girl. "If he wasn't so big and heavy I would get him for you," remarked the Stork. "He isn't heavy a bit," said Dorothy eagerly, "for he is stuffed with straw; and if you will bring him back to us, we shall thank you ever and ever so much." "Well, I'll try," said the Stork, "but if I find he is too heavy to carry I shall have to drop him in the river again." So the big bird flew into the air and over the water till she came to where the Scarecrow was perched upon his pole. Then the Stork with her great claws grabbed the Scarecrow by the arm and carried him up into the air and back to the bank, where Dorothy and the Lion and the Tin Woodman and Toto were sitting. When the Scarecrow found himself among his friends again, he was so happy that he hugged them all, even the Lion and Toto; and as they walked along he sang "Tol-de-ri-de-oh!" at every step, he felt so gay. "I was afraid I should have to stay in the river forever," he said, "but the kind Stork saved me, and if I ever get any brains I shall find the Stork again and do her some kindness in return." "That's all right," said the Stork, who was flying along beside them. "I always like to help anyone in trouble. But I must go now, for my babies are waiting in the nest for me. I hope you will find the Emerald City and that Oz will help you." "Thank you," replied Dorothy, and then the kind Stork flew into the air and was soon out of sight. They walked along listening to the singing of the brightly colored birds and looking at the lovely flowers which now became so thick that the ground was carpeted with them. There were big yellow and white and blue and purple blossoms, besides great clusters of scarlet poppies, which were so brilliant in color they almost dazzled Dorothy's eyes. "Aren't they beautiful?" the girl asked, as she breathed in the spicy scent of the bright flowers. "I suppose so," answered the Scarecrow. "When I have brains, I shall probably like them better." "If I only had a heart, I should love them," added the Tin Woodman. "I always did like flowers," said the Lion. "They seem so helpless and frail. But there are none in the forest so bright as these." They now came upon more and more of the big scarlet poppies, and fewer and fewer of the other flowers; and soon they found themselves in the midst of a great meadow of poppies. Now it is well known that when there are many of these flowers together their odor is so powerful that anyone who breathes it falls asleep, and if the sleeper is not carried away from the scent of the flowers, he sleeps on and on forever. But Dorothy did not know this, nor could she get away from the bright red flowers that were everywhere about; so presently her eyes grew heavy and she felt she must sit down to rest and to sleep. But the Tin Woodman would not let her do this. "We must hurry and get back to the road of yellow brick before dark," he said; and the Scarecrow agreed with him. So they kept walking until Dorothy could stand no longer. Her eyes closed in spite of herself and she forgot where she was and fell among the poppies, fast asleep. "What shall we do?" asked the Tin Woodman. "If we leave her here she will die," said the Lion. "The smell of the flowers is killing us all. I myself can scarcely keep my eyes open, and the dog is asleep already." It was true; Toto had fallen down beside his little mistress. But the Scarecrow and the Tin Woodman, not being made of flesh, were not troubled by the scent of the flowers. "Run fast," said the Scarecrow to the Lion, "and get out of this deadly flower bed as soon as you can. We will bring the little girl with us, but if you should fall asleep you are too big to be carried." So the Lion aroused himself and bounded forward as fast as he could go. In a moment he was out of sight. "Let us make a chair with our hands and carry her," said the Scarecrow. So they picked up Toto and put the dog in Dorothy's lap, and then they made a chair with their hands for the seat and their arms for the arms and carried the sleeping girl between them through the flowers. On and on they walked, and it seemed that the great carpet of deadly flowers that surrounded them would never end. They followed the bend of the river, and at last came upon their friend the Lion, lying fast asleep among the poppies. The flowers had been too strong for the huge beast and he had given up at last, and fallen only a short distance from the end of the poppy bed, where the sweet grass spread in beautiful green fields before them. "We can do nothing for him," said the Tin Woodman, sadly; "for he is much too heavy to lift. We must leave him here to sleep on forever, and perhaps he will dream that he has found courage at last." "I'm sorry," said the Scarecrow. "The Lion was a very good comrade for one so cowardly. But let us go on." They carried the sleeping girl to a pretty spot beside the river, far enough from the poppy field to prevent her breathing any more of the poison of the flowers, and here they laid her gently on the soft grass and waited for the fresh breeze to waken her. CHAPTER IX The Queen of the Field Mice We cannot be far from the road of yellow brick, now," remarked the Scarecrow, as he stood beside the girl, "for we have come nearly as far as the river carried us away." The Tin Woodman was about to reply when he heard a low growl, and turning his head (which worked beautifully on hinges) he saw a strange beast come bounding over the grass toward them. It was, indeed, a great yellow Wildcat, and the Woodman thought it must be chasing something, for its ears were lying close to its head and its mouth was wide open, showing two rows of ugly teeth, while its red eyes glowed like balls of fire. As it came nearer the Tin Woodman saw that running before the beast was a little gray field mouse, and although he had no heart he knew it was wrong for the Wildcat to try to kill such a pretty, harmless creature. So the Woodman raised his axe, and as the Wildcat ran by he gave it a quick blow that cut the beast's head clean off from its body, and it rolled over at his feet in two pieces. The field mouse, now that it was freed from its enemy, stopped short; and coming slowly up to the Woodman it said, in a squeaky little voice: "Oh, thank you! Thank you ever so much for saving my life." "Don't speak of it, I beg of you," replied the Woodman. "I have no heart, you know, so I am careful to help all those who may need a friend, even if it happens to be only a mouse." "Only a mouse!" cried the little animal, indignantly. "Why, I am a Queen—the Queen of all the Field Mice!" "Oh, indeed," said the Woodman, making a bow. "Therefore you have done a great deed, as well as a brave one, in saving my life," added the Queen. At that moment several mice were seen running up as fast as their little legs could carry

them, and when they saw their Queen they exclaimed: "Oh, your Majesty, we thought you would be killed! How did you manage to escape the great Wildcat?" They all

bowed so low to the little Queen that they almost stood upon their heads. "This funny tin man," she answered, "killed the Wildcat and saved my life. So hereafter you must

all serve him, and obey his slightest wish." "We will!" cried all the mice, in a shrill chorus. And then they scampered in all directions, for Toto had awakened from his sleep,

and seeing all these mice around him he gave one bark of delight and jumped right into the middle of the group. Toto had always loved to chase mice when he lived in Kansas,

and he saw no harm in it. But the Tin Woodman caught the dog in his arms and held him tight, while he called to the mice, "Come back! Come back! Toto shall not hurt

you." At this the Queen of the Mice stuck her head out from underneath a clump of grass and asked, in a timid voice, "Are you sure he will not bite us?" "I will not let him,"

said the Woodman; "so do not be afraid." One by one the mice came creeping back, and Toto did not bark again, although he tried to get out of the Woodman's arms, and

would have bitten him had he not known very well he was made of tin. Finally one of the biggest mice spoke. "Is there anything we can do," it asked, "to repay you for saving

the life of our Queen?" "Nothing that I know of," answered the Woodman; but the Scarecrow, who had been trying to think, but could not because his head was stuffed with

straw, said, quickly, "Oh, yes; you can save our friend, the Cowardly Lion, who is asleep in the poppy bed." "A Lion!" cried the little Queen. "Why, he would eat us all up."

"Oh, no," declared the Scarecrow; "this Lion is a coward." "Really?" asked the Mouse. "He says so himself," answered the Scarecrow, "and he would never hurt anyone

who is our friend. If you will help us to save him I promise that he shall treat you all with kindness." "Very well," said the Queen, "we trust you. But what shall we do?" "Are

there many of these mice which call you Queen and are willing to obey you?" "Oh, yes; there are thousands," she replied. "Then send for them all to come here as soon as

possible, and let each one bring a long piece of string." The Queen turned to the mice that attended her and told them to go at once and get all her people. As soon as they

heard her orders they ran away in every direction as fast as possible. "Now," said the Scarecrow to the Tin Woodman, "you must go to those trees by the riverside and make

a truck that will carry the Lion." So the Woodman went at once to the trees and began to work; and he soon made a truck out of the limbs of trees, from which he chopped

away all the leaves and branches. He fastened it together with wooden pegs and made the four wheels out of short pieces of a big tree trunk. So fast and so well did he work

that by the time the mice began to arrive the truck was all ready for them. They came from all directions, and there were thousands of them: big mice and little mice and

middle-sized mice; and each one brought a piece of string in his mouth. It was about this time that Dorothy woke from her long sleep and opened her eyes. She was greatly

astonished to find herself lying upon the grass, with thousands of mice standing around and looking at her timidly. But the Scarecrow told her about everything, and turning

to the dignified little Mouse, he said: "Permit me to introduce to you her Majesty, the Queen." Dorothy nodded gravely and the Queen made a curtsy, after which she became

quite friendly with the little girl. The Scarecrow and the Woodman now began to fasten the mice to the truck, using the strings they had brought. One end of a string was tied around the neck of each mouse and the other end to the truck. Of course the truck was a thousand times bigger than any of the mice who were to draw it; but when all the mice had been harnessed, they were able to pull it quite easily. Even the Scarecrow and the Tin Woodman could sit on it, and were drawn swiftly by their queer little horses to the place where the Lion lay asleep. After a great deal of hard work, for the Lion was heavy, they managed to get him up on the truck. Then the Queen hurriedly gave her people the order to start, for she feared if the mice stayed among the poppies too long they also would fall asleep. At first the little creatures, many though they were, could hardly stir the heavily loaded truck; but the Woodman and the Scarecrow both pushed from behind, and they got along better. Soon they rolled the Lion out of the poppy bed to the green fields, where he could breathe the sweet, fresh air again, instead of the poisonous scent of the flowers. Dorothy came to meet them and thanked the little mice warmly for saving her companion from death. She had grown so fond of the big Lion she was glad he had been rescued. Then the mice were unharnessed from the truck and scampered away through the grass to their homes. The Queen of the Mice was the last to leave. "If ever you need us again," she said, "come out into the field and call, and we shall hear you and come to your assistance. Good-bye!" "Good-bye!" they all answered, and away the Queen ran, while Dorothy held Toto tightly lest he should run after her and frighten her. After this they sat down beside the Lion until he should awaken; and the Scarecrow brought Dorothy some fruit from a tree near by, which she ate for her dinner. CHAPTER X The Guardian of the Gates It was some time before the Cowardly Lion awakened, for he had lain among the poppies a long while, breathing in their deadly fragrance; but when he did open his eyes and roll off the truck he was very glad to find himself still alive. "I ran as fast as I could," he said, sitting down and yawning, "but the flowers were too strong for me. How did you get me out?" Then they told him of the field mice, and how they had generously saved him from death; and the Cowardly Lion laughed, and said: "I have always thought myself very big and terrible; yet such little things as flowers came near to killing me, and such small animals as mice have saved my life. How strange it all is! But, comrades, what shall we do now?" "We must journey on until we find the road of yellow brick again," said Dorothy, "and then we can keep on to the Emerald City." So, the Lion being fully refreshed, and feeling quite himself again, they all started upon the journey, greatly enjoying the walk through the soft, fresh grass; and it was not long before they reached the road of yellow brick and turned again toward the Emerald City where the Great Oz dwelt. The road was smooth and well paved, now, and the country about was beautiful, so that the travelers rejoiced in leaving the forest far behind, and with it the many dangers they had met in its gloomy shades. Once more they could see fences built beside the road; but these were painted green, and when they came to a small house, in which a farmer evidently lived, that also was painted green. They passed by several of these houses during the afternoon, and sometimes people came to the doors and looked at them as if they would like to ask questions; but no one came near them nor spoke to them because of the great Lion, of which they were very much afraid. The people were all dressed in clothing of a lovely emerald-green color and wore peaked hats like those of the Munchkins. "This must be the Land of Oz," said Dorothy, "and we are surely getting near the Emerald City." "Yes," answered the Scarecrow. "Everything is green here, while in the country of the Munchkins blue was the favorite color. But the people do not seem to be as friendly as the Munchkins, and I'm afraid we shall be unable to find a place to pass the night." "I should like something to eat besides fruit," said the girl, "and I'm sure Toto is nearly starved. Let us stop at the next house and talk to the people." So, when they came to a good-sized farmhouse, Dorothy walked boldly up to the door and knocked. A woman opened it just far enough to look out, and said, "What do you want, child, and why is that great Lion with you?" "We wish to pass the night with you, if you will allow us," answered Dorothy; "and the Lion is my friend and comrade, and would not hurt you for the world." "Is he tame?" asked the woman, opening the door a little wider. "Oh, yes," said the girl, "and he is a great coward, too. He will be more afraid of you than you are of him." "Well," said the woman, after thinking it over and taking another peep at the Lion, "if that is the case you may come in, and I will give you some supper and a place to sleep." So they all entered the house, where there were, besides the woman, two children and a man. The man had hurt his leg, and was lying on the couch in a corner. They seemed greatly surprised to see so strange a company, and while the woman was busy laying the table the man asked: "Where are you all going?" "To the Emerald City," said Dorothy, "to see the Great Oz." "Oh, indeed!" exclaimed the man. "Are you sure that Oz will see you?" "Why not?" she replied. "Why, it is said that he never lets anyone come into his presence. I have been to the Emerald City many times, and it is a beautiful and wonderful place; but I have never been permitted to see the Great Oz, nor do I know of any living person who has seen him." "Does he never go out?" asked the Scarecrow. "Never. He sits day after day in the great Throne Room of his Palace, and even those who wait upon him do not see him face-to-face." "What is he like?" asked the girl. "That is hard to tell," said the man thoughtfully. "You see, Oz is a Great Wizard, and can take on any form he wishes. So that some say he looks like a bird; and some say he looks like an elephant; and some say he looks like a cat. To others he appears as a beautiful fairy, or a brownie, or in any other form that pleases him. But who the real Oz is, when he is in his own form, no living person can tell." "That is very strange," said Dorothy, "but we must try, in some way, to see him, or we shall have made our journey for nothing." "Why do you wish to see the terrible Oz?" asked the man. "I want him to give me some brains," said the Scarecrow eagerly. "Oh, Oz could do that easily enough," declared the man. "He has more brains than he needs." "And I want him to give me a heart," said the Tin Woodman. "That will not trouble him," continued the man, "for Oz has a large collection of hearts, of all sizes and shapes." "And I want him to give me courage," said the Cowardly Lion. "Oz keeps a great pot of courage in his Throne Room," said the man, "which he has covered with a golden plate, to keep it from running over. He will be glad to give you some." "And I want him to send me back to Kansas," said Dorothy. "Where is Kansas?" asked the man, with surprise. "I don't know," replied Dorothy sorrowfully, "but it is my home, and I'm sure it's somewhere." "Very likely. Well, Oz can do anything; so I suppose he will find Kansas for you. But first you must get to see him, and that will be a hard task; for the Great Wizard does not like to see anyone, and he usually has his own way. But what do *you* want?" he continued, speaking to Toto. Toto only wagged his tail; for, strange to say, he could not speak. The woman now called to them that supper was ready, so they gathered around the table and Dorothy ate some delicious porridge and a dish of scrambled eggs and a plate of nice white bread, and enjoyed her meal. The Lion ate some of the porridge, but did not care for it, saying it was made from oats and oats were food for horses, not for lions. The Scarecrow and the Tin Woodman ate nothing at all. Toto ate a little of everything, and was glad to

get a good supper again. The woman now gave Dorothy a bed to sleep in, and Toto lay down beside her, while the Lion guarded the door of her room so she might not be

disturbed. The Scarecrow and the Tin Woodman stood up in a corner and kept quiet all night, although of course they could not sleep. The next morning, as soon as the sun

was up, they started on their way, and soon saw a beautiful green glow in the sky just before them. "That must be the Emerald City," said Dorothy. As they walked on, the

green glow became brighter and brighter, and it seemed that at last they were nearing the end of their travels. Yet it was afternoon before they came to the great wall that

surrounded the City. It was high and thick and of a bright green color. In front of them, and at the end of the road of yellow brick, was a big gate, all studded with emeralds

that glittered so in the sun that even the painted eyes of the Scarecrow were dazzled by their brilliancy. There was a bell beside the gate, and Dorothy pushed the button and

heard a silvery tinkle sound within. Then the big gate swung slowly open, and they all passed through and found themselves in a high arched room, the walls of which

glistened with countless emeralds. Before them stood a little man about the same size as the Munchkins. He was clothed all in green, from his head to his feet, and even his

skin was of a greenish tint. At his side was a large green box. When he saw Dorothy and her companions the man asked, "What do you wish in the Emerald City?" "We

came here to see the Great Oz," said Dorothy. The man was so surprised at this answer that he sat down to think it over. "It has been many years since anyone asked me to

see Oz," he said, shaking his head in perplexity. "He is powerful and terrible, and if you come on an idle or foolish errand to bother the wise reflections of the Great Wizard,

he might be angry and destroy you all in an instant." "But it is not a foolish errand, nor an idle one," replied the Scarecrow; "it is important. And we have been told that Oz

is a good Wizard." "So he is," said the green man, "and he rules the Emerald City wisely and well. But to those who are not honest, or who approach him from curiosity, he

is most terrible, and few have ever dared ask to see his face. I am the Guardian of the Gates, and since you demand to see the Great Oz I must take you to his Palace. But first

you must put on the spectacles." "Why?" asked Dorothy. "Because if you did not wear spectacles the brightness and glory of the Emerald City would blind you. Even those

who live in the City must wear spectacles night and day. They are all locked on, for Oz so ordered it when the City was first built, and I have the only key that will unlock

them." He opened the big box, and Dorothy saw that it was filled with spectacles of every size and shape. All of them had green glasses in them. The Guardian of the Gates

found a pair that would just fit Dorothy and put them over her eyes. There were two golden bands fastened to them that passed around the back of her head, where they were

locked together by a little key that was at the end of a chain the Guardian of the Gates wore around his neck. When they were on, Dorothy could not take them off had she

wished, but of course she did not wish to be blinded by the glare of the Emerald City, so she said nothing. Then the green man fitted spectacles for the Scarecrow and the

Tin Woodman and the Lion, and even on little Toto; and all were locked fast with the key. Then the Guardian of the Gates put on his own glasses and told them he was ready

to show them to the Palace. Taking a big golden key from a peg on the wall, he opened another gate, and they all followed him through the portal into the streets of the

Emerald City. CHAPTER XI The Wonderful Emerald City of Oz Even with eyes protected by the green spectacles, Dorothy and her friends were at first dazzled by the brilliancy of the wonderful City. The streets were lined with beautiful houses all built of green marble and studded everywhere with sparkling emeralds. They walked over a pavement of the same green marble, and where the blocks were joined together were rows of emeralds, set closely, and glittering in the brightness of the sun. The windowpanes were of green glass; even the sky above the City had a green tint, and the rays of the sun were green. There were many people—men, women, and children— walking about, and these were all dressed in green clothes and had greenish skins. They looked at Dorothy and her strangely assorted company with wondering eyes, and the children all ran away and hid behind their mothers when they saw the Lion; but no one spoke to them. Many shops stood in the street, and Dorothy saw that everything in them was green. Green candy and green popcorn were offered for sale, as well as green shoes, green hats, and green clothes of all sorts. At one place a man was selling green lemonade, and when the children bought it Dorothy could see that they paid for it with green pennies. There seemed to be no horses nor animals of any kind; the men carried things around in little green carts, which they pushed before them. Everyone seemed happy and contented and prosperous. The Guardian of the Gates led them through the streets until they came to a big building, exactly in the middle of the City, which was the Palace of Oz, the Great Wizard. There was a soldier before the door, dressed in a green uniform and wearing a long green beard. "Here are strangers," said the Guardian of the Gates to him, "and they demand to see the Great Oz." "Step inside," answered the soldier, "and I will carry your message to him." So they passed through the Palace Gates and were led into a big room with a green carpet and lovely green furniture set with emeralds. The soldier made them all wipe their feet upon a green mat before entering this room, and when they were seated he said politely: "Please make yourselves comfortable while I go to the door of the Throne Room and tell Oz you are here." They had to wait a long time before the soldier returned. When, at last, he came back, Dorothy asked: "Have you seen Oz?" "Oh, no," returned the soldier; "I have never seen him. But I spoke to him as he sat behind his screen and gave him your message. He said he will grant you an audience, if you so desire; but each one of you must enter his presence alone, and he will admit but one each day. Therefore, as you must remain in the Palace for several days, I will have you shown to rooms where you may rest in comfort after your journey." "Thank you," replied the girl; "that is very kind of Oz." The soldier now blew upon a green whistle, and at once a young girl, dressed in a pretty green silk gown, entered the room. She had lovely green hair and green eyes, and she bowed low before Dorothy as she said, "Follow me and I will show you your room." So Dorothy said good-bye to all her friends except Toto, and taking the dog in her arms followed the green girl through seven passages and up three flights of stairs until they came to a room at the front of the Palace. It was the sweetest little room in the world, with a soft comfortable bed that had sheets of green silk and a green velvet counterpane. There was a tiny fountain in the middle of the room, that shot a spray of green perfume into the air, to fall back into a beautifully carved green marble basin. Beautiful green flowers stood in the windows, and there was a shelf with a row of little green books. When Dorothy had time to open these books she found them full of queer green pictures that made her laugh, they were so funny. In a wardrobe were many green dresses, made of silk and satin and velvet; and all of them fitted Dorothy exactly. "Make yourself perfectly at home," said the green girl, "and if you wish for anything ring the bell. Oz will send for you tomorrow morning." She left Dorothy alone and went back to the others. These she also led to rooms, and each one of them found himself lodged in a very pleasant part of the Palace. Of course this politeness was wasted on the Scarecrow; for when he found himself alone in his room he stood stupidly in one spot, just within the doorway, to wait till morning. It would not rest him to lie down, and he could not close his eyes; so he remained all night staring at a little spider which was weaving its web in a corner of the room, just as if it were not one of the most wonderful rooms in the world. The Tin Woodman lay down on his bed from force of habit, for he remembered when he was made of flesh; but not being able to sleep, he passed the night moving his joints up and down to make sure they kept in good working order. The Lion would have preferred a bed of dried leaves in the forest, and did not like being shut up in a room; but he had too much sense to let this worry him, so he sprang upon the bed and rolled himself up like a cat and purred himself asleep in a minute. The next morning, after breakfast, the green maiden came to fetch Dorothy, and she dressed her in one of the prettiest gowns, made of green brocaded satin. Dorothy put on a green silk apron and tied a green ribbon around Toto's neck, and they started for the Throne Room of the Great Oz. First they came to a great hall in which were many ladies and gentlemen of the court, all dressed in rich costumes. These people had nothing to do but talk to each other, but they always came to wait outside the Throne Room every morning, although they were never permitted to see Oz. As Dorothy entered they looked at her curiously, and one of them whispered: "Are you really going to look upon the face of Oz the Terrible?" "Of course," answered the girl, "if he will see me." "Oh, he will see you," said the soldier who had taken her message to the Wizard, "although he does not like to have people ask to see him. Indeed, at first he was angry and said I should send you back where you came from. Then he asked me what you looked like, and when I mentioned your Silver Shoes he was very much interested. At last I told him about the mark upon your forehead, and he decided he would admit you to his presence." Just then a bell rang, and the green girl said to Dorothy, "That is the signal. You must go into the Throne Room alone." She opened a little door and Dorothy walked boldly through and found herself in a wonderful place. It was a big, round room with a high arched roof, and the walls and ceiling and floor were covered with large emeralds set closely together. In the center of the roof was a great light, as bright as the sun, which made the emeralds sparkle in a wonderful manner. But what interested Dorothy most was the big throne of green marble that stood in the middle of the room. It was shaped like a chair and sparkled with gems, as did everything else. In the center of the chair was an enormous Head, without a body to support it or any arms or legs whatever. There was no hair upon this head, but it had eyes and a nose and mouth, and was much bigger than the head of the biggest giant. As Dorothy gazed upon this in wonder and fear, the eyes turned slowly and looked at her sharply and steadily. Then the mouth moved, and Dorothy heard a voice say: "I am Oz, the Great and Terrible. Who are you, and why do you seek me?" It was not such an awful voice as she had expected to come from the big Head; so she took courage and answered: "I am Dorothy, the Small and Meek. I have come to you for help." The eyes looked at her thoughtfully for a full minute. Then said the voice: "Where did you get the Silver Shoes?" "I got them from the Wicked Witch of the East, when my house fell on her and killed her," she replied. "Where did you get the mark upon your forehead?"

continued the voice. "That is where the Good Witch of the North kissed me when she bade me good-bye and sent me to you," said the girl. Again the eyes looked at her

sharply, and they saw she was telling the truth. Then Oz asked, "What do you wish me to do?" "Send me back to Kansas, where my Aunt Em and Uncle Henry are," she

answered earnestly. "I don't like your country, although it is so beautiful. And I am sure Aunt Em will be dreadfully worried over my being away so long." The eyes winked

three times, and then they turned up to the ceiling and down to the floor and rolled around so queerly that they seemed to see every part of the room. And at last they looked

at Dorothy again. "Why should I do this for you?" asked Oz. "Because you are strong and I am weak; because you are a Great Wizard and I am only a little girl." "But you

were strong enough to kill the Wicked Witch of the East," said Oz. "That just happened," returned Dorothy simply; "I could not help it." "Well," said the Head, "I will give

you my answer. You have no right to expect me to send you back to Kansas unless you do something for me in return. In this country everyone must pay for everything he

gets. If you wish me to use my magic power to send you home again you must do something for me first. Help me and I will help you." "What must I do?" asked the girl.

"Kill the Wicked Witch of the West," answered Oz. "But I cannot!" exclaimed Dorothy, greatly surprised. "You killed the Witch of the East and you wear the Silver Shoes,

which bear a powerful charm. There is now but one Wicked Witch left in all this land, and when you can tell me she is dead I will send you back to Kansas—but not before."

The little girl began to weep, she was so much disappointed; and the eyes winked again and looked upon her anxiously, as if the Great Oz felt that she could help him if she

would. "I never killed anything, willingly," she sobbed. "Even if I wanted to, how could I kill the Wicked Witch? If you, who are Great and Terrible, cannot kill her yourself,

how do you expect me to do it?" "I do not know," said the Head; "but that is my answer, and until the Wicked Witch dies you will not see your uncle and aunt again.

Remember that the Witch is Wicked—tremendously Wicked—and ought to be killed. Now go, and do not ask to see me again until you have done your task." Sorrowfully

Dorothy left the Throne Room and went back where the Lion and the Scarecrow and the Tin Woodman were waiting to hear what Oz had said to her. "There is no hope

for me," she said sadly, "for Oz will not send me home until I have killed the Wicked Witch of the West; and that I can never do." Her friends were sorry, but could do nothing

to help her; so Dorothy went to her own room and lay down on the bed and cried herself to sleep. The next morning the soldier with the green whiskers came to the

Scarecrow and said: "Come with me, for Oz has sent for you." So the Scarecrow followed him and was admitted into the great Throne Room, where he saw, sitting in the

emerald throne, a most lovely Lady. She was dressed in green silk gauze and wore upon her flowing green locks a crown of jewels. Growing from her shoulders were wings,

gorgeous in color and so light that they fluttered if the slightest breath of air reached them. When the Scarecrow had bowed, as prettily as his straw stuffing would let him,

before this beautiful creature, she looked upon him sweetly, and said: "I am Oz, the Great and Terrible. Who are you, and why do you seek me?" Now the Scarecrow, who

had expected to see the great Head Dorothy had told him of, was much astonished; but he answered her bravely. "I am only a Scarecrow, stuffed with straw. Therefore I have no brains, and I come to you praying that you will put brains in my head instead of straw, so that I may become as much a man as any other in your dominions." "Why should

I do this for you?" asked the Lady. "Because you are wise and powerful, and no one else can help me," answered the Scarecrow. "I never grant favors without some return,"

said Oz; "but this much I will promise. If you will kill for me the Wicked Witch of the West, I will bestow upon you a great many brains, and such good brains that you will

be the wisest man in all the Land of Oz." "I thought you asked Dorothy to kill the Witch," said the Scarecrow, in surprise. "So I did. I don't care who kills her. But until she

is dead I will not grant your wish. Now go, and do not seek me again until you have earned the brains you so greatly desire." The Scarecrow went sorrowfully back to his

friends and told them what Oz had said; and Dorothy was surprised to find that the Great Wizard was not a Head, as she had seen him, but a lovely Lady. "All the same,"

said the Scarecrow, "she needs a heart as much as the Tin Woodman." On the next morning the soldier with the green whiskers came to the Tin Woodman and said: "Oz has

sent for you. Follow me." So the Tin Woodman followed him and came to the great Throne Room. He did not know whether he would find Oz a lovely Lady or a Head, but

he hoped it would be the lovely Lady. "For," he said to himself, "if it is the head, I am sure I shall not be given a heart, since a head has no heart of its own and therefore

cannot feel for me. But if it is the lovely Lady I shall beg hard for a heart, for all ladies are themselves said to be kindly hearted." But when the Woodman entered the great

Throne Room he saw neither the Head nor the Lady, for Oz had taken the shape of a most terrible Beast. It was nearly as big as an elephant, and the green throne seemed

hardly strong enough to hold its weight. The Beast had a head like that of a rhinoceros, only there were five eyes in its face. There were five long arms growing out of its

body, and it also had five long, slim legs. Thick, woolly hair covered every part of it, and a more dreadful-looking monster could not be imagined. It was fortunate the Tin

Woodman had no heart at that moment, for it would have beat loud and fast from terror. But being only tin, the Woodman was not at all afraid, although he was much

disappointed. "I am Oz, the Great and Terrible," spoke the Beast, in a voice that was one great roar. "Who are you, and why do you seek me?" "I am a Woodman, and made

of tin. Therefore I have no heart, and cannot love. I pray you to give me a heart that I may be as other men are." "Why should I do this?" demanded the Beast. "Because I

ask it, and you alone can grant my request," answered the Woodman. Oz gave a low growl at this, but said, gruffly: "If you indeed desire a heart, you must earn it." "How?"

asked the Woodman. "Help Dorothy to kill the Wicked Witch of the West," replied the Beast. "When the Witch is dead, come to me, and I will then give you the biggest

and kindest and most loving heart in all the Land of Oz." So the Tin Woodman was forced to return sorrowfully to his friends and tell them of the terrible Beast he had seen.

They all wondered greatly at the many forms the Great Wizard could take upon himself, and the Lion said: "If he is a Beast when I go to see him, I shall roar my loudest,

and so frighten him that he will grant all I ask. And if he is the lovely Lady, I shall pretend to spring upon her, and so compel her to do my bidding. And if he is the great

Head, he will be at my mercy; for I will roll this head all about the room until he promises to give us what we desire. So be of good cheer, my friends, for all will yet be well."

The next morning the soldier with the green whiskers led the Lion to the great Throne Room and bade him enter the presence of Oz. The Lion at once passed through the door, and glancing around saw, to his surprise, that before the throne was a Ball of Fire, so fierce and glowing he could scarcely bear to gaze upon it. His first thought was that Oz had by accident caught on fire and was burning up; but when he tried to go nearer, the heat was so intense that it singed his whiskers, and he crept back tremblingly to a spot nearer the door. Then a low, quiet voice came from the Ball of Fire, and these were the words it spoke: "I am Oz, the Great and Terrible. Who are you, and why do you seek me?" And the Lion answered, "I am a Cowardly Lion, afraid of everything. I came to you to beg that you give me courage, so that in reality I may become the King of Beasts, as men call me." "Why should I give you courage?" demanded Oz. "Because of all Wizards you are the greatest, and alone have power to grant my request," answered the Lion. The Ball of Fire burned fiercely for a time, and the voice said, "Bring me proof that the Wicked Witch is dead, and that moment I will give you courage. But as long as the Witch lives, you must remain a coward." The Lion was angry at this speech, but could say nothing in reply, and while he stood silently gazing at the Ball of Fire it became so furiously hot that he turned tail and rushed from the room. He was glad to find his friends waiting for him, and told them of his terrible interview with the Wizard. "What shall we do now?" asked Dorothy sadly. "There is only one thing we can do," returned the Lion, "and that is to go to the land of the Winkies, seek out the Wicked Witch, and destroy her." "But suppose we cannot?" said the girl. "Then I shall never have courage," declared the Lion. "And I shall never have brains," added the Scarecrow. "And I shall never have a heart," spoke the Tin Woodman. "And I shall never see Aunt Em and Uncle Henry," said Dorothy, beginning to cry. "Be careful!" cried the green girl. "The tears will fall on your green silk gown and spot it." So Dorothy dried her eyes and said, "I suppose we must try it; but I am sure I do not want to kill anybody, even to see Aunt Em again." "I will go with you; but I'm too much of a coward to kill the Witch," said the Lion. "I will go too," declared the Scarecrow; "but I shall not be of much help to you, I am such a fool." "I haven't the heart to harm even a Witch," remarked the Tin Woodman; "but if you go I certainly shall go with you." Therefore it was decided to start upon their journey the next morning, and the Woodman sharpened his axe on a green grindstone and had all his joints properly oiled. The Scarecrow stuffed himself with fresh straw and Dorothy put new paint on his eyes that he might see better. The green girl, who was very kind to them, filled Dorothy's basket with good things to eat, and fastened a little bell around Toto's neck with a green ribbon. They went to bed quite early and slept soundly until daylight, when they were awakened by the crowing of a green cock that lived in the backyard of the Palace, and the cackling of a hen that had laid a green egg. CHAPTER XII The Search for the Wicked Witch The soldier with the green whiskers led them through the streets of the Emerald City until they reached the room where the Guardian of the Gates lived. This officer unlocked their spectacles to put them back in his great box, and then he politely opened the gate for our friends. "Which road leads to the Wicked Witch of the West?" asked Dorothy. "There is no road," answered the Guardian of the Gates. "No one ever wishes to go that way." "How, then, are we to find her?" inquired the girl. "That will be easy," replied the man, "for when she knows you are in the country of the Winkies she will find you, and make you all her slaves." "Perhaps not," said the Scarecrow, "for we mean to destroy her." "Oh, that is different," said the Guardian of the Gates. "No one has ever destroyed her before, so I naturally thought she would make slaves of you, as she has of the rest. But take care; for she is wicked and fierce, and may not allow you to destroy her. Keep to the West, where the sun sets, and you cannot fail to find her." They thanked him and bade him good-bye, and turned toward the West, walking over fields of soft grass dotted here and there with daisies and buttercups. Dorothy still wore the pretty silk dress she had put on in the palace, but now, to her surprise, she found it was no longer green, but pure white. The ribbon around Toto's neck had also lost its green color and was as white as Dorothy's dress. The Emerald City was soon left far behind. As they advanced the ground became rougher and hillier, for there were no farms nor houses in this country of the West, and the ground was untilled. In the afternoon the sun shone hot in their faces, for there were no trees to offer them shade; so that before night Dorothy and Toto and the Lion were tired, and lay down upon the grass and fell asleep, with the Woodman and the Scarecrow keeping watch. Now the Wicked Witch of the West had but one eye, yet that was as powerful as a telescope, and could see everywhere. So, as she sat in the door of her castle, she happened to look around and saw Dorothy lying asleep, with her friends all about her. They were a long distance off, but the Wicked Witch was angry to find them in her country; so she blew upon a silver whistle that hung around her neck. At once there came running to her from all directions a pack of great wolves. They had long legs and fierce eyes and sharp teeth. "Go to those people," said the Witch, "and tear them to pieces." "Are you not going to make them your slaves?" asked the leader of the wolves. "No," she answered, "one is of tin, and one of straw; one is a girl and another a Lion. None of them is fit to work, so you may tear them into small pieces." "Very well," said the wolf, and he dashed away at full speed, followed by the others. It was lucky the Scarecrow and the Woodman were wide awake and heard the wolves coming. "This is my fight," said the Woodman, "so get behind me and I will meet them as they come." He seized his axe, which he had made very sharp, and as the leader of the wolves came on the Tin Woodman swung his arm and chopped the wolf's head from its body, so that it immediately died. As soon as he could raise his axe another wolf came up, and he also fell under the sharp edge of the Tin Woodman's weapon. There were forty wolves, and forty times a wolf was killed, so that at last they all lay dead in a heap before the Woodman. Then he put down his axe and sat beside the Scarecrow, who said, "It was a good fight, friend." They waited until Dorothy awoke the next morning. The little girl was quite frightened when she saw the great pile of shaggy wolves, but the Tin Woodman told her all. She thanked him for saving them and sat down to breakfast, after which they started again upon their journey. Now this same morning the Wicked Witch came to the door of her castle and looked out with her one eye that could see far off. She saw all her wolves lying dead, and the strangers still traveling through her country. This made her angrier than before, and she blew her silver whistle twice. Straightway a great flock of wild crows came flying toward her, enough to darken the sky. And the Wicked Witch said to the King Crow, "Fly at once to the strangers; peck out their eyes and tear them to pieces." The wild crows flew in one great flock toward Dorothy and her companions. When the little girl saw them coming she was afraid. But the Scarecrow said, "This is my battle, so lie down beside me and you will not be harmed." So they all lay upon the ground except the Scarecrow, and he stood up and stretched out his arms. And when the crows saw him they were frightened, as these birds always are by scarecrows, and did not dare to come any nearer. But the King Crow said: "It is only a stuffed man. I will peck his eyes out." The King Crow flew at the Scarecrow, who caught it by the head and twisted its neck until it died.

And then another crow flew at him, and the Scarecrow twisted its neck also. There were forty crows, and forty times the Scarecrow twisted a neck, until at last all were lying

dead beside him. Then he called to his companions to rise, and again they went upon their journey. When the Wicked Witch looked out again and saw all her crows lying in

a heap, she got into a terrible rage, and blew three times upon her silver whistle. Forthwith there was heard a great buzzing in the air, and a swarm of black bees came flying

toward her. "Go to the strangers and sting them to death!" commanded the Witch, and the bees turned and flew rapidly until they came to where Dorothy and her friends

were walking. But the Woodman had seen them coming, and the Scarecrow had decided what to do. "Take out my straw and scatter it over the little girl and the dog and the

Lion," he said to the Woodman, "and the bees cannot sting them." This the Woodman did, and as Dorothy lay close beside the Lion and held Toto in her arms, the straw

covered them entirely. The bees came and found no one but the Woodman to sting, so they flew at him and broke off all their stings against the tin, without hurting the

Woodman at all. And as bees cannot live when their stings are broken that was the end of the black bees, and they lay scattered thick about the Woodman, like little heaps of

fine coal. Then Dorothy and the Lion got up, and the girl helped the Tin Woodman put the straw back into the Scarecrow again, until he was as good as ever. So they started

upon their journey once more. The Wicked Witch was so angry when she saw her black bees in little heaps like fine coal that she stamped her foot and tore her hair and

gnashed her teeth. And then she called a dozen of her slaves, who were the Winkies, and gave them sharp spears, telling them to go to the strangers and destroy them. The

Winkies were not a brave people, but they had to do as they were told. So they marched away until they came near to Dorothy. Then the Lion gave a great roar and sprang

towards them, and the poor Winkies were so frightened that they ran back as fast as they could. When they returned to the castle the Wicked Witch beat them well with a

strap, and sent them back to their work, after which she sat down to think what she should do next. She could not understand how all her plans to destroy these strangers had

failed; but she was a powerful Witch, as well as a wicked one, and she soon made up her mind how to act. There was, in her cupboard, a Golden Cap, with a circle of diamonds

and rubies running round it. This Golden Cap had a charm. Whoever owned it could call three times upon the Winged Monkeys, who would obey any order they were given.

But no person could command these strange creatures more than three times. Twice already the Wicked Witch had used the charm of the Cap. Once was when she had made

the Winkies her slaves, and set herself to rule over their country. The Winged Monkeys had helped her do this. The second time was when she had fought against the Great

Oz himself, and driven him out of the land of the West. The Winged Monkeys had also helped her in doing this. Only once more could she use this Golden Cap, for which

reason she did not like to do so until all her other powers were exhausted. But now that her fierce wolves and her wild crows and her stinging bees were gone, and her slaves

had been scared away by the Cowardly Lion, she saw there was only one way left to destroy Dorothy and her friends. So the Wicked Witch took the Golden Cap from her

cupboard and placed it upon her head. Then she stood upon her left foot and said slowly: "Ep-pe, pep-pe, kak-ke!" Next she stood upon her right foot and said: "Hil-lo, hol-lo, hel-lo!" After this she stood upon both feet and cried in a loud voice: "Ziz-zy, zuz-zy, zik!" Now the charm began to work. The sky was darkened, and a low rumbling

sound was heard in the air. There was a rushing of many wings, a great chattering and laughing, and the sun came out of the dark sky to show the Wicked Witch surrounded

by a crowd of monkeys, each with a pair of immense and powerful wings on his shoulders. One, much bigger than the others, seemed to be their leader. He flew close to the

Witch and said, "You have called us for the third and last time. What do you command?" "Go to the strangers who are within my land and destroy them all except the Lion,"

said the Wicked Witch. "Bring that beast to me, for I have a mind to harness him like a horse, and make him work." "Your commands shall be obeyed," said the leader. Then,

with a great deal of chattering and noise, the Winged Monkeys flew away to the place where Dorothy and her friends were walking. Some of the Monkeys seized the Tin

Woodman and carried him through the air until they were over a country thickly covered with sharp rocks. Here they dropped the poor Woodman, who fell a great distance

to the rocks, where he lay so battered and dented that he could neither move nor groan. Others of the Monkeys caught the Scarecrow, and with their long fingers pulled all

of the straw out of his clothes and head. They made his hat and boots and clothes into a small bundle and threw it into the top branches of a tall tree. The remaining Monkeys

threw pieces of stout rope around the Lion and wound many coils about his body and head and legs, until he was unable to bite or scratch or struggle in any way. Then they

lifted him up and flew away with him to the Witch's castle, where he was placed in a small yard with a high iron fence around it, so that he could not escape. But Dorothy

they did not harm at all. She stood, with Toto in her arms, watching the sad fate of her comrades and thinking it would soon be her turn. The leader of the Winged Monkeys

flew up to her, his long, hairy arms stretched out and his ugly face grinning terribly; but he saw the mark of the Good Witch's kiss upon her forehead and stopped short,

motioning the others not to touch her. "We dare not harm this little girl," he said to them, "for she is protected by the Power of Good, and that is greater than the Power of

Evil. All we can do is to carry her to the castle of the Wicked Witch and leave her there." So, carefully and gently, they lifted Dorothy in their arms and carried her swiftly

through the air until they came to the castle, where they set her down upon the front doorstep. Then the leader said to the Witch: "We have obeyed you as far as we were

able. The Tin Woodman and the Scarecrow are destroyed, and the Lion is tied up in your yard. The little girl we dare not harm, nor the dog she carries in her arms. Your

power over our band is now ended, and you will never see us again." Then all the Winged Monkeys, with much laughing and chattering and noise, flew into the air and were

soon out of sight. The Wicked Witch was both surprised and worried when she saw the mark on Dorothy's forehead, for she knew well that neither the Winged Monkeys

nor she, herself, dare hurt the girl in any way. She looked down at Dorothy's feet, and seeing the Silver Shoes, began to tremble with fear, for she knew what a powerful

charm belonged to them. At first the Witch was tempted to run away from Dorothy; but she happened to look into the child's eyes and saw how simple the soul behind them

was, and that the little girl did not know of the wonderful power the Silver Shoes gave her. So the Wicked Witch laughed to herself, and thought, "I can still make her my

slave, for she does not know how to use her power." Then she said to Dorothy, harshly and severely: "Come with me; and see that you mind everything I tell you, for if you do not I will make an end of you, as I did of the Tin Woodman and the Scarecrow." Dorothy followed her through many of the beautiful rooms in her castle until they came

to the kitchen, where the Witch bade her clean the pots and kettles and sweep the floor and keep the fire fed with wood. Dorothy went to work meekly, with her mind made

up to work as hard as she could; for she was glad the Wicked Witch had decided not to kill her. With Dorothy hard at work, the Witch thought she would go into the

courtyard and harness the Cowardly Lion like a horse; it would amuse her, she was sure, to make him draw her chariot whenever she wished to go to drive. But as she opened

the gate the Lion gave a loud roar and bounded at her so fiercely that the Witch was afraid, and ran out and shut the gate again. "If I cannot harness you," said the Witch to

the Lion, speaking through the bars of the gate, "I can starve you. You shall have nothing to eat until you do as I wish." So after that she took no food to the imprisoned Lion;

but every day she came to the gate at noon and asked, "Are you ready to be harnessed like a horse?" And the Lion would answer, "No. If you come in this yard, I will bite

you." The reason the Lion did not have to do as the Witch wished was that every night, while the woman was asleep, Dorothy carried him food from the cupboard. After he

had eaten he would lie down on his bed of straw, and Dorothy would lie beside him and put her head on his soft, shaggy mane, while they talked of their troubles and tried

to plan some way to escape. But they could find no way to get out of the castle, for it was constantly guarded by the yellow Winkies, who were the slaves of the Wicked Witch

and too afraid of her not to do as she told them. The girl had to work hard during the day, and often the Witch threatened to beat her with the same old umbrella she always

carried in her hand. But, in truth, she did not dare to strike Dorothy, because of the mark upon her forehead. The child did not know this, and was full of fear for herself and

Toto. Once the Witch struck Toto a blow with her umbrella and the brave little dog flew at her and bit her leg in return. The Witch did not bleed where she was bitten, for

she was so wicked that the blood in her had dried up many years before. Dorothy's life became very sad as she grew to understand that it would be harder than ever to get

back to Kansas and Aunt Em again. Sometimes she would cry bitterly for hours, with Toto sitting at her feet and looking into her face, whining dismally to show how sorry

he was for his little mistress. Toto did not really care whether he was in Kansas or the Land of Oz so long as Dorothy was with him; but he knew the little girl was unhappy,

and that made him unhappy too. Now the Wicked Witch had a great longing to have for her own the Silver Shoes which the girl always wore. Her bees and her crows and

her wolves were lying in heaps and drying up, and she had used up all the power of the Golden Cap; but if she could only get hold of the Silver Shoes, they would give her

more power than all the other things she had lost. She watched Dorothy carefully, to see if she ever took off her shoes, thinking she might steal them. But the child was so

proud of her pretty shoes that she never took them off except at night and when she took her bath. The Witch was too much afraid of the dark to dare go in Dorothy's room

at night to take the shoes, and her dread of water was greater than her fear of the dark, so she never came near when Dorothy was bathing. Indeed, the old Witch never

touched water, nor ever let water touch her in any way. But the wicked creature was very cunning, and she finally thought of a trick that would give her what she wanted.

She placed a bar of iron in the middle of the kitchen floor, and then by her magic arts made the iron invisible to human eyes. So that when Dorothy walked across the floor she stumbled over the bar, not being able to see it, and fell at full length. She was not much hurt, but in her fall one of the Silver Shoes came off; and before she could reach it, the Witch had snatched it away and put it on her own skinny foot. The wicked woman was greatly pleased with the success of her trick, for as long as she had one of the shoes she owned half the power of their charm, and Dorothy could not use it against her, even had she known how to do so. The little girl, seeing she had lost one of her pretty shoes, grew angry, and said to the Witch, "Give me back my shoe!" "I will not," retorted the Witch, "for it is now my shoe, and not yours." "You are a wicked creature!" cried Dorothy. "You have no right to take my shoe from me." "I shall keep it, just the same," said the Witch, laughing at her, "and someday I shall get the other one from you, too." This made Dorothy so very angry that she picked up the bucket of water that stood near and dashed it over the Witch, wetting her from head to foot.

Instantly the wicked woman gave a loud cry of fear, and then, as Dorothy looked at her in wonder, the Witch began to shrink and fall away. "See what you have done!" she screamed. "In a minute I shall melt away." "I'm very sorry, indeed," said Dorothy, who was truly frightened to see the Witch actually melting away like brown sugar before her very eyes. "Didn't you know water would be the end of me?" asked the Witch, in a wailing, despairing voice. "Of course not," answered Dorothy. "How should I?" "Well, in a few minutes I shall be all melted, and you will have the castle to yourself. I have been wicked in my day, but I never thought a little girl like you would ever be able to melt me and end my wicked deeds. Look out—here I go!" With these words the Witch fell down in a brown, melted, shapeless mass and began to spread over the clean boards of the kitchen floor. Seeing that she had really melted away to nothing, Dorothy drew another bucket of water and threw it over the mess. She then swept it all out the door. After picking out the silver shoe, which was all that was left of the old woman, she cleaned and dried it with a cloth, and put it on her foot again. Then, being at last free to do as she chose, she ran out to the courtyard to tell the Lion that the Wicked Witch of the West had come to an end, and that they were no longer prisoners in a strange land. CHAPTER XIII The Rescue The Cowardly Lion was much pleased to hear that the Wicked Witch had been melted by a bucket of water, and Dorothy at once unlocked the gate of his prison and set him free. They went in together to the castle, where Dorothy's first act was to call all the Winkies together and tell them that they were no longer slaves. There was great rejoicing among the yellow Winkies, for they had been made to work hard during many years for the Wicked Witch, who had always treated them with great cruelty. They kept this day as a holiday, then and ever after, and spent the time in feasting and dancing. "If our friends, the Scarecrow and the Tin Woodman, were only with us," said the Lion, "I should be quite happy." "Don't you suppose we could rescue them?" asked the girl anxiously. "We can try," answered the Lion. So they called the yellow Winkies and asked them if they would help to rescue their friends, and the Winkies said that they would be delighted to do all in their power for Dorothy, who had set them free from bondage. So she chose a number of the Winkies who looked as if they knew the most, and they all started away. They traveled that day and part of the next until they came to the rocky plain where the Tin Woodman lay, all battered and bent. His axe was near him, but the blade was rusted and the handle broken off short. The Winkies lifted him tenderly in their arms, and carried him back to the Yellow Castle again, Dorothy shedding a few tears by the way at the sad plight of her old friend, and the Lion looking sober and sorry. When they reached the castle Dorothy said to the Winkies: "Are any of your people tinsmiths?" "Oh, yes. Some of

us are very good tinsmiths," they told her. "Then bring them to me," she said. And when the tinsmiths came, bringing with them all their tools in baskets, she inquired, "Can

you straighten out those dents in the Tin Woodman, and bend him back into shape again, and solder him together where he is broken?" The tinsmiths looked the Woodman

over carefully and then answered that they thought they could mend him so he would be as good as ever. So they set to work in one of the big yellow rooms of the castle and

worked for three days and four nights, hammering and twisting and bending and soldering and polishing and pounding at the legs and body and head of the Tin Woodman,

until at last he was straightened out into his old form, and his joints worked as well as ever. To be sure, there were several patches on him, but the tinsmiths did a good job,

and as the Woodman was not a vain man he did not mind the patches at all. When, at last, he walked into Dorothy's room and thanked her for rescuing him, he was so pleased

that he wept tears of joy, and Dorothy had to wipe every tear carefully from his face with her apron, so his joints would not be rusted. At the same time her own tears fell

thick and fast at the joy of meeting her old friend again, and these tears did not need to be wiped away. As for the Lion, he wiped his eyes so often with the tip of his tail that

it became quite wet, and he was obliged to go out into the courtyard and hold it in the sun till it dried. "If we only had the Scarecrow with us again," said the Tin Woodman,

when Dorothy had finished telling him everything that had happened, "I should be quite happy." "We must try to find him," said the girl. So she called the Winkies to help

her, and they walked all that day and part of the next until they came to the tall tree in the branches of which the Winged Monkeys had tossed the Scarecrow's clothes. It was

a very tall tree, and the trunk was so smooth that no one could climb it; but the Woodman said at once, "I'll chop it down, and then we can get the Scarecrow's clothes." Now

while the tinsmiths had been at work mending the Woodman himself, another of the Winkies, who was a goldsmith, had made an axe-handle of solid gold and fitted it to the

Woodman's axe, instead of the old broken handle. Others polished the blade until all the rust was removed and it glistened like burnished silver. As soon as he had spoken,

the Tin Woodman began to chop, and in a short time the tree fell over with a crash, whereupon the Scarecrow's clothes fell out of the branches and rolled off on the ground.

Dorothy picked them up and had the Winkies carry them back to the castle, where they were stuffed with nice, clean straw; and behold! here was the Scarecrow, as good as

ever, thanking them over and over again for saving him. Now that they were reunited, Dorothy and her friends spent a few happy days at the Yellow Castle, where they found

everything they needed to make them comfortable. But one day the girl thought of Aunt Em, and said, "We must go back to Oz, and claim his promise." "Yes," said the

Woodman, "at last I shall get my heart." "And I shall get my brains," added the Scarecrow joyfully. "And I shall get my courage," said the Lion thoughtfully. "And I shall

get back to Kansas," cried Dorothy, clapping her hands. "Oh, let us start for the Emerald City tomorrow!" This they decided to do. The next day they called the Winkies

together and bade them good-bye. The Winkies were sorry to have them go, and they had grown so fond of the Tin Woodman that they begged him to stay and rule over

them and the Yellow Land of the West. Finding they were determined to go, the Winkies gave Toto and the Lion each a golden collar; and to Dorothy they presented a beautiful bracelet studded with diamonds; and to the Scarecrow they gave a gold-headed walking stick, to keep him from stumbling; and to the Tin Woodman they offered a silver oilcan, inlaid with gold and set with precious jewels. Every one of the travelers made the Winkies a pretty speech in return, and all shook hands with them until their arms ached. Dorothy went to the Witch's cupboard to fill her basket with food for the journey, and there she saw the Golden Cap. She tried it on her own head and found that it fitted her exactly. She did not know anything about the charm of the Golden Cap, but she saw that it was pretty, so she made up her mind to wear it and carry her sunbonnet in the basket. Then, being prepared for the journey, they all started for the Emerald City; and the Winkies gave them three cheers and many good wishes to carry with them. CHAPTER XIV The Winged Monkeys You will remember there was no road—not even a pathway—between the castle of the Wicked Witch and the Emerald City. When the four travelers went in search of the Witch she had seen them coming, and so sent the Winged Monkeys to bring them to her. It was much harder to find their way back through the big fields of buttercups and yellow daisies than it was being carried. They knew, of course, they must go straight east, toward the rising sun; and they started off in the right way. But at noon, when the sun was over their heads, they did not know which was east and which was west, and that was the reason they were lost in the great fields. They kept on walking, however, and at night the moon came out and shone brightly. So they lay down among the sweet-smelling yellow flowers and slept soundly until morning—all but the Scarecrow and the Tin Woodman. The next morning the sun was behind a cloud, but they started on, as if they were quite sure which way they were going. "If we walk far enough," said Dorothy, "I am sure we shall sometime come to some place." But day by day passed away, and they still saw nothing before them but the scarlet fields. The Scarecrow began to grumble a bit. "We have surely lost our way," he said, "and unless we find it again in time to reach the Emerald City, I shall never get my brains." "Nor I my heart," declared the Tin Woodman. "It seems to me I can scarcely wait till I get to Oz, and you must admit this is a very long journey." "You see," said the Cowardly Lion, with a whimper, "I haven't the courage to keep tramping forever, without getting anywhere at all." Then Dorothy lost heart. She sat down on the grass and looked at her companions, and they sat down and looked at her, and Toto found that for the first time in his life he was too tired to chase a butterfly that flew past his head. So he put out his tongue and panted and looked at Dorothy as if to ask what they should do next. "Suppose we call the field mice," she suggested. "They could probably tell us the way to the Emerald City." "To be sure they could," cried the Scarecrow. "Why didn't we think of that before?" Dorothy blew the little whistle she had always carried about her neck since the Queen of the Mice had given it to her. In a few minutes they heard the pattering of tiny feet, and many of the small gray mice came running up to her. Among them was the Queen herself, who asked, in her squeaky little voice: "What can I do for my friends?" "We have lost our way," said Dorothy. "Can you tell us where the Emerald City is?" "Certainly," answered the Queen; "but it is a great way off, for you have had it at your backs all this time." Then she noticed Dorothy's Golden Cap, and said, "Why don't you use the charm of the Cap, and call the Winged Monkeys to you? They will carry you to the City of Oz in less than an hour." "I didn't know there was a charm," answered Dorothy, in surprise. "What is it?" "It is written inside the Golden Cap," replied the Queen of the Mice.

"But if you are going to call the Winged Monkeys we must run away, for they are full of mischief and think it great fun to plague us." "Won't they hurt me?" asked the girl

anxiously. "Oh, no. They must obey the wearer of the Cap. Good-bye!" And she scampered out of sight, with all the mice hurrying after her. Dorothy looked inside the

Golden Cap and saw some words written upon the lining. These, she thought, must be the charm, so she read the directions carefully and put the Cap upon her head. "Ep-pe,

pep-pe, kak-ke!" she said, standing on her left foot. "What did you say?" asked the Scarecrow, who did not know what she was doing. "Hil-lo, hol-lo, hel-lo!" Dorothy went

on, standing this time on her right foot. "Hello!" replied the Tin Woodman calmly. "Ziz-zy, zuz-zy, zik!" said Dorothy, who was now standing on both feet. This ended the

saying of the charm, and they heard a great chattering and flapping of wings, as the band of Winged Monkeys flew up to them. The King bowed low before Dorothy, and

asked, "What is your command?" "We wish to go to the Emerald City," said the child, "and we have lost our way." "We will carry you," replied the King, and no sooner

had he spoken than two of the Monkeys caught Dorothy in their arms and flew away with her. Others took the Scarecrow and the Woodman and the Lion, and one little

Monkey seized Toto and flew after them, although the dog tried hard to bite him. The Scarecrow and the Tin Woodman were rather frightened at first, for they remembered

how badly the Winged Monkeys had treated them before; but they saw that no harm was intended, so they rode through the air quite cheerfully, and had a fine time looking

at the pretty gardens and woods far below them. Dorothy found herself riding easily between two of the biggest Monkeys, one of them the King himself. They had made a

chair of their hands and were careful not to hurt her. "Why do you have to obey the charm of the Golden Cap?" she asked. "That is a long story," answered the King, with

a laugh; "but as we have a long journey before us, I will pass the time by telling you about it, if you wish." "I shall be glad to hear it," she replied. "Once," began the leader,

"we were a free people, living happily in the great forest, flying from tree to tree, eating nuts and fruit, and doing just as we pleased without calling anybody master. Perhaps

some of us were rather too full of mischief at times, flying down to pull the tails of the animals that had no wings, chasing birds, and throwing nuts at the people who walked

in the forest. But we were careless and happy and full of fun, and enjoyed every minute of the day. This was many years ago, long before Oz came out of the clouds to rule

over this land. "There lived here then, away at the North, a beautiful princess, who was also a powerful sorceress. All her magic was used to help the people, and she was

never known to hurt anyone who was good. Her name was Gayelette, and she lived in a handsome palace built from great blocks of ruby. Everyone loved her, but her greatest

sorrow was that she could find no one to love in return, since all the men were much too stupid and ugly to mate with one so beautiful and wise. At last, however, she found

a boy who was handsome and manly and wise beyond his years. Gayelette made up her mind that when he grew to be a man she would make him her husband, so she took

him to her ruby palace and used all her magic powers to make him as strong and good and lovely as any woman could wish. When he grew to manhood, Quelala, as he was

called, was said to be the best and wisest man in all the land, while his manly beauty was so great that Gayelette loved him dearly, and hastened to make everything ready for

the wedding. "My grandfather was at that time the King of the Winged Monkeys which lived in the forest near Gayelette's palace, and the old fellow loved a joke better than a good dinner. One day, just before the wedding, my grandfather was flying out with his band when he saw Quelala walking beside the river. He was dressed in a rich costume of pink silk and purple velvet, and my grandfather thought he would see what he could do. At his word the band flew down and seized Quelala, carried him in their arms until they were over the middle of the river, and then dropped him into the water. "'Swim out, my fine fellow,' cried my grandfather, 'and see if the water has spotted your clothes.' Quelala was much too wise not to swim, and he was not in the least spoiled by all his good fortune. He laughed, when he came to the top of the water, and swam in to shore. But when Gayelette came running out to him she found his silks and velvet all ruined by the river. "The princess was angry, and she knew, of course, who did it. She had all the Winged Monkeys brought before her, and she said at first that their wings should be tied and they should be treated as they had treated Quelala, and dropped in the river. But my grandfather pleaded hard, for he knew the Monkeys would drown in the river with their wings tied, and Quelala said a kind word for them also; so that Gayelette finally spared them, on condition that the Winged Monkeys should ever after do three times the bidding of the owner of the Golden Cap. This Cap had been made for a wedding present to Quelala, and it is said to have cost the princess half her kingdom. Of course my grandfather and all the other Monkeys at once agreed to the condition, and that is how it happens that we are three times the slaves of the owner of the Golden Cap, whosoever he may be." "And what became of them?" asked Dorothy, who had been greatly interested in the story. "Quelala being the first owner of the Golden Cap," replied the Monkey, "he was the first to lay his wishes upon us. As his bride could not bear the sight of us, he called us all to him in the forest after he had married her and ordered us always to keep where she could never again set eyes on a Winged Monkey, which we were glad to do, for we were all afraid of her. "This was all we ever had to do until the Golden Cap fell into the hands of the Wicked Witch of the West, who made us enslave the Winkies, and afterward drive Oz himself out of the Land of the West. Now the Golden Cap is yours, and three times you have the right to lay your wishes upon us." As the Monkey King finished his story Dorothy looked down and saw the green, shining walls of the Emerald City before them. She wondered at the rapid flight of the Monkeys, but was glad the journey was over. The strange creatures set the travelers down carefully before the gate of the City, the King bowed low to Dorothy, and then flew swiftly away, followed by all his band. "That was a good ride," said the little girl. "Yes, and a quick way out of our troubles," replied the Lion. "How lucky it was you brought away that wonderful Cap!" CHAPTER XV The Discovery of Oz, the Terrible The four travelers walked up to the great gate of Emerald City and rang the bell. After ringing several times, it was opened by the same Guardian of the Gates they had met before. "What! are you back again?" he asked, in surprise. "Do you not see us?" answered the Scarecrow. "But I thought you had gone to visit the Wicked Witch of the West." "We did visit her," said the Scarecrow. "And she let you go again?" asked the man, in wonder. "She could not help it, for she is melted," explained the Scarecrow. "Melted! Well, that is good news, indeed," said the man. "Who melted her?" "It was Dorothy," said the Lion gravely. "Good gracious!" exclaimed the man, and he bowed very low indeed before her. Then he led them into his little room and locked the spectacles from the great box on all their eyes, just as he had done before. Afterward they passed on through the gate into the Emerald City. When the people heard from the Guardian of the Gates that Dorothy had melted the Wicked Witch of the West, they all gathered around the travelers and followed them in a great crowd to the Palace of Oz. The soldier with the green whiskers was still on guard before the door, but he let them in at once, and they were again met by the beautiful green girl, who showed each of them to their old rooms at once, so they might rest until the Great Oz was ready to receive them. The soldier had the news carried straight to Oz that Dorothy and the other travelers had come back again, after destroying the Wicked Witch; but Oz made no reply. They thought the Great Wizard would send for them at once, but he did not. They had no word from him the next day, nor the next, nor the next. The waiting was tiresome and wearing, and at last they grew vexed that Oz should treat them in so poor a fashion, after sending them to undergo hardships and slavery. So the Scarecrow at last asked the green girl to take another message to Oz, saying if he did not let them in to see him at once they would call the Winged Monkeys to help them, and find out whether he kept his promises or not. When the Wizard was given this message he was so frightened that he sent word for them to come to the Throne Room at four minutes after nine o'clock the next morning. He had once met the Winged Monkeys in the Land of the West, and he did not wish to meet them again. The four travelers passed a sleepless night, each thinking of the gift Oz had promised to bestow on him. Dorothy fell asleep only once, and then she dreamed she was in Kansas, where Aunt Em was telling her how glad she was to have her little girl at home again. Promptly at nine o'clock the next morning the green-whiskered soldier came to them, and four minutes later they all went into the Throne Room of the Great Oz. Of course each one of them expected to see the Wizard in the shape he had taken before, and all were greatly surprised when they looked about and saw no one at all in the room. They kept close to the door and closer to one another, for the stillness of the empty room was more dreadful than any of the forms they had seen Oz take. Presently they heard a solemn Voice, that seemed to come from somewhere near the top of the great dome, and it said: "I am Oz, the Great and Terrible. Why do you seek me?" They looked again in every part of the room, and then, seeing no one, Dorothy asked, "Where are you?" "I am everywhere," answered the Voice, "but to the eyes of common mortals I am invisible. I will now seat myself upon my throne, that you may converse with me." Indeed, the Voice seemed just then to come straight from the throne itself; so they walked toward it and stood in a row while Dorothy said: "We have come to claim our promise, O Oz." "What promise?" asked Oz. "You promised to send me back to Kansas when the Wicked Witch was destroyed," said the girl. "And you promised to give me brains," said the Scarecrow. "And you promised to give me a heart," said the Tin Woodman. "And you promised to give me courage," said the Cowardly Lion. "Is the Wicked Witch really destroyed?" asked the Voice, and Dorothy thought it trembled a little. "Yes," she answered, "I melted her with a bucket of water." "Dear me," said the Voice, "how sudden! Well, come to me tomorrow, for I must have time to think it over." "You've had plenty of time already," said the Tin Woodman angrily. "We shan't wait a day longer," said the Scarecrow. "You must keep your promises to us!" exclaimed Dorothy. The Lion thought it might be as well to frighten the Wizard, so he gave a large, loud roar, which was so fierce and dreadful that Toto jumped away from him in alarm and tipped over the screen that stood in a corner. As it fell with a crash they looked that way, and the next moment all of them were filled with wonder. For they saw, standing in just the spot the screen had hidden, a little old man, with a bald head and a wrinkled face, who seemed to be as much surprised as they were. The Tin Woodman, raising his axe, rushed toward the little man and cried out, "Who are you?" "I am Oz, the Great and Terrible," said the little man, in a trembling voice. "But don't strike me—please don't—and I'll do anything you want me to." Our friends looked at him in surprise and dismay. "I thought Oz was a great Head," said Dorothy. "And I thought Oz was a lovely Lady," said the Scarecrow. "And I thought Oz was a terrible Beast," said the Tin Woodman. "And I thought Oz was a Ball of Fire," exclaimed the Lion. "No, you are all wrong," said the little man meekly. "I have been making believe." "Making believe!" cried Dorothy. "Are you not a Great Wizard?" "Hush, my dear," he said. "Don't speak so loud, or you will be overheard—and I should be ruined. I'm supposed to be a Great Wizard." "And aren't you?" she asked. "Not a bit of it, my dear; I'm just a common man."

"You're more than that," said the Scarecrow, in a grieved tone; "you're a humbug." "Exactly so!" declared the little man, rubbing his hands together as if it pleased him. "I am a humbug." "But this is terrible," said the Tin Woodman. "How shall I ever get my heart?" "Or I my courage?" asked the Lion. "Or I my brains?" wailed the Scarecrow, wiping the tears from his eyes with his coat sleeve. "My dear friends," said Oz, "I pray you not to speak of these little things. Think of me, and the terrible trouble I'm in at being found out." "Doesn't anyone else know you're a humbug?" asked Dorothy. "No one knows it but you four—and myself," replied Oz. "I have fooled everyone so long that I thought I should never be found out. It was a great mistake my ever letting you into the Throne Room. Usually I will not see even my subjects, and so they believe I am something terrible." "But, I don't understand," said Dorothy, in bewilderment. "How was it that you appeared to me as a great Head?" "That was one of my tricks," answered Oz. "Step this way, please, and I will tell you all about it." He led the way to a small chamber in the rear of the Throne Room, and they all followed him. He pointed to one corner, in which lay the great Head, made out of many thicknesses of paper, and with a carefully painted face. "This I hung from the ceiling by a wire," said Oz. "I stood behind the screen and pulled a thread, to make the eyes move and the mouth open." "But how about the voice?" she inquired. "Oh, I am a ventriloquist," said the little man. "I can throw the sound of my voice wherever I wish, so that you thought it was coming out of the Head. Here are the other things I used to deceive you." He showed the Scarecrow the dress and the mask he had worn when he seemed to be the lovely Lady. And the Tin Woodman saw that his terrible Beast was nothing but a lot of skins, sewn together, with slats to keep their sides out. As for the Ball of Fire, the false Wizard had hung that also from the ceiling. It was really a ball of cotton, but when oil was poured upon it the ball burned fiercely. "Really," said the Scarecrow, "you ought to be ashamed of yourself for being such a humbug." "I am—I certainly am," answered the little man sorrowfully; "but it was the only thing I could do. Sit down, please, there are plenty of chairs; and I will tell you my story." So they sat down and listened while he told the following tale. "I was born in Omaha—" "Why, that isn't very far from Kansas!" cried Dorothy. "No, but it's farther from here," he said, shaking his head at her sadly. "When I grew up I became a ventriloquist, and at that I was very well trained by a great master. I can imitate any kind of a bird or beast." Here he mewed so like a kitten that Toto pricked up his ears and looked everywhere to see where she was. "After a time," continued Oz, "I tired of that, and became a balloonist." "What is that?"

asked Dorothy. "A man who goes up in a balloon on circus day, so as to draw a crowd of people together and get them to pay to see the circus," he explained. "Oh," she said, "I know." "Well, one day I went up in a balloon and the ropes got twisted, so that I couldn't come down again. It went way up above the clouds, so far that a current of air struck it and carried it many, many miles away. For a day and a night I traveled through the air, and on the morning of the second day I awoke and found the balloon floating over a strange and beautiful country. "It came down gradually, and I was not hurt a bit. But I found myself in the midst of a strange people, who, seeing me come from the clouds, thought I was a great Wizard. Of course I let them think so, because they were afraid of me, and promised to do anything I wished them to. "Just to amuse myself, and keep the good people busy, I ordered them to build this City, and my Palace; and they did it all willingly and well. Then I thought, as the country was so green and beautiful, I would call it the Emerald City; and to make the name fit better I put green spectacles on all the people, so that everything they saw was green." "But isn't everything here green?" asked Dorothy. "No more than in any other city," replied Oz; "but when you wear green spectacles, why of course everything you see looks green to you. The Emerald City was built a great many years ago, for I was a young man when the balloon brought me here, and I am a very old man now. But my people have worn green glasses on their eyes so long that most of them think it really is an Emerald City, and it certainly is a beautiful place, abounding in jewels and precious metals, and every good thing that is needed to make one happy. I have been good to the people, and they like me; but ever since this Palace was built, I have shut myself up and would not see any of them. "One of my greatest fears was the Witches, for while I had no magical powers at all I soon found out that the Witches were really able to do wonderful things. There were four of them in this country, and they ruled the people who live in the North and South and East and West. Fortunately, the Witches of the North and South were good, and I knew they would do me no harm; but the Witches of the East and West were terribly wicked, and had they not thought I was more powerful than they themselves, they would surely have destroyed me. As it was, I lived in deadly fear of them for many years; so you can imagine how pleased I was when I heard your house had fallen on the Wicked Witch of the East. When you came to me, I was willing to promise anything if you would only do away with the other Witch; but, now that you have melted her, I am ashamed to say that I cannot keep my promises." "I think you are a very bad man," said Dorothy. "Oh, no, my dear; I'm really a very good man, but I'm a very bad Wizard, I must admit." "Can't you give me brains?" asked the Scarecrow. "You don't need them. You are learning something every day. A baby has brains, but it doesn't know much. Experience is the only thing that brings knowledge, and the longer you are on earth the more experience you are sure to get." "That may all be true," said the Scarecrow, "but I shall be very unhappy unless you give me brains." The false Wizard looked at him carefully. "Well," he said with a sigh, "I'm not much of a magician, as I said; but if you will come to me tomorrow morning, I will stuff your head with brains. I cannot tell you how to use them, however; you must find that out for yourself." "Oh, thank you—thank you!" cried the Scarecrow. "I'll find a way to use them, never fear!" "But how about my courage?" asked the Lion anxiously. "You have plenty of courage, I am sure," answered Oz. "All you need is confidence in yourself. There is no living thing that is not afraid when it faces danger. True courage is in facing danger when you are afraid, and that kind of courage you have in plenty." "Perhaps I have, but I'm scared just the same," said the Lion. "I shall really be very unhappy

unless you give me the sort of courage that makes one forget he is afraid." "Very well, I will give you that sort of courage tomorrow," replied Oz. "How about my heart?"

asked the Tin Woodman. "Why, as for that," answered Oz, "I think you are wrong to want a heart. It makes most people unhappy. If you only knew it, you are in luck not

to have a heart." "That must be a matter of opinion," said the Tin Woodman. "For my part, I will bear all the unhappiness without a murmur, if you will give me the heart."

"Very well," answered Oz meekly. "Come to me tomorrow and you shall have a heart. I have played Wizard for so many years that I may as well continue the part a little

longer." "And now," said Dorothy, "how am I to get back to Kansas?" "We shall have to think about that," replied the little man. "Give me two or three days to consider the

matter and I'll try to find a way to carry you over the desert. In the meantime you shall all be treated as my guests, and while you live in the Palace my people will wait upon

you and obey your slightest wish. There is only one thing I ask in return for my help—such as it is. You must keep my secret and tell no one I am a humbug." They agreed

to say nothing of what they had learned, and went back to their rooms in high spirits. Even Dorothy had hope that "The Great and Terrible Humbug," as she called him,

would find a way to send her back to Kansas, and if he did she was willing to forgive him everything. CHAPTER XVI The Magic Art of the Great Humbug Next morning

the Scarecrow said to his friends: "Congratulate me. I am going to Oz to get my brains at last. When I return I shall be as other men are." "I have always liked you as you

were," said Dorothy simply. "It is kind of you to like a Scarecrow," he replied. "But surely you will think more of me when you hear the splendid thoughts my new brain is

going to turn out." Then he said good-bye to them all in a cheerful voice and went to the Throne Room, where he rapped upon the door. "Come in," said Oz. The Scarecrow

went in and found the little man sitting down by the window, engaged in deep thought. "I have come for my brains," remarked the Scarecrow, a little uneasily. "Oh, yes; sit

down in that chair, please," replied Oz. "You must excuse me for taking your head off, but I shall have to do it in order to put your brains in their proper place." "That's all

right," said the Scarecrow. "You are quite welcome to take my head off, as long as it will be a better one when you put it on again." So the Wizard unfastened his head and

emptied out the straw. Then he entered the back room and took up a measure of bran, which he mixed with a great many pins and needles. Having shaken them together

thoroughly, he filled the top of the Scarecrow's head with the mixture and stuffed the rest of the space with straw, to hold it in place. When he had fastened the Scarecrow's

head on his body again he said to him, "Hereafter you will be a great man, for I have given you a lot of bran-new brains." The Scarecrow was both pleased and proud at the

fulfillment of his greatest wish, and having thanked Oz warmly he went back to his friends. Dorothy looked at him curiously. His head was quite bulged out at the top with

brains. "How do you feel?" she asked. "I feel wise indeed," he answered earnestly. "When I get used to my brains I shall know everything." "Why are those needles and pins

sticking out of your head?" asked the Tin Woodman. "That is proof that he is sharp," remarked the Lion. "Well, I must go to Oz and get my heart," said the Woodman. So

he walked to the Throne Room and knocked at the door. "Come in," called Oz, and the Woodman entered and said, "I have come for my heart." "Very well," answered the little man. "But I shall have to cut a hole in your breast, so I can put your heart in the right place. I hope it won't hurt you." "Oh, no," answered the Woodman. "I shall not

feel it at all." So Oz brought a pair of tinsmith's shears and cut a small, square hole in the left side of the Tin Woodman's breast. Then, going to a chest of drawers, he took

out a pretty heart, made entirely of silk and stuffed with sawdust. "Isn't it a beauty?" he asked. "It is, indeed!" replied the Woodman, who was greatly pleased. "But is it a

kind heart?" "Oh, very!" answered Oz. He put the heart in the Woodman's breast and then replaced the square of tin, soldering it neatly together where it had been cut.

"There," said he; "now you have a heart that any man might be proud of. I'm sorry I had to put a patch on your breast, but it really couldn't be helped." "Never mind the

patch," exclaimed the happy Woodman. "I am very grateful to you, and shall never forget your kindness." "Don't speak of it," replied Oz. Then the Tin Woodman went

back to his friends, who wished him every joy on account of his good fortune. The Lion now walked to the Throne Room and knocked at the door. "Come in," said Oz. "I

have come for my courage," announced the Lion, entering the room. "Very well," answered the little man; "I will get it for you." He went to a cupboard and reaching up to

a high shelf took down a square green bottle, the contents of which he poured into a green-gold dish, beautifully carved. Placing this before the Cowardly Lion, who sniffed

at it as if he did not like it, the Wizard said: "Drink." "What is it?" asked the Lion. "Well," answered Oz, "if it were inside of you, it would be courage. You know, of course,

that courage is always inside one; so that this really cannot be called courage until you have swallowed it. Therefore I advise you to drink it as soon as possible." The Lion

hesitated no longer, but drank till the dish was empty. "How do you feel now?" asked Oz. "Full of courage," replied the Lion, who went joyfully back to his friends to tell

them of his good fortune. Oz, left to himself, smiled to think of his success in giving the Scarecrow and the Tin Woodman and the Lion exactly what they thought they

wanted. "How can I help being a humbug," he said, "when all these people make me do things that everybody knows can't be done? It was easy to make the Scarecrow and

the Lion and the Woodman happy, because they imagined I could do anything. But it will take more than imagination to carry Dorothy back to Kansas, and I'm sure I don't

know how it can be done." CHAPTER XVII How the Balloon Was Launched For three days Dorothy heard nothing from Oz. These were sad days for the little girl,

although her friends were all quite happy and contented. The Scarecrow told them there were wonderful thoughts in his head; but he would not say what they were because

he knew no one could understand them but himself. When the Tin Woodman walked about he felt his heart rattling around in his breast; and he told Dorothy he had

discovered it to be a kinder and more tender heart than the one he had owned when he was made of flesh. The Lion declared he was afraid of nothing on earth, and would

gladly face an army or a dozen of the fierce Kalidahs. Thus each of the little party was satisfied except Dorothy, who longed more than ever to get back to Kansas. On the

fourth day, to her great joy, Oz sent for her, and when she entered the Throne Room he greeted her pleasantly: "Sit down, my dear; I think I have found the way to get you

out of this country." "And back to Kansas?" she asked eagerly. "Well, I'm not sure about Kansas," said Oz, "for I haven't the faintest notion which way it lies. But the first

thing to do is to cross the desert, and then it should be easy to find your way home." "How can I cross the desert?" she inquired. "Well, I'll tell you what I think," said the little man. "You see, when I came to this country it was in a balloon. You also came through the air, being carried by a cyclone. So I believe the best way to get across the desert will be through the air. Now, it is quite beyond my powers to make a cyclone; but I've been thinking the matter over, and I believe I can make a balloon." "How?" asked Dorothy. "A balloon," said Oz, "is made of silk, which is coated with glue to keep the gas in it. I have plenty of silk in the Palace, so it will be no trouble to make the balloon. But in all this country there is no gas to fill the balloon with, to make it float." "If it won't float," remarked Dorothy, "it will be of no use to us." "True," answered Oz. "But there is another way to make it float, which is to fill it with hot air. Hot air isn't as good as gas, for if the air should get cold the balloon would come down in the desert, and we should be lost." "We!" exclaimed the girl. "Are you going with me?" "Yes, of course," replied Oz. "I am tired of being such a humbug. If I should go out of this Palace my people would soon discover I am not a Wizard, and then they would be vexed with me for having deceived them. So I have to stay shut up in these rooms all day, and it gets tiresome. I'd much rather go back to Kansas with you and be in a circus again." "I shall be glad to have your company," said Dorothy. "Thank you," he answered. "Now, if you will help me sew the silk together, we will begin to work on our balloon." So Dorothy took a needle and thread, and as fast as Oz cut the strips of silk into proper shape the girl sewed them neatly together. First there was a strip of light green silk, then a strip of dark green and then a strip of emerald green; for Oz had a fancy to make the balloon in different shades of the color about them. It took three days to sew all the strips together, but when it was finished they had a big bag of green silk more than twenty feet long. Then Oz painted it on the inside with a coat of thin glue, to make it airtight, after which he announced that the balloon was ready. "But we must have a basket to ride in," he said. So he sent the soldier with the green whiskers for a big clothes basket, which he fastened with many ropes to the bottom of the balloon. When it was all ready, Oz sent word to his people that he was going to make a visit to a great brother Wizard who lived in the clouds. The news spread rapidly throughout the city and everyone came to see the wonderful sight. Oz ordered the balloon carried out in front of the Palace, and the people gazed upon it with much curiosity. The Tin Woodman had chopped a big pile of wood, and now he made a fire of it, and Oz held the bottom of the balloon over the fire so that the hot air that arose from it would be caught in the silken bag. Gradually the balloon swelled out and rose into the air, until finally the basket just touched the ground. Then Oz got into the basket and said to all the people in a loud voice: "I am now going away to make a visit. While I am gone the Scarecrow will rule over you. I command you to obey him as you would me." The balloon was by this time tugging hard at the rope that held it to the ground, for the air within it was hot, and this made it so much lighter in weight than the air without that it pulled hard to rise into the sky. "Come, Dorothy!" cried the Wizard. "Hurry up, or the balloon will fly away." "I can't find Toto anywhere," replied Dorothy, who did not wish to leave her little dog behind. Toto had run into the crowd to bark at a kitten, and Dorothy at last found him. She picked him up and ran toward the balloon. She was within a few steps of it, and Oz was holding out his hands to help her into the basket, when, crack! went the ropes, and the balloon rose into the air without her. "Come back!" she screamed. "I want to go, too!" "I can't come back, my dear," called Oz from the basket. "Good-bye!" "Good-bye!" shouted everyone, and all eyes were turned upward to where the Wizard was riding in the basket, rising every moment farther and farther into the sky. And that was the last any of them ever saw of Oz, the Wonderful Wizard, though he may have reached Omaha safely, and be there now, for all we know. But the people remembered him lovingly, and said to one another: "Oz was always our friend. When he was here he built for us this beautiful Emerald City, and now he is gone he has left the Wise Scarecrow to rule over us." Still, for many days they grieved over the loss of the Wonderful Wizard, and would not be comforted. CHAPTER XVIII Away to the South Dorothy wept bitterly at the passing of her hope to get home to Kansas again; but when she thought it all over she was glad she had not gone up in a balloon. And she also felt sorry at losing Oz, and so did her companions. The Tin Woodman came to her and said: "Truly I should be ungrateful if I failed to mourn for the man who gave me my lovely heart. I should like to cry a little because Oz is gone, if you will kindly wipe away my tears, so that I shall not rust." "With pleasure," she answered, and brought a towel at once. Then the Tin Woodman wept for several minutes, and she watched the tears carefully and wiped them away with the towel. When he had finished, he thanked her kindly and oiled himself thoroughly with his jeweled oilcan, to guard against mishap. The Scarecrow was now the ruler of the Emerald City, and although he was not a Wizard the people were proud of him. "For," they said, "there is not another city in all the world that is ruled by a stuffed man." And, so far as they knew, they were quite right. The morning after the balloon had gone up with Oz, the four travelers met in the Throne Room and talked matters over. The Scarecrow sat in the big throne and the others stood respectfully before him. "We are not so unlucky," said the new ruler, "for this Palace and the Emerald City belong to us, and we can do just as we please. When I remember that a short time ago I was up on a pole in a farmer's cornfield, and that now I am the ruler of this beautiful City, I am quite satisfied with my lot." "I also," said the Tin Woodman, "am well-pleased with my new heart; and, really, that was the only thing I wished in all the world." "For my part, I am content in knowing I am as brave as any beast that ever lived, if not braver," said the Lion modestly. "If Dorothy would only be contented to live in the Emerald City," continued the Scarecrow, "we might all be happy together." "But I don't want to live here," cried Dorothy. "I want to go to Kansas, and live with Aunt Em and Uncle Henry." "Well, then, what can be done?" inquired the Woodman. The Scarecrow decided to think, and he thought so hard that the pins and needles began to stick out of his brains. Finally he said: "Why not call the Winged Monkeys, and ask them to carry you over the desert?" "I never thought of that!" said Dorothy joyfully. "It's just the thing. I'll go at once for the Golden Cap." When she brought it into the Throne Room she spoke the magic words, and soon the band of Winged Monkeys flew in through the open window and stood beside her. "This is the second time you have called us," said the Monkey King, bowing before the little girl. "What do you wish?" "I want you to fly with me to Kansas," said Dorothy. But the Monkey King shook his head. "That cannot be done," he said. "We belong to this country alone, and cannot leave it. There has never been a Winged Monkey in Kansas yet, and I suppose there never will be, for they don't belong there. We shall be glad to serve you in any way in our power, but we cannot cross the desert. Good-bye." And with another bow, the Monkey King spread his wings and flew away through the window, followed by all his band. Dorothy was ready to cry with disappointment. "I have wasted the charm of the Golden Cap to no purpose," she said, "for the Winged Monkeys cannot help me." "It is certainly too bad!" said the tender-hearted Woodman. The Scarecrow was thinking again, and his head bulged out so horribly that Dorothy feared it would burst. "Let us call in the soldier with the green whiskers," he said, "and ask his advice." So the soldier was summoned and entered the Throne Room timidly, for while Oz was alive he never was allowed to come farther than the door. "This little girl," said the Scarecrow to the soldier, "wishes to cross the desert. How can she do so?" "I cannot tell," answered the soldier, "for nobody has ever crossed the desert, unless it is Oz himself." "Is there no one who can help me?" asked Dorothy earnestly. "Glinda might," he suggested. "Who is Glinda?" inquired the Scarecrow. "The Witch of the South. She is the most powerful of all the Witches, and rules over the Quadlings. Besides, her castle stands on the edge of the desert, so she may know a way to cross it." "Glinda is a Good Witch, isn't she?" asked the child. "The Quadlings think she is good," said the soldier, "and she is kind to everyone. I have heard that Glinda is a beautiful woman, who knows how to keep young in spite of the many years she has lived." "How can I get to her castle?" asked Dorothy. "The road is straight to the South," he answered, "but it is said to be full of dangers to travelers. There are wild beasts in the woods, and a race of queer men who do not like strangers to cross their country. For this reason none of the Quadlings ever come to the Emerald City." The soldier then left them and the Scarecrow said: "It seems, in spite of dangers, that the best thing Dorothy can do is to travel to the Land of the South and ask Glinda to help her. For, of course, if Dorothy stays here she will never get back to Kansas." "You must have been thinking again," remarked the Tin Woodman. "I have," said the Scarecrow. "I shall go with Dorothy," declared the Lion, "for I am tired of your city and long for the woods and the country again. I am really a wild beast, you know. Besides, Dorothy will need someone to protect her." "That is true," agreed the Woodman. "My axe may be of service to her; so I also will go with her to the Land of the South." "When shall we start?" asked the Scarecrow. "Are you going?" they asked, in surprise. "Certainly. If it wasn't for Dorothy I should never have had brains. She lifted me from the pole in the cornfield and brought me to the Emerald City. So my good luck is all due to her, and I shall never leave her until she starts back to Kansas for good and all." "Thank you," said Dorothy gratefully. "You are all very kind to me. But I should like to start as soon as possible." "We shall go tomorrow morning," returned the Scarecrow. "So now let us all get ready, for it will be a long journey." CHAPTER XIX Attacked by the Fighting Trees The next morning Dorothy kissed the pretty green girl good-bye, and they all shook hands with the soldier with the green whiskers, who had walked with them as far as the gate. When the Guardian of the Gates saw them again he wondered greatly that they could leave the beautiful City to get into new trouble. But he at once unlocked their spectacles, which he put back into the green box, and gave them many good wishes to carry with them. "You are now our ruler," he said to the Scarecrow; "so you must come back to us as soon as possible." "I certainly shall if I am able," the Scarecrow replied; "but I must help Dorothy to get home, first." As Dorothy bade the good-natured Guardian a last farewell she said: "I have been very kindly treated in your lovely City; everyone has been good to me. I cannot tell you how grateful I am." "Don't try, my dear," he answered. "We should like to keep you with us, but if it is your wish to return to Kansas, I hope you will find a way." He then opened the gate of the outer wall, and they walked forth and started upon their journey.

The sun shone brightly as our friends turned their faces toward the Land of the South. They were all in the best of spirits, and laughed and chatted together. Dorothy was once more filled with the hope of getting home, and the Scarecrow and the Tin Woodman were glad to be of use to her. As for the Lion, he sniffed the fresh air with delight and whisked his tail from side to side in pure joy at being in the country again, while Toto ran around them and chased the moths and butterflies, barking merrily all the time. "City life does not agree with me at all," remarked the Lion, as they walked along at a brisk pace. "I have lost much flesh since I lived there, and now I am anxious for a chance to show the other beasts how courageous I have grown." They now turned and took a last look at the Emerald City. All they could see was a mass of towers and steeples behind the green walls, and high up above everything the spires and dome of the Palace of Oz. "Oz was not such a bad Wizard, after all," said the Tin Woodman, as he felt his heart rattling around in his breast. "He knew how to give me brains, and very good brains, too," said the Scarecrow. "If Oz had taken a dose of the same courage he gave me," added the Lion, "he would have been a brave man." Dorothy said nothing. Oz had not kept the promise he made her, but he had done his best, so she forgave him. As he said, he was a good man, even if he was a bad Wizard. The first day's journey was through the green fields and bright flowers that stretched about the Emerald City on every side. They slept that night on the grass, with nothing but the stars over them; and they rested very well indeed. In the morning they traveled on until they came to a thick wood. There was no way of going around it, for it seemed to extend to the right and left as far as they could see; and, besides, they did not dare change the direction of their journey for fear of getting lost. So they looked for the place where it would be easiest to get into the forest. The Scarecrow, who was in the lead, finally discovered a big tree with such wide-spreading branches that there was room for the party to pass underneath. So he walked forward to the tree, but just as he came under the first branches they bent down and twined around him, and the next minute he was raised from the ground and flung headlong among his fellow travelers. This did not hurt the Scarecrow, but it surprised him, and he looked rather dizzy when Dorothy picked him up. "Here is another space between the trees," called the Lion. "Let me try it first," said the Scarecrow, "for it doesn't hurt me to get thrown about." He walked up to another tree, as he spoke, but its branches immediately seized him and tossed him back again. "This is strange," exclaimed Dorothy. "What shall we do?" "The trees seem to have made up their minds to fight us, and stop our journey," remarked the Lion. "I believe I will try it myself," said the Woodman, and shouldering his axe, he marched up to the first tree that had handled the Scarecrow so roughly. When a big branch bent down to seize him the Woodman chopped at it so fiercely that he cut it in two. At once the tree began shaking all its branches as if in pain, and the Tin Woodman passed safely under it. "Come on!" he shouted to the others. "Be quick!" They all ran forward and passed under the tree without injury, except Toto, who was caught by a small branch and shaken until he howled. But the Woodman promptly chopped off the branch and set the little dog free. The other trees of the forest did nothing to keep them back, so they made up their minds that only the first row of trees could bend down their branches, and that probably these were the policemen of the forest, and given this wonderful power in order to keep strangers out of it. The four travelers walked with ease through the trees until they came to the farther edge of the wood. Then, to their surprise, they found before them a high wall which seemed to be made of white china. It was smooth, like the surface of a dish, and higher than their heads. "What shall we do now?" asked Dorothy.

"I will make a ladder," said the Tin Woodman, "for we certainly must climb over the wall." CHAPTER XX The Dainty China Country While the Woodman was making

a ladder from wood which he found in the forest Dorothy lay down and slept, for she was tired by the long walk. The Lion also curled himself up to sleep and Toto lay beside

him. The Scarecrow watched the Woodman while he worked, and said to him: "I cannot think why this wall is here, nor what it is made of." "Rest your brains and do not

worry about the wall," replied the Woodman. "When we have climbed over it, we shall know what is on the other side." After a time the ladder was finished. It looked clumsy,

but the Tin Woodman was sure it was strong and would answer their purpose. The Scarecrow waked Dorothy and the Lion and Toto, and told them that the ladder was

ready. The Scarecrow climbed up the ladder first, but he was so awkward that Dorothy had to follow close behind and keep him from falling off. When he got his head over

the top of the wall the Scarecrow said, "Oh, my!" "Go on," exclaimed Dorothy. So the Scarecrow climbed farther up and sat down on the top of the wall, and Dorothy put

her head over and cried, "Oh, my!" just as the Scarecrow had done. Then Toto came up, and immediately began to bark, but Dorothy made him be still. The Lion climbed

the ladder next, and the Tin Woodman came last; but both of them cried, "Oh, my!" as soon as they looked over the wall. When they were all sitting in a row on the top of

the wall, they looked down and saw a strange sight. Before them was a great stretch of country having a floor as smooth and shining and white as the bottom of a big platter.

Scattered around were many houses made entirely of china and painted in the brightest colors. These houses were quite small, the biggest of them reaching only as high as

Dorothy's waist. There were also pretty little barns, with china fences around them; and many cows and sheep and horses and pigs and chickens, all made of china, were

standing about in groups. But the strangest of all were the people who lived in this queer country. There were milkmaids and shepherdesses, with brightly colored bodices

and golden spots all over their gowns; and princesses with most gorgeous frocks of silver and gold and purple; and shepherds dressed in knee breeches with pink and yellow

and blue stripes down them, and golden buckles on their shoes; and princes with jeweled crowns upon their heads, wearing ermine robes and satin doublets; and funny clowns

in ruffled gowns, with round red spots upon their cheeks and tall, pointed caps. And, strangest of all, these people were all made of china, even to their clothes, and were so

small that the tallest of them was no higher than Dorothy's knee. No one did so much as look at the travelers at first, except one little purple china dog with an extra-large

head, which came to the wall and barked at them in a tiny voice, afterwards running away again. "How shall we get down?" asked Dorothy. They found the ladder so heavy

they could not pull it up, so the Scarecrow fell off the wall and the others jumped down upon him so that the hard floor would not hurt their feet. Of course they took pains

not to light on his head and get the pins in their feet. When all were safely down they picked up the Scarecrow, whose body was quite flattened out, and patted his straw into

shape again. "We must cross this strange place in order to get to the other side," said Dorothy, "for it would be unwise for us to go any other way except due South." They

began walking through the country of the china people, and the first thing they came to was a china milkmaid milking a china cow. As they drew near, the cow suddenly gave a kick and kicked over the stool, the pail, and even the milkmaid herself, and all fell on the china ground with a great clatter. Dorothy was shocked to see that the cow had

broken her leg off, and that the pail was lying in several small pieces, while the poor milkmaid had a nick in her left elbow. "There!" cried the milkmaid angrily. "See what

you have done! My cow has broken her leg, and I must take her to the mender's shop and have it glued on again. What do you mean by coming here and frightening my

cow?" "I'm very sorry," returned Dorothy. "Please forgive us." But the pretty milkmaid was much too vexed to make any answer. She picked up the leg sulkily and led her

cow away, the poor animal limping on three legs. As she left them the milkmaid cast many reproachful glances over her shoulder at the clumsy strangers, holding her nicked

elbow close to her side. Dorothy was quite grieved at this mishap. "We must be very careful here," said the kindhearted Woodman, "or we may hurt these pretty little people

so they will never get over it." A little farther on Dorothy met a most beautifully dressed young Princess, who stopped short as she saw the strangers and started to run away.

Dorothy wanted to see more of the Princess, so she ran after her. But the china girl cried out: "Don't chase me! Don't chase me!" She had such a frightened little voice that

Dorothy stopped and said, "Why not?" "Because," answered the Princess, also stopping, a safe distance away, "if I run I may fall down and break myself." "But could you

not be mended?" asked the girl. "Oh, yes; but one is never so pretty after being mended, you know," replied the Princess. "I suppose not," said Dorothy. "Now there is Mr.

Joker, one of our clowns," continued the china lady, "who is always trying to stand upon his head. He has broken himself so often that he is mended in a hundred places, and

doesn't look at all pretty. Here he comes now, so you can see for yourself." Indeed, a jolly little clown came walking toward them, and Dorothy could see that in spite of his

pretty clothes of red and yellow and green he was completely covered with cracks, running every which way and showing plainly that he had been mended in many places.

The Clown put his hands in his pockets, and after puffing out his cheeks and nodding his head at them saucily, he said, *"My lady fair, Why do you stare At poor old Mr. Joker?*

You're quite as stiff And prim as if You'd eaten up a poker!" "Be quiet, sir!" said the Princess. "Can't you see these are strangers, and should be treated with respect?" "Well,

that's respect, I expect," declared the Clown, and immediately stood upon his head. "Don't mind Mr. Joker," said the Princess to Dorothy. "He is considerably cracked in

his head, and that makes him foolish." "Oh, I don't mind him a bit," said Dorothy. "But you are so beautiful," she continued, "that I am sure I could love you dearly. Won't

you let me carry you back to Kansas, and stand you on Aunt Em's mantel? I could carry you in my basket." "That would make me very unhappy," answered the china

Princess. "You see, here in our country we live contentedly, and can talk and move around as we please. But whenever any of us are taken away our joints at once stiffen, and

we can only stand straight and look pretty. Of course that is all that is expected of us when we are on mantels and cabinets and drawing-room tables, but our lives are much

pleasanter here in our own country." "I would not make you unhappy for all the world!" exclaimed Dorothy. "So I'll just say good-bye." "Good-bye," replied the Princess.

They walked carefully through the china country. The little animals and all the people scampered out of their way, fearing the strangers would break them, and after an hour

or so the travelers reached the other side of the country and came to another china wall. It was not so high as the first, however, and by standing upon the Lion's back they all managed to scramble to the top. Then the Lion gathered his legs under him and jumped on the wall; but just as he jumped, he upset a china church with his tail and smashed it all to pieces. "That was too bad," said Dorothy, "but really I think we were lucky in not doing these little people more harm than breaking a cow's leg and a church. They are all so brittle!" "They are, indeed," said the Scarecrow, "and I am thankful I am made of straw and cannot be easily damaged. There are worse things in the world than being a Scarecrow." CHAPTER XXI The Lion Becomes the King of Beasts After climbing down from the china wall the travelers found themselves in a disagreeable country, full of bogs and marshes and covered with tall, rank grass. It was difficult to walk without falling into muddy holes, for the grass was so thick that it hid them from sight. However, by carefully picking their way, they got safely along until they reached solid ground. But here the country seemed wilder than ever, and after a long and tiresome walk through the underbrush they entered another forest, where the trees were bigger and older than any they had ever seen. "This forest is perfectly delightful," declared the Lion, looking around him with joy. "Never have I seen a more beautiful place." "It seems gloomy," said the Scarecrow. "Not a bit of it," answered the Lion. "I should like to live here all my life. See how soft the dried leaves are under your feet and how rich and green the moss is that clings to these old trees. Surely no wild beast could wish a pleasanter home." "Perhaps there are wild beasts in the forest now," said Dorothy. "I suppose there are," returned the Lion, "but I do not see any of them about." They walked through the forest until it became too dark to go any farther. Dorothy and Toto and the Lion lay down to sleep, while the Woodman and the Scarecrow kept watch over them as usual. When morning came, they started again. Before they had gone far they heard a low rumble, as of the growling of many wild animals. Toto whimpered a little, but none of the others was frightened, and they kept along the well-trodden path until they came to an opening in the wood, in which were gathered hundreds of beasts of every variety. There were tigers and elephants and bears and wolves and foxes and all the others in the natural history, and for a moment Dorothy was afraid. But the Lion explained that the animals were holding a meeting, and he judged by their snarling and growling that they were in great trouble. As he spoke several of the beasts caught sight of him, and at once the great assemblage hushed as if by magic. The biggest of the tigers came up to the Lion and bowed, saying: "Welcome, O King of Beasts! You have come in good time to fight our enemy and bring peace to all the animals of the forest once more." "What is your trouble?" asked the Lion quietly. "We are all threatened," answered the tiger, "by a fierce enemy which has lately come into this forest. It is a most tremendous monster, like a great spider, with a body as big as an elephant and legs as long as a tree trunk. It has eight of these long legs, and as the monster crawls through the forest he seizes an animal with a leg and drags it to his mouth, where he eats it as a spider does a fly. Not one of us is safe while this fierce creature is alive, and we had called a meeting to decide how to take care of ourselves when you came among us." The Lion thought for a moment. "Are there any other lions in this forest?" he asked. "No; there were some, but the monster has eaten them all. And, besides, they were none of them nearly so large and brave as you." "If I put an end to your enemy, will you bow down to me and obey me as King of the Forest?" inquired the Lion. "We will do that gladly," returned the tiger; and all the other beasts roared with a mighty roar: "We will!" "Where is this great spider of yours now?" asked the

Lion. "Yonder, among the oak trees," said the tiger, pointing with his forefoot. "Take good care of these friends of mine," said the Lion, "and I will go at once to fight the monster." He bade his comrades good-bye and marched proudly away to do battle with the enemy. The great spider was lying asleep when the Lion found him, and it looked so ugly that its foe turned up his nose in disgust. Its legs were quite as long as the tiger had said, and its body covered with coarse black hair. It had a great mouth, with a row of sharp teeth a foot long; but its head was joined to the pudgy body by a neck as slender as a wasp's waist. This gave the Lion a hint of the best way to attack the creature, and as he knew it was easier to fight it asleep than awake, he gave a great spring and landed directly upon the monster's back. Then, with one blow of his heavy paw, all armed with sharp claws, he knocked the spider's head from its body. Jumping down, he watched it until the long legs stopped wiggling, when he knew it was quite dead. The Lion went back to the opening where the beasts of the forest were waiting for him and said proudly: "You need fear your enemy no longer." Then the beasts bowed down to the Lion as their King, and he promised to come back and rule over them as soon as Dorothy was safely on her way to Kansas. CHAPTER XXII The Country of the Quadlings The four travelers passed through the rest of the forest in safety, and when they came out from its gloom saw before them a steep hill, covered from top to bottom with great pieces of rock. "That will be a hard climb," said the Scarecrow, "but we must get over the hill, nevertheless." So he led the way and the others followed. They had nearly reached the first rock when they heard a rough voice cry out, "Keep back!" "Who are you?" asked the Scarecrow. Then a head showed itself over the rock and the same voice said, "This hill belongs to us, and we don't allow anyone to cross it." "But we must cross it," said the Scarecrow. "We're going to the country of the Quadlings." "But you shall not!" replied the voice, and there stepped from behind the rock the strangest man the travelers had ever seen. He was quite short and stout and had a big head, which was flat at the top and supported by a thick neck full of wrinkles. But he had no arms at all, and, seeing this, the Scarecrow did not fear that so helpless a creature could prevent them from climbing the hill. So he said, "I'm sorry not to do as you wish, but we must pass over your hill whether you like it or not," and he walked boldly forward. As quick as lightning the man's head shot forward and his neck stretched out until the top of the head, where it was flat, struck the Scarecrow in the middle and sent him tumbling, over and over, down the hill. Almost as quickly as it came the head went back to the body, and the man laughed harshly as he said, "It isn't as easy as you think!" A chorus of boisterous laughter came from the other rocks, and Dorothy saw hundreds of the armless Hammer-Heads upon the hillside, one behind every rock. The Lion became quite angry at the laughter caused by the Scarecrow's mishap, and giving a loud roar that echoed like thunder, he dashed up the hill. Again a head shot swiftly out, and the great Lion went rolling down the hill as if he had been struck by a cannonball. Dorothy ran down and helped the Scarecrow to his feet, and the Lion came up to her, feeling rather bruised and sore, and said, "It is useless to fight people with shooting heads; no one can withstand them." "What can we do, then?" she asked. "Call the Winged Monkeys," suggested the Tin Woodman. "You have still the right to command them once more." "Very well," she answered, and putting on the Golden Cap she uttered the magic words. The Monkeys were as prompt as ever, and in a few moments the entire band stood before her. "What are your commands?" inquired the King of the Monkeys, bowing low. "Carry us over the hill to the country of the Quadlings," answered the girl. "It shall be done," said the King, and at once the Winged Monkeys caught the four

travelers and Toto up in their arms and flew away with them. As they passed over the hill the Hammer-Heads yelled with vexation, and shot their heads high in the air, but

they could not reach the Winged Monkeys, which carried Dorothy and her comrades safely over the hill and set them down in the beautiful country of the Quadlings. "This

is the last time you can summon us," said the leader to Dorothy; "so good-bye and good luck to you." "Good-bye, and thank you very much," returned the girl; and the

Monkeys rose into the air and were out of sight in a twinkling. The country of the Quadlings seemed rich and happy. There was field upon field of ripening grain, with

well-paved roads running between, and pretty rippling brooks with strong bridges across them. The fences and houses and bridges were all painted bright red, just as they

had been painted yellow in the country of the Winkies and blue in the country of the Munchkins. The Quadlings themselves, who were short and fat and looked chubby and

good-natured, were dressed all in red, which showed bright against the green grass and the yellowing grain. **The Monkeys had set them down near a farmhouse, and the four**

travelers walked up to it and knocked at the door. It was opened by the farmer's wife, and when Dorothy asked for something to eat the woman gave them all a good dinner,

with three kinds of cake and four kinds of cookies, and a bowl of milk for Toto. "How far is it to the Castle of Glinda?" asked the child. "It is not a great way," answered the

farmer's wife. "Take the road to the South and you will soon reach it." Thanking the good woman, they started afresh and walked by the fields and across the pretty bridges

until they saw before them a very beautiful Castle. Before the gates were three young girls, dressed in handsome red uniforms trimmed with gold braid; and as Dorothy

approached, one of them said to her: "Why have you come to the South Country?" "To see the Good Witch who rules here," she answered. "Will you take me to her?" "Let

me have your name, and I will ask Glinda if she will receive you." They told who they were, and the girl soldier went into the Castle. After a few moments she came back

to say that Dorothy and the others were to be admitted at once. CHAPTER XXIII Glinda The Good Witch Grants Dorothy's Wish Before they went to see Glinda,

however, they were taken to a room of the Castle, where Dorothy washed her face and combed her hair, and the Lion shook the dust out of his mane, and the Scarecrow

patted himself into his best shape, and the Woodman polished his tin and oiled his joints. When they were all quite presentable they followed the soldier girl into a big room

where the Witch Glinda sat upon a throne of rubies. She was both beautiful and young to their eyes. Her hair was a rich red in color and fell in flowing ringlets over her

shoulders. Her dress was pure white but her eyes were blue, and they looked kindly upon the little girl. "What can I do for you, my child?" she asked. Dorothy told the Witch

all her story: how the cyclone had brought her to the Land of Oz, how she had found her companions, and of the wonderful adventures they had met with. "My greatest

wish now," she added, "is to get back to Kansas, for Aunt Em will surely think something dreadful has happened to me, and that will make her put on mourning; and unless

the crops are better this year than they were last, I am sure Uncle Henry cannot afford it." Glinda leaned forward and kissed the sweet, upturned face of the loving little girl.

"Bless your dear heart," she said, "I am sure I can tell you of a way to get back to Kansas." Then she added, "But, if I do, you must give me the Golden Cap." "Willingly!"

exclaimed Dorothy; "indeed, it is of no use to me now, and when you have it you can command the Winged Monkeys three times." "And I think I shall need their service just those three times," answered Glinda, smiling. Dorothy then gave her the Golden Cap, and the Witch said to the Scarecrow, "What will you do when Dorothy has left us?" "I will return to the Emerald City," he replied, "for Oz has made me its ruler and the people like me. The only thing that worries me is how to cross the hill of the Hammer-Heads." "By means of the Golden Cap I shall command the Winged Monkeys to carry you to the gates of the Emerald City," said Glinda, "for it would be a shame to deprive the people of so wonderful a ruler." "Am I really wonderful?" asked the Scarecrow. "You are unusual," replied Glinda. Turning to the Tin Woodman, she asked, "What will become of you when Dorothy leaves this country?" He leaned on his axe and thought a moment. Then he said, "The Winkies were very kind to me, and wanted me to rule over them after the Wicked Witch died. I am fond of the Winkies, and if I could get back again to the Country of the West, I should like nothing better than to rule over them forever." "My second command to the Winged Monkeys," said Glinda "will be that they carry you safely to the land of the Winkies. Your brain may not be so large to look at as those of the Scarecrow, but you are really brighter than he is—when you are well polished—and I am sure you will rule the Winkies wisely and well."

Then the Witch looked at the big, shaggy Lion and asked, "When Dorothy has returned to her own home, what will become of you?" "Over the hill of the Hammer-Heads," he answered, "lies a grand old forest, and all the beasts that live there have made me their King. If I could only get back to this forest, I would pass my life very happily there." "My third command to the Winged Monkeys," said Glinda, "shall be to carry you to your forest. Then, having used up the powers of the Golden Cap, I shall give it to the King of the Monkeys, that he and his band may thereafter be free for evermore." The Scarecrow and the Tin Woodman and the Lion now thanked the Good Witch earnestly for her kindness; and Dorothy exclaimed: "You are certainly as good as you are beautiful! But you have not yet told me how to get back to Kansas." "Your Silver Shoes will carry you over the desert," replied Glinda. "If you had known their power you could have gone back to your Aunt Em the very first day you came to this country." "But then I should not have had my wonderful brains!" cried the Scarecrow. "I might have passed my whole life in the farmer's cornfield." "And I should not have had my lovely heart," said the Tin Woodman. "I might have stood and rusted in the forest till the end of the world." "And I should have lived a coward forever," declared the Lion, "and no beast in all the forest would have had a good word to say to me." "This is all true," said Dorothy, "and I am glad I was of use to these good friends. But now that each of them has had what he most desired, and each is happy in having a kingdom to rule besides, I think I should like to go back to Kansas." "The Silver Shoes," said the Good Witch, "have wonderful powers. And one of the most curious things about them is that they can carry you to any place in the world in three steps, and each step will be made in the wink of an eye. All you have to do is to knock the heels together three times and command the shoes to carry you wherever you wish to go." "If that is so," said the child joyfully, "I will ask them to carry me back to Kansas at once." She threw her arms around the Lion's neck and kissed him, patting his big head tenderly. Then she kissed the Tin Woodman, who was weeping in a way most dangerous to his joints. But she hugged the soft, stuffed body of the Scarecrow in her arms instead of kissing his painted face, and found she was crying herself at this sorrowful parting from her loving comrades. Glinda the Good stepped down from her ruby throne to give the little girl a good-bye kiss, and Dorothy thanked her for all the kindness she had shown to her friends and herself. Dorothy now took Toto up solemnly in her arms, and having said one last good-bye she clapped the heels of her shoes together three times, saying: "Take me home to Aunt Em!" Instantly she was whirling through the air, so swiftly that all she could see or feel was the wind whistling past her ears. The Silver Shoes took but three steps, and then she stopped so suddenly that she rolled over upon the grass several times before she knew where she was. At length, however, she sat up and looked about her. "Good gracious!" she cried. For she was sitting on the broad Kansas prairie, and just before her was the new farmhouse Uncle Henry built after the cyclone had carried away the old one. Uncle Henry was milking the cows in the barnyard, and Toto had jumped out of her arms and was running toward the barn, barking furiously. Dorothy stood up and found she was in her stocking feet. For the Silver Shoes had fallen off in her flight through the air, and were lost forever in the desert. CHAPTER XXIV Home Again Aunt Em had just come out of the house to water the cabbages when she looked up and saw Dorothy running toward her. "My darling child!" she cried, folding the little girl in her arms and covering her face with kisses. "Where in the world did you come from?"

"From the Land of Oz," said Dorothy gravely. "And here is Toto, too. And oh, Aunt Em! I'm so glad to be at home again!" LITTLE WIZARD STORIES OF OZ The Cowardly Lion and the Hungry Tiger In the splendid palace of the Emerald City, which is in the center of the fairy Land of Oz, is a great Throne Room, where Princess Ozma, the Ruler, for an hour each day sits in a throne of glistening emeralds and listens to all the troubles of her people, which they are sure to tell her about. Around Ozma's throne, on such occasions, are grouped all the important personages of Oz, such as the Scarecrow, Jack Pumpkinhead, Tiktok the Clockwork Man, the Tin Woodman, the Wizard of Oz, the Shaggy Man and other famous fairy people. Little Dorothy usually has a seat at Ozma's feet, and crouched on either side the throne are two enormous beasts known as the Hungry Tiger and the Cowardly Lion. These two beasts are Ozma's chief guardians, but as everyone loves the beautiful girl Princess there has never been any disturbance in the great Throne Room, or anything for the guardians to do but look fierce and solemn and keep quiet until the Royal Audience is over and the people go away to their homes. Of course no one would dare be naughty while the huge Lion and Tiger crouched beside the throne; but the fact is, the people of Oz are very seldom naughty. So Ozma's big guards are more ornamental than useful, and no one realizes that better than the beasts themselves. One day, after everybody had left the Throne Room except the Cowardly Lion and the Hungry Tiger, the Lion yawned and said to his friend: "I'm getting tired of this job. No one is afraid of us and no one pays any attention to us." "That is true," replied the big Tiger, purring softly. "We might as well be in the thick jungles where we were born, as trying to protect Ozma when she needs no protection. And I'm dreadfully hungry all the time." "You have enough to eat, I'm sure," said the Lion, swaying his tail slowly back and forth. "Enough, perhaps; but not the kind of food I long for," answered the Tiger. "What I'm hungry for is fat babies. I have a great desire to eat a few fat babies. Then, perhaps, the people of Oz would fear me and I'd become more important." "True," agreed the Lion. "It would stir up quite a rumpus if you ate but *one* fat baby. As for myself, my claws are sharp as needles and strong as crowbars, while my teeth are powerful enough to tear a person to pieces in a few seconds. If I should spring upon a man and make chop suey of him, there would

be wild excitement in the Emerald City and the people would fall upon their knees and beg me for mercy. That, in my opinion, would render me of considerable importance."

"After you had torn the person to pieces, what would you do next?" asked the Tiger sleepily. "Then I would roar so loudly it would shake the earth and stalk away to the

jungle to hide myself, before anyone could attack me or kill me for what I had done." "I see," nodded the Tiger. "You are really cowardly." "To be sure. That is why I am

named the Cowardly Lion. That is why I have always been so tame and peaceable. But I'm awfully tired of being tame," added the Lion, with a sigh, "and it would be fun

to raise a row and show people what a terrible beast I really am." The Tiger remained silent for several minutes, thinking deeply as he slowly washed his face with his left

paw. Then he said: "I'm getting old, and it would please me to eat at least one fat baby before I die. Suppose we surprise these people of Oz and prove our power. What do

you say? We will walk out of here just as usual and the first baby we meet I'll eat in a jiffy, and the first man or woman you meet you will tear to pieces. Then we will both

run out of the city gates and gallop across the country and hide in the jungle before anyone can stop us." "All right; I'm game," said the Lion, yawning again so that he showed

two rows of dreadfully sharp teeth. The Tiger got up and stretched his great, sleek body. "Come on," he said. The Lion stood up and proved he was the larger of the two,

for he was almost as big as a small horse. Out of the palace they walked, and met no one. They passed through the beautiful grounds, past fountains and beds of lovely

flowers, and met no one. Then they unlatched a gate and entered a street of the city, and met no one. "I wonder how a fat baby will taste," remarked the Tiger, as they stalked

majestically along, side by side. "I imagine it will taste like nutmegs," said the Lion. "No," said the Tiger, "I've an idea it will taste like gumdrops." They turned a corner,

but met no one, for the people of the Emerald City were accustomed to take their naps at this hour of the afternoon. "I wonder how many pieces I ought to tear a person

into," said the Lion, in a thoughtful voice. "Sixty would be about right," suggested the Tiger. "Would that hurt any more than to tear one into about a dozen pieces?" inquired

the Lion, with a little shudder. "Who cares whether it hurts or not?" growled the Tiger. The Lion did not reply. They entered a side street, but met no one. Suddenly they

heard a child crying. "Aha!" exclaimed the Tiger. "There is my meat." He rushed around a corner, the Lion following, and came upon a nice fat baby sitting in the middle

of the street and crying as if in great distress. "What's the matter?" asked the Tiger, crouching before the baby. "I—I—I—lost my m—m—mama!" wailed the baby. "Why,

you poor little thing," said the great beast, softly stroking the child's head with its paw. "Don't cry, my dear, for mama can't be far away and I'll help you to find her." "Go

on," said the Lion, who stood by. "Go on where?" asked the Tiger, looking up. "Go on and eat your fat baby." "Why, you dreadful creature!" said the Tiger reproachfully;

"would you want me to eat a poor little lost baby, that doesn't know where its mother is?" And the beast gathered the little one into its strong, hairy arms and tried to comfort

it by rocking it gently back and forth. The Lion growled low in his throat and seemed very much disappointed; but at that moment a scream reached their ears and a woman

came bounding out of a house and into the street. Seeing her baby in the embrace of the monster Tiger the woman screamed again and rushed forward to rescue it, but in her haste she caught her foot in her skirt and tumbled head over heels and heels over head, stopping with such a bump that she saw many stars in the heavens, although it was

broad daylight. And there she lay, in a helpless manner, all tangled up and unable to stir. With one bound and a roar like thunder the huge Lion was beside her. With his strong

jaws he grasped her dress and raised her into an upright position. "Poor thing! Are you hurt?" he gently asked. Gasping for breath the woman struggled to free herself and

tried to walk, but she limped badly and tumbled down again. "My baby!" she said pleadingly. "The baby is all right; don't worry," replied the Lion; and then he added: "Keep

quiet, now, and I'll carry you back to your house, and the Hungry Tiger will carry your baby." The Tiger, who had approached the place with the child in its arms, asked in

astonishment: "Aren't you going to tear her into sixty pieces?" "No, nor into six pieces," answered the Lion indignantly. "I'm not such a brute as to destroy a poor woman

who has hurt herself trying to save her lost baby. If you are so ferocious and cruel and bloodthirsty, you may leave me and go away, for I do not care to associate with you."

"That's all right," answered the Tiger. "I'm not cruel—not in the least—I'm only hungry. But I thought *you* were cruel." "Thank heaven I'm respectable," said the Lion,

with dignity. He then raised the woman and with much gentleness carried her into her house, where he laid her upon a sofa. The Tiger followed with the baby, which he safely

deposited beside its mother. The little one liked the Hungry Tiger and grasping the enormous beast by both ears the baby kissed the beast's nose to show he was grateful and

happy. "Thank you very much," said the woman. "I've often heard what good beasts you are, in spite of your power to do mischief to mankind, and now I know that the

stories are true. I do not think either of you have ever had an evil thought." The Hungry Tiger and the Cowardly Lion hung their heads and did not look into each other's

eyes, for both were shamed and humbled. They crept away and stalked back through the streets until they again entered the palace grounds, where they retreated to the pretty,

comfortable rooms they occupied at the back of the palace. There they silently crouched in their usual corners to think over their adventure. After a while the Tiger said

sleepily: "I don't believe fat babies taste like gumdrops. I'm quite sure they have the flavor of raspberry tarts. My, how hungry I am for fat babies!" The Lion grunted

disdainfully. "You're a humbug," said he. "Am I?" retorted the Tiger, with a sneer. "Tell me, then, into how many pieces you usually tear your victims, my bold Lion?" The

Lion impatiently thumped the floor with his tail. "To tear anyone into pieces would soil my claws and blunt my teeth," he said. "I'm glad I didn't muss myself up this

afternoon by hurting that poor mother." The Tiger looked at him steadily and then yawned a wide, wide yawn. "You're a coward," he remarked. "Well," said the Lion, "it's

better to be a coward than to do wrong." "To be sure," answered the other. "And that reminds me that I nearly lost my own reputation. For, had I eaten that fat baby I would

not now be the Hungry Tiger. It's better to go hungry, seems to me, than to be cruel to a little child." And then they dropped their heads on their paws and went to sleep.

LITTLE DOROTHY AND TOTO Dorothy was a little Kansas girl who once accidentally found the beautiful Land of Oz and was invited to live there always. Toto was

Dorothy's small black dog, with fuzzy, curly hair and bright black eyes. Together, when they tired of the grandeur of the Emerald City of Oz, they would wander out into

the country and all through the land, peering into queer nooks and corners and having a good time in their own simple way. There was a little Wizard living in Oz who was a faithful friend of Dorothy and did not approve of her traveling alone in this way, but the girl always laughed at the little man's fears for her and said she was not afraid of anything that might happen. One day while on such a journey, Dorothy and Toto found themselves among the wild wooded hills at the southeast of Oz—a place usually avoided by travelers because so many magical things abounded there. And, as they entered a forest path, the little girl noticed a sign tacked to a tree, which said: "Look out for Crinklink." Toto could not talk, as many of the animals of Oz can, for he was just a common Kansas dog; but he looked at the sign so seriously that Dorothy almost believed he could read it, and she knew quite well that Toto understood every word she said to him. "Never mind Crinklink," said she. "I don't believe anything in Oz will try to hurt us, Toto, and if I get into trouble you must take care of me." "Bow-wow!" said Toto, and Dorothy knew that meant a promise. The path was narrow and wound here and there between the trees, but they could not lose their way, because thick vines and creepers shut them in on both sides. They had walked a long time when, suddenly turning a curve of the pathway, they came upon a lake of black water, so big and so deep that they were forced to stop. "Well, Toto," said Dorothy, looking at the lake, "we must turn back, I guess, for there is neither a bridge nor a boat to take us across the black water." "Here's the ferryman, though," cried a tiny voice beside them, and the girl gave a start and looked down at her feet, where a man no taller than three inches sat at the edge of the path with his legs dangling over the lake. "Oh!" said Dorothy; "I didn't see you before." Toto growled fiercely and made his ears stand up straight, but the little man did not seem in the least afraid of the dog. He merely repeated: "I'm the ferryman, and it's my business to carry people across the lake." Dorothy couldn't help feeling surprised, for she could have picked the little man up with one hand, and the lake was big and broad. Looking at the ferryman more closely she saw that he had small eyes, a big nose, and a sharp chin. His hair was blue and his clothes scarlet, and Dorothy noticed that every button on his jacket was the head of some animal. The top button was a bear's head and the next button a wolf's head; the next was a cat's head and the next a weasel's head, while the last button of all was the head of a field mouse. **When Dorothy looked into the eyes of these animals' heads, they all nodded and said in a chorus: "Don't believe all you hear, little girl!"** "Silence!" said the small ferryman, slapping each button head in turn, but not hard enough to hurt them. Then he turned to Dorothy and asked: "Do you wish to cross over the lake?" "Why, I'd like to," she answered, hesitating; "but I can't see how you will manage to carry us, without any boat." "If you can't see, you mustn't see," he answered with a laugh. "All you need do is shut your eyes, say the word, and—over you go!" Dorothy wanted to get across, in order that she might continue her journey. "All right," she said, closing her eyes; "I'm ready." Instantly she was seized in a pair of strong arms—arms so big and powerful that she was startled and cried out in fear. "Silence!" roared a great voice, and the girl opened her eyes to find that the tiny man had suddenly grown to a giant and was holding both her and Toto in a tight embrace while in one step he spanned the lake and reached the other shore. Dorothy became frightened, then, especially as the giant did not stop but continued tramping in great steps over the wooded hills, crushing bushes and trees beneath his broad feet. She struggled in vain to free herself, while Toto whined and trembled beside her, for the little dog was frightened, too. "Stop!" screamed the girl. "Let me down!" But the giant paid no attention. "Who are you…

Canterbury Classics

An imprint of Printers Row Publishing Group

10350 Barnes Canyon Road, Suite 100, San Diego, CA 92121

www.thunderbaybooks.com

Printers Row Publishing Group is a division of Readerlink Distribution Services, LLC. The Canterbury Classics and Novel Journal names and logos are registered trademarks of Readerlink Distribution Services, LLC.

All correspondence concerning the content of this book should be addressed to Canterbury Classics, Editorial Department, at the above address.

Publisher: Peter Norton

Publishing Team: Lori Asbury, Ana Parker, Laura Vignale, Kathryn Chipinka

Editorial Team: JoAnn Padgett, Melinda Allman, J. Carroll

Production Team: Jonathan Lopes, Rusty von Dyl, Lidija Tomas

A Novel Journal: The Wizard of Oz
ISBN: 978-1-62686-606-5

$14.99 U.S.
ISBN 978-1-62686-606-5

Printed in China

20 19 18 17 16 2 3 4 5 6